snapshots

brian **waddington**

*snap*shots

a novel by brian **waddington**

Copyright © 2011 by Brian Waddington.
All rights are reserved. Standard Copyright Licence.
No part of this book can be stored on a retrieval system or transmitted in any form or by whatever means without the prior permission in writing from the publisher.
The moral right of Brian Waddington to be identified as the author of this work has been asserted in accordance with the Standard Copyright Licence.
This book is a work of fiction. All names, characters, businesses, organizations and events are either the product of the authors imagination or are used fictitiously. Any resemblance to actual persons, living or dead, events or locales is entirely coincidental.

HB.ISBN: 978-1-4475-1473-2
HB.ID 10310272
PB.ISBN: 978-1-4467-4856-5
PB.ID 9954283

Printed and bound by Lulu Publishing.

www.lulu.com

Acknowledgements

I first began planning and writing snapshots in the late winter of 2006. The following year I was diagnosed with cancer and underwent an arduous round of diagnostic investigations over a period of several months, followed by an operation to remove my oesophagus. Having spent several weeks in intensive care, which involved one to one nursing care, I eventually made a full recovery. There are many people I have to thank for their unflinching care during this period. They are my local GP, Dr Mike Wallwork, (Lets have a look), the consultant surgeon Mr May and colleagues, and the many nurses, physiotherapists, and support staff at the Intensive Care Unit at Bradford Royal Infirmary. They saved my life, without them this book would never have been completed.

I would also like to thank the many friends and relatives who rallied round me during this period. My sister Patricia and her husband Mick, Lesley, Carl, Joanne and Mario from Cyprus. My brother Peter and his wife Christine, Ben and Jemma. My brother-in-law David and his wife Shirley, Robert, Lucy, Leo, Daisy, Samantha and Molly. Also my brother-in-law Mike who painstakingly reviewed the copy and made numerous suggestions, and Lyn, Antony, Amanda, Simon and Kelly. A special thank you to my dear old friend Roger Ownsworth and his wife Patsy.

One person stands out, to whom I owe a huge debt of gratitude. Someone who visited me every day, cared for me unconditionally throughout my long, long convalescence, and whom I love dearly; my wife Shirley. When I was eventually able to return to the novel it was Shirley who advised me, corrected copy and made invaluable suggestions. It was Shirley who accompanied me on the field trips to research the many places featured in the novel. Thanks also to my two stepsons; Chris for his encouragement and John Paul for designing the cover and for helping me with numerous creative suggestions. Also thanks to John Paul and his wife Cheryl for our two wonderful granddaughters, Carrie and Maya, who put smiles on grandma and grandad's faces every day.

A special thanks to Phil Tyrrell for his encouragement after reading the early script, and my good friend, Mr Bill Case who has been a constant source of support. Finally I would like to mention two friends who have journeyed on during the writing of my novel; Andrew Milner and Brian Brooke, I can hear your laughter still.

P.S. To all the readers who take the time to read my book, thank you. Can I suggest that you might enhance the pleasure of reading about the lovely locations by following them on Google Earth. All the villages, pubs and hotels I have featured really exist. Whereever possible I have tried to be authentic in my descriptions, only occasionally using artistic licence where it suited the story.

Brian Waddington.

For Carrie and Maya.

You are special.

Snapshot 1

Everything was the same as the last time Nick had visited the restaurant, the tables were neatly laid with clean linen. The kitchen, with its busy chefs, was situated at one end of the rectangular room. Waitresses moved between tables taking orders and bringing food. Enough people, just enough to keep the staff busy.
The food was very good, Italian; the Beef Carpaccio he had just finished was superb.
Nick looked towards the small corridor, in the middle of the room, which led to the reception area where the owner, an amiable old man who leant on his elbow studying a Su Doku puzzle, manned the till. A heavy glass door led out onto a deserted patio entrance where drizzles of rain slithered down the glass panes.

Snapshot 2

It had been a good lunchtime with lots of passing shoppers and workpeople, faceless people, each with their own lives, trudging slowly by in both directions. This was her patch; she sat here with legs outstretched, beguiling face upturned to passing strangers, appealing to their better nature. Being young helped, already she had collected over thirty quid, another hour and she would stop for the day.

Snapshot 3

Detective Chief Inspector Martin was enjoying his lunch while poring over reports of last night's arrests. An amiable man, he could be described as an old fashioned copper. Finished, he threw the report onto the next desk, saying 'Jack, there's nothing here of interest, check it out, file and forget'
Jack had been a Detective Sergeant for four years and was looking forward to promotion; he loved the job, loved working with Martin and was generally happy with his lot.
'Are you still meeting with the old man this afternoon?' asked Jack.
Martin glanced towards his sergeant, 'Yes, another bloody wasted meeting'.

Snapshot 4

'Did you enjoy your meal, sir?' The man at the till pushed away the puzzle, then his sparkling eyes suddenly widened as he noticed the gun between the folded newspaper pointing in his direction. 'Put the money in the bag', Nick pushed a cloth shoulder bag toward the startled owner,
  'Remember the bags under the till, notes only, no coins.'
The gun muzzle waved to the man to get on with the instructions. Quickly, and without betraying any nervousness, the man at the till pushed everything into the bag.
  'Right, now bring the bag and walk in front of me towards the patio.'
He handed the bag to Nick and followed the instructions, moving out of the doorway into the drizzle.
  'Good, now walk on towards Main Street, stop at the kerbside.'
As the man walked on, Nick pushed the gun and the folded newspaper into the shoulder bag.
Being lunchtime, there were plenty of pedestrians moving along the pavement, so the man slowed his pace on approaching them.
  'Keep moving forward,' barked Nick.

Snapshot 5

Life on the pavement gives a different perspective to life; to most passers-by she was invisible.
She could pick out expensive shoes from the everyday shoe, so when she spotted a new pair of Italian shoes she gave the owner a special look, hoping for at least a quid. So when a pair of trainers, followed by a smart pair of brogues, walked across the pavement, she followed their progress until they came to a halt at the pavement's edge. She recognized the trainers as belonging to Luigi from the restaurant, and thought he looked agitated.
  Suddenly, there was a metallic sound, a fountain of pound coins hit the floor, bouncing and rolling in all directions, followed by the scuffling of feet as passers-by's groping hands reached down to retrieve the glistening coins. It was pandemonium. Her nimble fingers, used to retrieving coins thrown onto the cold wet

Yorkshire stone, quickly gathered all that were within her reach, and thrust them into her coat pocket.

Looking up through and in-between the moving, grabbing people she tried to see who had dropped the coins, then, out of the corner of her eye she saw Luigi go headlong into the road. He had been pushed, pushed by the owner of the brogues.

Before she could raise herself and gather her possessions, there was a sickening thud, followed by the sound of screeching tyres. Screams pierced the damp air as passers-by, realizing the horror of the moment, looked aghast, first at each other, and then at the passengers on the bus, who stared out in disbelief, through the rain-covered windows.

The brogue shoes made off through the crowd of shocked onlookers.

Snapshot 6

He could see his reflection in the shop windows as he walked away from the throng of people; onlookers crying for help, others, too shocked, recoiling from the sight of the blood trickling on the wet tarmac from beneath the bus.

'What happened?' 'Did anyone see…' the voices grew fainter with each passing stride.

Normally he loved the feel of the street; the people, the noise, the movement, it all gelled together to produce a rich buzz that thrilled his senses.

He turned into the small deserted alleyway, where halfway down he moved between two large plastic corporation green bins.

With one movement he removed the wig and moustache. Off came the coat, then on with a pair of designer glasses and a baseball cap.

From inside the coat he took out a folded hemp sports bag and quickly pushed everything inside, including the bag containing the money.

The sound of a siren grew louder as it raced to the scene of the accident.

After a quick check to make sure the alleyway was clear before moving off, he reached and turned into a crowded shopping esplanade, which swallowed him into its midst so that now he was surrounded on each side by brightly lit shops, selling the latest fashions in clothes, phones, travel and electrical goods.

Snapshot 7

Nick never tired of riding on escalators, with their gentle silent movement between floors. Soon he was in the kitchen and china department, from where he made his way towards the exit and into the enclosed car park.

He knew, from previous visits, that the toilets had more than a dozen cubicles, and, more importantly, the security camera was out of order due to vandalism.

Once inside a cubicle, it was time for a rapid change. He had rehearsed the changes many times, each one designed to alter his age and appearance; off came the casual jacket, baseball cap and glasses, these were then pushed into the bag, to which he attached a shoulder strap which made it easier to carry.

Ruffling his hair, he once again joined the shopping mall, the job was done.

He made off towards the Viking café where he could relax until it was time to join 'Rosemary'.

Snapshot 8

The girl decided to follow the brogues; they belonged to someone who was wearing a raincoat, had a thick mop of greying hair and carried a bulky shoulder bag. She was sure that this person with the brogues had pushed Luigi into the road and the oncoming bus, but why?

Luigi had always been kind to her. Often he would bring her a little parcel of brown paper all tied neatly with string, which made a bow so that it could be carried easily. Inside would be pasta, spaghetti or pizza.

Sometimes, when everyone had left the restaurant he would invite her in to enjoy a mug of hot coffee. He would tell her of his time in Napoli, where, as a child he would fish with his father late at night under the stars, where the gentle lapping of the water would send him to sleep. As he told her each story, his eyes would glaze over and his head would gently rock from side to side as if he was reliving those times with his father again.

After one story he took her face in both his hands and kissed her, full on the lips, but very gently. It was not her who he really kissed, it was someone from the past, far away, long forgotten. He never told her who it was, but she liked to imagine it was some first forbidden love, long forgotten.

Snapshot 9

The brogues turned left into the alley, which was full of large refuse bins that were emptied each night by the council.
Sirens from an ambulance racing to the scene of the accident grew louder. She peered around the corner just in time to see a figure disappear out into the esplanade at the bottom of the alleyway.
She rushed down as fast as her legs would take her, but by the time she joined the busy street scene, her man was gone.

Snapshot 10

Looking around the busy shopping centre drew a blank.
Cold and hungry she sat down on one of those uncomfortable metal seats that have become a fashionable accessory in most modern shopping arcades.

A mother and daughter shuffled away from her like she was some disease that they might catch. Such reactions occurred everyday. As a street person she lived, not out of choice, on the fringe of society. She enjoyed her own company, and held her own counsel; she also knew the boundaries she could cross, and those that were out of bounds.

She lived in one small room, unlike most street people, who inhabited hostels, or shop doorways. Her possessions were few.
Food and warmth were what she required most; being pretty frugal, the money she had bought her enough food, most times.

She spent quite a lot of her time in the main library, which was warm and non-threatening. Reading was her passion, a sanctuary where she could escape her dreary surroundings.

Her meandering thoughts and mind-wandering suddenly came to halt when a pair of brown brogues passed in front of her, but the owner looked different wearing a rugby shirt with blond hair and a yellow sports bag over his shoulder, he moved away from her with jaunty self-assured strides.

Snapshot 11

Detective Chief Inspector Martin took a sip of the steaming hot coffee, and walked through the corridor to the restaurant, where he looked around.

'No one remembers seeing anyone leaving with Mr. Portolini?' he continued, without waiting for a reply.

'The till is empty of all notes, together with the week's takings from under the counter. Mr. Portolini is lying dead under a bus, no money is found on him, no tape in the indoor camera. Jack, talk to me,'

Jack was used to Martin's manner, and gave him a quick summary of the situation; the call-out was less than thirty minutes old, the area has been sealed, there were plenty of witnesses from the accident scene, but from inside the restaurant it was less than clear.

No one recalled seeing anything unusual or even seeing old Portolini leave the premises, he explained.

'I've sent for footage from the street CCTV, forensic are going to contact me as soon as they find anything. We are taking the details of witnesses as we speak'.

'OK Jack. As soon as my meeting is over I'll see you in the office. Ring me if you find anything of interest.'

Jack watched him leave. He looked around the room; tables with half eaten meals and glasses of unfinished wine were waiting to be cleared. He had a bad feeling about the case, but then he usually did.

His mobile rang, he looked at the screen. It was his wife, probably wanting to know if he would be home today.

Snapshot 12

Pouring the tea, Nick watched it swirl around the cup, as wisps of steam curled upwards.

Reflecting on the last hour, his adrenalin was still flowing, making him high. Now it was time to chill-out, slip back into a relaxed mood. Everything had gone well.

Settling back into the Winchester leather settee, he was aware, for the first time, of the chatter drifting around the room.

Snapshot 13

Nick Hartford was in his thirty-second year. He was rugged, of average build, with a fresh complexion. His striking blue eyes and mop of blond hair were his most noticeable features. His early years had been spent in Hampshire with his parents, who were both teachers.

After graduating from university, with a double first in history, he moved to London, where he worked in a large auction house.

His mum and dad were killed when a lorry hit their car. After settling his parents' estate, which left him well provided for, Nick decided to make a complete break and open a new chapter in his life.

That was four years ago; after making no announcements, he settled all his affairs in London and moved to the Yorkshire Dales. There he purchased a country house with two acres of land, a comfortable distance from the thriving market town of Hawes.

Shortly after he settled in the house, he had opened an antique shop in the busy main street. This meant he spent a lot of time away from home promoting his business, keeping the shop well stocked with beautiful objects de art.

Snapshot 14

Her peers at the all-girls-college had always thought that George was by far the brightest, the one most likely to succeed. More than desirable to the opposite sex, George was a popular young woman who excelled at her studies, enjoyed a wide range of sporting activities, and, like most students of her age, partied into the night.

Unfortunately, this carefree life was brought to an abrupt end when her best friend threw herself from the roof of a multipurpose building. Her death, and the resulting finality of a beautiful rich friendship, was unbearable for George, and there followed a long period of grieving.

Her parents, after two months of, what seemed to them, an interminable long period of grieving, expected her to resume her studies by returning to her life at college. They failed to appreciate how the sudden death of her friend had left her in an emotional turmoil; it was though a curtain had descended, to separate her from the normality of what had been her previous life.
Numerous arguments followed, and soon the rift between them was beyond repair. One day George gathered together a few possessions, and, leaving no note of explanation, walked away.

She had never heard from, or seen them, since that day.

Snapshot 15

Approaching him in the café would be better than in the street, as the surroundings would inhibit any aggressive reaction, that's what George hoped.

She was going to approach him. Why did he push Luigi? She had to know.

George purchased a coffee, and then weaved her way between neatly laid tables, to where Nick Hartford was slouched on a comfortable settee.

Snapshot 16

Chief Inspector Martin opened the door to his office, to find his sergeant fiddling with a remote control. Video pictures from the main street played on a monitor.

'Well, Jack, have you anything for me?'

'Well, after interviewing the witnesses from the street and the passengers on the bus, there are a few common leads', the sergeant turned pages in his notebook and continued.

'Six witnesses from the street remember pound coins falling to the pavement just before the accident; this could have been a deliberate ploy to cause a diversion! Three witnesses remember seeing a street girl sat on the pavement, but following the ensuing panic, she had left the scene of the accident. No one actually saw the old man fall into the road'.

'Tell me that's not all you got Jack,' growled Martin.
The sergeant turned on the video to reveal the street scene just after the accident.

'Here, sir', the sergeant pointed to the screen. 'This is the street girl who witnesses recalled leaving the scene of accident, she seems to be in a hurry'.

'Perhaps she's squeamish at the sight of blood' snorted Martin.

'See how she stops, turns and moves into the alleyway.'

'Rewind the tape Jack.'

After a few button pushing moves the tape started again. Martin leant forward and then pointed at the screen.

'There. Stop the tape.'

The Sergeant looked where Martin's finger remained pointing on the screen. 'See the male in a raincoat with the shoulder bag, he turns into the alleyway before the girl'.

'Is she following him? Run it again'.

They both followed the street scene on the monitor.

'Jack, get me enlarged images of the girl and the man in a raincoat. Send D.C. Ripley round to the CCTV office, I want him to view all the video tapes available, let's see if we can pick out these two, and if they meet'.

'Take the photos and show them to the staff in the restaurant, let's see if anyone recognizes these two. I'm going to the post-mortem, you can meet me there'.

'Have we got any biscuits?'

Jack shuffled in a desk drawer, and threw a packet of Digestives to Martin.

Snapshot 17

'Excuse me, is this seat free?' asked George.

Nick glanced towards the young woman. She wore a long, sixties-style combat jacket with a fur hood and a woolly scarf, tied French-style. As she sat, he could see that she was wearing a pair of Doc Marten boots. She pulled back the hood, and shook her head lightly. Her hair was fair, a light ash colour that set off her fresh complexion.

Drinking her tea, she settled into the soft leather cushions while looking around the café and absorbing the warm atmosphere. Smiling, she leant towards Nick.

'I just watched you knock Luigi into the road.'

He could feel the warmth of her breath, as the words, delivered in a low voice, pierced into him like steel slivers.

'I saw you drop the pound coins. I saw Luigi fall, watched you leave, and then I followed you. I lost you, but later I picked you up in the shopping arcade!'

Nick was stunned, his insides ached and his head whirled as he listened to each word.

'Who are you?' he whispered.

'People call me a street girl, but I don't sell 'Big Issue', I just beg a few quid each day. My spot's just outside the restaurant.'

He took a gulp of tea and looked around. People at the other tables were busily passing the time chattering and drinking tea.

The drizzle continued outside so that rivulets of rainwater ran, snake-like, down the shop window. Shoppers, carrying bags and parcels, passed by the window. Some glanced in, others just continued on their journey with heads bowed.

'Do you know how I was able to follow you even after you changed your appearance?' She seemed to revel in her success, leaning toward him she whispered,

'Your brogue shoes.'

If she had wanted to drive a nail straight into him to cause as much pain as possible, she had just succeeded. Bloody Hell, how could he have been so careless. No time for regret, he had to respond. He had to get out of here and fast.

'What do you want?'

'Why did you do it?'

'Do what?'

'Push the old man under the bus!'

'It was an accident, someone pushed me into him, he fell.'

'I don't believe you.'

'Its true, I dropped the coins as a decoy to facilitate my leaving without being noticed'

George stared; could he have been pushed into Luigi, was it an accident? She wanted to believe him.

'If that is true, then why did you change your clothes?'

'Look, I can't explain here, there are too many people.'

'That makes me feel safe,' she said, taking a long drink of her coffee while watching his reaction.

'I'm going to leave, if you want to come with me, fine. You will be quite safe'.

He slung his bag over his shoulder and walked slowly to the exit.

Uncertain, George gathered her belongings and followed.

Snapshot 18

The dreary drizzle had given way to meagre pockets of sunlight piercing through a grey blanket of cloud.

It had been a long time since George had been interested in anyone. She cursed her involuntary thoughts; was he responsible for Luigi's fall or was it an accident as he had suggested, who was he, why had he changed his appearance; so many questions.

Having left the main town centre, they walked over a very elegant, high, arched cast iron footbridge, and then alongside an old converted warehouse towards the canal basin.

People were fishing along the waters edge. Each of them stared into the black murky waters, contemplating God knows what; perhaps it was their way of escaping from a bad day, or a bad life. Perhaps they even enjoyed it!

George and Nick trudged on, until, at last, the canal waters widened out into a marina. On one side was a riverside restaurant, and on the other, were moored several narrow boats, each one in shining livery that made them look serene.

She followed as he made his way to the nearest boat where he pressed a remote control. Lights came on, and he pushed open a door and disappeared down some steps. From inside, his voice called out

'Come on in, and close the door behind you'.

Snapshot 19

A gentle ripple of water moved away from the hull of the boat as she stepped into the bow section.

The light from the open French doors glowed on the brass Yale lock face, as she stepped into a narrow, oak-furnished lounge. On one side, separated by a coffee table, were two Queen Anne ox-blood leather chairs. Opposite, against the wall, was a low, rectangular sideboard. An oak panelled wall, with a bevelled glass door, divided the room.

'Make yourself at home', he called out.

His voice made her inwardly jolt back to reality.

'What the hell am I doing here, I should never have followed him'. But she knew, from that first meeting in the café, that he intrigued her.

Glancing out of the porthole, across the dark stretch of water, she could see people dining in a dimly lit restaurant. So near, yet so far away.

Snapshot 20

Jack was busy at his desk when the door opened with such force it ruffled papers in his filing tray.

Chief Inspector Martin leant over him.

'You will never believe what the *old man* has just offered me. A bloody desk job – with promotion – but confined to the seventh floor. Me!' He dropped into his chair with a jolt.

Jack was silent as usual.

'I told him No,' Martin continued. 'God! I've waited long enough for promotion, but not this way Jack. I'm not an administrator, the streets are my desk'.

The sergeant, with a look of surprise glanced up, his eyes met Martin's staring at him.

'Handling a squad of dedicated pale-faced computer nerds, can you imagine Jack, a mouse in one hand, and a pen in the other? The Boss reckons this is the future, well not for me, its a load of bollocks!'

Snapshot 21

Detective Constable Ripley was tall and slender, with straight black hair. Renowned for keeping cool in difficult circumstances, he was always well groomed.

He felt sure the photographs, which he had selected, would be of some interest to Chief Inspector Martin.
Unfortunately, most of the CCTV cameras were fixed, so they only delivered surveillance video of their respective target street, and the total area of the town they covered was limited.

Snapshot 22

Snuggled in the deep-buttoned chair, drinking a steaming hot mug of tea smoothed away any immediate fear.

Nick, having drunk from his mug of tea, leaned forward and placed it on the oak table. Reaching behind the chair, he retrieved a cloth shoulder bag and tipped out the contents onto the table.

George, wide-eyed, smiled with her lips tightly closed, as the bundles of notes spewed across the table top.

'I took them from the Italian restaurant' he said, in a matter-of fact voice.

'That's what I do, some of the time.'

'Is this what you killed Luigi for?' George said, staring at the bundles of notes.

'I've already told you that I did not push the old man deliberately. The coins were a decoy to distract pedestrians from noticing my departure, but suddenly everyone was diving around trying to catch the coins. I was pushed into him, he must have stumbled and fallen under the bus, it was an accident'.

'Tell that to Luigi,' said George.

'You knew him?'

'Yes, he was a friend'. She stared at him with piercing brown eyes.

'I'm sorry'. His eyes met hers.

'Look, if there was anything I could do to bring him back, I would, honest.'

George stood; taking off her scarf, she loosened her combat jacket.

'If I thought for one minute you had purposely pushed him,' her voice trailed as she removed the heavy coat, 'I wouldn't be here.'

'Now what's all this? ' She said, sitting in the chair and pointing to the notes on the table.

For the first time he could see the hint of a curvaceous outline beneath the green rugby shirt, but he had no time to mull over such matters, she was expecting answers.

'This is money, I take it from establishments who have plenty,' he said picking up a bundle of notes.

'I've done six over the last two years,' he said smiling.

'I take it that you've never been caught,' she ventured.

'Careful planning, its part of the thrill, being caught doesn't enter into the equation,' he replied.

'Oh, I see' she said shaking her head in a mimicking manner, 'It's part of the thrill'.

'Look,' he said. 'I don't really need the money. It's my way of putting two fingers up at Society, you can have the money,' he pushed the bundle of notes towards her. It was more money than George had ever seen. Even so, she had no intention of taking it. Nick, without waiting for a reply, said, 'Lets have something to eat,' and disappeared.

Snapshot 23

D.C. Ripley walked into the office in a way that suggested to Jack that he was pleased with himself. Jack watched, as Ripley carefully hung his jacket on a vacant hook, before placing a brown folder on the desk in front of Jack.

'I managed to get some images of the street girl.' Leaning over, he fanned out the photographs.

'This one shows the girl sat down in the shopping centre. Here, we see her leaving the shopping centre.'

Jack gazed at the pictures.

'What about the man in the raincoat?'

'Nothing on him after he leaves the main street, but look, here, where she's leaving the shopping centre, there's a male in front, could that be him?'

'This male is much younger than the man in a raincoat,' said Jack looking closely at the picture.

'Yes, but he could have changed his clothes,' said Ripley.

Jack moved towards the door. 'Get your coat, bring those photographs, we are going to pay a visit to the restaurant, lets see if anyone there recognizes this man of yours.'

'Any chance of getting some food while we're there?' asked Ripley, following.

'No chance,' Jack called out, 'I ate yesterday.'

Snapshot 24

George reflected on the cold lonely life she led on the street. She was happy enough, but she had always known that the time would come when she had to move on. The warmth and comfort of the surroundings, the meal and wine she had just enjoyed were the right ingredients to induce a desire for a change of direction. Meeting Nick had stirred those feelings that she thought were best left dormant. The room with its three-quarter bed, a beautiful thick duvet and soft snug pillows, was just sheer heaven. She was beginning to succumb to tiredness.

Snapshot 25

Nick, having finished making the boat ready for the night, switched the outside security system to active, then moved to the lounge where, after pouring himself a malt whisky, with water, he enjoyed a long drink.

He was pleased George had agreed to accept his offer of staying the night, as once over the initial exploratory chit chat, they had enjoyed a pleasant over-the-meal conversation.

His plans for future jobs required two people to do them successfully; would she be prepared to join him? 'I certainly hope so', he thought, as he sipped the whisky.

'Of course,' he mused, 'it will be strictly business.' If she agrees, I will take her through the looking glass.

Snapshot 26

Chief Inspector Martin carried the tray of drinks to a quiet corner, where his Sergeant and Detective Constable Ripley were waiting in anticipation.

'A celebratory drink for my promotion,' he said, putting the tray in the middle of the table.

Jack and Ripley each took a glass.

'Congratulations,' said Ripley, as he raised his glass.

'Actually, I've turned it down, Ripley,' said Martin, 'Would you like to know why?' he continued.

'Yes, sir,' said Ripley, looking confused.

'Because I hate progress, Ripley, it ignores real life situations. Everything is viewed on a flat screen, from behind a desk. Jack, I hope, when your time comes for promotion, they don't drag you away from what matters most, the streets.'

Ripley waited for the Chief Inspector to continue, but nothing followed.

'Did you get a report on the old man from the restaurant Sir,' asked Jack, changing the conversation.

'Don't hold your breath, Jack, it's just what you would expect when someone's been flattened by a bus. There is nothing to suggest it was foul play. What have you got?' asked Martin.

'Well, sir, interviews with witnesses at the scene of the accident have failed to produce any substantial evidence of foul play. It looks like he may have just lost his footing when people scrambled to grab the coins that someone dropped.'

Jack took a drink, and then continued.

'Our only solid link with the restaurant is the man in the raincoat. The waitress remembers serving him, but no one saw him leave.'

'What about the video images, anything there?' Martin asked.

'Afraid not, the man in the raincoat was in the restaurant, but we have no ID and he disappeared off CCTV. The street girl is well known, but there is no evidence to link her to the crime.' Jack finished his drink.

'Inside job?' offered Ripley.

'No chance,' Jack shook his head. 'The owner dies under a bus, and the cash disappears. No, the two are linked, I know they are.'

'Let's look at it with fresh eyes tomorrow,' suggested Martin, 'but right now, Ripley, it's your round.'

Snapshot 27

'Good morning.' Nick knocked on the door.

George woke slowly. The sun shone through the porthole, highlighting the pattern on the duvet. Nick called out again, 'Good morning.' The door opened a little; on seeing she was awake, he entered, with a tray.

'Breakfast, I hope you like soldiers with your boiled eggs,' he said as he placed the tray on the bedside table.

'Do you take milk with your tea?' he asked. Tears welled into the corners of her eyes. The last time she had enjoyed breakfast like this, was when she lived at home with her parents. And boiled eggs!

'It has been so long since I had boiled eggs,' she giggled.
He poured the tea.
'Milk?' he asked.
'Please, this is wonderful. Thank you,' she smiled.
A low, intermittent buzz startled Nick.
'Sorry, I must go,' he said dashing out of the door.
'What's the problem?' shouted George.
'It's the autopilot telling me there is something ahead, another boat probably. Enjoy your breakfast, I'll see you later.'
George looked out of the porthole, to see the countryside moving slowly past.

'Autopilot on a canal-barge. I did not even know we were moving,' she thought. Carefree, she dipped a soldier into the yolk. Now this was idyllic.

Snapshot 28

George had little experience with boats. She looked around curiously, before going to the kitchen to make some more tea. She then showered, and had no trouble in finding anything she wanted, apart from one thing; her clothes.
She did not have to wait too long before Nick returned.

'There is a swing bridge ahead which we have to negotiate, would you give me a hand please,' he asked.

'Well, I would, but you may have noticed that I am not dressed, because I can't find my clothes,' she said in a taunting manner.

'Ah.' He held up one arm in acknowledgement, left the room for a moment, only to return holding a bundle of clothes, which he handed her.
George looked at the trousers and shirt, and asked irritably,

'Where are my clothes?'

Nick pulled a face and rocked his head from side to side, before blurting out,

'I burnt them, your possessions are in the bag,' he handed the bag to George, who looked nonplussed at him.

'You burnt my clothes, what the bloody hell are you playing at, you asshole.'

'It was absolutely necessary, we were both at the scene of the accident, when the police check the CCTV they may think you were involved, you would be easily identified in those clothes.' he stressed.

'Why would they think I was involved?' she said disbelievingly.

'You left the scene of a crime, you were a witness, and they may want to interview you.'

'Oh great, that's my patch, everyone knows me,' she said.

'Exactly, and when you don't return, they will put two and two together.'

'You still had no right to burn my clothes, absolutely no right.'

'Look, I'm sorry, go out and buy new clothes. Shop till you drop.'

'You had absolutely no right,' she repeated.

'In those clothes, everyone knew you. But look at you now, in my rugby shirt, you look great. No one, in a million years, would think you were a street girl,' he smiled and held out the clothes once more.

'It is a long time since anyone paid me a compliment,' George mused.

'Shop till you drop, he said, well he just might regret that,' she thought. 'You should have talked to me first, I don't like being taken for granted.'

She scooped up the shirt and trousers. 'If you need help with the swing bridge, I need to dress,' she said.

'Right, meet you topside,' he said.

'Oh, and by the way, I like my eggs boiled for five minutes.'

Snapshot 29

Ripley held up the police tape that cordoned off the scene of the accident, both Jack and Chief inspector Martin bent low and made their way through to the restaurant. Once inside, all three sat down in the reception area, opposite the till.

'Forensics have failed to find anything, no prints, fibres or footprints. We have so far failed to identify the 'man in the raincoat'. Interviews with witnesses, searches, and CCTV material have likewise failed to produce any evidence. So, we are looking for a needle in a haystack, except, we have no idea where the bloody haystack is,' said Martin.
Jack stood and surveyed the immediate area.

'Our suspect finishes a meal, walks over to the till, then, he persuades Luigi to hand over the takings.' Jack walked over to the till.

'He then guides the old man outside, where he ends up under the bus. He leaves no clues, evades CCTV, and disappears.'
Martin walked over to join Jack.

'Well, lets get out there and catch him. Jack I want you to contact other departments, let's check on crimes with a similar modus operandi. Ripley, I want you to check the CCTV footage of major stores around town for any sightings of this man in the raincoat.'

Snapshot 30

It was a beautiful afternoon. George lay on the roof of the boat as it drifted lazily along a stretch of still water. The sky was cloudless. In the distance, a passenger jet moved slowly through the sky, leaving behind a white vapour trail that gradually dispersed. The breeze that swept over her was warm as she looked down past the hull of the boat, and saw trees reflected in the sparkling water. Her thoughts drifted along with the passing images.

Her recent life had become so monotonous. Begging was so demeaning and degrading, even though it had been necessary for survival. The fact that she was a street girl didn't mean she had lost her sense of morals or social sensibility.

It was time to leave. Meeting Nick had reawakened a zest for life. It was now time for a new direction. His adventurous, carefree life appealed to her more than she cared to admit.

But for now, she was happy to drift along, especially on this lazy afternoon.

Snapshot 31

Nick was busy mapping their progress on the canal. The attraction for him, of cruising on a narrow boat, was the leisurely pace of life. The boat had a top speed of 5 mph, which meant there was plenty of time for reflection.

He estimated that they should reach the next mooring in two hours. First, he had to successfully navigate a passage through a five-rise lock system that would lift the boat over sixty feet to the next water level. George seemed to have settled into boat life, he pondered. He enjoyed her company. When the boat had been successfully moored he would take her on the promised shopping trip, after which Nick would have to leave for the next job. Perhaps George would agree to join him.

Snapshot 32

As an antique dealer he was used to long hours in the auction houses, but shopping with George was a much more tiresome business. Despite not having had the opportunity to shop for a few years, she had lost none of the enthusiasm that her sex was blessed with when it came to spending money.

An exhausted Nick poured himself a malt whisky, and then dropped into the Queen Anne chair.

A jubilant George poured a drink. 'Guess how many bags?'

'I've no idea.'

'Fourteen, I haven't enjoyed myself so much for ages.' she said, prodding Nick.

'Now, I'll show you what I bought,' she said laughing.

'All that.' He asked incredulously, pointing at a pile of bags.

'Absolutely.' She carefully lifted out a limp garment from its box. Nick helped himself to another whisky. George placed the dress against her body and half turned.

'What do you think?'

'Its beautiful.'

She tossed the dress aside and opened another parcel.

'I just love this colour,' she said spinning round to show him another dress. After many twirls and swirls and an indeterminate number of changes, the show finally came to end. George slumped in a chair and threw off her shoes.

'Thanks Nick, for a most wonderful, absolutely superfragalistic type of amazing day.' Her voice grew ever fainter then trailed off, as she relaxed.

Nick watched her as she fell asleep. He reflected on how fortunate he was to have met her, even though the circumstances of that meeting were a little unusual. He had liked her the first time she had thrown him her friendly smile, for she had a vitality that he found charming.

However, he thought, tomorrow I must talk to her. When she's listened to my plans, then she'll have to decide whether to stay and join me, or move on.

Snapshot 33

After checking the mooring pins and ropes, Nick walked the full length of the boat to make sure everything was in order. Satisfied the boat was moored correctly, he made his way down to the lounge. George had just finished making a snack of tea and corned beef sandwiches.

'That was good timing,' she smiled.
Nick pushed a CD into a player and adjusted the volume.

'George, I need to talk.'

'OK,' she sensed a degree of seriousness in his voice. She joined him in the lounge, setting down the tray on the oak table between the two chairs.

'I hope you like corned beef,' she said, pushing a mug of tea in his direction.

'I do, thank you.' He said taking a bite.

'You're welcome.'

'Really tasty.'

'You have something to tell me,' she said curiously.

'Yes,' he sighed. 'Look, if I didn't like you so much, this would be really easy,' he blurted out in a low voice.

'Wow, corned beef can work wonders,' she giggled.

'I have to leave.'

'I know.'

'I'd like you to come with me.' They both ate in silence, as a track of soft, gentle music by Carmine D'Amico played in the background.

George had anticipated this moment, the time when she would be faced with having to make a decision. She had only known Nick briefly, but already was becoming addicted to the thrill of his unpredictability; his unchoreographed attitude to life appealed to her more and more, and the excitement of his 'out-of-the-blue' moments was increasingly tempting to her.

Her jumbled thoughts were spinning around. Did she really want to walk away? Yes. There was another side to him, that which had brought them together. There was so much she really didn't know.

Her street life phase had ended. Should she stay with Nick, or walk away.

Nick felt uncertain about what her answer would be. He knew at this moment he really wanted her to stay. Previously his emotions had been strictly controlled, put away for another day, well that day had finally arrived. He reached and took her hand.

'You want to know more about me, before you can make a decision?'

She looked at his hand lightly grasping hers, and said with a gentle nod. 'Yes.'

Snapshot 34

Nick had suggested that they both pack, and be ready to leave, so whichever decision George made, they would either leave the boat separately, or together.

Nick did not have to wait too long. George brought in her bags and joined him in the lounge. Dressed in black stretch jeans and a zip-up chunky cardigan, with her hair hung loose around her shoulders, she slumped into the chair opposite Nick.

After passing a few pleasantries, Nick began what he knew would be a make or break explanation. He took a drink, and shuffled back into his chair.

'After leaving University, where I studied History, I moved to London where I worked in a leading auction house.'

'Life was good to me, I moved over to New York for a short time with the company, and shortly after my return I was promoted. Everything was fine, I enjoyed my work and I had a good social life with a great circle of friends.'

'But then my parents were killed in a road accident. The driver of a lorry fell asleep, crossed the central reservation and hit their car head on, they were both killed instantly.'

'Oh God,' murmured George, standing and looking out of the window, 'Please stop, I'm so sorry, you don't have to go on.'

'George it's OK, I want to continue.' Nick motioned to her to sit down.

'As the only child, I inherited everything.'

'I took a lot for granted when I was young, perhaps, even right up to my parents' death. They were both hard-working teachers, they lived in a beautiful house in Hampshire, and enjoyed a comfortable standard of living.'

'I know my father inherited some money from a distant uncle when I was about seventeen, but it was never mentioned, so I assumed it was a modest amount. Actually, they could have retired, and lived off the interest, but instead, they chose to put it away for me.'

Reflective for a moment, Nick sighed, then continued.

'So, suddenly I found myself very well off. I was able to give up my job in London and move back to my parents' house.'

'I spent a couple of months taking stock of everything that had happened, searching for answers about my parents' death.'

'I attended the trial of the lorry driver who had crashed into mum and dad. He was just an ordinary man in his late 30's, married with four children. He was employed by a multi national firm 'East West Transportation Co', whose tight delivery schedules made it very difficult for him to keep within the legal requirements governing the time he was allowed to drive during any one shift.'
'The firm hired the best defence lawyers that money could buy, they hung the lorry driver out to dry; he lost his licence, his job and was sentenced to nine months imprisonment. The Company directors walked out of court without a blemish to their name or reputation.'

'The driver hung himself in prison.'

'After a while, I knew that I wanted to hurt large companies like the one that had, in my mind, been responsible for the death of my parents, and the driver.'

'Apart from myself, the innocent victims of this tragic accident were the family that the driver had left behind. I had to see them before I could close this chapter of my life and move on. I visited the wife and her children. They rented a small two bedroom terraced house on a council estate.'

'I went as a welfare officer from her husband's previous company.'

'She was living on benefits, the home was clean and tidy, the children were happy. We talked, she expressed no bitterness about what had happened, on the contrary, she expressed sorrow for the elderly couple that had died as a result of the *'accident'*.'

'You gave her money didn't you,' interrupted George.
Nick smiled,

'There was pain in the woman's eyes, she was lonely. I don't know why, but I shared her pain. Yes, I sent her the keys to a detached house, and she later learnt that her husband had been awarded a pension.'

'Oh yes, that is just wonderful. Did you see her again?' Without waiting for a reply George continued, 'You did, didn't you, tell me.'

'Yes, some months later, I called. They were happy in their new home; the children loved their new school, and the pain had left the woman's eyes.'

'Oh wow, that is really cool,' said George.
Nick smiled but was determined to conclude the final part of his narrative.

'I travelled around quite a bit, looking for somewhere to settle down, before eventually finding the ideal place in Wensleydale.
I bought a house and started a small antique business in Hawes; it's a small market town nestled in the hills of the Yorkshire Dales.'

'It's from here that I decide which firms to hit. I plan everything down to the last detail, then carry it out while I am away, supposedly buying antiques.'

'How many jobs have you done?' asked George curiously.
'Six,' replied Nick.

'But the restaurant you robbed is not a large business,' George protested.

'I know, I did that to divert attention. If the Police think there are a number of small businesses being targeted, they will concentrate a lot of their resources in that area. I have one more job to do before the big one against 'Computer International'.'

George listened to Nick's matter-of-fact manner, describing in detail how he planned each robbery. Instead of being repelled by his actions against the multi-nationals, she found herself excited by the element of risk; she was being drawn into his web.

'Nick. You don't have to explain anymore' she said interrupting him. Nick stopped talking, he stared at her. He could feel his heart beating faster while he waited for her to give him her decision.

'I'm staying with you.' she said decisively.

Snapshot 35

Heavy clouds blocked out the moonlight, tree branches danced against a chill wind. Through a gap in the trees, they could see the front of the late seventeenth century building that was now a private country club with exclusive membership. The windows on the ground floor were black, and a solitary light shone from one window upstairs. The revellers had left fifteen minutes ago.

Nick glanced at his watch. 'One forty-five, the steward and his wife will be leaving soon,' he whispered.

'Are you sure?' asked George.

'Absolutely, they meet their friends at the Casino every Saturday, like clockwork,'

George waited patiently at Nick's side. She felt rather awkward in her dark disposable jump suit; she pulled down her wool hat to keep her ears warm.

'Here they come,' Nick pointed; they watched as the couple climbed into their car, started the engine, then drove off down the drive and into the road.

Once the headlights had disappeared, Nick and George moved to the front door. Nick opened the haversack; passed a torch, and then he inserted a master key into the lock and with a few twists, the door opened.

Once inside, George followed Nick down a wood-panelled corridor and into a side office. Using the torchlight, he searched round until he came to a large desk, on top of which were two till drawers.

'Unbelievable how people can be so careless with money,' said Nick. They quickly put the notes into the haversack.

'I can't believe it,' George said excitedly.

Finished, they moved along the corridor and back into the night air. Nick closed the front door, and they set off across the drive.
It did not take too long before they reached the car and sped off into the night.

Snapshot 36

George could hardly believe she was walking on the same streets that she had used as a street girl. Familiar faces still occupied the same spots on the pavement, but none recognized her as she gave each one some coins.

They had visited the church in the centre of town, where they had left an envelope for the church appeal for the disabled, then another one for music therapy for children with autism; for almost an hour they had toured through the town, dropping off donations to various charitable organizations.
Finally, they called into the Viking, where they had first met.

'That was a really great afternoon,' said George.

'A lot of people are going to be surprised,' smiled Nick.

'Absolutely,' replied George.

'Now for the big one,' said Nick.

Snapshot 37

Chief Inspector Martin turned the car into the tree-lined drive of the country club.

'How much do you think it will cost to be a member here?' asked Martin.

'A lot more than I can afford on my wage,' answered the sergeant.

'My father's a member,' chirped Ripley.

'Is he now, then you'll know who's who, I suppose,' said Martin sternly.

'Not really, sir,' answered Ripley nervously.

The car came to a halt in front of the grand building. The three of them walked towards a young constable waiting at the front entrance.

'First on the scene, were you constable?' Martin asked.

'Yes sir, I got here at 11.19 am,' the constable answered confidently.

'What have you to tell me?'

'It looks like the suspect or suspects came in through the front door, here, sir,' the constable said as he pointed to the door lock. 'No sign of forced entry; it seems they walked into the unlocked office, took the money from the desk and left sir.'

'Witnesses,' asked Martin.

'None at the time of entry, sir, but four people were on the premises when I arrived, they are waiting in the bar. I secured the immediate area, sir, although there were some members already on the golf course.'

'Bloody Hell, Ripley, secure the whole area, and get those people off the course,' barked Martin, before returning his attention to the constable.

'Tell me about the witnesses.'

The constable opened his notebook. 'There is Mr. Rolling and his wife, they are the live-in stewards, a Mr. Marshall the barman, and finally Mrs. Dixon, a cleaner.'

'Well done. Now go down the drive and secure the entrance,' said Martin.

Inspector Martin and the sergeant entered the hallway.

'Jack, ask Mr. Rolling if he will join me, you look after the other three with Ripley.'

Martin needed only a few minutes with the steward to realize that slack security had been a major factor in the robbery. He turned to Jack, who had joined him in the office.

'Leaving the money on top of the desk was gross stupidity Jack, but there is more; the safe is in need of repair and the security camera hasn't worked for ages.'

'Apparently the committee had postponed repairs because they felt that their isolation and the fact that they had not had any break-ins lessened the urgency.' said Jack.

'Bloody fools' Martin retorted.

'That apart, Jack, does anything strike you as being familiar?'

'Yes, the simplicity; it's clean, they leave very little evidence, it reminds me of the Italian job.'

'Exactly,' agreed Martin, 'good local knowledge, leaves very little to chance, he's going to hit us again Jack, but the question is, where?'

Snapshot 38

This was a side of him that she had not seen before today. The break-in at the club had been relatively easy for her, all she had to do was follow him, but now she had a role, and Nick had rehearsed her through every stage of the job, until she could repeat it word for word.

'I'm exhausted,' said George leaning back in her chair.

'Sorry, I've been too hard on you.' said Nick.

'I forgive you,' she teased.

'In the past, I've only had myself to consider,' he explained.

'And now you have me,' she grinned.

'Yes, and tomorrow we are really going to hurt Computer International,' he said.

'Do you really believe taking the money will hurt them?' asked George.

'Oh yes, it's not just losing the money George, but the way we will have removed it, that will hurt them most. It undermines their credibility.'

'Well that is tomorrow, right now, I think we should go for something to eat.' she said.

'Just what the doctor ordered,' he laughed.

'No. George.'

Snapshot 39

Chief Inspector Martin was struggling with some paperwork on the computer, Jack was leant over a filing cabinet as Ripley entered carrying the local Metro paper.

'Sarge, have you seen the paper today?' he said, approaching Jack, who shut the filing cabinet with a clatter.

'No' answered Jack, 'I never read the papers on Monday.'

'How much money was taken from the restaurant and the golf club, asked Ripley.

'Exactly £27,000,' replied Jack.

Chief Inspector Martin, listening, suddenly showed some interest.

'Why do you want to know,' asked the sergeant.

'Look,' Ripley spread the newspaper on the desk, 'someone has been leaving donations around the town, and guess how much?

'Would it be £27,000, asked Jack, looking at the Inspector who had grabbed the paper?

Martin, having read the piece, dropped the paper.

'Well, Jack looks like Robin Hood's returned.' They both stared at each other.

'Grab your coats,' said Martin, 'we're going to be charitable and collect some envelopes and cash.'

Snapshot 40

'Sarah, I have packed your clothes, will you please choose what you want to wear for travelling,' called Sheila Hawks to her daughter.

'OK mum. Have you seen my Molly Moon book?' asked Sarah.

Sheila was looking forward to the mid-week break in Scotland. She carried the luggage through to the hall ready for a quick getaway. Sheila and her husband had been married for fourteen years, and they made a habit of taking as many weekend breaks as work would allow.

'Sarah, your book's next to the computer in the study,' she called out to her daughter.

Snapshot 41

Stephen was forty, slightly overweight, with dark hair that was receding steadily. He was manager of a busy store selling the latest in computer technology. The last three days of the sale had seen a huge increase in people buying last minute bargains.

He would be glad when the last customers left, and he could close the store. He was looking forward to meeting his wife and daughter and then driving to Selkirk overnight, where he would relax and enjoy a few days fishing.

Snapshot 42

'We should arrive in about five minutes,' said Nick, without taking his eyes off the road.

George felt nervous, but prevented it from showing by smiling. She watched the countryside gradually giving way from a sprinkling of private dwellings amongst the fields, to a sudden mass of housing estates.

'Are you OK?' asked Nick.

'Yes,' she replied.

She knew there was no going back, but something nagged deep inside, telling her that this was wrong. They were going to dive inside someone's life and turn it upside down; for three hours they were going to hold two people against their will and cause untold suffering. But, of course, they would not be harmed in any way, they would soon be reunited, and as a result of the experience they might be closer as a family, she told herself, attempting to justify what was about to unfold.

Nick pulled the Ford Galaxy into a lay by.

'The house is just round the corner,' he said.

He reached over to the rear seat for a parcel and a clipboard.

'As soon as I am in the house I will ring you, then bring the car into the drive and join me in the house'. His voice was firm and betrayed no emotion. She watched him go towards the house.

Alone, she felt very vulnerable. Part of her felt like running away. Quickly she moved into the driving seat and dismissed any doubt, for the next few hours she had to remain focused. Looking into the vanity mirror on the visor, she admired the skilfully applied makeup and wig that made her look fifteen years older. Nick had aged himself twenty years. The preparation and application of the make-up had taken over two hours, but the transformation was amazing, she hardly recognized herself.

Snapshot 43

The gravel crunched beneath his feet, as he walked down the drive. He gazed over a neatly cut lawn, surrounded by a square border in which rudbeckia, dahlias and asters vied with each other to display their beauty.
He approached the front door and pressed the doorbell once.
He heard the chime from inside, a moment passed, then the door opened and Mrs. Sheila Hawks appeared.

'Hello, I have a parcel for Mrs. Hawks,' Nick said, holding out the gift-wrapped parcel.

'Would you sign here please?' Nick passed the clipboard to a surprised looking Mrs. Hawks. She tried to sign, but the pen was empty.

'It rather looks like your pen has run out of ink' she said.

'Oh, I am sorry,' said Nick, acting surprised.

'I have one inside, just one moment.' She disappeared, leaving Nick alone at the door. Quickly he moved inside, then closed the door gently. He found himself in a spacious warm hallway; a coat stand, chair and table occupied one side of the hall. He saw two suitcases and some jackets laid under the table. On the other side of the hall, a large mirror hung at the bottom of a staircase, and at the end of the hall another door led into a kitchen.

Nick could see Mrs. Hawks moving about in this room through a chink in the door. He moved down and met her as she was returning with a pencil. A gasp of surprise turned to anger, as she realized the stranger had entered her home.

'What on earth do you think you are doing?' she asked angrily. Nick pulled out a gun and pointed it at the woman.

'Don't make a noise and you will come to no harm, just do as I say. Move into the sitting room right now.' He waved the gun towards the room. Mrs. Hawks looked in horror at the nozzle of the gun pointing in her direction. She moved slowly into the room.

'Sit down. Now, I want you to call your daughter and ask her to join you,' Nick asked firmly.

How did this man, whom she had never seen before today, know that she had a daughter? Who was he, and what did he want?

'Look, what do you want? Who are you?' she cried.

'I'll explain everything to you when your daughter is here, now call her,' he asked again.

'Sarah, will you come down please' she called before sitting on the edge of the settee.

'Now I'm going to put this in my pocket, but remember you must do exactly what I say, we mean you no harm.' Nick put the gun away.

'OK, mummy, what do you want? Oh,' the young girl ran into the room, but halted quickly when she saw her mum with a stranger standing at the side of her.

'Hello,' she said, looking at Nick.

'Mummy, what's the matter? Who is this?' She climbed on her mother's knee, but kept a very careful eye on the stranger.
Nick took out a mobile phone, pressed a button, and waited for George to answer. After what seemed an age, he heard her say 'Hello'.

'We're ready' he said, and finished the call.
The girl looked at him the whole time with an unnerving gaze.

'In a few moments we will be leaving, I want you both to wear warm coats. When my colleague arrives, I'll explain what we want you to do. Do you understand?

'Yes, but what do you want, if its money, I have some you can have....' Nick interrupted the woman.

'I'll explain everything in a moment. I don't want your money.' Sheila Hawks was frightened for the safety of herself and her daughter, but already it was apparent to her that this was no ordinary robbery, and she did not feel threatened in a sexual way. She had to keep calm.

Her thoughts were interrupted by the sound of the front door opening and someone coming into the room. Who could it be, was it a neighbour, or even Stephen, coming home from work early? The door opened and her hopes were dashed.

Nick turned to Sarah. 'Will you put on a warm coat and gloves, this lady will go with you to find them, then we are going to take a short car journey.'

The girl clung tightly to her mother, and shook her head to signify her reluctance.

Nick motioned to the mother. 'Please?' he asked.

The woman told her daughter that everything was all right, and that she should accompany the lady, and return as soon as she found her clothes.

' Thank you for that,' he said, before continuing,

'Briefly, this is what we are going to do. Your husband is the manager of Computer International. We are going to visit the store, where we will explain to him that we have you with us; he will give us money for your safe return. That's it.'

'You'll not hurt us?' the woman asked.

'Not at all, it will be all over in a couple of hours. Believe me, if there was another way of persuading your husband to hand over the money, I would do it, but he is a company man, and this is the only way,' Nick said.

There was something in his explanation that rang true. She believed he meant them no harm, but he had no right invading their privacy. She felt helpless against him, but she had to play along. Sarah and the woman came back into the room, her daughter looked calm.

'Would you please get your coat, Mrs. Hawks, and be sure to bring your mobile,' Nick said, as he led the way into the hall. Once they had put their coats on, Nick gave them some woollen hats.

'Put these on please.' He motioned to George, 'Bring the clip board and parcel.'

Once outside, he opened the rear door of the Galaxy, lifted the seat, and motioned to the girl and Mrs. Hawks to sit in the third row. George moved into the driving seat, turned the key and the engine spluttered to life.

Snapshot 44

Sheila Hawks sat motionless, in the rear of the car. It seemed unreal; they were being driven away by two complete strangers. She hugged her daughter as a source of comfort for both of them.

The man who sat in the passenger seat turned round, and gave them both a pair of headphones. She recognised them straight away as similar to the Bose Quietcomfort they had at home.

'Put these on over your hats please,' once they had put them on, he continued, his voice coming through the headphones.

'Thank you, I have chosen the latest Wallace and Gromit film for you to watch, Sarah, I hope you like it.' He flicked a switch on the console between the front seats and continued, 'From now on all communication between us will only be through your headset.'

It was so unreal, they had planned everything. The credits started to roll as the DVD played on the small screens fitted into the rear of the headrests. Through the tinted side window she looked out upon familiar streets; there were people going about their business, everyone was oblivious to their plight. She was really angry inside, but her instincts told her to sit quietly. Hopefully, her cooperation could lead to a quick conclusion of this damned business.

The man turned to face her, 'Please pass me your mobile,' he asked.

She passed him the phone. 'Thank you, I'll be using this to speak to your husband.'

He made it sound like it was so ordinary.

The voice of Peter Sallis as Wallace babbled over the headphones.

Snapshot 45

Walking around the store, Stephen Hawks noticed instinctively, which displays required attention and stock replenishment, as well as the customers whose body language suggested that they required the help of a sales assistant.

He caught the eye of a number of assistants, and despatched them to assist waiting customers in various parts of the store.

Once inside the office, he automatically refreshed his computer screen in order to observe the latest ongoing sales figures for the day. As the manager of a large retail outlet, a large proportion of his day was related to observing the stores performance targets. His success was measured by the outcome of such figures.

The familiar ring of his mobile broke his concentration. He glanced at the screen, it was his wife on the phone.

'Hello Sheila' he sat back in his chair, and looked out through the large smoked glass window into the store.

'Mr Hawks, I have your wife Sheila and your daughter Sarah here with me. Now listen, very carefully, to what I'm about to say.' The hairs on the nape of Hawks neck stood out, as he listened to the intrusive, unemotional voice.

'Don't talk to anyone, don't do anything to draw attention to yourself, do you understand?'

'How do I know...' unable to continue Hawks listened as the voice said firmly,

'Mr Hawks, when I ask a question, you had better answer me or else you will never see your family alive, do you understand?'

'Yes.' He responded meekly, his gut knotted tight in revulsion at the submissive response.

'Proceed to the front entrance of the store immediately,' the voice ordered him, 'stand to the right of the door. You will see your wife and daughter. Remember, do not speak to anyone, we are watching you Mr. Hawks.' The mysterious caller rang off.

Not even sure his legs would carry him, he began the walk, as instructed, to the front of the store. Tears of fear were beginning to form in the corner of his eyes; he consciously jerked himself upright, fighting the anxiety for his beloved wife and lovely Sarah. *'What were they feeling, oh God, please don't let anything happen to them. I must behave normally,'* he said to himself. He reached the large plate glassed entrance and peered out into the darkness of the car park.

The phone rang.

'Hello' said Mr Hawks.

'Look to your right Stephen.'

He didn't like the familiarity the voice had adopted towards him, as if they were chums. The voice continued.

'You will see a car moving slowly towards you soon, it will halt in front of you. Don't call out; you may press your hand onto the window in acknowledgement when you see your wife and daughter. I will be in touch.'

His heart was racing when he saw the vehicle approaching, it was a Ford Galaxy. It moved slowly towards the store with its headlights on full beam, which made it difficult for Stephen to see the driver. The windows were tinted, making it impossible to see inside. The car stopped directly in front of him, and as he stared intently at the rear window, it opened slowly to reveal two faces; his wife and daughter. For one moment, their eyes made contact.

Mr Hawks pressed his right hand onto the glass in recognition, then the car pulled away. His heart sank as he watched the window slowly close. The sight of his wife and daughter in the clutches of some fanatic was really scary, the thought of what they might have to endure tormented him.

Suddenly, a voice returned him to the present.

'Stephen, I put the business figures on your desk.'

The voice belonged to his senior sales assistant Paul, who was waiting for a response.

'Thanks Paul, I'll be with you shortly.'

'Sure,' the young man said as he left.

His mobile rang once more.

'Stephen,' the voice continued. 'Your family will be safe providing you do exactly what I say. Do you understand?'

'Yes,' said Hawks.

'Now listen carefully Stephen, remember the safety of your family is in your hands. If you follow my instructions, you should be reunited soon. Close the store by 8-15 prompt, get rid of all the staff, including security, tell them you are waiting for some special downloads from Head Office, which means you have to stay behind. I will be watching you Stephen.'

Stephen put the mobile in his pocket. *'This person has inside knowledge of the store,'* he thought, no one, except staff, knew anything about the habits of Head Office. *'He still hasn't told me what he wants,'* he thought.

The last customer had left and some staff were tidying up ready for the morning, while others checked and closed down the tills. He thanked the staff and explained to them that they could leave early. They did not need to be told twice, and soon the last member of staff had said goodnight.

Alone, Stephen switched the lighting over to night mode. *'Should I ring the police,'* he thought, *'no, there was the possibility that the man holding his family might hurt them.'*

'They will be hurting now, oh God,' the thought of them suffering was unbearable. *'What next, he said he would ring, where are they,'* thoughts buzzing round and round, he was losing control.

Brrrrr, brrrrr, brrrr.

He grabbed the mobile, and with hands shaking he pressed the green 'accept call' button.

'Hello' he croaked.

'Is the store empty?' the voice asked.

'Yes, my wife an....'

'No questions, remember, no questions' the voice interrupted.

'Right, I just wanted to know that they are OK' he blurted out angrily, he was not used to taking a subordinate role.

'Look, we have a lot of work to do, now listen carefully. If you do exactly what I say, you will be with your family soon, OK' the voice said.

'Yes' Stephen rapped.

'Walk over to the finance office, tell me when you have arrived,' the voice ordered. Stephen made his way to the office, careful not to collide with any displays in the subdued lighting. *'This guy definitely has inside knowledge,'* he thought.

'I've arrived,' he called out over the phone.

'Good. Now, open the safe, take out all, and I mean all the bags from the last three days takings. Is that clear?'

'Yes, quite clear,' retorted Stephen.

'Good. Keep the cheques and coins separate. I only want notes, put these into two bags.'

Stephen opened the safe and carried out the stranger's instructions. He could remember exactly the number of staff who had left the store, during his time as manager, but not one of them could pull a stunt like this.

'Finished' he told the stranger.

'Good, now tie the tops, then place them inside a bin liner,' he ordered.

'A bin liner?' Stephen was not sure he could lay his hands on one.

'Go to the cleaner's cupboard, failing that, empty the bin by the tills and use that,' the voice said.

'Right.' Stephen was sure he detected a hint of mirth in the instructions. This man was relishing revealing his inside knowledge of the store. Back in the office he put the bags in the bin liner as ordered.

'That's done,' he said.

'Now remove the current video tape from the security machine and place it in the bag,' he said.

Stephen smiled, *'clever'* he thought, *without the tape, we have no film of customer movement in the store, and more importantly, outside the front entrance.*

'Tapes in the bag'

'I will be checking the tape for today's date' the voice said.

'It's the correct tape, believe me, I am not about to play with my family's safety,' Stephen replied.

'Good. Make sure the bag is secure, go wait in the front entrance. I will contact you in a moment,' the voice said.

Stephen carried the bin liner into the vestibule of the front entrance. The car park was dark and empty except for his car, a Ford Cobra. He longed to see Sheila and little Sarah. *'Please God keep them safe,'* he thought.

Lights swept, arc-like in the night, as a vehicle moved along the long drive and into the car park, where it came to a halt. Stephen watched and waited until the expected ring tone on his mobile played its familiar tone.

'Hello,' he said in anticipation.

'Do you have the bag?' the voice asked.

'Yes' he replied.

'When the Ranger stops outside the store, put the bag under the tanneau cover. Signal that you have done this by hitting the side panel, then stand back. Go to your car, I'll ring you in six minutes. Is that clear?' the voice said.

'Completely,' said Stephen. He watched the vehicle as it began to move slowly toward the store. *'He is inside, I could rush him, no, the doors will be locked, besides Sheila and Sarah were in the Ford Galaxy. Bloody Hell, there's two of them!'* his head ached with all this contemplation.

The blood red Ranger came to a halt opposite him.

He moved out into the night, the chill in the air brought a single shiver. He lifted the cover, threw in the bag, and gave the tailgate a swift crack. The vehicle moved off leaving Stephen surrounded in a cloud of white exhaust gasses.

Snapshot 46

Nick watched through the rear mirror as the store manager receded into the distance, surrounded by plumes of white exhaust smoke. It looked like a magician had just materialized on some giant stage.

The journey was a short one, and soon he was pulling the Ranger into the rear of the disused sports centre, where George was waiting in the Ford Galaxy with an increasingly anxious Mrs Hawks.

He lowered the window so he could speak with George.

'Everything went smoothly, are the passengers all right?' he whispered.

'Yes,' she replied.

'Good, then deliver them as arranged, I'll see you in a short while.' He closed the window and drove off.

George followed, after a short drive, she pulled into the drive leading to the store.

'Mrs Hawks, your husband is in the car outside the store, waiting for you,' she said, 'please put your hats and headphones on the seat in front of you. The door is unlocked, you may leave, do not look behind.'

Mrs Hawks heard the words with a huge sense of relief. Taking Sarah's headphones and hat, she leaned over and placed them with her own on the seat as instructed. There was a click as she pressed the door handle, she pushed the seat forward and climbed out. She held Sarah as she jumped down into the driveway. Suddenly the fresh air, although chilly, felt really good.

They walked quickly, almost in a run, towards the car, when she saw her husband get out of the car and stumble forward to meet them. Crying with relief, she grabbed Sarah and they ran the final few yards until they all met in a welcome embrace.

Snapshot 47

Nick parked the Ford Ranger on the deserted hillside road while waiting for George to join him with the Ford Galaxy.

He reached over and looked inside the bag stuffed full of notes, took out the videotape, and emptied the money into a sports bag.

She parked, as arranged, further down the hill. She jumped out of the cab and went to meet him.

'Are you alright?' he asked.

'Yes,' she said, out of breath from the uphill walk.

Nick gave her a small welcome hug, which she reciprocated.

'If you take this up to the BMW, I will clear up here,' he said, handing her the sports bag. He watched her set off for the car that they had left earlier.

'You were terrific,' he called after her.

He gathered all the evidence; headphones, hats, jackets and wigs, together with mobiles and the videotape, and threw them into the rear seat.

From the back of the Ranger he pulled out two large petrol cans. With one of them, he walked down the hill to the Galaxy. Quickly, he emptied the contents of the can over the upholstery, and shut the door.

Back at the Ranger, he emptied the second can in the same way. Starting the engine, he held down the clutch and at the same time jammed the accelerator with a pre-made bracket. The engine screamed as the revolutions increased.

Poised carefully on the side styling bar step, he flicked the car into gear, and jumped clear as the vehicle, tyres screeching, rushed down the hill at great speed.

Already moving up the hill to join George, he watched as the two cars met with a deafening explosion. A ball of flame burst into the air. Nick climbed into the BMW, and as the car moved off, he sank into the seat and gazed at the images reflected in the door mirror; flames from the cars danced fiercely in the chill of the night.

Snapshot 48

Detective Chief Inspector Martin pulled up the collar of his coat against the chill night air. He walked together with his sergeant to the front of the store, where revolving lights from the parked police vehicles reflected onto the large glass frontage.

A policeman from inside signalled to them to use the lower door. As they walked along the frontage, Martin glanced irritably at his reflection.

The glass door opened, and they were greeted by Ripley.

'Evening sir, I think you'll be interested in this particular robbery.'

'Do you now, even at 9.30 at night,' said Martin mischievously.

'I think our friend's been at it again, sir,' said Ripley.

'He's not exactly our friend, is he Ripley,' Martin said, smiling at Jack.

'No sir, I was speaking metaphorically,' replied Ripley.

'Get on with it Ripley, get on with it,' said Martin.

Ripley gave an outline of the robbery to Martin and the sergeant.

'Only took bank notes again,' remarked Martin. 'Tiger kidnapping; now that requires cunning, stealth and meticulous planning Jack.'

'Mr and Mrs Hawks and the girl are waiting in the canteen,' said Ripley.

'Jack, ask Mr Hawks to join me, you talk with the wife; not the girl though, we will have to wait for a specially trained officer. We can do that tomorrow. OK?'

Ripley led the sergeant to the canteen.

Martin walked round, looking at the various displays of printers, scanners and computers. The technology he observed did not endear him to the modern store. It was his first exposé; though he had often heard his children talk about their visits.

'Mr Martin.' Stephen Hawks called out.

'Detective Chief Inspector Martin, you must be Mr Hawks, the store manager,' Martin replied, reaching out and shaking his hand.

'I would like to ask you a few questions Mr Hawks.'

Stephen Hawks was tired, the last few hours had been draining. The wonderful reconciliation with his wife and daughter seemed an age away. Once the police had arrived, there had been photographs, fingerprints, explanations and statements, phone calls to the regional manager to explain the evening's events, and further questions, questions, questions.

He explained everything to the Detective Chief Inspector. From the tone of some of the questions he realized for the first time that he was a possible suspect, in that he could have conspired to rob his own store. The mere thought that he was under suspicion appalled him.

'So you did not see his face at all?' asked Martin.

'Like I said, not at all,' replied Hawks.

'And you cannot remember hearing this voice before tonight?' said Martin, probingly.

'No, never,' replied a very anxious Mr Hawks.

'That will be all for the moment, we'll talk some more tomorrow. The forensic team have finished "doing the necessary" at your house, so please take your family home.'

Martin noticed two men leaving the finance office with a large case. He signalled to Ripley, who rushed over.

'Who are they, Ripley?' he asked.

'Company security sir,' said Ripley.

'Get them off the premises Ripley, we are investigating a crime here, get rid of them,' he shouted so the two security men heard, and were left in no doubt they had overstepped the mark.

Martin turned to Hawks.

'Your daughter has suffered a terrible psychological ordeal, tomorrow a specialist officer will talk with her, until then, try and get a good nights sleep,'

'She's remarkably well. My wife thinks watching 'Wallace and Gromit' in the car soothed and relaxed her, I don't think she really comprehended what was going on,' said Mr Hawks.

Martin nodded. As far as he was concerned Wallace and Gromit were just lumps of plasticine. He watched the Hawks family leave.

'The perpetrator of this crime obviously thought through the best way to reduce the victims stress levels chipped in Ripley.

'Yes, and you ought to be considering my stress levels, Ripley,' retorted Martin.

'Jack, lets take advantage of this twenty four hour drinking, come on Ripley, it's your round.'

Snapshot 49

Back on board the boat, George flung herself into one of the deep-buttoned Queen Anne chairs. Nick sat opposite, he poured out two large brandies.

'Everything went just like clockwork, I told you it would,' Nick said, taking a long drink.

'How much do you think we have?' she asked.

'I have no idea,' he said, leaving briefly and then returning with a sports bag. He poured the money at George's feet.

'I never realised there was so much,' she laughed, tossing the money in the air, 'there are some charities in for a big surprise.'

'We can't give any of this money away just yet, the police will be watching local charities, any donations and they will pounce, so we'll sit on it for a while,' Nick explained.

'Fine, and in the mean time what do we do,' she asked.

'We go through the looking glass,' he said.

'Through the what?'

'The looking glass; in my real life I am a respectable antiques dealer, it's time I returned, with my latest acquisitions,' Nick said, with a glint in his eye.

'I hope you don't think of me as one of your acquisitions Nick,' she teased him.

'One of the best I've ever made,' he laughed.

'I'll see you in the morning, I'm whacked,' she picked up some of the money and threw it onto the table in front of Nick. 'Don't forget to clear up the evidence,' she leant over and planted a kiss on the top of his forehead,

'Goodnight.'

Snapshot 50

'When I was young I disliked riding on roundabouts, sitting on some great big painted horse just whizzing around, my mother waving each time I passed her. Going round in the same direction, and never going anywhere,' said Martin to Jack who was looking reflectively into a cup of tea.

'Can't say it's something I ever gave a lot of thought to,' said the sergeant, pouring spilt tea from his saucer back into the cup.

'For me, it's the smell of carborundum from the dodgem's electric contacts which brings back memories,' recalled Ripley.

Both Martin and Jack looked at each other with raised eyebrows.

'I feel,' said Martin ignoring the detective constables comments, 'that we are going round in circles, and I don't like it Jack, somebody is making bloody fools of us, and I don't bloody like it, do you hear me Ripley?' shouted Martin. 'He kidnaps two people, there are no fingerprints, the identity pictures are next to useless, he entertains them to a bloody premier of a film which is still not out on general release. Then he gets the manager of the store to drop £165,000 into the rear of a vehicle, and disappears. We find both vehicles burned out, leaving us with Sweet Fanny Adams. Is that summary to your liking Ripley?' bellowed Martin.
'Never mind your carborundum, we have a conundrum here Ripley. As coppers we are expected to solve this crime, but the clues are eluding us, so let's go out there and do some detective work, let's go catch a thief.' Martin slammed down his cup and stormed out of the room.

Jack finished his tea calmly. He knew that Martin was under a lot of pressure; the press wanted statements and the Detective Chief Inspector wanted results.

But this was no local thief. Jack felt sure he was from out of town, the planning of the robberies and the kidnapping was meticulous, he had obviously done a lot of minute observation of the victims and the premises. None of the local villains, who regularly gave them information, could throw any light on these latest thefts.
He dipped a biscuit into his tea and devoured it whole.

'You heard what he said, lets go catch a thief. Go down to the store and check all the people who have left in the last year, run them through records, lets see what we come up with. When you have finished that contact all local charities, we want to be informed of any large donations. OK?'

'Yes Sarge' said Ripley, collecting his coat.

'I love Digestive biscuits,' he said to the departing constable, 'bring me another packet.'

Snapshot 51

Ripley put the phone down, and began scribbling ferociously, he had taken several calls in the last half hour. When he contacted other forces with details of the recent thefts, he never believed that he would receive such a good response. The printer had been churning out accounts of similar robberies in various northern towns. The common factors in each robbery were that only notes were taken, and there was lack of forensic evidence.

There was a lot of work to do analysing the information, but first, he had better inform his sergeant and the Detective Chief Inspector about his findings.

'Oh God,' he thought, 'perhaps I should have consulted them before I contacted the other forces.' He was used to the sergeant and the Detective Chief Inspector's moods, the shouting and their idiosyncrasies. But still he was apprehensive.

'Bugger it, let's face them head on,' he thought. The Detective Chief Inspector said 'go out and catch a thief,' well that's exactly what he had been doing.

He gathered up the documents, together with a packet of Digestive biscuits.

Snapshot 52

'I bumped into Clarke from 'C squad' down the corridor; he wore a smile like a banana.
"Have you found Robin Hood yet," he shouted after me. They're laughing at us, Jack,' said Martin, angrily.

'Ignore him,' said Jack, 'he's always been a pillock.'

'I want all known local villains leaned on, Jack. Tell them life is going to be hard on the streets from now on. If our thief is out there, and they know him, I want him,' said Martin, leaning towards the sergeant.

Ripley walked in, tossed the biscuits onto Jacks desk, and sat down clutching some folders.

'Be careful, Ripley, you'll break them,' said Jack trying to open the biscuits.

'I don't like them when they are all in bits.'

'I have some information, Sir,' said Ripley in a less than confident voice. He passed some files to Jack and Martin.

'These are reports of similar thefts in York, Chesterfield, Bury and Rochdale. In each case only notes were taken, and no forensic evidence was left.'

Martin looked at Jack.

'Where did you get this information Ripley?' asked Martin.

'I contacted various forces, asking for information on any robberies where only notes were taken,' said Ripley.

'On your own initiative?' asked Martin.

'Yes, sir,'

'Well done, Ripley. Well Jack, you can forget about contacting local villains. Let's follow this lad's initiative, contact all forces, and let's find out where our man has been busy. Maybe there's a pattern, Jack, something that will tell us where he may strike next,' said a smiling Martin.

'Ripley, get me some mapping pins, and well done,' said the sergeant, struggling to open his packet of biscuits.

Snapshot 53

Nick pulled the BMW X5 into the parking bay.

'Where are we?' asked George, stretching after the long drive.

'Ingleton,' said Nick.

'What a wonderful place,' she said, looking up the narrow, long, main street with its black and white painted shops and inns.

'We can grab a sandwich, and sample the local brew,' said Nick, leading the way up the narrow street.

This was the first time that George had visited the Yorkshire dales. She was thrilled with the rich tapestry of green undulating fields, divided by higgledy-piggledy dry-stone walls.

'There is the 'Wheatsheaf,' pointed Nick, 'it used to be the local court house, a long time ago.'

In keeping with its surroundings, it had black and white painted timbers and rough-hewn stone walls. As they approached the building, George pointed to two converted gas street lamps, with their warm artificial flickering flames attached above the entrance.

'They are so welcoming,' she smiled.

'Wait till you see inside,' said Nick, opening the door for her.

Inside, a large log fire gave the room a warm glow. Nick ordered two drinks and brought them to George who had chosen to sit in a corner seat.

'I hope you like this,' he smiled, passing the glass of amber beer to her.

'Does it have a name?' she asked.

'Black Sheep,' he replied.

'Oh well, that's definitely me,' she laughed, 'this is so oldie worldly, I really like it.'

'The inn itself dates back to the mid sixteen hundreds,' said Nick, pointing to the arched beams in the ceiling.

'Have we passed through the looking glass yet?'

'Almost. Next, we have to climb over Dodd's Fell, a very remote area, then we are in Wensleydale,' he explained.

'Sounds very Christmassy,' she giggled.

'Wait until it snows; we are often cut off for days,' he laughed.

'As long as I have a good book,' she said, looking at the burning logs, 'and a warm fire like this one, I'll be fine.'

Nick cut short their conversation and walked over to a table at the other end of the fireplace.

'Excuse me, have you finished with this paper?' he asked the middle-aged man with silver hair. As he returned, he looked anxiously around the bar, which was sprinkled with customers, some eating, others deep in conversation.

'While we were talking I caught sight of this headline.' He held up the newspaper for her to read. The bold headline proclaimed, "Robin Hood Strikes Again. Three Injured". The article went on to describe how a '24 hour' store had been robbed, and three members of staff had been badly beaten before the raiders fled with the day's takings.

'Nick, they can't blame this on us,' she said, sipping her drink.

'Papers often make assumptions, but then again, they are often given leads by the investigating officers,' explained Nick.

'You would think the police would recognise a different approach, it's so blatantly obvious,' she whispered, suddenly feeling vulnerable.

'Of course they will know. The police have deliberately leaked the story to the press; it suits them to let everyone think we are responsible. They don't have any idea who we are, and they will be hoping that by blaming this robbery on us, we may react,' he said, folding the paper. He finished his drink and returned the newspaper to the elderly gentleman.

'I think we should go,' he said, and waited for George. He then followed her out into the street and placed his arm around her shoulder.

'Don't worry about that newspaper article,' he reassured her. George felt a warm glow of contentment. The article had at first unnerved her, but Nick soon dispelled any lingering fear with his confident approach.

As they continued their journey, she watched as the countryside flew by. Flower-filled meadows gave way to high fells scattered with stone barns and the endless dry-stone walls and sheep that grazed on the wild grass of the fells.

Eventually, after many miles of driving along small, twisting, climbing passes, they reached the bare summit of Dodd's Fell. Ahead they could see the winding road, stretching for what seemed miles before merging into the seamless landscape.

'Once we start descending, then you'll be able to see where I live,' said Nick, his voice bringing her back from a trance-like state, induced by the rolling vista.

'So we'll pass through the looking glass,' she jibed.

'Yes, you passed through when we left Ingleton.' He pointed at the windscreen; before them, deep in the valley, lay a scattered array of stone dwellings separated by a road on one side, and on the other side a river wound snake-like through green fields.

'Welcome to wonderland,' he smiled.

Snapshot 54

'What's that you're reading, Ripley?' asked the sergeant.

'Fatal fetish,' replied Ripley, smiling.

'What's that about when it's at home?'

'A fetishist died from heat stroke after putting on a rubber suit and zipping himself into a latex body bag, his death is not being treated as suspicious,' Ripley read out from the newspaper.

'Bloody Hell,' retorted the sergeant.

'I wonder if he found it orgasmic,' laughed the detective constable.

'More like he found it very hot, just like we will, if we don't finish this paperwork,' said the sergeant.

'There's a report on the 24 Hour shop robbery. "Robin Hood Beatings" the paper report tells how the robbers have turned to violence in pursuit of gain.' Ripley threw the paper down. 'Rubbish!'

'Have you finished your analysis on the cross robberies?'

'Yes, I fed all the information into the computer, here's the report.' Ripley passed over the papers to Jack, who read the conclusion on the final page.

'In all the years I have been on the force, I have never come across a case like this; meticulous planning, the execution of the robberies carried out like clockwork and no forensic evidence,' moaned the sergeant.

'They all make mistakes eventually,' said Ripley, trying to reassure the sergeant.

'But this one is different. His planning is something else, he knows that he is going to succeed before he commits the crime, Ripley. He has no fear of us.'

'They all fear being caught, Sarge.'

'Did you get the artist impressions from Mrs Hawks and her daughter?' asked the sergeant.

'Yes, this one shows a women in her late thirties, and the man in his forties.' Ripley passed the sheets to the sergeant, who studied each carefully.

'Lets go see if anyone recognises them, Ripley,' the sergeant said, as he pulled on his coat, and waited for the constable to join him.

Snapshot 55

The drab wallpaper and ill-fitted faded curtains were from the seventies; the room furnishings likewise, they had seen better times.

Two men sat at a table, in the centre of the room, counting money; neatly stacked piles of coins formed a line down one side of the tabletop, bundled notes, each secured with a rubber band, formed a second row.

Fray, otherwise known as Barry Pugh, was about five foot six inches tall; he had a large prominent Roman nose and ears that stuck out. The only criminal job he had ever personally planned was on a warehouse, allegedly full of laundered money. Having gained entry with his handpicked specialists, they then found the boxes were full of 'Fray Bentos' corned beef rather than money, hence his nickname 'Fray'.

He was counting the notes.

Lumpy, otherwise known as Kevin Simpson, was of average height, but was built like the side of a shed. His nickname originated from his poor hygiene as a child; he washed infrequently, which resulted in blocked facial pores, which in turn gave rise to dozens of small lumps. Not very bright, but sociable, he'd been a mate of Fray's since school.

He was counting the coins.

Their attention was interrupted when Ronson, the third member of their 'little gang', entered the room. He was the tallest of the three. Otherwise known as Matthew Lewis, he had gained his nickname from the methods he used when mugging people. To make them part with their money and valuables, he poured lighter fuel into their jacket pockets, then terrified them into submission by threatening to set it alight.

'I've been down to the snooker hall. We must leave straight away. No one wants to know us, we're bad news.' Ronson brought a small briefcase to Fray at the table.

'Put the money in the bag and then pack some clothes, we're off.'

'What's the panic?' asked Fray, curiously.

'The cops are leaning heavily on everyone, according to the boys down at the snooker hall, someone's going to blab sooner or later to get the pressure off.'

'Bloody Hell, where are we going?' asked Lumpy, pushing a few clothes into a sports bag.

'I don't know, anywhere, we'll go off into the countryside until things cool down, I'll ring the boys later to see when it's safe to return,' growled Ronson.

'Anybody tells on us and I'll spread'em,' yelled Lumpy.

'Yea, just like you did on the last job. That's why we're in this mess,' Fray replied.

'C'mon you two, this is not the time to start arguing, let's go.' Ronson pushed the two out of the room and closed the door with a bang.

Snapshot 56

Having breakfasted alone, George walked into the garden to survey the surroundings. The morning air was brisk and crisp. She turned to look at the house; inscribed over the door was the year 1854. High-pitched gables with verge-boards pieced the skyline, and blue grey slates together with Yorkshire stone walls gave the house a solid appearance. Rolling lawns pushed up to tall chestnut and ash trees that shimmered in the morning sunlight, and the path on which she walked meandered off between rose and flower beds down to the fast flowing rivers edge.

'Do you like my garden?' she recognised Nick's voice.

'I really do, it's so peaceful,' she said.

'Yes, when I first set eyes on the house and the gardens I just knew it was right for me,' Nick said, inspecting the gardens.

'The house was built by a rather well-off retired clergymen-come-explorer in the nineteenth century.'

'I saw the date above the door. It really is wonderful, and the house, well, it's so large,' she laughed.

'Did you get a chance to look around?' he asked.

'No, after breakfast I came straight into the garden. When you have spent so long on the streets, a garden like this is intoxicating.' She walked off towards the riverbank.

'I'll you give you a personal tour,' he said, as he walked besides her. 'Afterwards we'll take a trip into Hawes, where I will introduce you to Mrs Spencer; she looks after the business while I'm away collecting.'

'I would much rather stay here and watch the water pass by,' she said, sitting down on the riverbank.

'There will be plenty of time for that. Village's soon know when someone new is around, so the sooner we introduce you the better,' he explained.

'And who am I?'

'I've been thinking about that. Perhaps, to avoid awkward questions, it would be best, if I introduce you as my girlfriend,' he looked at George, waiting for some reaction.

'Someone you've picked up on your travels?'

'Baggage more like,' he laughed, running off towards the house.

'BAGGAGE!' she cried, 'Just you wait.'

Snapshot 57

'Its lovely to meet you,' she said, with a twinkle in her eye. She leaned over to George and whispered, 'I'm so pleased he's finally met someone who makes him happy.'

Mrs Spencer, known to her friends as 'Spence', was in her forties, married with two teenage daughters. Her husband was a cheese maker. With her knowledge of antiques, she had quickly become indispensable to Nick, who had made her a junior partner in the business. Showing George around the various displays, her warm disposition soon became apparent.

'This is a Tsimshian puppet from around 1856, next to it is a Crow War shirt, from 1850; both are American.' She carefully adjusted a small printed description. 'This chest of drawers was also made in America, Boston actually, about 1770. Beautiful mahogany, the ball and claw feet and cabriole leg are typical of the craftsmen from this city,' she explained with an appreciative smile.

'Fascinating,' George said as she pointed in another direction. 'I noticed this earlier.' She moved in the direction of a small porcelain figure.

'Ah. The Meissen Harlequinn, mid eighteenth century from Germany. The colours are so strong despite it's age.'

'You must hate it when someone comes in and buys them.'

'No. That is why we are here, to sell. All of our items go to good homes, so we know they are well cared for.'

'You make it sound like they are alive,' laughed George.

'When you have travelled long distances, searching and buying, you do get attached, but it doesn't end there. We make our own arrangements for them to despatched back home, and then wait, for what sometimes feels like an eternity, for them to arrive.

But when you unpack the cases and see them, well, they are special, but you have to let them go, providing the price is right.' Mrs Spencer put her hand on to George's arm. 'Providing the price is right, it makes parting with them so much easier,' she laughed.

Nick walked into the showroom and waved in their direction. 'I hope Spence has not given you any inside information,' he said as he joined them, and placed his arm on Mrs Spencer's shoulder.

'Of course not, apart from telling me about you that is.' George gave a sly wink in Mrs Spencer's direction.

'I've booked us a room and table at the Golden Lion in Settle, you can tell me what confidences have been betrayed this evening over dinner.'

'My lips will remain sealed, Spence,' replied George.

'I hope you both have a wonderful time.' Mrs Spencer watched them both leave, then began to prepare the shop for closing.

Snapshot 58

'Where exactly are we going?' asked Fray.

'Settle. I've booked us a room at the Golden Lion,' replied Ronson.

'Where's that then?' asked a curious Lumpy.

'It's in the middle of the Yorkshire Dales,' said Ronson.

'Yorkshire Dales, I've never been there before,' said Lumpy, looking out of the rear passenger window. 'I've never seen so many sheep and cows, there's hundreds of them, people up 'ere must eat a lot of meat.'

'Well, where do you think your meat comes from' Fray said.

'From the supermarket,' laughed Lumpy.

'Forget it Fray,' said Ronson.

'Do you think we'll be safe here?' asked Fray.

'Yes, the police won't be looking up here, they'll focus on the town.'

'Did you make arrangements for someone to contact us when it's safe to return.'

'There is to be no contact, no one knows where we are. I told them at the snooker hall we were heading south.'

'Fine,' said Fray obediently.

'Did you hear that Lumpy? No contact with anyone from home,' Ronson turned, looking for a sign of acknowledgement.

'Sure Ronson, no problem, I was thinking, with all these sheep around Fray, we should be able to buy a sheepskin coat really cheaply up 'ere. I've always fancied one of them coats, real class.'

Ronson and Fray momentarily looked at each other in a moment of disbelief.

Snapshot 59

The car headlights picked out the narrow winding road ahead, as Nick negotiated the bends and steep inclines. Oddly shaped hedgerows loomed up, ghost-like, on either side, and then disappeared as the car passed them by. Outside the splay of the headlights the countryside was pitch black.

'This room that you booked, don't you think you are taking this 'girlfriend' story too far?'

'Don't worry, I booked the room with twin beds' Nick chuckled.

'H'mm, well as long as the food is as good as you say, I'll forgive you, this once.'

'You'll love this place. It was built in 1640, and is next to the old market place. We have some very good customers who live round about,' said Nick.

'Sounds good, please tell me there is no hidden agenda,' she murmured.

'Absolutely not, this is me taking my girlfriend out for a romantic meal,' he laughed.

George smiled. Secretly, she enjoyed this charade.

Snapshot 60

The dining room was small; it held about twelve tables, each laid out with a starched tablecloth and napkins. In the centre of each table was a narrow glass vase, each with two pink rose buds. Nick and George were seated at the corner table, opposite the dining room entrance.

'Nick, it's very good to see you again.' A tall thin man, dressed in a smart dark blue pinstripe suit, with a dark blue silk tie, delivered the greeting.

'Hello Nigel, please let me introduce George,' Nick stood as he introduced her. 'I've told her all about the excellent food and hospitality, so I do hope you don't let me down.'

'I hope you enjoy your evening George, the last lady he brought here was delighted.' He smiled as he placed the napkin on her knee, and gave her a large blue menu, 'and so was her husband.'

'He always tries to embarrass me, its his little way of making me feel welcome,' Nick laughed.

'Tonight we have a special menu, I hope you find something you like,' he said as he gave Nick a menu.

'Could we please have two 'La Fin Du Monde' while we choose,' asked Nick.

'Certainly.'

'What on earth is 'La Fin' whatever it is?' asked George.

' 'La Fin Du Monde', or 'The End of the World', it's a beer from Canada, a real treat, though very strong.'

'I may not like it.'

'You will, I promise, it's smooth, slightly tart, with a good head and quite a kick if you drink more than two,' he smiled.

Nigel returned with the drinks, which he poured carefully into two glasses, each with a thick twisted green stem.

'Cheers,' Nick raised his glass towards George. After allowing her to savour the first mouthful, he asked, 'What do you think?'

'Strong, I can taste apple and tangerine, h'mm very nice.'

They both studied the menu, enjoying the moment. George looked up to see that Nigel was busy taking an order from three men sat at a table on the same side as herself and Nick, but separated by a highly polished large Victorian sideboard.

'Have you made your choice?' asked Nick, gaining her attention.

'Yes. To start with, I'm going with the Crispy Tofu and Rice Cake, then I shall have the Grilled Lamb Loin marinated in Curry and Lemongrass.'

'Wow, sounds very good.'

'What have you chosen?'

'Well, to start with I've chosen the Sautéed Calamari, then the Pan Roasted Beef Fillet.' Nick raised his glass. 'To a very successful partnership.'

'To a successful partnership,' George laughed, as she lifted her glass in a toast.

Snapshot 61

Having completed their main courses, George and Nick relaxed over another bottle of wine, enjoying the evening. Nigel and his staff moved unobtrusively between tables serving customers, then after what he considered an appropriate time, he presented the dessert menu to Nick.

'Are you ready to order dessert?' He slipped a menu to both of them. 'Of course I know what you will be ordering Nick.'

'And what might that be?' asked George full of curiosity.

'My one weakness. Warm Valrhona chocolate cake served with dried cherry Armagnac ice cream.'

'Sounds delicious.' George seemed to hesitate in mid-sentence. 'Sorry, I'll go with the Caramel Chocolate Dome please,' she said, looking over towards the table at the other side of the Victorian sideboard. 'Nick, did you hear what one of those men sat behind you just said?' she leant closer as if to catch his ear only. 'He said, "…they are calling us Robin Hood…"'

'Just relax George, don't make it obvious that you are listening,' said Nick.

'Listen,' she looked at Nick, but all the time, she was listening to the scraps of conversation from the table. 'They have just referred to the large man as 'Little John', Nick, they could be 'you know who,' what the bloody hell are they doing here?'

'George,' Nick took hold of her hand, 'as far as anyone here is concerned we are just two people having a romantic meal. These characters, whoever they are, seem to be enjoying themselves, the alcohol has loosened their tongues, let's listen calmly.'

It soon became obvious to both George and Nick that these three men could be the ones who they had read about in the paper they had borrowed from the old gentleman at Ingleton.

'This is really weird, what are we going to do?' asked George.

Nick had been listening to snatches of the jovial banter, and a quick glance at their table told him they had consumed several bottles of La Fin Du Monde each, at 9% volume, this beer was very strong.

'First we can enjoy the finale; here comes the dessert,' said Nick.

'You are amazing, you must have ice in your veins,' whispered George.

'As soon as I've finished this I'm going for a wander. If any of those three leave their table, ring me immediately.'

'What are you up to?'

'Just curious.'

'Nick, I may look cool, but I'm shaking like a leaf.'

'You look terrific, this Armagnac ice cream is delicious,' smiled Nick, taking another spoonful.

They both watched as Nigel, assisted by two waitresses, brought the three men their main course and some more bottles of La Fin Du Monde. Nick finished off the last of his dessert. 'Perfect time for me to excuse myself,' he whispered. He left the room, leaving George to finish her chocolate dome.

Snapshot 62

Once outside, Nick approached his friend Nigel. 'Just popping up to the room.'

'Fine, you know where the key is, shall I serve coffee?'

'Please.' Nick moved inside the small office, he looked for and found the Hotel Register, a quick check told him the three men were in Room 17. Removing the key, he made his way up the winding wooden staircase. He walked past the large oak longcase clock by Jason Duncan of Old Meldrum at the top of the stairs. He had tried to buy the clock from Nigel several times without success. Once inside room 17, Nick quickly scanned the family room. Each bed was cluttered with clothes and magazines. They were travelling lightly, small bags, left open, lay scattered around the room. He moved quickly, opening bedside cabinet drawers. In the first two he found nothing more than the prerequisite 'Gideon' bible, but in the third drawer he found wads of money.

'You really are amateurs,' thought Nick. Swiftly, he grabbed the money and returned, via the stairs, to the small office where he replaced the key. Back in the dining room Nigel had just finished serving coffee.

'Everything alright Nick?' asked George, raking her fingers through her hair nervously.

Nick smiled and moved closer to her, at the same time holding the lapel of his jacket open so she could see the wads of money.

George stared wide-eyed, then brought herself to smile the type of smile that portrayed fear. 'You are mad taking such a massive risk,' she said through clenched teeth.

'I don't think so. They can't call the police, what are they going to do?'

'Why take the money?'

'I want to teach them a lesson.' Nick took hold of her hand. 'To let them know that someone else knows who they are. If they have any sense they'll move on.'

'But you can't be sure they'll just leave. What ever happened to the idea that we were going to be....' Too anxious, she was unable to finish.

'Look,' Nick, moved closer to George, 'they will reason that whoever took the money could also ring the police. The last thing they're going to do is cause a fuss.'

'We're supposed to be keeping our heads low, we moved to your home because we thought it was a refuge. And what happens, they turn up!' She flashed a sideward glance towards the three men.

'Let's take our coffee through to the lounge.' Nick waited for George to leave the dining room. He was pleased they had the residential lounge to themselves.

'You'll have to trust me, George, on this matter.' He drained the last of his coffee, and then poured himself some more. 'These people, for whatever reason, have turned up on my patch, presumably, because they feel safe here. Once they discover the money is missing, that safety cushion disappears.'

George finished her coffee, she had not taken her eyes off Nick while he had been talking. In the short while she had known him he had not let her down. On the contrary, he seemed to go out of his way to put her first. She rationalized that he would make decisions which best represented both their interests.

'I don't agree with taking the money. But it's done now, so we will have to make the best of it.'

'That's right.' He took hold of her hand and gave it a gentle squeeze.

'I would like a G&T, a big one, and don't spare the ice,' she said, wresting her hand free from his, 'the night is still young.'

Snapshot 63

'Fray wake up, Fray.' Ronson shook the prostrate figure hidden under a blue duvet.

'Fray, come on, if we don't hurry we're going to miss the last call for breakfast.'
Ronson walked over to Lumpy and repeated the call. Having finished his shower, Ronson found the others starting to surface, each looking the worse for the previous nights drinking.

'I feel as rough as a bear's arse. What time is it?' asked a sorry-looking Fray.

'Eight-fifteen,' replied Ronson pulling on his sweater. 'I'm off down to get a paper, I'll meet you both in the breakfast room.'

'Fine,' replied Fray, never being one for a lot of conversation in the morning.

Snapshot 64

The morning sun shone through the window in the breakfast room. The rays cast long shadows, which fell at an angle across the empty tables, chairs and woven carpet.

'Lumpy, have you fallen out with that bacon, cos' if you 'ave, then I'll 'ave it,' said Fray, eyeing up the three rashers of bacon on Lumpy's plate.

'I haven't fallen out with nobody,' replied Lumpy.

'Yes, I know you haven't fallen out with anybody, it's just a figure of speech, right,' said Fray.

'Lumpy, are you going to eat your bacon?' asked Ronson.

'No. Do you want it?' asked Fray.

'Yes, that would be nice, thank you Lumpy, give it 'ere.' Ronson transferred the bacon to his plate, watched by a wide-eyed Fray.

'Oy, I asked first. I asked him first,' cried Fray disconsolately.
'Bit of hard luck you're havin',' laughed Lumpy.
'It's not bloody fair, I asked first.'
'Oh shut up Fray, you're like a big tart,' growled Ronson.
'Well,' sulked Fray.
'Big Tart,' chuckled Lumpy.

Snapshot 65

'Have you enjoyed your stay with us Sir,' asked Nigel, placing the cash in the till.
'Very nice place, very welcoming,' said Ronson.
'Are you staying in the area, or are you moving on?'
'Oh, we're moving on, but it's been very nice,' replied Ronson. '*I 'aint telling him anything*', he thought, as he made his way back to the room, '*especially now that we've got a cottage where we're going to stay.*'
'Everybody ready then,' he asked, not really looking at anyone in particular. He pushed a few clothes and a magazine into his bag, then opened the bedside cabinet drawer, which, to his surprise, was empty.
'Fray, have you taken the money from the drawer?'
'I haven't touched it,' replied Fray, eyeing Ronson suspiciously.
'Lumpy?'
'Not me, I haven't been near the drawer. You must have put it somewhere else Ronson,' said Lumpy.
'But I left it here last night. I haven't been in the drawer since.' They all three stared at each other, then at the drawer, then back at each other in disbelief.
'We've bin robbed,' squawked Lumpy.

Snapshot 66

George buttered a slice of toast and then reached over for the marmalade. Breakfast was a quiet affair, she had expected to see the men from the night before, but as yet they had not come down to the dining room. Nick read the sports pages, and ate his scrambled egg, without making any conversation.

'Have you ever tried tree felling on ski's?' asked George.

'No,' mumbled Nick from behind the paper.

'Really, do I look stupid to you?'

'George,' Nick said in an exasperating voice. 'You are not making much sense, what did you say?'

'Don't believe everything you read.'

'I don't.'

'Good.'

'George, I'm a little confused, are you trying to tell me something?'

'Yes I am. In future, I'll eat breakfast alone, I would hate to come between you and your paper.'

Nick looked at her and realised that she was not amused at being ignored. He folded the newspaper. 'You've made your point,' he said, impishly.

'Do you think they've discovered the money is missing yet?'

'Perhaps.'

'They don't seem to be very bright.'

'Lucky for us.'

'Nick, I just wish we were out of here.'

'Ok, look, you put the bags in the car while I settle the bill with Nigel.' He grabbed a slice of toast. 'Here are the car keys, you drive, I'll meet you out front.'

George gave a sigh of relief. She clutched the keys and left the dining room.

Snapshot 67

Sally Martin came in from the garden and deposited three large clay pots on the table just inside the patio doors. Ever since she had suggested to her husband, David, that a large conservatory would be useful, she had lay sole claim to it. This was where she could lovingly tend to her favourite plants, and put into effect her plans for the seasons ahead. At forty-six years old, she was three years younger than her husband, who she had married twenty-one years ago. They had two children, Carrie and Nicole, who were eighteen and seventeen years of age respectively. She reached down and filled each pot to the brim with compost, from a bag of John Innes. Gently, she firmed down the soil in each pot, then carefully lifted some cuttings from a plastic bag and pushed them, one by one, into the soil. Carrie walked in carrying a mug of tea.

'Hi mum, here's some tea.'

'Thank you Carrie,' she said as she wiped her hands on a towel, 'just give these beauties a few weeks and we'll have a dozen or so more plants ready for planting out. She lifted a pot to show her daughter the healthy cuttings.

'Do you think I'll ever get 'green fingers,' like you mum?'

'Who knows, one day perhaps, when you have your own place.'

'That'll be the day. Nicole and I are off into town, shopping, mum. Can I get you anything?'

'No, thank you. Say cheerio to your Dad, he's going to work soon.'

'I have. He's absorbed in finishing his latest painting for the competition.'

'He always is. Then he'll decide at the last minute, that it isn't good enough to enter,' she laughed. 'Take care driving'

Sally stood back and admired the full pots of cuttings. She carefully gave each one a little water, then wiped her hands and took off her gardening apron. She then climbed the stairs to join her husband in his small studio at the top of the house.

'Carrie tells me you are going to exhibit this one.' She leant round her husband to view the painting. 'It's very good. You've captured the light very well on the bottles.'

'Do you really like it?' Martin stood back to view his work.

'Absolutely, you have a lot of ability, but until you show them, well, you won't know if they'll stand up to competition.'

'People may not like it, I'm not sure that I'm ready.'

'David, exhibit the painting, then you'll know what people think of your work. If you adopted the same hesitancy at work you would never solve any crimes.' She gave her husband a large hug. 'Did you say Jack was picking you up at 4 o'clock?'

'Yes, we're working late tonight.'

'Well, you go and get your shower while I make you some tea.' Sally Martin had been very supportive of her husband throughout his career with the force, and the stability of their marriage was largely due to her understanding of the pressures of her husband's work.

Snapshot 68

Jack had knocked at the door a hundred times before. He had known Sally before she had married the young David Martin, the copper who personally arrested a gang of bank robbers while still on the beat. Shortly afterwards he was transferred to plain clothes where he met Jack, himself a young man who had done well in uniform.

Sally opened the door and welcomed him. 'Come in Jack, he's just getting ready.'

'Jenny's sent you these cuttings of the 'Black Velvet Red' geranium that you admired when you came to our anniversary party.'

'Oh wonderful, I'll ring Jenny later and thank her, it's time we had a chat. Would you like a cup of tea while you wait, I've just made a pot?' She took hold of the cuttings and took them through to the conservatory.

Chief Inspector Martin came in and motioned to his sergeant. 'Hello Jack, sorry I'm running a bit late, I got involved with my painting and just got carried away. You really should try it Jack, it's great for relaxing.' He sat down next to Jack and passed him his latest painting. 'This is the one I have just finished.' Jack examined the picture. 'Well, what do you think?'

'It's very good. Bottles,' he mused. 'I've never been much good at drawing.' He handed the painting back to Martin, who looked slightly disappointed at his colleague's lack of interest. Sally came in with a tray of tea and biscuits.

'Ah, I see you've been looking at his latest work of art.' She poured tea and handed a cup to each of them. 'We're going to enter this one in an exhibition.' She held up the painting admiringly. 'I'm off to pot those cuttings you brought, Jack. David I'll see you later.'

'Are you ready for an evening touring the clubs, Jack?' asked Martin, smiling mischievously.

'Well, it does have a certain appeal,' said Jack, sipping his tea.

'Especially as Ripley's driving,' laughed Martin.

Snapshots 69

Martin and Jack walked through the swing doors, into the dimly lit snooker hall. Only a third of the tables were occupied and a canopy of light shone over each of the tables in use. Half a dozen customers sat at a long bar. The barman looked up, and his gaze followed Jack and Martin as they made their way towards the bar. Ripley waited at the entrance.

'Hello Baggett, long time since we last met,' said Martin, leaning on the bar facing the nervous looking barman.

'Hello Inspector, can I get you anything?' Baggett asked, wiping the bar surface clean.

'Did you hear that, Jack? He's offering to buy us a drink,' snarled Martin.

'We'll have two bitters in two very clean glasses.' Jack threw a five pound note onto the bar. 'We can't accept your offer Baggett, it might be construed as a bribe.'

'That's right Jack, but I'm sure you weren't trying to buy favours, were you Baggett?'

'No, of course not.' Baggett pulled two pints and pushed them towards the unwanted visitors.

'Has Matthew Lewis been in?' asked Jack.

'Matthew Lewis?' exclaimed Baggett in surprise.

'Otherwise known as Ronson. Don't act dumb, we know he's been here.' Martin said banging his glass onto the bar.

'He hasn't been here for a few days. Honest' said the barman.

'So you do know him. Where is he then?' asked Jack.

'Word is they're out of town.'

'They?' asked Jack, pointedly.

'Ronson and his two mates, they come in for a game of snooker'

Martin took a drink and looked around the hall. Everyone at the snooker tables avoided his gaze, but carried on playing as if nothing was amiss. Martin walked over to a table in the middle of the room.

'Mickey the dodger, I haven't seen you for a long time'

'Just passing through Inspector, visiting my old mates.' The man addressed the table, as if he was going to play a shot.

'Didn't know you had any mates Mickey. Have you come across Ronson?' asked Martin.

'No,' replied Mickey.

Martin picked up the black ball. 'Where is he?'

'I haven't seen him.'

Martin rolled the ball down the table splaying other balls as it collided with them.

'I can make it very awkward for you and your mates Mickey. Make sure you tell me if you come across him. You don't want to be blackballed, do you?' Martin walked back towards the bar. 'Drink up Jack, we'd better leave these lads to ponder over what we've said.'

He turned towards Baggett, 'Contact me if you see him. If I find out he's been here and you haven't told me, I'll close you down. Don't forget. Come on, Jack, let's get some fresh air.'

Once outside, they walked two hundred yards and entered the 'Barley Mow'. Once inside, they looked round the smoke-filled room. 'Jack, you do the talking, I'm going to sit over here.' Martin walked over to a small empty table. 'Ripley, mine's a bitter.'

Snapshot 70

Fray and Lumpy had been wandering around the small village for most of the afternoon. They had taken a ride on a steam engine, and had visited a well-known local deep cave from which they had just emerged.

'Bloody hell, I never knew it was so cold down them caves,' remarked Lumpy.

'You can say that again,' said Fray rubbing his hands.

'I never knew it was so cold down them caves,' repeated Lumpy.

'Silly bugger, you really are stupid.'

'No I'm not. You said....'

'Never mind. Let's get back to the car,' interrupted Fray, irritably.

'Do you think Ronson will want us back yet?' asked Lumpy.

'There's only one way to find out,' said Fray.

'I don't like it when he's thinking, he can get really mad.'

'Look, someone's just bloody taken all our money. He's got plenty to think about, Ronson will sort it out, that's why he needs time to think,' said Fray, reassuringly.

'Yea, he always knows what to do,' agreed Lumpy.

'It's not like we could go to the police and report a theft, is it.' scoffed Fray.

'No, not really, in fact No,' laughing out loud, 'not at all, not bloody likely.' Having walked down the street for what seemed the twentieth time, they turned into the car park to be met by Ronson.

'You've been a bloody long time, I've been looking everywhere for you,' he growled, obviously still in a bad mood.

'You said disappear to give you time to sort things out. We've been down a cave,' said Fray sheepishly.

'What the hell did you do down a cave' asked Ronson.

'It was really cold,' chirped in Lumpy, 'and dark, but they had lights on so we could see like.'

Ronson stared at Fray who just shrugged his shoulders.

'Well while you two have been gallivanting down holes, I've been trying to think how we can get our money back. There's a twenty-four-hour café up at the roundabout at the end of the village next to a garage that does nice business. I've been up there and it was packed with tourists, I reckon it's a gold mine. And tonight, when its quiet, we are going to pay it a little visit.'

'Great, a bit of action, now that's what I've been missing,' laughed Fray digging Lumpy in the ribs.

'Yer a bit of action,' agreed Lumpy.

Snapshot 71

The church clock struck a single chime on the quarter hour.
A lone dog barked somewhere in the dark empty street. Leaves danced as if in frenzy, along the pavement, pushed by a northerly breeze. The village was asleep, the normal silence was broken by the odd sound of a far distant engine pulling away and fading into the night so stillness returned. This was how it was every night, nothing much ever happened in this sleepy tranquil part of the Dales.

Snapshot 72

Ronson parked the car opposite the entrance to the all-night café and garage. Pale lights from the windows spilt out onto the front of the building. A few cars were parked just outside the café entrance adorned by a few shrubs blowing in the cold northerly wind.

'Everyone alright?'

Fray and Lumpy nodded in acknowledgement, 'as soon as we get inside the entrance, pull up your masks, I'll do the talking, Fray, you go straight into the kitchen and bring any staff you find in there through to the sitting area. Don't forget Lumpy, no rough stuff.'

'Let's go.'

Leaving the car, they moved swiftly over to the entrance, adjusted their coats and pulled on the hastily made masks. Once inside the door to the café, they could see that diners occupied only two tables. Two staff idled their time away around the serving counter. One girl was cooking on a large griddle plate.

'This is a hold-up. Everyone stay where you are,' shouted Ronson.

Fray rushed through the cooking area into the kitchen. Lumpy pointed a sawn-off shotgun at the two tables occupied by the late night diners and the two waitresses.

'Who's in charge?' Ronson pointed his shotgun at the frightened staff. 'Who's in charge? I won't ask again,' he said, menacingly.

'I am,' stuttered a pale-faced woman of about thirty.

'Safe, quickly.' Ronson pushed the gun into the ribs of the terrified woman, who led him to the office and pointed to the floor-safe.

Fray came back into the dining room with another woman. He motioned to the remaining staff to lay on the floor, arms outstretched. Lumpy brought the diners over to join the staff.

Ronson returned to the room and motioned to the women in charge to join the others, then barked out, 'Place your mobile phones in front of you, now.' Fray moved round and collected them.

'We're going to leave. Stay on the floor for fifteen minutes. If we see anyone move we will return and hurt you all,' shouted Ronson. They made their way out into the night and scrambled into the car, then drove off into the darkness.

Snapshot 73

Still half-asleep, June Berry reached out and grasped the phone, dragging it back underneath the warm sheets.

'Hello, Sergeant J. Berry,' she answered, croakily.

Listening to the caller quickly removed the sleepiness associated with a warm bed. She sat upright and looked at the clock. 'Stay where you are, don't let anyone leave, I'll be with you in ten minutes.' Replacing the receiver, she shook her husband, who awoke to see his wife dressing.

'What's happened?' he asked, anxiously.

'Armed robbery up at the White Cross Café and Garage'

'Oh God, is anyone hurt?'

'No, but I'd like you to join me, they'll be shook up'

'Right, I'll join you as soon as I've rung Mum to baby-sit.'

'Great, see you.' Already dressed, she was fastening her belt, vest and radio, as she rushed out and into her police car.

As a local doctor, Chris Berry was used to occasionally helping his wife. She was a Police Sergeant in charge of the small satellite police station in Settle, along with a police constable. Together they covered the whole village and the local surrounding area.

'Mum, Hi, sorry to wake you at this time in the morning, but we've been called out, can you come round and look after the kids please? Wonderful, you're a peach; yes I'll have some tea ready, bye and thanks.'

Snapshot 74

Sergeant Berry was calling in to report the incident to the local head office in Skipton.

'Yes sir, they just rushed in and pretty much surprised the staff and four diners who were having a late night snack. The suspects had three sawn-off shotguns. A couple of the girls are badly shocked, but no one was physically hurt. They made a clean getaway. No witnesses saw the vehicle leave. Yes, sir, Dr. Berry is on his way.'

Her husband came in, wearing a white coverall gown to avoid any contamination of the crime scene.

'Has mum arrived?' she asked her husband quietly.

'Yes. Is there anyone who needs attention?'

'The manager is in a bit of a state, a couple of diners seem to be a bit traumatised, if you could see to them first. I'll take the others over into this corner of the room and take some initial statements. Forensics should be here within the hour. Would you like some coffee, we might as well make use of the facilities.'

'That would be great.'

June Berry looked at her watch, it was 2.20 am. Taking out her notebook she wrote a quick summary of her initial survey of the crime scene, after which she started to interview the witnesses.

Snapshot 75

Having snatched a few hours sleep, June, a mother of eight-year-old twins, had prepared breakfast and supervised the getting up and the getting ready for school routine. Her mum took them to school everyday, a 'chore' she loved. Her husband Chris had already left for his morning surgery.

Laughter, and the sound of running tiny feet, signalled the twins were on their way from the bathroom to breakfast, which consisted of cereal, toast and fresh juice.

'Mum, the phone is ringing in your office', said Nathan.

'Hi mum,' called Jessica.

'Hi, you two, eat your breakfasts without any books or arguing please.'

The sound of the front door opening and the familiar voice of her mum calling out 'Hello its only me,' brought the usual chorus of 'Hello granny' from the twins. She started telling her daughter about the village gossip concerning the robbery before coming into the kitchen.

'It's all anyone is talking about. An armed robbery in Settle. Who would ever have thought it, goodness me? You must catch them, goodness me?'

'We will mum don't worry. Look, I really must be off.'

'Bye Nathan, bye Jessica, bye mum.'
She reached over and planted a kiss on all their cheeks.
'Bye, mum,' cried the twins, in unison.

Snapshot 76

As Sergeant in the usually quiet town of Settle, a large part of her duties were extending liaisons with the community, meeting with school children, attending meetings with Neighbourhood Watch coordinators, as well as routine policing.

She parked her BMW 4x4 squad car alongside P.C. Dunstan's car.

'Good morning, Patrick, what have you got for me?'

'Like I said on the phone Sarge, we have some pretty angry residents.'

'Understandable. It's not everyday we have people held up at gunpoint. Look I want you to go through the licence details of everyone in the area who has a shotgun. Check them out, I want you personally to inspect each weapon.'

'Everyone?' exclaimed Dunstan.

'All of them, we have to account for all of them, if you find anyone who cannot produce their shotgun, let me know immediately.'

'Thanks Sarge, will do.'

Snapshot 77

Having driven up the three-quarter-mile, ancient, lime avenue which leads to Grice Hall, George and Nick stared enviously at the Hall, an imposing building of mellow, soft, red brickwork, giving an air of timeless tranquillity.

'Wow, this is a really cool. What is this place? Asked George.

'It used to be owned by a Lord, but he sold the place about a year ago to cover debts. Spence received a call asking me to visit, with a view to looking at some pieces they have for sale.'

'Perhaps it's the house,' teased George.

'I wish,' said Nick.

They walked up the marble stairs to the entrance, an imposing double oak panelled door with twisted wrought iron hinges. Nick rang the bell and almost immediately a tall, wiry man in a grey uniform opened the door. Having introduced themselves, they were ushered into the library.

'Quite a collection.' Nick gazed over the hundreds of leather bound books on the dark wood shelves. He pulled out one edition and turned the pages. 'This is interesting, 'The Young Angler Naturalist', and 'Pigeon and Rabbit Fancier', wonderful illustrations.'

'Is it worth much?' asked George.

'Not really, about £300. It's not the monetary value, it's more about owning such a lovely book.'

'Give me a good Agatha Christie anytime,' said George, looking at a book she pulled from the shelves.

'Let me see. Ah, yes, 'Sad Cypress', a Poirot novel, first edition from 1940 with its original dust jacket.'

'Is that good?' asked George.

'Oh yes, it will be worth about, hmm, £2800, give or take a quid or two,' he said.

'Good God. So much?' She returned the book to its rightful place on the shelf. The door opened and a well-dressed man in his mid thirties entered the room.

'Nick Hartford,' he walked towards Nick with his hand outstretched.

'Yes, pleased to meet you, Mr...' Nick hesitated.

'Blandford, Reginald Blandford, and you are?' he looked towards George.

'George.'

'Pleased to meet you George,' he shook her hand vigorously.

'We thought you might be interested in a few pieces that were left by the previous owner, Lord Saville. The new owner has selected what he wishes to keep, but these are, how shall we say, surplus to requirements.'

He walked over to the window where a large cloth covered what appeared to be several items of furniture. Nick loved surprises and walked over eagerly to join Blandford, who whipped the cloth off skilfully. Nick gasped in surprise as he immediately recognised a few items of interest. He moved over to one in particular, and gently brushed his fingers over the cabriole leg, up over the serpentine top and Sevres-style porcelain panels.

'You like that, do you,' asked Blandford, who clearly had no interest in the furniture.

Nick nodded in assent, and moved over to a three-legged tea table with an over elaborate scrolled fluted shaft. Next, he turned to a Rosewood Canterbury, then a Burr elm chest. George watched, fascinated, as he moved between the pieces, touching each one gently, almost like a caress she thought; he seemed to recognise each like a long lost friend.

'Well?' asked Blandford, as if in a hurry.

'Why would anyone leave such pieces behind? asked Nick. 'Lord Saville left a considerable amount of belongings in the Hall as part of an agreement to clear all his debts. It was not an insignificant sum,' replied Blandford haughtily.

'Well,' said Nick. 'Very fine, very fine. And what figure does the new owner have in mind?'

'I think he was hoping you would make an offer. As I said, he does not want these items, so he is willing to listen to a reasonable figure.'

Nick surveyed the items. He couldn't help but feel that if the owner wanted to really move these items, he would be better off putting them into an auction house.

'£12,000.' Nick looked at Blandford to test his reaction; not a flinch.

'Thank you. If you will excuse me for one moment.' Blandford left the room. Nick motioned George over to the window.

'There's something not right, he never even twitched so much as an eyelid when I made him an offer. He is too detached, it's like he's selling fish.'

'Perhaps that's because these items are of no particular interest to him.'

'No, it isn't that. Normally, when you are dealing with people over a piece of furniture, they'll have a figure in mind. If you don't get near that with your first offer, they'll jump in straight away. My offer was ridiculously low, but he didn't flinch and he is supposed to be representing the best interests of the owner.'

'But he said the furniture was left by the previous owner so they feel no attachment.'

Nick moved over to the bureau and beckoned her to join him.

'George, look at this 19th century Kingwood bureau-de-dame. It's exquisite, the workmanship is unique; I could sell that for £9,000 without any effort.'

'Really? Wow, then your offer was ridiculously low,' exclaimed George, looking at the bureau with a new eye.

'Exactly.' As Nick stood upright, his eye caught something outside. He looked out of the window to see two people arriving in a black Bentley. 'I'm sure I've seen that man before. George, do you recognise the man in the grey suit?'

George glimpsed out of the window onto the forecourt. 'Yes, he looks familiar. I know, its Henry Burton, the Home Secretary,' said George, watching the two men climbing the stairway, followed by a chauffeur carrying suitcases.

'So it is. Now, why would he be staying here?' Mused Nick.

'You are dreadfully inquisitive,' smiled George.

The door opened and Blandford entered. He was immaculately dressed in a pin stripe navy blue suit with a silk handkerchief in his top pocket. George couldn't help but notice that he used Ea de Cologne, perhaps rather too much, she thought.

'We've just observed some guests arriving, and recognised one of them as the Home Secretary, Henry Burton,' remarked Nick, in a probing voice.

'Mr Viktor Luzhkov has a large number of influential house guests. We are very pleased to accept your offer for these items of furniture,' said Blandford, in a matter-of-fact way.

'Good. How long has Mr Luzhkov lived at Grice Hall?' asked Nick.

'Mr Luzhkov bought the Hall last year, but has only recently taken up residence. Now, if you will pardon me, I have other business,' said Blandford, cutting off conversation about his employer.

'I'll send someone round to collect the furniture on Monday if that's convenient. About payment, who shall I make the cheque out to?' asked Nick.

'East West Global Investments. Mr Luzhkov believes the sky's the limit with all his business transactions.' Blandford gave a little giggle, as if enjoying a private joke.

Nick wrote out a cheque and passed it to the heavily scented Blandford.

'Thank you Mr Hartford, it has been a pleasure doing business with you.'

'The pleasure is all mine,' said Nick, raising his eyebrows to George.

Snapshot 78

Leaving the Hall, they drove down the lime avenue. George sensed that Nick was very tense; he seemed to be absorbing every detail of the grounds on either side of the driveway. Unhappy with the silence, she asked. 'What's the problem? You've just struck a very good deal.'

'I know. My intuition tells me that not everything is as it seems at the Hall. I would like to find out a little more about Mr Viktor Luzhkov.'

'What good would that do?' asked George, sensing that this was not a good idea.

'That's just it, I don't know. It's a feeling. Perhaps I'm wrong. Look, you see the hill at the other side of the road?'

They had reached the large gates at the end of the driveway. Ahead lay the main route back to Hawes; just ahead she could see a hill covered in straggling thick shrubbery and twisted hawthorn trees bent by seasons of vicious winds.

'What of it?'

'It would make a perfect place to observe the comings and goings at the hall.'

'What! Don't you think you are taking this just a little too far?' she protested.

'Perhaps,' he smiled.

Snapshot 79

Nick closed the oyster shell mobile and pushed it into his jacket pocket. He walked into the study, where George was sat on a dark blue chaise long, reading.

'Spence has just told me the most incredible news.' Nick related the news about the robbery.

'Have they caught anyone?' asked George.

'No, but *we* know who is responsible,' said Nick, sitting next to her.

'Tell me, is life always so interesting for you?' she marked her place with a bookmark.

'Only since I met you,' he laughed.

'Somehow, I find that hard to believe.'

Snapshot 80

Ronson led the way towards Malham Cove; a curved crag of carboniferous limestone formed after the last ice age. The ground underfoot was soft and springy. A river ran away from the cove in a winding trail, it's progress impeded by hundreds of small stones laying on the riverbed. The sound of the running water accompanied the three companions as they made their way towards the towering crag. Lumpy was walking ahead of Ronson and Fray.

'How did Lumpy get those scratches on his face?' asked Ronson curiously.

'Scratches?' repeated Fray, trying to avoid the subject.

'Fray, you and Lumpy went out for a drink last night, I told you to avoid any trouble, what happened?' His patience was running out.

'Well, we had a drink, then when we were leaving, he got into an argument with this woman outside.'

'What woman?'

'She was in the pub, we bought her some drinks. We were simply having a laugh. Anyway when we left she followed us out, and Lumpy wanted a bit of, well you know, but she didn't want to know, and she called him names.'

'So?'

'Well he shoved her around and she gave him a right clout with her handbag and ran off,' he added.

'Bloody hell, a handbag, it would be farcical if it wasn't so bloody important.' Ronson stopped and grabbed Fray's arm.

'It was his rough tactics in the supermarket job that got us all the unnecessary publicity. He's got to go. We'll never be safe with him around.'

'What do you mean?' asked Fray alarmed by the suggestion.

'You know I'm right, if we are going to keep a low profile until the heats off, then we have to get rid of Lumpy.'

'Send him away?'

'Permanent.'

'This is heavy, man.'

'The alternative doesn't bear thinking about. If we're caught, we face time, Fray.'

'No, I can't do that again Ronson,' said Fray, agitated at the very mention of time.

'Together we can survive, together, Fray, we *will* be safe. If we let Lumpy go, and he gets caught, he'll talk.'

'OK, OK,' murmured Fray.

'Back me up when the time comes,' rapped Ronson.

Once they reached the cove face, the steep wall of limestone towered over them. Water seeped down the many fissures, making any ascent of the face almost impossible to all but the most skilled climber.

'What happens now?' asked Lumpy.

'Now we are going up there,' Ronson pointed to the top of the cove.

'We can't climb that, and I left my wings behind,' laughed Lumpy.

'There's a way up the waterfall, it's the easy way to the top,' explained Ronson.

'But we'll get soaked,' croaked Lumpy indignantly.

'You're not frightened of getting wet, are you? Follow me, I'll show you the way,' said Ronson, standing astride two boulders at the foot of the waterfall.

'Look, there are some women over there, when they see you at the top they'll think you're bloody Spiderman.'

'Yeah, right, let's go,' yelled Lumpy, scrambling over the boulders.

The ascent was slow; while not as steep as the cove face, it still presented the three villains with considerable obstacles. The path, such as it was, zigzagged up the side of the waterfall, the rocks were covered in sodden lichen and moss, which made them slippery. Every foothold, each negotiated grip taken by Ronson was copied by the others. In this way, they slowly made their way up the waterfall. Once at the top they collapsed in a crumpled, sweaty heap; breathless, but triumphant. A brisk breeze soon cooled them. Looking up at the sky, Fray counted the criss-crossing trails left by highflying aircraft.

'I wish we were on one of those planes, flying to somewhere on the other side of the world.'

'This is high enough for me,' coughed a still-breathless Lumpy.

'That was really good, I feel great,' said Ronson.

'How high are we?' asked Lumpy.

'250 feet,' replied Ronson.

'Is that all, feels like we climbed Everest,' said Lumpy, sulkily.

'I'm going to take your photograph, Lumpy, so you can show everyone.' Ronson rummaged inside his haversack and pulled out a camera. He looked through the lens, then moved over to Fray giving him a sly smile.

'Come on Lumpy,' cried Ronson.

They walked over the deeply fissured channels of the limestone pavement towards the edge of the cove. Looking down, Ronson surveyed the scene, then waved to someone below.

'Who are you waving to?' asked Lumpy.

'Those women we saw walking earlier, they're waving. Come over here, Lumpy, and I'll take a photo. Hold your arms out.' Ronson showed Lumpy where to stand. Lumpy posed, Ronson moved around as if looking for the best shot.

'That's great, one more, just step back a little.'

'Those women are watching you Lumpy,' yelled Fray.

'Yea, make it good Ronson,' called Lumpy, excitably as he held out his arms, making a 'Y' shape.

'That's it, brilliant, take one more step, that's it, another Lumpy, this is going to look great.'

Lumpy, caught up in the thrill of the occasion, took one large step back and suddenly, without a sound, disappeared over the cove edge, arms still outstretched.

Ronson and Fray looked at each other.

'He did say he'd forgotten his wings,' one said to the other.

Snapshot 81

The door opened and P.C. Dunstan shuffled in, carrying a folder tucked under each elbow and a steaming mug of tea in each hand.

'You could have made two journeys,' said Sergeant Berry taking one mug of tea.

'I've found out where the man who died on Malham Cove came from?' Dunstan raised his eyebrows, 'Guess where?'

'Huddersfield,' said Sgt Berry.

'That's right, but how did you know?' Dunstan felt deflated.

'I ran his fingerprints through the computer. The deceased is called Kevin Simpson, he has a record, mostly petty theft.'

'So he, could be one of the three men involved in the White Cross robbery?'

'We'll know for sure after you've paid a visit to White Cross and shown the staff his photograph. Sgt Berry took a long drink of tea.

'Where are the other two?' asked Dunstan.

'My guess is they are still in the area. After I have contacted the force in Huddersfield, I'm going to visit the hotels to see if anyone recognises the photo of Mr Simpson.'

She took one more drink, flashing Dunstan a glance he recognized as 'it's all over, get moving.' He took a hurried drink, collected his helmet and jacket and left, reflecting on her words.

Snapshot 82

George pushed open the shop door and admired the ringing of the brass bell above it. The sound took her back to her childhood, when she would visit the corner shop with her mother to buy bread. For one brief moment, she experienced the aromas of the freshly baked bread from yesteryear.

'Hello, you're just in time for the grand opening.' Spence appeared from behind a maple bookcase with a multi-coloured feather duster.

'What opening would that be, Spence?' asked Nick.

'Exquisite Furs,' laughed Spence. 'The grand opening is accompanied with a parade, by models wearing a selection of fur coats, outside the new premises.'

'Models wearing fur coats in Hawes,' laughed Nick, 'are they mad? How many do they really expect to sell?'

'I remember someone asked you a similar question when you opened the antique shop,' said Spence, still dusting.

'Sounds fun, I think we should have a look,' said George.

'OK, come on Spence, shut up shop, we're going to watch the parade.' Nick took the duster and led both George and Spence to the door.

A small crowd of both curious locals and tourist visitors was gathered outside the premises of 'Exquisite Furs,' when George, Spence and Nick joined the small throng to see tall, slender, attractive models wearing full-length fur coats parading on the pavement.

'Are they local young women, Spence?' asked Nick.

'No, not one of them that I recognise,' answered Spence.

'You're supposed to be looking at the coats,' said George nudging Spence.

The crowd, appreciating the display, applauded the girls as each turned smartly and repeated the walk along the shop front. Waitresses moved along the spectators, handing out drinks. Nick took three glasses and handed one each to Spence and George.

'Nick, don't make it obvious, but if you look just inside the entrance, do you recognise anyone?' whispered George.

Following the models progress along the shop front, Nick scanned the entrance, and then quickly turned to George.

'Blandford and Henry Burton, and if I'm not mistaken that will be Mr Viktor Luzhkov with them.'

'Who?' asked Spence curiously. 'The new owner of Grice Hall,' explained Nick.

'And of Exquisite Furs, it seems,' said George.

The three of them made their way back up the main street towards the shop. Spence motioned to Nick, 'Isn't that P.C. Patrick Dunstan from Settle looking in the shop window.'

'Hello, Patrick, are you looking for something for your wife?' Dunstan looked up, and smiled when he recognised Mrs Spencer.

'Afraid not, I was just looking, you have some beautiful things. I am circulating photographs of a man who fell from the top of Malham Cove. He is a suspect in a robbery.'

'Do you have a photograph?' asked Nick. P.C. Dunstan pulled out a photograph and Nick nodded, 'We've seen him,'

Nick flashed the photograph to George. 'He was in the Golden Lion when we were there the other night.'

'Really, oh I say, that's terrific. Thank you very much. I'll be on my way to the Lion, See you, and thank you, Mr Hartford once again.'

Snapshot 83

'Jack, the chief wants us to travel up to Settle to investigate a body that the Craven Force have found, and listen to this, we're travelling up there in the Police helicopter,' Martin spoke fast to Jack, excited at the prospect of the trip.

'Helicopter, how the hell did you manage that?' said Jack, surprised but delighted at the prospect.

'The Chief Detective Inspector of North Yorkshire is an old mate of our Chief Superintendent and he wants us up there to identify the body. And guess what Jack? It's Kevin Lumpy Simpson.'

'What the hell is he doing up there?' Jack was surprised at the news. 'So much for local intelligence. He was supposed to be down south.'

'Well, at the moment he's lying on a mortuary slab. Apparently he fell off the top of Malham Cove.'

'Hell of a way to squeeze your spots,' retorted Jack, dryly.

Snapshot 84

June Berry stood by the car in the hospital grounds as she watched the helicopter hover overhead. The downdraft from the rotor-blades created a whirlwind that lifted fallen leaves above the blades of grass in a crazy symphonic flurry as the aircraft landed. There was no mistaking the two figures she had been told to meet and brief, they looked every inch, seasoned coppers.

After the usual introductions, Berry took them to the mortuary. Once inside, she took them over to where a technician stood waiting with the body. He pulled the sheet back to reveal the corpse.

'Definitely Lumpy,' said Jack

'Lumpy?' asked Sgt Berry, puzzled.

'Simpson's nickname,' explained Martin, 'it's definitely him, no mistaking that face. We suspect he and two pals have pulled a couple of hold-ups at supermarkets back home.'

'Three men held up the White Cross Cafe, we have a positive ID on Simpson,' said Sgt Berry.

'So where are Fray and Ronson?' pondered Jack, ignoring Sgt Berry.

'We know that Simpson and two other men stayed at the Golden Lion for one night. We're checking all rented cottages with estate agents and the local Tourist Information office.' Sgt Berry passed a bag, containing the dead man's personal possessions, to Jack.

'These were found on him. We have been unable to trace next-of-kin.'

Jack examined the contents of the bag. 'I doubt if anyone would own up to being related to Lumpy.' He passed the bag to Martin who looked briefly at the belongings before passing them back to his sergeant.

'I agree with Jack, if there is nothing in it for them, no one will claim him. When the coroner has finished his inquest, pass him on to the local undertaker.'

June Berry did not like the matter-of-fact attitude the Chief Inspector and the Sergeant displayed towards the deceased, they could have easily been talking about a lump of meat. She decided to wind everything up as soon as possible.

'If you've finished here I'll take you back to the station.'

'We'll need to find some accommodation for the night,' said Martin.

'I've already arranged a couple of rooms for you at the station.' She sensed from the blank look she received that they were far from impressed. 'It's about a hundred yards from the Golden Lion, and they have a very commendable restaurant.'

'Thank you for everything you have done, Sergeant Berry, I'm sure that everything will be just fine. Perhaps you could join us for a drink and a meal this evening?' said Martin.

'Afraid not, I have two children to chauffeur. But I'll be around tomorrow if you require any further information.'

Snapshot 85

Nick rang the doorbell. The heavy door opened and he was addressed, snootily by Blandford.

'It really would be more convenient if you could use the rear entrance, Mr Hartford, we have a shooting party expected back at the Hall within the hour.'

Nick was angry at being spoken to in this way, but stifled any reaction. He signalled to his men in the van to go round to the rear of the hall. He then deftly moved past a startled Blandford into the reception hall.

'Is the furniture still in the library?' asked Nick, pointing towards the door.

Blandford threw his head sideways in annoyance at this intrusion, and led Nick into the library.

'I will get someone to bring your men round. He pointed to some French windows, 'you can access the rear of the hall through these.' It was obvious from his matter-of-fact manner that he wanted them out of the way as soon as possible.

'We'll be finished in no time,' said Nick.

'I didn't expect you to be here in person,' snapped Blandford.

'With such delicate workmanship, I like to supervise personally,' smiled Nick, running his hand over the Kingwood bureau de dame.

'Of course.'

'Didn't I see you and Mr Luzhkov in Hawes yesterday?'

Blandford, still with a strong hint of Ea de Cologne, looked uncomfortable with the small talk and shifted about, tapping his foot.

'Yes. Mr Luzhkov opened a fur salon, it was quite an occasion.'

If you don't mind me saying so, it seems rather out of place, a fur shop in the high street of Hawes.'

'I should imagine much the same was said when you opened your antique shop,' smirked Blandford.

'Touché,'

'I really must be attending to my duties, Mr Hartford. I will, no doubt, see you before you leave.' He retreated hurriedly.

Left alone at last, Nick pulled out a scan meter and carefully walked around the library pointing the instrument in all directions. The meter told him the room was clean of any hidden cameras. He pulled out a small pouch from inside his Berghaus jacket and went straight to Agatha Christies 'Sad Cypress' that George had admired a few days previously. From the pouch he took out a sensor listening device, no larger than a small pea; on one side was a fine tungsten spike which he pushed into the rear panel and replaced the book.

Moving over to a large desk, he carefully placed another listening device on the underside of the leather covered desktop. Through the French windows he saw his two men being shown the way to the library by a young woman in a black uniform with a white frilly apron; they were enjoying an amicable conversation. Judging he had time, he removed the back from the digital phone and inserted a small wafer microchip onto the underside of the microcircuit board, then replaced the battery and clicked the back in place with moments to spare.

The packing was uneventful, and soon complete. Nick left with his men and joined the vehicle at the rear of the hall. It gave him the brief opportunity to survey the immediate area. The hall had suffered from years of neglect, so he easily spotted new cabling to two security cameras. Blandford made a brief appearance, brandishing papers for Nick's signature to conclude the sale of the furniture.

Snapshot 86

Nick found George reading in the study. 'Hello, did everything go alright collecting the furniture from Grice Hall?'

'Oh yes,' he said throwing off his Berghaus and slumping into the deep cushions.

'I recognise that tone, what have you been up to?' she asked curiously.

'George, you have a suspicious mind.'

'Nick, it pays to be curious where you are concerned. It's like being with Biggles, Dan Dare and Jason Bourne all at the same time, except they were fiction.'

'Did you ever see the film 'Panic Room' with Jodie Foster'?'

'No, but I did read about it. Where is this leading?' she asked.

Nick walked over to the fire place and pointed to the wall.

'What can you see?'

George walked over to Nick and surveyed the fireplace and the surrounding wall carefully.

'Don't tell me, you have a room concealed behind the wall, but why?'

'As a precaution,' he shrugged, moving towards the mirror.

Nick looked into the mirror over the fireplace and placed the palm of his hand onto the bottom left side of the glass.

The bookcase to the left of the fireplace swung open silently and Nick ushered George into the room. On the wall facing her, a table supported three monitor screens, on another table, various pieces of electric apparatus surrounded a widescreen laptop.

'You're full of surprises,' said George looking around the room.

'All surfaces are lined with Kevlar; a substance ten times stronger than steel.

The room has its own power source.' Nick walked over to a corner of the room, pressed a red pad and immediately, part of the floor slid open to reveal a stainless steel-lined chute.

'In an emergency, press the red pad and drop down the chute. In a few moments, you will find yourself in a small room by the riverbank.'

George gazed down the hole and then fixed her eyes on Nick.'

'Have you tried this?'

'Oh yes, it's good fun, reminds me of being on a slide when I was young. But it is only to be used in an emergency.'

'Nick, exactly what is this room?'

'It is a secure space to stay in, undetected, in the event of intrusion from whoever.'

'*Whoever* being the police.'

'Yes, it could be the police. It also acts as a secure area where I keep a number of computers that provide me with secure access and monitoring. When I'm planning a job, this is where I can access a firm's communications system, computers, etc.'

'It's all beyond me, I'm afraid,' said George, examining a set of monitors.

'Let me show you.' He sat down at a computer and typed in a few commands. 'Today I planted two UHF listening devices in the library of Grice Hall, and a small microcircuit board into the digital phone. Now all conversation in the room will be picked up and transferred by the phone to this computer's hard disk'

'Now why should I be so surprised?' George shook her head, not in disbelief, but amazed acceptance.

'It gets better; by typing in keywords, for example, my name, the software will sort out all conversations where my name is mentioned, and trash the rest. It really is quite simple,' smiled Nick.

'Of course, everyone I know carries bugs round with them and surveillance is the latest fashion.' George said

'There's more,' said Nick sheepishly

'What?'

'You remember when we left Grice Hall, I briefly mentioned that the hill opposite would make a very good vantage point for observing the Hall.'

'Yes.'

'Well I am going there tonight.'

'You know, there must be hundreds of reasons why I should leave you, but right now, I can't think of one. What time do we go?'

'Now where have I heard that line before?'

Snapshot 87

It was just after twilight when Nick had put up the hide, in which they were both now watching for activity in Grice Hall, through a APO-Televid linked to a laptop.

'There are a lot of people moving about, some are drinking, others standing around in groups talking,' commented George looking through the lens.

'Blandford mentioned they had a shooting party. Our Mr Luzhkov likes entertaining.'

'There are plenty of girls.' George handed the scope to Nick who scanned the hall windows.

'I'm sure some those girls are the ones who were modelling the furs,' said Nick.

'Perhaps they are, so what does that tell us?'

'That he likes pretty girls,'

'Wonderful, so we spend an evening in the country, in a tent not much bigger than a clothes horse, to observe pretty girls' she growled.

'You remember clothes horse's' he said in a surprised tone.

'Yea, we were a pretty old-fashioned family.' George felt a pang of regret at mentioning her family; it wasn't as if she thought about them often.

'Eureka!' he cried.

'What have you seen, let me look,' George cried, eagerly moving over to look through the lens. 'Henry Burton, the home secretary. Nick, he likes very long-legged blonds. They look very well acquainted,' she giggled.

Nick took hold of the scope. 'It seems to me our friend Mr Luzhkov is providing a lot of comforts for his guests. Have you noticed there are no middle-aged female guests?'

'Now you come to mention it, not one,' she yawned.

'I'd love to know the identity of the other guests. Let's hope we can get some good quality prints from the hard drive.' Nick closed the lid of the laptop. 'Time to go home.'

'Great, I'm freezing cold and in need of a big brandy,' said George rubbing her hands.

Snapshot 88

The front entrance of the Golden Lion was bathed in warm autumn sunshine when DCI Martin and his Sergeant walked out into the main street.

'Nice place that Jack, a very warm, typical, countryside pub. The manager has made a positive ID on the three suspects; we know where Lumpy is, but where are the other two?'
Martin stood at the kerbside and looked up and down the narrow town street.

'Ronson is the brains. I think, after Lumpy's accident they will be lying low somewhere,' said Jack, in a matter-of-fact manner.

'I agree Jack, and with the local constabulary checking all the main hotels and bed and breakfasts, my betting is they will be in private rented accommodation.'

Martin set off at a brisk pace towards the police station, leaving his sergeant still standing at the kerbside.

'Come on Jack, let's take a ride.' When Martin said they were going for a ride, it usually meant that someone else was going to do the driving. Usually it fell to Ripley, but today it fell to Jack; he climbed into the local station's BMW 4x4, put at their disposal by Sgt Berry.

'Nice vehicle,' Jack said as he eased it into gear and steered into the road, 'I could get used to this, mind you, up here, they'll need this in the winter snows, probably the only way they can get around,' pondered Jack admiringly.

'My wife used to cycle in the Dales every weekend when she was a teenager,' said Martin, staring out of the window. 'She belonged to a club called 'The Pudsey Owlers.' Can you imagine it, setting off and cycling two abreast along these roads. Jack, in today's traffic it would be impossible. Mind you, the very thought of six hours physical exercise would be totally alien to most of today's teenagers. My wife still loves this area. Every time we visit, she points out where they used to stop for a rest, or some hill that they used to race up.'

'Plenty of them up here.'

'What?'

'Hills. Just the thought of all that exertion; peddling like hell, and only moving a few yards. No, it makes me feel tired just thinking about it,' mused Jack.

'You used to play a good game of football.'

'H'mm. There are some cottages ahead, do you want to stop?' asked Jack, ending the reminiscence.

'No, the chances of finding them this way are slim, there are cottages spread over every valley. They have to eat Jack, and there aren't a lot of shops, so let's visit and see if any of the shopkeepers recognise the photo shots.'

'Good idea, they'll probably be living off ready-cooked meals,' suggested Jack.

'Great, put the siren on Jack, let's have some fun.'

'The siren, are you sure?'

'Yes, all this empty space with nothing but sheep, get it going,' chuckled Martin, excitedly.

'Right,' Jack looked at the array of switches, 'but which one turns it on?'

'Try them all Jack. Try them all.'

Snapshot 89

Sergeant Berry saw the station BMW parked in the square just before she caught sight of the two figures ambling down the street. She did not like the idea of two cops from another force tramping around her streets, but she had been told to give them her full cooperation in their investigation. If they were successful then that would immediately clear two crimes off the books, and that would please her Detective Chief Inspector at headquarters. Berry was a placid person who easily endeared herself to the local community, but she found these two detectives abrasive, a pair of rough diamonds.

Their ways were not hers, but at the end of the day she reasoned, they shared a common goal through their work in the police force.

Snapshot 90

Martin walked past the tall display cabinets, and waited his turn at the counter behind a couple of young teenagers who were sharing texts on their mobiles while being served by a middle-aged, healthy looking woman with neatly plaited auburn hair. Jack hovered by the magazine section, having spotted a Railway magazine, a lifelong interest.

Having been served, the two teenagers squeezed past Martin, still preoccupied with their mobiles.

'Good afternoon, whatever do they find so fascinating with those things?' Martin passed a few pleasantries with the lady before introducing himself and Jack. He passed some photographs to the lady who studied them diligently.

'No, I have not served either of them. I'm so sorry, I am very good with faces, but no I haven't served them in the shop. Maxine,' the lady faced towards a side door and called out the name once again.

'Maxine, can you come into the shop, love.'

After only a moment a young woman in her early twenties came into the shop through a curtain of beads. She had a rounded face, large eyes and a skin that was noticeably smooth and free from blemishes. Martin handed her the photographs, which she studied closely.

'Is this the only copy you have?' she asked Martin.

'No, why?'

'Can I just draw some glasses on this one?'

'Yes, if you think that will help,' Martin glanced towards Jack, who had joined him.

The girl rummaged through a drawer and found the pencil she was looking for and started to draw carefully on the image. Having produced the desired effect, she held the photo at arms' length and studied the finished result.

'Yes, I served that man yesterday.' She handed the photo back to Martin, who peered at the altered image.

'Fray,' he said, handing Jack the photo.

'It's really important that you tell me everything you can remember about this man. Is there somewhere we can talk without disturbing your customers?'

The young woman, pleased that she had been of help, pointed Martin towards the beaded curtains.

'Could I have this please?' Jack paid for the magazine on railways, and followed Martin.

Snapshot 91

Berry waited for the two detectives outside the shop, they were taking much longer than she had expected. She acknowledged local passers-by with a nod or with a wave of her hand.

Settle, being a market town, was a regular shopping spot for people who lived and worked around the local dales. It was a common occurrence for people to huddle in small groups exchanging information and catching up on local news, and Sgt Berry was part of the community.

Eventually, the two detectives emerged from the shop, and upon recognising her, walked over to join her. Each had a wide smile and looked in a happy mood.

'I saw you go into the shop, so I thought I'd wait for you,' she explained to Martin.

'I'm glad you did, Sergeant. We've been visiting general provision shops and asking the staff if they recognise the suspects from the photographs, and guess what, we have a positive confirmation right here on your doorstep.'

Martin was positively gushing with enthusiasm.

'A very bright young shop assistant in this shop remembers Fray buying quite a large order of frozen goods the same day as you found Lumpy at the bottom of Malham Tarn. He was wearing sunglasses, but could not sort out his money without lifting them to get a clear sight of his money. The girl thought at the time this was strange, because most people would have taken the glasses off completely.' He handed her the photograph on which the girl had drawn glasses.

'Smart girl,' said Berry, full of admiration.

'They're staying somewhere in the vicinity. I suggest we run some copies of this and circulate it as widely as possible,' suggested Martin to the sergeant.

'Right sir, will do. Have you finished with the car for today?'

'Yes I think so, thank you.'

'Good. I've had a number of reports about a squad car driving over the dales with sirens and lights on full blast,' she said.
Martin and Jack looked at each other sheepishly.

'We did have problem with some of the switches at one point,' said Jack to the sergeant, by way of a simple explanation.

'Boys with their toys,' she called, as she left them standing outside the shop.

Snapshot 92

Fray poked his stick into the undergrowth; he wasn't looking for anything in particular, just poking around, passing time that seemed to have stood still since they had been in the cottage. Every minute seemed to pass ever so slowly and he was totally bored out here in the countryside; there was so little to do. He missed his friend, Lumpy, and could not wipe out the memory of him disappearing over the tarn edge. He had been so happy in those final moments, having his photograph taken.
Fray didn't mention his feelings to Ronson.

A magpie flew into a patch of the scrub opposite to where Fray was standing and surveyed the undergrowth, its black wings and tail showing off a hint of iridescent green and blue in the sunlight, and his deep black eyes flitted back and forth. Fray looked around, anxiously trying to catch a glimpse of another bird, for he knew they mated for life, but he was unable to spot a partner. The magpie hopped from one twig to another, probably looking for grubs and worms.

He knew the rhyme, 'one for sorrow, two for joy.' Perhaps it was superstitious mumbo-jumbo, but it left him nervous and he hurried back indoors.

'You look as if you've seen a ghost, are you alright?' asked Ronson.

'I've just seen a magpie.'

'So?'

'Well, if you only see one it's supposed to be unlucky.'

'Rubbish, that's an old wives tale.'

''One for sorrow', that's what they say,' said Fray, becoming more agitated.

'And you only saw one.'

'Yes, I told you.'

'Perhaps it was Lumpy come back as a magpie, he's always been a thief, and a loner,' laughed Ronson.

'There's a lot of truth in them old tales,' snapped Fray, irritably.

'Oh yea, and I'm the bogeyman,' added Ronson, sarcastically.

'Well I don't like it, there must be another one out there somewhere,' Fray said, looking anxiously out of the window into the overgrown land.

'Let's take a trip into the village, we need some more food,' suggested Ronson.

'Great, I'm fed up of this dump,' said Fray, grabbing his jacket.

'Don't forget your sunglasses,' called out Ronson.

Snapshot 93

George moved around the various bookcases, tables, cabinets and chairs. A walnut and floral marquetry longcase clock made a familiar tick tock sound that seemed to her to be the perfect accompaniment for the surroundings.

It had begun to rain, and the all too familiar rivulets of raindrops running down the window, reminded her of the Viking café, and the day she had first met Nick.

'Gosh, that seems an age away,' she thought, and smiled at the change in her fortune. Dressed in a fitted, beige, ribbed jumper with a slashed neck and light khaki combat style trousers she was almost unrecognisable from the image of the now forgotten street girl. She picked up an art deco silvered figure of a female with a discus on a green and black marble base. The figure felt cold to touch, and as she carefully replaced it she noticed two men looking in through the front picture window. The rain was falling quite heavily now as the two men made their way through the front door into the shop.

'Good afternoon,' she greeted the men who both removed their sunglasses to wipe away the wet.

'Afternoon, alright if we just look around?' asked the tall man, without really waiting for her to answer.

'Please do, if you need any help please don't hesitate to ask,' she said, mimicking Spence, who had just popped out for lunch. She sat down and started to flick through a journal while keeping an eye on the two men who were admiring some silver sauceboats. They looked familiar, but why should they, she hardly knew anyone around these parts, but the more she looked, the more she was sure she had seen them before.

'Oh my God,' she thought, suddenly realising they were from the Golden Lion, 'these were two of the men that Nick had stolen the money from.

Calmly, she went into the back where Nick was working.

'Nick, look at those two men in the shop,' she said, shaking his arm. Nick looked at the security monitor.

'Well, well, our friends from the dining room.'

'What shall we do?' she asked, anxiously.

'I want you to go back into the shop, and when you see me, play along, everything will be OK, you'll see.'

He ushered her back into the room, where the two men were now looking at a 1920's mushroom top millefiore table lamp.

George returned to the desk and pretended to be looking at the trade journals. She had hardly turned more than a couple of pages before the door opened and in walked another customer wearing a beige raincoat and a felt hat.

'Oh my goodness, what a horrible day,' the man said as he shook his coat and removed his hat.

'Good afternoon everybody, I suppose we get used to the sun and dry weather so when it rains it takes us all by surprise,' he said as he moved around the shop.

'You have some lovely things. But talking about the weather, well I study the clouds coming off the fells. Today I thought to myself, those clouds look like rain clouds, so I brought my raincoat.'

The man moved near the two men and stood admiring a Victorian sampler. It was Nick.

'Now this is superb, embroidered in silk,' Nick said, as he held it up to the light, 'the standard of needlework is very high.' Turning to George, he continued in a loud voice. '

These samplers are very interesting examples of social history, they tell us so much about how people lived. How much is it? Oh my goodness, £450.' He wiped his brow and replaced the sampler. 'A little too much for my pocket, though I would dearly love to own it. Now if I had been as lucky as the old Russian in the Fur shop, then money would be no object.'

The two men listened, interested in any story about money.

'Did you hear what happened? There he was, taking a stroll the other night and finds a bundle of notes on the pavement. Now how

lucky is that? When he counted the notes, there was £17,000. The police have said that no one has reported losing any money, and if it is not claimed within six months, he can keep it. Now doesn't that prove how good exercise is for you gentlemen? Oh look, the rain is not as heavy now.'
He replaced the sampler.

'Best be off before it starts again, I'll be sure to pop in next week, bye.' He rushed out, pushing his arms through the sleeves of his raincoat as he moved out of the door and onto the pavement.

The two men whispered to each other excitedly; the tall man half turned towards George and raised his arm in a farewell gesture. They shuffled towards the door, both putting on their sunglasses before they left.
George watched in disbelief.

'How on earth does he do it?' Her mobile rang.

'Hello.'

'It's me, listen, Spence will be back soon, hang around the shop with her until I return, I'll...' his voice was faint and was breaking up.

'Where are you?'

'In the BMW..following our friends. When they left the shop..... went straight..... to the Fur shop. I just want to....know... they are staying....'

The crackling signalled an abrupt end to the call that must be due to a very poor signal in the fells, she reasoned.

Snapshot 94

The BMW engine purred quietly as Nick followed the car in front that belonged to the two men from the fur shop. It was raining heavily once again.

The two men had left Hawes driving up Pike hill before turning into the B6255, after about half a mile they turned into Mossy Lane; a small, extremely narrow road. Nick stayed well back, guessing that they would drive straight on. The road was barely wider than the average car; with a high, irregular gritty Yorkshire stone wall on either side.

The rain was lashing fiercely against the windscreen. Nick knew that Bands Lane, a turning up ahead, went up past the disused quarries, then over the fells to Hollin Keld Spring.

There was nothing up there except a couple of working farms; Nick guessed once again that the two men must be heading for Faw's Head Farmhouse; that had been converted into accommodation.

This local knowledge meant he could drive slowly without fear of being spotted. If they did turn into Bands Lane he would soon be able to pick them out as they climbed up the steep narrow road. The wind was still screaming around the car as the windscreen wipers worked incessantly to clear the lashings of rain being hurled at the screen. Nick drove slowly until at last he approached a sheepfold and barn at Faw Head.

He switched off the engine, opened the door and went out into the foul lashing rain. From behind the barn wall, which afforded him some shelter from the biting wind and rain, he could just make out the men's vehicle pulling into the empty farmyard. He watched and waited until the two men had made their way up the path, and entered the front door. The warm glow of the lights from the cottage windows told him they were inside. He had presumed right, now he could put the next part of his plan into action.

Snapshot 95

The main street, with shops and pubs on either side, was deserted. The light from the street lamps reflected off the wet, empty roadway as the rain continued to fall. Ronson and Fray stood in a shop doorway looking across the street towards the Exquisite Furs shop window.

'This looks as good a time as any, go and fetch the car, don't forget to freewheel it, and don't put the lights on,' Ronson whispered to Fray, who nodded in acknowledgement, and then moved out of the doorway and made his way up the street. Ronson watched his colleague leave until he disappeared into the rain sodden night.

Looking around once more to check the street was clear, he picked up a bag and moved across the street until he was standing in front of the display window of the fur shop.

When he saw Fray rolling the car down the street, he opened the bag and took out two building bricks. With one movement he flung both bricks against the glass pane. The impact and sound of shattered glass falling onto the pavement broke the silence of the night with a resounding crash. Fray stopped the car and jumped out to join Ronson in grabbing as many coats as he could hold and flinging them inside the car. Glass cracked underfoot as they dashed to and fro with the coats. They did not speak, they just got on with the job, and after an exhausting few minutes they had finished.

Wiping sweat from his brow, Ronson nodded to Fray. Soon they were speeding off, lights blazing, leaving behind what they thought was a deserted street.

Nick emerged from the shadows of his own shop doorway and watched the car speed off into the night. His hunch had been correct; he suspected that they would be unable to resist the bait of the story he had told in the shop.

Now there was just one more piece to put into place before he could return home.

Snapshot 96

It had been a long night. Sgt Berry had returned home just in time to have breakfast with the twins before her mum took them to school. In her office, she was dealing with routine reports when Dennis the village postman called and left the post. As she sorted through the various letters, one letter without a stamp caught her attention. She opened the letter, and as she read the neat typeface her heart beat a little faster.

'Chief Inspector Martin will like this', she thought, as she walked through to the living quarters of the station. She found the detectives enjoying breakfast, each reading a newspaper.

'Good morning, I've just received this letter telling us where the two suspects are staying.' They both looked up from reading. Martin took the letter and read the short message, then handed it to Jack, who read it while sipping tea.

'How did you receive the letter, sergeant?' asked Martin.

'It came with the morning post, but without a stamp,' she answered, surprised by the lack of interest shown by either man.

'I understand you were busy last night sergeant, some break-in at a fur shop,' said Martin folding his newspaper.

'Yes, a shop in Hawes had its front window smashed in with a couple of bricks, and someone made off with £12,000 worth of fur coats.'

The chief inspector and his sergeant were remarkably well informed she thought, then realised that P.C. Dunstan would have called at the station earlier.

'Well, Sergeant Berry, where is this farmhouse?' Martin asked.

'Its called Faw Head Farm off Mossy Lane about 4 miles outside Hawes.' Sgt Berry unfolded a map and placed it onto the table.

'Here it is sir,' she pointed out the farmhouse on the map.

'Someone's done us a great service sergeant, when can we go?' asked Martin, suddenly fired up.

'What about back-up?'

'We can't wait for back-up sergeant, there's only two of them. They've been up all night, the sooner we get there the better.'

'But sir, they have shotguns, we really should ring in for back-up.'

'Sgt Berry. Jack and I know these villains, they've been around for a long time and not once have they used firearms. They carry round those shotguns like you carry your gloves. Now let's get off, before it's too late,' said Martin.

'I'll still have to ring in to headquarters,' she said, surprised at Martin's disregard of the threat from the shotguns.

'Fine, sergeant, we'll wait for you in the car,' said Martin.

'Come on, Jack, finish your tea.'

Snapshot 97

The two squad cars pulled up just before they reached the sheepfold and barn. Martin and Sgt Berry had travelled in one car and Jack and P.C. Dunstan in the other. They walked down the road and peered over the stone wall at the building. Sgt Berry used a pair of binoculars.

'No sign of movement sir,' said Sgt Berry.

'Jack, take P.C. Dunstan and go round the back to cover any exits, Sgt Berry and I will take the front entrance. Wait for me to call you on the radio,' ordered Martin. Jack and the constable moved off as instructed.

'We'll give them a couple of minutes,' smiled Martin.

'Still no movement in any of the front windows.'

'Good, with any luck we'll take them by surprise. Follow me.'

They made steady progress up the farm driveway. There were deep furrows on either side, made by vehicles sinking into the clay drive, which made walking difficult. Martin surveyed the scene; a stone built farmhouse was surrounded by a large overgrown garden through which a stone flagged path led to the front door.

Berry reached the door first and waited for Martin to join her. He peered into each window, looking from side to side at each room. Sgt Berry was growing impatient with the Chief Inspector, she still would have preferred to wait for back-up. Martin signalled to her to join him.

'There are the fur coats,' he pointed to the coats, which lay in a heap on the floor.

They reached the four-panelled door.

'Shall we break the door down?' asked Sgt Berry.

'Always try the easy way first, sergeant,' whispered Martin as he turned the door handle and pushed the door open. He walked in, followed by an embarrassed Sgt Berry. There was no sound except for the squawking of some crows in the distant trees. Moving carefully down the hall, Martin looked in each room, then stopped, listened and signalled to the Sergeant to join him.

'This is the room,' he whispered.

He gently opened the door; there were two beds, both occupied by sleeping figures. Martin crept in until he was at side of one bed and prodded the dormant Fray, who looked up, sleepily surprised to see Sgt Berry then Martin.

'Oh no, Inspector Martin!' gasped Fray.

'Chief Inspector to you, my lad. You're nicked.' Martin signalled to Sgt Berry to stay with Fray and at the same time he moved quickly to Ronson's bedside.

'Wakey, wakey, Ronson.' Ronson tried to get out of bed but was knocked back by Martin.

'Now now lad, no sudden movements. Hold out your hands. Sgt, cuff them please.'

Sgt Berry handcuffed both men, who, to her surprise, showed no resistance. Martin looked under Ronson's bed and pulled out three shotguns wrapped in sacking.

'Sgt Berry, call the others on the radio and ask them to join us.' After a moment, Jack and the constable came in to the room.

'Recognise them Jack?' asked Martin, teasingly.

'Oh yes sir, Fray and Ronson, otherwise known as Barry Pugh and Matthew Lewis,' replied Jack. Ronson and Fray looked at each other, sleepily, in disbelief.

Martin addressed Jack once more. 'Arrest them Sergeant, then we can be on our way.'

Martin moved into another room with Sgt Berry.

'I want to thank you and your Detective Chief Inspector for letting us take charge of them, and thank you for all your cooperation.' Sgt Berry smiled, and watched as the two were led out and put into the car by Jack and P.C. Dunstan.

'Thank you sir, we'll be glad to have these villains off our patch,' she replied.

'I wonder who sent that letter Sergeant.' Martin asked loudly, as he got into the car with Jack.

'I wonder,' said Berry, relieved that it was all over.

' Come on Patrick, we'll put the fur coats in the back of the car, then we'll take them back to the station,' said Sgt Berry.

'When they leave tomorrow, we'll get back to our normal routine.'

'Oh yes, our local residents have rather been neglected, they'll be glad to see us back on the beat,' said P.C. Dunstan enthusiastically, carrying out the coats.

'You mean you've missed your regular chats and mugs of tea.'

'All part of the caring community service offered by yours truly, Sarge.'

Snapshot 98

Fray shuffled in the back of the police car and wriggled his wrists in the handcuffs to ease the nipping. He glanced out of the half open window over the undergrowth and was disturbed to see a lone magpie staring at him with its deep black eyes.

He remembered his encounter with the bird yesterday, and what Ronson had said. The bird hopped nearer, and then its harsh, uneasy call rang out '*kyack, kyack, kyack.*' Fray stared back uneasily, then with one last call, '*kyack,*' the bird flew off, free.

Snapshot 99

Nick sifted through the thick ream of papers until he found what he was looking for.

'One of these days I really must sit down and file this lot,' he thought, 'before it becomes unmanageable, which it almost is.'

He quickly scanned the article, then returned it to the pile. He picked up the phone, punched in a number and waited a few moments until a voice answered in a familiar New York drawl.

'Gallery 567, good morning, Mark Webber speaking, how can I help you?'

'Hello Mark, it's Nick Hartford calling from Hawes in Yorkshire.'

'Hi there Nick, how is Yorkshire today?' he said, emphasizing the 'shire'.

'Wet and cold. Did you receive my e-mail?'

' Yes, I did, thank you. When can you despatch the bureau?'

'Tomorrow; it should arrive at Newark in three days.'

'Great, I can't wait to pick it up. I'll wire your money.'

'No need Mark, I'm coming over tomorrow, I'll collect it in person.'

'Hey, that's great, we'll have to get a steak at the Madison Square Gardens Steak House.'

'Let's make that a yes, book a table for three,' said Nick.

'Three?'

'Yes, I'll be bringing my girl.'

'Great, can't wait to meet her.'

'Ok, Mark, I'll see you in a couple of days, bye.'

'You can count on it, bye.'

Nick replaced the phone and smiled. The thought of the juicy steak was already whetting his appetite. Now all he had to do was tell George that they were travelling to New York tomorrow.

Snapshot 100

'Now, you two have a lovely time,' said Spence, warmly.

'Oh, we will, he doesn't realise how much serious shopping we're going to do,' laughed George, excitedly.

'It did cross my mind,' said Nick. 'Part of my trip is business, so I'll be busy at auctions some of the time.'

'Well, as long as there's some room in the container for my shopping, and I must visit the top of the Empire State building,' smiled George, winking at Spence.

'Do you know how long they queue to get to the top?' asked Nick.

'No, but we'll be finding out soon enough,' she said.

'Spence, do you want to come with us to New York?' asked Nick, putting his arm around Spence.

'Certainly not, you two get off and enjoy the trip. Oh, by the way, the police caught two men for the fur shop robbery.' Spence said.

'Did they, well that's good news, glad to hear that the village is safe again,' said Nick giving George a sly wink.

Snapshot 101

'Ripley, thank God you're 'ere, now we can get off,' growled Martin impatiently to the detective constable.

'Hello sir, enjoyed your stay in the country?' asked Ripley donning a wide grin.

'We've been too busy to enjoy ourselves, Ripley, besides, the air up 'ere, stinks of cow shit,' said Martin, checking his watch.

'Ah, they'll 'ave been mucking out sir, it's what they do to replenish goodness back to the land,' said Ripley, pleased with himself.

'Mucking out,' Martin gasped. 'Ripley, the air up here is obviously not good for you, you seem to be hyperventilating a load of crap. Now if you don't mind, report to Jack. Make sure that Fray and Ronson are ready to leave, then we can make our way back home, to some good old pollution.'

Martin walked slowly into the station and joined Sgt Berry, to finalise the paperwork, while Jack and Ripley escorted Fray and Ronson to the van that would take them back to Huddersfield.

Sgt Berry and P.C. Dunstan, both relieved, came out of the station to see the departure of the visiting officers and their prisoners. 'Come on Patrick, I'll make the tea,' said a happy Sgt Berry, 'now I might see more of my family.'

Snapshot 102

'What time is it?' asked George.

'Back home it's midnight, here in New York it's 7pm,' answered Nick, taking the bags out of the yellow cab, and paying the driver. 'Well here we are, the Hotel Pennsylvania, made famous by Glen Miller who wrote a song about the telephone number.'

'Well Nick, I don't know the song, but who cares.'
After signing in with the reception staff, Nick and George took the elevator to their suite on the seventeenth floor.

'Oh my God, look at that view. I feel like we're still on the aircraft,' George said, staring out of the windows.

'Why don't we freshen up, grab a cab down to Times Square, where we can eat in a local diner, and watch the world go by.'

'We've only been here two minutes, and you're already talking like an American,' she teased him.

'When in Rome,' laughed Nick.

Snapshot 103

This was the first time that Jack had taken a day off for over three weeks, and only then because Martin had insisted. Having accompanied his wife, Jenny, on a shopping expedition, he was now back home, sorting through a collection of railway postcards that he had bought, at a local church fete, several months ago. His interest in railways went back to when he was a schoolboy. He still possessed his original Ian Allen train spotting books, though that was not something he would broadcast.

'Jack, it's David on the phone for you,' Jenny handed him the phone.

'Hello.'

'Jack I'm sorry to bother you at home. Fray wants to make a confession, but he'll only talk to you, and he says that he must do it now.'

'Can't it wait until tomorrow?' asked Jack.

'He won't talk; he says it must be you. I explained to him that you were busy, but he said if he can't talk to you today, he won't talk to anyone at all.'

'It had better be good,' said Jack. 'Tell him I'm on my way.'

'Jack?'

'Yes.'

'Would you do me a favour on your way in?'

'What's that?'

'Would you call in Patsy's Bakery, and get me a ham salad in brown. I haven't eaten since breakfast.'

'Right.'

'Oh and Jack. Could you get me a paradise slice as well? Thanks.'

Jack put the phone down and walked through to see his wife, who was preparing some food.

'Sorry love, but I have to go in.'

Snapshot 104

Jenny and Jack had been happily married for 23 years and had two grown up children; the elder, Travis, was twenty-one, while Samantha, at two years younger was nineteen. Both were away, studying at university.

Jenny, at forty-five years of age, had thick, blond, shoulder length hair, swept back. With deep blue eyes, she had a wicked sense of humour, and no doubt, through the years, this had helped with the raising of their two children, often alone, while her husband was away on duty. Jack was a loving father, and had often put the family first, which had possibly gone against him rising through the ranks.

She stared down at the keyboard of her laptop, and, after a moment's hesitation to gather her thoughts, she continued to write her weekly agony aunts column for the Weekly News. Her smile revealed faint lines around her mouth, as she reflected on how often she had drawn on personal experiences to offer some comfort to her readers. For Jack to be called back into work on his day off, while not a regular occurrence, was nevertheless not unusual.

Snapshot 105

Martin paced up and down the corridor, impatiently waiting for Jack to arrive. It irked him that Fray would only talk to his sergeant. The swing doors opened and Jack walked through, carrying his coat and a couple of paper bags with the familiar logo of Patsy's bakery. Martin reached out and grabbed a bag.

'I forgot to ask you for some salad cream,' said Martin, diving into the bag and pulling out a huge teacake.

'Look in the bottom of the bag.'

'Oh, Jack, thank you. Salad doesn't taste the same without salad cream.'

'What about Fray?' asked Jack as he watched as the chief inspector struggled to bite open the sachet of salad cream.

'He's in the interview room. Ripley is sat with him.'

Martin, having taken a bite of the sandwich, was left with excess salad cream around his mouth. 'I'll wait for you in the office. Thanks for the sandwich, Jack. You didn't forget the paradise slice, did you?' The sergeant handed him another bag and watched as he disappeared along the dimly lit corridor to the office.

Snapshot 106

Fray looked up expectantly as Jack walked into the interview room. He looked like a comic figure, with his big bat-like ears and prominent bent nose, leaning over the table. Ripley, who was sitting opposite the man, moved to allow Jack to sit down.

'Fetch us some tea will you please, Ripley?' asked Jack, sitting down. 'I expect you would like a cup of tea Fray, wouldn't you?'

'Oh yeah, that would be great, thank you,' said Fray nervously. Ripley left the room, thankful to stretch his legs.

'Now then, what have you got to tell me that wouldn't wait until tomorrow?' asked Jack.

Fray rolled his eyes, and looked around the room. His ears twitched, and he clasped his hands tight until the skin covering his knuckles was white.

'Well, we did them jobs in the supermarkets,' he said with his head bowed. Jack could hardly see his mouth move as he spoke because of his large nose.

'Yes, I know that Fray. I already know that.' Jack leaned forward. 'I do hope for your sake you're not wasting my time.'

'It was Lumpy who did the pushing around, he lost it.'

'Is that so?' snapped Jack.

'We did the fur shop, as well,' he said meekly. 'And the café and garage.'

'Fray, I know all this. What about Computer International?' he asked, pointedly.

'Did you pull that job?'

Fray's eyes were scrunched together as he listened to the sergeant. Shaking his head from side to side, he said, 'No, no, we didn't do that job, definitely not that.'

'What is it you want to tell me, Fray?'

'It's about Lumpy.'

Ripley entered the room carrying a tray with three mugs of tea, which he placed onto the table. Jack pushed a mug of tea towards Fray.

'What about Lumpy,' he asked quietly.

Fray, holding the mug of tea in both hands, took a sip of tea.

'After we did our last job we went up to the dales to lay low. The first night we stayed at this pub, in Settle, and we had our money stolen.'

'How much?'

'About £17,000.'

Jack looked at Ripley. 'So the money you stole from the supermarkets was stolen from you?'

Fray nodded. 'Yea, somebody took it, then he must have lost it, 'cause it was found by a man; some Russian bloke, who runs a fur shop in Hawes.'

'How did you know this?' asked Jack.

'Well, it was raining and we went into this junk shop, an' we heard this bloke telling the shop-keeper this tale about how this guy was lucky 'cos he found this money in the street'

'So that's why you did the fur shop?'
'Yeah.'

Jack shook his head. He had heard many stories down the years, so very little surprised him.

'But Lumpy didn't do the fur shop, because he was already dead wasn't he?'

'Yea. He was my best mate. I'd known him since we were at school together; we were good friends, always together. But he'd started to get really rough; he was always losing his temper, especially when he couldn't get his own way. He knew that if he got really nasty, then people gave in to him. So he did it more. But Ronson blamed him for a lot of the trouble we were in, so he did him.'

'What do you mean, 'he did him',' asked Jack interested, at last, in what Fray was saying.

'We went for a walk, and climbed this waterfall, because Ronson said we could. There were some girls at the bottom watching us. Well, Lumpy got real excited, he liked showing off. Anyway it was a really difficult climb, we all got really wet. When we got to the top we just flopped out, then Ronson said the girls at the bottom were looking for us at the top of the cliff. So he suggested taking Lumpy's photo, he kept saying to him, I'll look after you, just go back a little bit more so the girls can see you.

Lumpy was stood with his back to the cliff waving his arms in the air. Ronson shouts to him. Back a little more, just a couple of more steps, then he was gone!' Fray hesitated and sipped his tea, and still holding on to his cup, he continued. 'He just disappeared, still waving his arms so the girls would see him. That was it.' Fray hung his head low in sadness, leaving Jack and Ripley staring at each other.

Jack drank his tea and gave Fray time to recover. After what seemed to be an appropriate interval Jack said, 'Are you telling me that Ronson was responsible for Lumpy's fall?'

'Yes, he was sergeant, he definitely did him.'

'You do realise you will be called upon to repeat this in court.' Fray nodded.

'Yes. I owe it to my mate.'

Martin smiled when Jack had finished reporting the detail of his interview with Fray. This meant that quite a few crimes could be cleared from the books, and a couple of local villains were going to be put away for quite some time, hopefully.

'The man upstairs is going to be very happy at this news,' chuckled Martin.

'Ripley, you're in for a treat. I want you to travel up to Settle, and meet with Sergeant Berry, inform her about the Fray's interview. Find this junk shop that Fray mentioned; find out what you can to substantiate his statement. Try and trace the man in the shop, interview the owner of the fur shop and so on. You know what to do. Let's have some names and information. While you're there, take another look at Malham Cove where Lumpy died. Can you think of anything else Jack?'

'I don't remember seeing any camera when we picked them up at the farmhouse. Try to find that camera Ripley,' added Jack.

'I'll leave by train first thing in the morning,' replied Ripley, trying to hide the excitement he felt at being given the task.

'Train?' exclaimed Martin.

'Yes sir. Leeds-Settle-Carlisle express, one of the most famous routes in the country.'

'How are we going to manage without him, Jack?' Martin joked.

'More to the point, how will he manage without us?' ribbed Jack.

'I'm sure I'll survive,' smiled Ripley.

'Tomorrow, Jack, ask Fray about that camera. Then, together, we'll interview Ronson, and see what he has to say when we confront him with Fray's statement.' Martin reached for his coat. 'I want this wrapped up as soon as possible. If anyone's interested, I'm buying the first round.' Jack and Ripley both grabbed their coats and followed Martin out of the building.

Snapshot 108

George emerged from the front of Macy's, clutching a handful of different sized bags, at the prearranged time, to find Nick studying a street map.

'New York is just so stimulating,' she said. Putting down all her bags, she gazed at the busy street scene with long dark limousines, commercial vehicles and the familiar yellow street cabs, all going about their daily business.

'I'm just surprised you came out of Macy's on time,' jibed Nick.

The sound of far-off sirens grew louder. They both craned their necks to look down the street, until a column of light blue police cars came into view. The growing cacophony of collective whirring sirens and lights almost bowled them over as the vehicles sped past them.

'Ah, ah,' she laughed, ignoring his comment 'it's just like the cavalry.'

'Reuben's Diner is just across the street, come on.'

Nick grabbed her bags and they rushed across the busy street. Once settled in the diner, George ordered a double burger with relish and fries and Nick settled for grilled corned beef, with Swiss cheese and sauerkraut, on rye bread, with coffee.

'How did your meeting with Mark Webber go?' George asked, biting into a saucer sized burger, while reading the New York Times.

'Really good, he was ecstatic about the bureau and is interested in buying a number of other items. Tomorrow, if you don't mind, I'm going to an auction in Brooklyn,' explained Nick.

'Oh my goodness, he's leaving me again. Oh well, there's always...' she stopped mid-sentence and scrutinized the paper. 'Nick, look at the wedding photograph.' She passed the paper to Nick, who stared at the picture as requested.

'It's the wedding of Henry Burton, the Home Secretary.'

'Yes, but look who he's marrying,' she gasped excitedly. Nick once again studied the photograph, his brow knitted and lips pursed. He shook his head as he failed to recognise the bride. 'No, I don't recognise her.'

'It's one of the women who modelled the fur coats from Exquisite Furs,' she prodded the photo, which Nick now examined more closely.

'I think you're right. He's old enough to be her father, lucky devil!' he said, still peering at the picture.

'Oh, men and their fantasies,' she laughed.

Ignoring the friendly ribbing, he said, 'Talking about happy occasions, Mark is taking us out for dinner tomorrow. He's really looking forward to meeting you. I told him you were the typical English rose,' he smiled.

'Prickly,' she quipped.

'Rambling, more like.'

Snapshot 109

Ripley had thoroughly enjoyed the train journey. As he walked from the station, along a path of old flagstones, towards the police station, he absorbed the atmosphere of the old country village. He stopped to admire the late nineteenth century shop fronts with their intricate carvings, scrolls and heavy doors with brass handles and letterboxes. Houses, surrounded by low walls enclosing small front gardens, stretched all down the street. On the top of each wall, he could see stubs of iron from railings that were cut down during the First World War. Ripley wondered if this was how the village had contributed to the manufacture of guns that mowed down thousands at the battlefronts on some foreign field, fields not so different from those he had just passed.

'Detective Constable Ripley.' The sudden calling of his name interrupted his reflections.

'Yes,' he said, surprised.

'I'm P.C. Dunstan, I was supposed to meet you at the station, but I was delayed, sorry.'

'How did you know me?' asked Ripley.

'Ah, you're not the only who can detect,' said Dunstan, tapping a finger on his nose. 'My sergeant wants to meet you before you start wondering around asking questions.'

'Fine,' replied Ripley. 'I meant to call and tell her about some new evidence that has come to light anyway.'

'As long as you've got those villains locked up. We're not used to their sort up here.'

'Don't worry, they won't be troubling anyone for quite a while.'

Snapshot 110

Sgt Berry listened to what Ripley had to say. She had no intention of spending too much time with the young detective constable, but, having listened to him, she was quite sure it would benefit Dunstan immeasurably if he accompanied the young man.

Snapshot 111

At first, Ripley was not wholly convinced that having Dunstan on his heels was a good idea, but, as the day wore on, he could see direct benefits. Firstly, the constable knew the area like the back of his hand, secondly, he did all the driving, and thirdly, he was quite good company.

Trying to check out Frays statement, they visited a number of 'junk shops', without any success. Ripley felt that the antique shop in Hawes was possibly the shop referred to in the statement, especially as the fur shop, whose owner was supposed to have found the money, was just down the road. However, Mrs Spencer, the lady who worked in the shop, had no recollection of any customers having the alleged conversation that Fray said had taken place in the shop on that rainy day. Similarly, the man who looked after Exquisite Furs said that the owner of the shop never actually worked in the shop. And he denied all knowledge of any money being found by anyone connected with the shop.

'Well, that blows a hole through the confession,' said Dunstan.

'Maybe, maybe not,' reasoned Ripley, thinking through the whole thing. 'Perhaps everything that Fray described in his statement occurred at lunchtime, when Mr. Hartford's girlfriend was covering for Mrs. Spencer.'

'H'mm, unfortunately, she's in New York,' said Dunstan cynically.

'So, the mobile works across the Atlantic.'

'Do you have her number?' asked the constable.

'Of course, once I explained how important it was to our investigation, Mrs Spencer gave me Miss Sanderson's mobile number.'

'But even if she did hear the conversation, the man in the fur shop denies any knowledge of the money,' chipped in Dunstan.

Ripley looked at the constable with slight annoyance. 'Look at the sequence of events. We know that, on the day of the conversation, Fray and Ronson robbed the fur shop. What would make two small-time villains, who had previously only done jobs for cash, suddenly take fur coats, which are difficult to move without contacts? I believe they did hear a conversation; I believe the robbery on the fur shop was an act of revenge. And I also believe that the man they listened to on that rainy afternoon set them up.'

'How did you work that out?' asked Dunstan, anxious to understand the young detective's thinking.

'As one famous detective is reputed to have said, 'logical deduction'. I think we can make a number of assumptions about the man who told the story in the antique shop. Let's call him 'X'. I believe Mr X stole the money from Fray and Ronson. He saw them in the shop, so he pretended to be a customer and told the tale. Having set the trap, X calculated they would rob the fur shop in revenge. He followed them, and once he knew where they were staying, X wrote the letter to Sgt Berry, which gave details of their hideout.'

Dunstan nodded his head as he followed Ripley's interpretation of events. 'Right, but how do we find this Mr X?' Dunstan asked.

'For the moment, my orders are to verify Fray's account of events, not chase after the elusive storyteller.'

'But that means he's going to get away with everything,' said Dunstan.

'Look, I'm sorry, but I have my orders,' replied Ripley. 'If it helps any, I think that Mr X is local to this area. So, why don't you investigate who he is or could be? Let me know if you come up with anything of interest.'

Snapshot 112

'Stay with him constable,' snapped Martin, shutting the door of the interview room.

'Well, Jack, it's not surprising that he denies any involvement in Lumpy's death. Let's leave him to stew awhile.' Martin led the way to the office. Once inside, he dropped into his chair. Jack filled the kettle.

'Let's hope that Ripley finds the camera.'

'H'mm, that rattled Ronson. Did you notice? It was as if he'd forgotten about the camera.'

'He turned white when you suggested how he'd been responsible for Lumpy's fall from the top of the cove,' recalled Jack, pouring hot water into two mugs.

'He realised that the photographs in that camera would condemn him. If he had destroyed the camera, he would have been quietly smug. Instead, he was visibly rattled, and very uncomfortable. Jack, get on to Ripley, we must find that camera.' The sergeant placed a mug of tea in front of the chief inspector.

'I'll get right on to it. Do you want some digestives?'

'Oh thanks,' said Martin, fiddling with the packet of biscuits. 'Some of these are broken.'

Snapshot 113

Having completed a tour of the United Nations buildings, Nick and George made their way down East 46th Street to the Captain's Table, a popular seafood restaurant, where Nick had booked a table for two. The mid-morning sun hung directly above them, it's rays hitting the buildings and casting huge shadows to one side.

'Did you enjoy the tour?' asked Nick.

'Very much, it's not a place I would have ever thought about visiting, but yes. The building itself is not very exciting, but once inside you realise that this is the seat of world power, where decisions affecting world peace are made, or broken.' She continued, 'I thought the half-melted sculpture from the ruins of Hiroshima and Nagasaki makes a very poignant statement to world leaders.'

Nick listened to George, while at the same time fumbling for his mobile, which he switched on and dealt with outstanding messages.

'Spence has left a message.' He glanced at his watch.

'Six-fifteen at home, I'll call her.' George watched him make the call. She was very happy and relaxed, the whole trip was so splendid. The sights of the Big Apple were so thrilling, so much so that the big shop she had planned had not really taken place, yet!

'Switch on your mobile, George, the police are going to call you,' he said, in a matter-of-fact voice.

The very mention of 'police' sent a chill right through her, and she felt the hairs at the nape of her neck stand out. Before she could utter a word, Nick continued.

'It's alright, it's just a routine call about a conversation you overheard in the shop when you covered for Spence.'

'Conversation,' she gulped.

'Remember when I imitated the old man,' he laughed. 'Apparently they are trying to trace the gentleman, so they want to know if you can identify him.'

'Oh great, you think it's funny. It must be serious if they are going to ring me here in New York.'

'George, stay cool. Spence told them she knew of no such conversation, but once she checked the diary, she realised that you had covered for her that day, while she had lunch. So, you just tell the officer what happened that lunchtime; you remember the man, but have never seen him before or since,' he said, as they reached the 'Captains Table' entrance.

'I do hope they have red snapper on the menu,' she whispered in his ear as they entered the restaurant.

'Ouch, that doesn't sound good.'

Snapshot 114

'Morning, Sgt Berry,' said Ripley cheerfully. 'I just called in to say 'cheerio', I'm leaving today, so I want to thank you for all your help with my enquiries.'

'Don't mention it, I'm just sorry that your trip was not more successful, Ripley.'

The hint of negativity didn't go down well with Ripley. He felt much more positive about his visit to the area and the crime scene; he was convinced that, if he had had more time, he would have discovered more about the identity of Mr X.

'Patrick is off today, he's taking me up to Malham Cove before I catch my train home.'

'So I understand, you seem to have made quite an impression with Dunstan. Just remember he's a rural copper, don't put any more ideas in his head about undertaking any mini-investigation. He has enough to keep him busy.'

'Right Sergeant, point taken,' Ripley said, leaving Sgt Berry at the front desk.

Snapshot 115

'So what did Miss Sanderson have to say about Mr X?' asked Dunstan.

'Not a lot. She was able to confirm Fray's statement, i.e. that the conversation took place, but she was unable to throw any light on the identity of X, she says she had never seen him before.'

'Well, our Mr X certainly covered his tracks. He leaves no ID, no clues, nothing,' spat out Dunstan, 'I know most locals, and the description rings no bells with me'.

The young constable's remarks had a familiar ring to them, Ripley thought as he watched him change gear several times as they made their way up the fells.

Could it be possible that two separate people, in two different geographical areas, would repeatedly pull jobs and leave no clues? Here we have someone who brazenly walks into a room, and takes all the cash belonging to Ronson. Then, disappears into thin air, only to reappear and be directly responsible, possibly, for the crooks' arrest. At home, a number of crimes are committed, and on each occasion the perpetrator leaves no evidence. His head was dizzy with ideas; could these crimes be linked? Could Mr X have committed them all?

'Are you alright?' asked Dunstan, throwing the vehicle round a steep U bend.

'Yes, I'm fine,' replied Ripley, putting his ideas away for the moment.

'Here's Malham Cove. We'll have to park the car and walk the rest of the way.'

Ripley looked out on the familiar landscape. As a child, he had spent a lot of time in this area, with the scout movement. He remembered being led by the dreaded Mr R, who used to lecture them on the Second World War. No matter what they did, or where they were, he would relate it as some wonderful wartime experience, as if the whole war had been one big adventure.

The walk over the coarse grass, with the path littered with rocks, was reminiscent of many a walk with Mr R. The scout leader seemed to purposely choose the most tortuous routes to test 'his boys'. 'This will sort out the men from the boys', he used to say, striding forth, regardless of the chaos he left behind him; usually, a string of exhausted boys struggling to keep up.

'This is the spot where we found the body of Mr. Whatshisname,' said Dunston.

'Lumpy, his nickname was Lumpy,' said Ripley, leaving behind reminiscences of his days in the scouts. He surveyed the rough terrain.

'Let's mark the spot where he landed after the fall so we can see it from the top of the cove,' Ripley walked away from the cove face and, when he was sure that he had found a suitable spot, pulled out a handkerchief, placed it on the ground, and held it in place with a couple of rocks.

'We'll see that from the top,' he said, looking up at the vertical limestone face.

'Come on, I'll race you to the top,' shouted Dunstan, as he set off running towards the waterfall at high speed.

'The man is mad,' thought Ripley, but as this was a question of pride, the scout in him took up the challenge. Recent rainfall meant the water was flowing fairly fast. Ripley estimated that the waterfall was about two hundred feet high.

The rock face was dangerously slippy, but fortunately the craggy limestone gave them good finger-grips, from which they could heave themselves upwards. Any thought of racing up to the top soon disappeared, it was going to be a slow climb.

'Bloody hell,' yelled Dunstan, obviously in some discomfort.

'Are you OK?' asked Ripley, anxiously holding onto a small ledge while looking up at his colleague.

'The damn water's running down the inside of my sleeves.' Ripley laughed

'Just like taking a cold shower.'

'A cold shower fully clothed, no thank you' said Dunstan, heaving himself upwards. Ripley followed, carefully double-checking each grip. Eventually, they reached the top and fell exhausted onto the fretted limestone surface.

'That was exhilarating, Mr R would have loved that,' he said, catching his breath.

'Who?' asked Dunstan.

'Forget it, just me thinking aloud.' After a short rest, Ripley pulled himself up and surveyed the scene.

'Come on, let's start looking for that camera.'

'This is my day off,' gasped the young cop, still breathless.

'Coppers are never off duty, Dunstan, you know that.'

'You sound just like my sergeant.'

'God forbid, my voice broke years ago.' They both laughed as they walked along the cove top. Eventually, they reached the point above the handkerchief, left as a marker on the ground below.

'Let's search around here,' said Ripley.

The limestone pavement reminded him of a slab of tripe and a quick cursory search revealed nothing unusual. Ripley looked around the bare scene; a few bent twisted hawthorn trees had manage to survive, their roots penetrating cracks and hollows in search of nourishment. Many of them took on a 'bonsai' form as a result of the stressful environment.

If Ronson had dropped the camera, it would have possibly been found by one of the many ramblers, but if he had decided to hide the camera, so that he could pick it up at some future date, then he would want a landmark, something easily recognisable. The trees, it had to be the trees.

Ripley stood in line with the handkerchief on the ground. With his back to the waterfall, he looked along the pavement. If, when Lumpy dropped off of the cliff face, they panicked, then they would want to get off the cove as soon as possible. Perhaps Ronson had looked upon the camera as a weapon that must be concealed.

He walked along the route he imagined they would have taken, stopping at the first tree he encountered. Searching around the base of the tree revealed nothing.

Just below the tree, the pavement fell away in steps and grikes. He pushed his arm into the hollows of the first grike where there was an abundance of 'hart's tongue' fern and the beautiful bloody crane's bill flowers growing. His fingers felt around the rough surfaces, and then suddenly, with his arm fully stretched, he felt something smooth. His fingers reached and slithered over the surface until he could found something to grab, and with one heave, he pulled it out. He shouted to Dunstan, who came running over excitably, and they both looked at the bag.

'Open it,' cried Dunstan. Ripley fumbled with the zip and pulled it open to reveal another bag, inside which laid a Canon Ixus camera. The detective constable, triumphant, placed in on the ground and wiped his arm free of soil. Both men beamed at the success of the find.

'See if it still works,' said Dunstan. Ripley picked up the camera and turned it over looking for the on/off button. Once he found it, one simple push and the screen burst into life.

'My brother has one of these.' Dunstan grabbed the camera and expertly manipulated a couple of the buttons, glared at the screen, and then passed it back to Ripley, who looked, wide-eyed, at the image.

Snapshot 116

This was the local train; consequently it stopped at every subway station along the line northwards to Penn Station. As far as George was concerned it was a very pleasant journey; she enjoyed watching the evening commuters boarding and leaving. New York was a truly cosmopolitan city. Smartly dressed business commuters mixed with everyday travellers, tourists and young people all going about their business. Some read newspapers or a book, while others listened to music on their iPods, or, like George, watched the world go by.

Nick was flicking through the latest edition of Newsweek, oblivious of the comings and goings of the many different travellers. He flicked over another page, and saw yet another column highlighting the wedding of the Home Secretary, Henry Burton and his wife Yekaterina. He was just about to turn the page when his eye caught the name 'East West Global Investments'.

His fingers tightened on the pages. As he read the account of how the bride's uncle was a successful entrepreneur, policy specialist and owner of the highly successful company, East West Global Investments. His name was Viktor Luzhkov.

He looked up from the paper and gazed out of the carriage window opposite. The tunnel walls flashed by as the train hurtled along the rails at high speed. Its motion rocked the carriage gently from side to side, then Nick was aware of the familiar screech from the wheels as it slowed down to stop at the 18th Street Station. The driver of the truck that collided with his parents' car had been employed by the East West Transportation Co. Was it possible that this was owned by Luzhkov?

Nick knew he had to find out.

Snapshot 117

Ripley opened the door to see both Chief Inspector Martin and his sergeant sat at their desks. Both looked up as the young constable made his entrance.

'What time do you call this lad?' asked the sergeant, looking at his watch.

'Sorry I'm late Sarge,' said Ripley, pulling up a chair.

'Well, did you enjoy your jaunt to the countryside, not forgetting your train excursion?' asked Martin in a jovial, but sarcastic way. 'I hope you've got something to make us forget the fact that you're late. We've even had to make our own tea, and we've run out of digestives,' he said, winking at Jack.

'Yes sir, I think I have just what you wanted to see,' Ripley hastily pulled out the brown paper bag.

'Well, what is it?' asked Martin impatiently.

'The camera, sir. I found the camera Ronson used to take photographs of Lumpy.'

'Did you now, well, that is good news,' said Martin, leaning over the desk to watch as Ripley slowly removed the camera, wrapped in clear plastic, from the brown paper bag. Ripley then proceeded to push a couple of buttons and suddenly the screen lit up.

'Let me see,' said Martin, impatiently.

Ripley pressed another button, juggled with the menu button, and then passed the camera to the Chief Inspector.

'We've got him, Jack, we've bloody got him. Arrange an interview with Ronson immediately,' Martin passed Jack the camera.

'Good work Ripley,' said Jack, viewing the last photo of Lumpy disappearing from the edge of the cove.

'What else have you got for me?' asked Martin, expectantly.

'Well sir, I spoke to a Miss Sanderson in New York who can verify...' Jack watched as Martin's jaw almost hit the desktop at the mere mention of the phone call. But there was no stopping Ripley, as he passed on the results of his investigation to the Chief Inspector.

Snapshot 118

Nick had spent most of the morning bent over his laptop. George had been out for a mini-shop, and having returned was surprised to see him still busy, looking at various company records and sending off e-mails.

'Any luck?' she asked chirpily.

'Its amazing the lengths some people will go to cover up their business footprints,' he said without looking up from the screen. 'This Luzhkov fellow is a really slippery individual.'

'Does he own the company who employed the driver who ran into your parents car?' she asked bluntly, standing behind him peering at the plasma widescreen.

'I'm pretty sure he does have interests in the company, but trying to unravel his business links is proving to be very difficult, it's going to take to some time to untangle.'

'Well I'm pretty sure that if there is a link, you'll find it,' she said, reassuringly.

'Thank you for that vote of confidence,' he said, closing the lid of the laptop.

'You're welcome. Now, if you'll excuse me, I'm going to get ready for our last evening in New York.'

'But it's only early afternoon,' he protested. But it was too late, she had already disappeared into the bathroom.

Snapshot 119

'What do you think of Ripley's ideas, Jack?' asked Martin.

'Interesting,' said the sergeant, downing the last remnants of his bitter.

'Well, he's established that Fray's statement of events is fairly accurate.'

'Yes, and he found the camera.'

'Bloody good detective work that. Something from the old school has rubbed off on him, eh, Jack?' said Martin laughing, having no hesitation in taking full credit for the initiative displayed by the young detective.

'What about his theory that Mr X could be the one who did the robberies down here on our patch?'

'Bollocks Jack, no substantive evidence to link the two. Forget that airy-fairy mumbo-jumbo. Let's stick to the facts. We can clean this one up. Ronson has now admitted his part in the killing of Lumpy, together with the supermarket robberies. Case solved.' Martin took one last gulp of bitter then held his glass out.

'Same again Jack.'

Jack trundled off to the bar, it had always been the same. Every time they cleared another case from the books, they drank in this pub.

While a case was ongoing they drank down at the Lord Wellington, but once it was solved, they drank here in the Plumbers. The décor was Victorian, all the doors and partitions were decorated with stained glass, each depicting a different picture of a tradesman from yesteryear. It was mainly used by professional types, not manual workers with lead piping stuck down their trousers, as the name suggests.

'You'll never guess what Sally has done,' Martin said, taking the pint from Jack.

'What?'

'She sent off my painting, to an exhibition in Hull.'

'What, and you didn't know!'

'No. The last thing I want is everybody gawping at my painting an' saying "Oh I could have done better than that."'

'Why did she do it?'

'Because she thinks it's good enough.'

'And you don't.'

'It's not that, Jack. It's personal, when I paint something,' Martin hesitated as if struggling to explain, 'something of me goes into the painting.'

'Is it that one with the bottles?' asked Jack taking a long drink.

'Yes, half a dozen bottles of 'Becks', set out on a table.'

'Ah,' said the sergeant, amused. 'Were they empty?'

'Yes.'

'Now I know what part of you is in the painting!' Laughing, they finished their drinks.

'Did we get a positive result from the finger prints on the camera?' asked Martin.

'Yes, they belonged to Ronson.'

'Now I'll get the next drinks,' said Martin.

Snapshot 120

The seven-hour flight from New York had left George very tired, especially as she had spent most of the flight watching films, unlike Nick, who slept the whole journey.

Having checked in with reception at the Jury Inn in Croydon, George collapsed onto her bed. It was 10 am. Nick had a quick shower, changed his clothes, had a black coffee, and then was in a taxi heading for the East West Transportation Co, whose headquarters were on the fringe of the old Croydon airfield.

His thoughts were fragmented; he had no plan, but was simply going to snoop around, to see what he could find out. He had to know if Luzhkov was the owner. The taxi stopped outside an unimposing two-storey white pebble-dashed building, with one entrance at the front and two rows of standard windows. Walking past the windows revealed nothing unusual.

Nick stopped by an empty bus shelter and put on a pair of thick-framed dark glasses and a hat. Then he walked into the building and checked in to reception.

'Morning.' The young woman behind the glass-topped desk was heavily built, and her dark hair had two beetroot coloured highlights.

'Can I help you sir?' Her accent was very 'east end'.

'Mr. Broom, Health and Safety Inspector, I have an appointment to check your safety notices.'

'To check the what?' she asked, puzzled.

'Young lady, my time is valuable. My office rang last week to notify you that I was calling today to make an inspection of your health and safety notices, to make sure they are displayed in the correct places, and that they are up to date.'

The receptionist checked her computer screen. 'Do you know who you spoke to, because I have no record of any appointment?'

'What! It is imperative I speak to someone in authority. This will have to go down in my report.' Nick fiddled with his glasses, peering at the receptionist.

'Young lady, do you know your chair is in the wrong position for you to operate that monitor? You must look down on the monitor, not up to it, as you do.'

'Really? Well, I much prefer it down 'ere Mr Bloom, it's much more comfortable. Just hold on, I'll speak with a manager. If you would like a coffee, please help yourself,' she pointed towards a table.

'Its Mr Broom,' said Nick, pouring himself a coffee, and then moving over to a display to study a collection of company photographs on the wall.

'Good morning, how can I help you? My name is Sam York.'

Nick turned to see a man in his mid thirties, wearing a pin stripe shirt, no tie, and trousers hung high above the waist without a crease.

'Mr Broom, Heath and Safety Inspector, my office rang last week and made an appointment for me to inspect all your current H&S certificates.' Nick went on to explain how under present legislation it was a requirement that all companies display the requisite information in the appropriate places etc, etc. Nick continued, 'Without this certificate to verify that your premises have been checked, you will be closed, until the aforesaid checks have been made.'

'Closed?' the young man uttered incredulously.

'I'm afraid so, it's the law.' Nick looked at Mr York over the top of his glasses.

'So, shall I start checking?' he smiled, while waiting for a reply.

'Well yes, I suppose so. Pauline, give Mr Broom a visitor's pass.' Turning to Nick, he continued, 'Tell Pauline where you would like to start, she will give you directions.'

'Here in reception will do to begin with, thank you. I should be finished in about two hours.' Nick marvelled at how easily he had managed to weave his way inside the company. He passed from office to office, taking notes and checking the requisite notices relating to Health and Safety. All the while he was picking up useful information about customers, freight and regular routes taken by the fleet of trucks. An enthusiastic employee gave Nick a tour round the loading bays and introduced him to the rolling stock foreman, who was just about to have his morning break. A small stocky man with a broad nose and black beard, he had a broad smile and strong forearms.

'Sit down. I was just on my way to the canteen. I'll bring you some tea and a bacon sandwich.' Once he had left, Nick looked round the untidy, windowless office. Files lay strewn on the desktop, mixed with clipboards. Above the desk was a row of hooks; each hook held a bunch of keys, each clearly labelled with the registration number of the vehicle to which it belonged. Two swivel chairs with worn, faded, red leather that had seen better times occupied the small floor space. Nick sat in one of the chairs and was surprised by how comfortable they were. He swung round, looking at the overcrowded walls; hardly an inch of the original wall could be seen beneath the array of faded memos, letters and photographs of trucks. The door burst open.

'Here we are, a nice mug of tea and the best bacon sandwich this side of the Thames,' the man sat down in the other swivel chair opposite Nick. 'Nobody will bother us here. Nobody ever comes to see me.'

'What do you do in here exactly?' asked Nick, taking a bite of the sandwich.

'Nothing,' he laughed, 'absolutely nothing.' 'I asked them to make me redundant, but they won't, it'll cost them too much. Many years ago, about twenty of us joined a private pension scheme. I'm the only one still left here working. I just come to work, sit in this room, keep the spare keys to the vehicles, book them in for a regular service when they're due, and that's it.'

'Don't you get bored?' asked Nick.

'Bored, me, nah. I do a lot of photography; it's my hobby you see, I just wander round taking photographs of the vehicles. If I get too fed up I go home. Nobody ever misses me, cos' I've nothing, really, to do, you see. I think I'm a bit of an embarrassment to them. A few years ago they tried to get to the pension scheme, said it was in my interest, but it's sealed as tight as my arse, another three years an' I'll be retired.'

'So you will have seen a lot of changes.'

'You can say that again, cor' blimey. This used to be a small family firm, we had no more than a dozen trucks. Then we expanded, gradually taking over other long distance companies who hit hard times. The old man died, his son sold out, one merger after another, then, five years ago, we were taken over by an investment company, an' they renamed us East West Transportation, I don't know who they are. Now managers and computers run us; they can find each truck on a computer screen at any time, day or night. There's no room for the likes of me. Here, let me show you some of my photographs.'

He pulled out several albums, each listed with the year, and proceeded to give Nick a running commentary of the many different lorries the company had used.

'You don't seem to have many of your colleagues,' commented Nick, inviting the old man to show him more snaps.

'No, I'd rather photograph the lorries. There are a few of my workmates, but I keep them separate from the lorries.' He fumbled in the filing cabinet and pulled out another album.

'Ere' we are, now let's have a look,' he flicked over the pages.

'This one is of me and the lads when we worked in the repair shop back in the fifties.' He enthusiastically described bygone years of the company, recalled through the photographs.

'A lot of them have gone now, I don't just mean from the company,' he laughed raucously, 'I mean from this earth. There were some good lads.' Nick was interested, but could hardly wait until the old man eventually reached the last few pages, where more formal photographs depicted staff and visiting dignitaries.
Nick scanned each one carefully, half listening to the old man describing each one.

With only two pages to go, Nick finally found the proof he was hoping for; there, amidst a formal photograph, taken at the front of the building, stood Luzhkov.

Nick stood up and glanced at his watch.

'Look at the time. I really have enjoyed talking with you, but I'm afraid I must be moving on,' Nick closed the album, while at the same time, snatching the photograph of Luzhkov and pushing it into his pocket.

'I understand,' chuckled the old man, 'it's been grand talking with yer, call in anytime. Come on, I'll walk you to reception, I could do with the exercise.'

At reception Nick said farewell to the old man and informed Pauline, the receptionist, he was leaving. Almost immediately, the manager, Sam York, appeared to see Nick.

'I hope you found everything well, Mr Broom,' he said, looking hopeful?

'Everything seems in order Mr York. However, there is one thing I am most unhappy with, and that is the lack of adequate accommodation for the service foreman. His present office breaks every rule in the book, I shall be returning in two weeks, and I will expect him to have an office that complies with H&S rules.'

'Who do you mean, the service foreman?' the manager asked, confused.

'Mr Strullyman,' snapped Nick.

'Who?'

'For goodness sake, Mr York, it's hardly surprising the poor man has to suffer outrageous conditions when you don't even know him.'

The manager broke off eye contact with Nick. His face took on a strawberry hue at this humiliating confrontation. He was rescued from further indignity by the intervention of Pauline, the receptionist.

'Mr Strullyman, he's the one who takes all the photographs, Mr York,' she whispered.

'Oh, that Mr Strullyman, of course,' he started laughing nervously, 'yes, he's part of the fixtures around here, really we are just waiting for him to retire.'

'That may or may not be the case Mr York, but his office environment is totally unacceptable and contravenes all regulations. I shall be back in two weeks time, and I will expect to see a great improvement in that quarter. Now, good day to you.' Nick turned and exited the building, leaving the exasperated manager.

Snapshot 121

Back in the hotel room, Nick found George still sleeping. He made two coffees and tried to wake her.

'George, wakey wakey, here's a coffee for you,' he said gently.

'What time is it?' she asked sleepily.

'Just after two,' replied Nick.

'In the morning?' she reached out for the coffee, eyes half shut. 'Are you kidding me?' she looked at her watch, bleary eyed. 'It's only 9 am, for God's sake.'

'That's New York time, we're back in London, remember,' he said, smiling, showing her the clock.

'Jet lag, I've got jet lag, leave me alone,' she moaned.

'OK, I thought you'd remember we had tickets for the premiere of 'Mission Impossible 4'. Tom Cruise will be attending in person.' After a slight pause, George threw back the duvet,

'You never told me that we had tickets for the premier?'

'Didn't I?'

'Let me see them,' she held out her hand expectantly. Nick placed the photograph of Luzhkov into her hand. She glanced at it, 'Nick, if you have woken me just to show me this, you are in deep trouble,' she tossed the photograph to one side.

'Oh sorry, wrong pocket,' he produced two tickets. She took them and pulled them up close for inspection. 'H'mm, Tom Cruise. Just what every girl would like!'

'He's due outside the theatre in two hours for a walkabout, before going inside to meet the guests.'

'Two hours, you must be joking, why didn't you wake me earlier, how can I be ready for Tom in two hours?' Nick watched as she rushed round, gathering essential items before disappearing into the bathroom.

'Are you interested in where the tickets came from?' he shouted after her.

'Of course, tell me later, then, you can also tell me about that photograph, I know you don't let me see something without there being a reason,' she shouted back from the shower.

Snapshot 122

For the last few days Ripley had enjoyed wallowing in praise after returning from his successful investigation in the Dales. This morning he was catching up on his paperwork. He liked being in the office alone as it meant he could clear his desk, file reports and sort out e-mails on his personal laptop.

Chief Inspector Martin and the Sergeant were in court at a preliminary hearing of the case against Fray and Ronson, and weren't expected back before lunch.

He opened an e-mail from P.C. Dunstan, which, after starting with the usual pleasantries, went on to describe how, when Fray and Ronson were apprehended at the farm cottage, he had noticed a deep impression of a tyre, which had a slash across the tread, in the mud at the side of the barn at Faw Head. At the time, he thought nothing of it, but recently, while on routine patrol, he came across another impression with the same feature, at the rear of the antique shop in Hawes.

Ripley rang the phone number that Dunstan had left, but when there was no answer he left a message. He reflected on the possible significance of the tyre impressions, if they were able to establish that the owner of the antique shop owned a vehicle that had a tyre that matched those impressions, then it was just possible...., his thought process came to a sudden halt.

'Oh God,' he thought, if Dunstan had not made a resin-cast, and photographed the tyre impressions, then there was no evidence. The phone rang, it was Dunstan returning Ripley's call.

'Hi there, thank you for the e-mail, with regard to the tyre impressions, did you make a cast and take photographs?' asked Ripley. There was a long silence.

'Well, I did take a photograph at the rear of the antique shop. Unfortunately the tyre impression at the farmhouse was no longer there,' said Dunstan.

'No cast?'

'No, I didn't think about that, sorry. But the photograph has come out really well, I'll send it to you as an attachment,' he said apologetically, realising his gaffe.

'Thanks. But you realise that as evidence it won't really be very good. Does the photograph have Meta data attached giving date, time etc.'

'Meta what?' asked Dunstan.

'Meta data, that is, information that is recorded by the camera, for each photograph you take.'

'No definitely not, it's just a cheap disposable I carry around in the car,' said Dunstan meekly.

'Never mind Dunstan, my Detective Chief Inspector is not over impressed with our theories of Mr X anyway.'

'Look, I'm sorry I let you down. I came across the tyre impression at the rear of the antique shop whilst I was on a routine patrol. Then, I remembered seeing the tyre impression on the roadside outside the farmhouse. Well, I thought, if we could identify the owner of the car, we might know the identity of the person who sent the letter to Sgt Berry, and possibly more.'

'Thanks, Dunstan, it may prove useful in the future. Look, I have to go. Thank you once again for everything you've done. I'll be in touch. Bye.' Ripley replaced the receiver. He laid back in his chair, and rubbed his eyes.

'Basics, that's all he had to do, routine recording of all the evidence.'

He let out a loud sigh, supporting his head on his arms.

Snapshot 123

The first class train compartment was only half full. George laid back in the sumptuous seat and sipped her coffee, while watching the countryside flash by as the train sped along the track at speeds in excess of 160 mph.

'Last night you showed me a photograph, who was it?' she asked putting the coffee down.

Nick smiled, 'Luzhkov. While you were asleep yesterday, I posed as a safety inspector and visited East West Transportation to see if I could establish whether Luzhkov had an interest in the company.'

'And does he?' she asked.

'Oh yes.'

'Right, so what now, as if I didn't know,' she took another sip of coffee while waiting for Nick to continue.

'This morning I posted a letter to the Office of Immigration at Scotland Yard.

It outlines an illegal operation, to bring Asylum Seekers into the country, posing as relief drivers, for guess who?' George shook her head.

'Has anyone ever said, you've got a beautiful mind.'

Nick smiled, and leaning toward her, whispered. 'It's not something I would ever 'crow' about.' They both laughed.

Snapshot 124

'From what I understand, the letter was anonymous. A forensic examination has failed to reveal any clues as to who sent it to the Yard.' The softly spoken voice continued, 'Henry has spoken to the commissioner, who is of the opinion that it is perhaps some ex-employee who bears a grudge and is being mischievous. If I hear anything else, I will ring you straight away, Viktor.'

'Thank you Yekaterina, please remember me to Henry.'

Luzhkov replaced the receiver, turned and looked out of the window overlooking his gardens.

Viktor Luzhkov was over six foot tall with a slight stoop. He was 42 years of age, with well chiselled, handsome features and piercing, steel blue eyes. Clean-shaven, he had blond hair that was thinning slightly and was swept back.

His family originated from St Petersburg, where his father and his grandfather had worked in the family business dealing in rare gemstones. A strict monarchist, his grandfather had fought against the Red Army, but after defeat, fled with his family to the Ukraine, only returning to his beloved St Petersburg after Stalin's death in 1953.

A knock at the door made him turn from the window. Reginald Blandford entered the room.

'You wanted to see me.'

As a personal assistant, Blandford had been with Luzhkov since he first came to live in England seven years ago.

Fiercely loyal, it was his job to ensure the smooth running of day-to-day business and social affairs.

'Yes, I have just been talking with Yekaterina; there is no information about who contacted Scotland Yard. Henry seems to think it may be the work of some disillusioned employee. I disagree. Send Lorenzo to Croydon, he is to investigate and report back to you within forty-eight hours,' said Luzhkov, coldly.

'I'll attend to it straight away,' Blandford turned to leave, as Luzhkov continued.

'When you brief Lorenzo, it is important he is realises the urgency. Someone out there is intent on causing trouble. I want a speedy conclusion to the whole business.'

'I will see to it,' said Blandford, who was in no doubt as to what inference to draw from 'speedy conclusion'.

Snapshot 125

Although George had enjoyed her sojourn to New York, she was pleased to be back at the house in Hawes. Having roamed around the garden and along the riverbank, she had returned to the large 'L' shaped lounge and deposited herself on the settee opposite the French windows, from where she could watch the birds foraging for food. The sun was shining sporadically between large fluffy white and grey clouds; the forecast was not good, with rain promised later in the afternoon, but who cared! Nick was doing a 'man thing', flitting in and out of the room carrying one of his gadgets, making some adjustment or other, and then disappearing again. It was, she felt, an idyllic arrangement; she was happy with her lot. A blackbird preened itself on the stone sun dial, lifting its wing in sharp jerky movements. It poked and pecked its feathers with its yellow bill, flapped its wings to restore the displaced feathers, and repeated the process.

George's thoughts drifted along easily, lightly touching past events and experiences without stopping too long to concentrate on any one for too long. A soft breeze lightly brushed by her, gently lifting pages of an open magazine. The blackbird let out a few stray mellow fluty song notes and flew off. Suddenly, she had no idea why, but her thoughts turned to her girlfriend who had tragically taken her own life.

Whatever possessed her that fateful day would never be known, but, she guessed, whatever it was, must have been unbearable. If only she could have shared her.... George pulled herself upright as Nick entered the room. She had no intention of revisiting this past traumatic period, it had caused her enough pain in the past, it was best left there.

'Nick, what are you doing?'

'Just running through these printouts,' he sat down beside her and unrolled sheets of continuous printout paper. 'Lots of information about East West Transportation Co,' he smiled in her direction, 'How about a coffee?'

'Yes please. What are you going to do with all this?' George looked at the printout.

'There is a lot of information about running schedules; destinations, times of departure and estimated times of arrival, all that sort of thing. I'll go make the coffee.'

George suspected he was evading her question so she left the comfort of the settee and followed him into the kitchen.

'You haven't answered my question.'

'I'm not sure; it has to be something that will upset him, Luzhkov. Stealing a truck, robbing his headquarters or even destroying part of the premises will not really hurt him personally. So, I'm undecided.'

He poured out the coffee, black and steaming, into two blue mugs.

'If you really want to annoy him, set fire to one of his trucks outside Grice Hall.' Nick passed her a mug of coffee, shook his head slightly and smiled.

'Outside the entrance, I like it. George, you have a beautiful mind.'

'Now that sounds familiar,' she said, making her way back to the lounge.

Snapshot 126

'Jack, where are you?' Martin's voice crackled over the phone in a hurried, snappy manner. Surrounded by rusting car wrecks, piled ten high in precarious rows, Jack hurried to the end of the row, where he hoped the phone reception would be clearer.

'Jack, can you hear me?'

'Yes,' he replied, breathlessly.

'Where are you?' Martin repeated impatiently.

'Moxey Bridge Scrap Yard, I've come to talk to Bertrand the owner. He knows a lot of people. I use him quite a lot for information.'

'Oh, right, well. Has he told you anything?' he asked expectantly.

'Not really, according to Bertrand, no one on the street knows anything about the jobs at Luigi's, the golf club or the robbery at Computer International. The word is, that everybody is nervous because of the pressure we're exerting, he says that if anyone knew anything, they would gladly give us information.'

'Almost makes you feel sorry for them,' snarled Martin sarcastically. 'How long are you going to be, I need to see you. Something's come up.'

'What?' asked Jack curiously?

'I've had a meeting with the new Deputy Chief Constable,' muttered Martin in a cowed way.

'What's she like?'

'She's on a crusade; look, I don't want to discuss this on the phone. Meet me in the Wellington in half an hour. Oh, and Jack, find Ripley and tell him to meet us there.'

Jack pocketed the mobile. The crane, which picked up the scrapped cars whirred and swung its long neck round and deposited what was left of a Discovery into the crushing machine.

Jack watched the large iron machine spring into action; pneumatics pushed the sides into the metal that folded accordion-like into a creaking, groaning rectangle of spent metal. Then, each end moved forward crushing and crunching the wreck until it was reduced to a two foot square cube, which the machine then spewed out, as if out of the depths of its bowels. It was rumoured that a number of villains who had 'crossed the boundary' had ended their days in this machine.

Snapshot 127

Jack pushed the bar-door open and walked inside. Glancing around, he spotted Martin sitting alone in the corner. He looked around the room, giving his eyes time to adjust to the dim light.

He recognised a few familiar faces and nodded greetings from a couple of regulars.

'Is it your usual Sarge?' Jack looked over to the direction of the voice to see Ripley ordering drinks at the bar, so he walked over to join him.

'Been here long?'

'Just arrived, I think he's been here a while,' Ripley nodded in the direction of the Chief Inspector. 'Seems to be a bit tense, do you know why he wants to see us?'

'No, but we'll soon find out,' Jack grabbed two beers, and together with Ripley, walked over to join Martin.

'Have you met the new Deputy Chief Constable Jack?' asked Martin, taking a long drink.

'No.' answered Jack, leaning back in his seat.

'A formidable woman, like I said to you earlier, she's on a crusade. Ripley's met and talked with her, haven't you lad?' said Martin, with a wry smile. Jack, surprised, looked over towards Ripley and growled.

'You've met with the Deputy Chief Constable and you never thought to mention it!'

'It wasn't really a meeting, I was working in the office and slipped out for a tea, when I returned she was there.'

'There?' snapped Jack.

'There in the office. She must have just wandered in, and...' Ripley hesitated, suddenly he realised the purpose of the meeting and before he could continue with his explanation, Martin interrupted.

'You see Jack, Ripley here was working on his laptop, and when he left the office, he left his work open, the Deputy wondered in and started reading his notes and e-mails, most intrigued she was. Isn't that so Ripley?'

'Yes, she was there when I returned. She started asking all these questions about the case.'

'Questions based on what she'd read on your laptop, because you didn't close it down before you left the office,' growled Martin angrily, downing the last remnants of bitter from his glass.

'From what I gather Jack, they had a long chat on Ripley's theory about Mr X, you do remember the drift of Ripley's theory?'

'Of course, we dismissed it because there was no substantive evidence to support such a theory.' Jack gathered in the empty glasses ready for another refill.

'Wait Jack. I want you to hear the rest; our esteemed 'new girl', after considering Ripley's ideas, thinks they are worth closer investigation, and after consulting the Deputy Chief Constables in the other districts where robberies have taken place, she has persuaded them to agree to part fund a further investigation.'

'Investigation into what?' asked Jack, puzzled.

'That Mr X committed the robberies and the kidnapping on our patch and elsewhere, leaving no evidence, and is the same person that robbed Ronson and Fray of their cash, and then appeared to them in the antique shop relating to them a story about how a stash of cash had been found by an old Russian man. Then we have this photo of a tyre with a slash across its tread, as seen at the farmhouse and the rear of the antique shop by P.C. Dunstan. The Deputy Chief Constable has reflected on her conversations with Ripley, looked at the case files and seems to think we should re-examine the case with a very special reference to the owner of the antique shop. And guess what, we three are relieved of all duties to conduct the investigation, starting with a visit to Settle.'

Martin reached over and collected the glasses.

'My round I believe.' He ambled off to the bar leaving Jack and Ripley.

'Bloody hell Ripley, you really have dropped a bollock, leaving your laptop on for anyone to see. I was going to a railway convention tomorrow evening, now I'm going to be stuck up there in the bloody wilderness. Bloody hell Ripley.'

'Sorry Sarge, but the DCC was so persistent with her questions.' Jack looked at Ripley and couldn't help but feel sorry for him; faced with a new Deputy Chief Constable who could easily pull rank, he didn't stand much of a chance.

'As long as you weren't trying to impress her with your Mr X theories.' Jack's broadside was fired with some finger wagging.

'No, it wasn't like that, Sarge. I just simply answered her questions. I should have closed my laptop lid, then none of this would have happened.'

'Too late now, just learn from your mistakes.'

'Sorry about you having to miss your convention,' said Ripley, meekly.

'There'll be others,' said Jack, looking round to see where Martin was with the refreshments. 'Some of them can be really boring, it's just the trains I like.'

Martin returned from the bar and placed the drinks on the table.

'I have more news, Jack; good and bad,' He sat back down, flashed a mischievous smile and asked, 'which would you like first?' Jack grimaced, looked across at Martin without being able to discern any clue as to what the 'news' could be.

'The good, I'll have the good news first,' Jack said nonchalantly.

'Well I've booked us in to the Golden Lion instead of us staying at the station, as before.'

'Oh that's a definite improvement, and the bad news?'

'You're sharing a room with Ripley,' Martin let out a peal of laughter, while Jack and Ripley looked at each other, before joining in with the laughter.

Snapshot 128

Luzhkov had left, with the guests, for a tour of the estate. There never seemed to be enough time in the day for Blandford to complete his work as a personal assistant.

Having checked with the chef that everything was on schedule for this evening's dinner in the great hall, he took tea in the library, his favourite room. He enjoyed these moments, surrounded by the books he so much loved to read. He had persuaded Mr Luzhkov to let him care for the library, amongst his many other duties, so that he could spend more time amongst his beloved authors.

He reflected on the day, which, despite Lorenzo's disappointing report from his investigation at East West Transport in Croydon, had gone well. He disliked dealing with Lorenzo, a Sicilian with a Mafiosi background; his demeanour made Blandford shudder. But he could take orders and he carried out his duties to the letter and without question.

However, he had not been able to bring his latest investigation to a satisfactory conclusion, the identity of who had sent the letter to Scotland Yard was still a mystery; perhaps it was a disgruntled former employee trying to cause mischief, but Blandford doubted it.

Lorenzo had established that Mr Broom was not a legitimate member of the Health and Safety Inspectorate. Blandford was sure they had not heard the last of Mr Broom, or whoever it was that was impersonating him.

Snapshot 129

'Do you remember the routine, it's imperative that you keep to the time. If you think for one moment it can't be done, you walk away, there'll be another day,' Nick spoke without looking at her, keeping his eyes fixed on the motorway ahead.

'Nick, don't worry. I've memorised each detail of the plan, I don't intend to take any chances, it will work,' George pulled down the sun visor and checked her disguise in the mirror.

'I have difficulty recognising myself. I love the way you're able to age me, though I'm not very happy about the teeth.'

'Well let's put it this way, when you bump into him and spill his lunch over him, one look at you and his heart will not be full of forgiveness,' Nick laughed at the truck driver's imminent fate.

'And you are absolutely sure he keeps to the same routine each day.'

'Definitely. Roast beef and Yorkshire pudding with lashings of gravy, treacle pudding and custard and one large mug of tea. Same meal, same time, same place, he parks the truck in the same spot, he never deviates from his routine.'

'Then there shouldn't be a problem.' She pushed the visor back. 'How long before we get there?'

'Fifteen minutes.'

Snapshot 130

Martin sat in the back of the car with Jack. They had passed the time going over specific details of the case, but now, with only a few miles to go, Jack was looking out of the window, looking at nothing in particular. Martin watched him, waiting for him to join in conversation again, but it was as if he was lost in some nook of a personal memory.

'Jack,' he called his name to bring him back on board. 'Jack, are you alright?' Slowly, the subdued Jack moved his gaze from the window and brought his frame round until he was facing Martin.

'Yes, I'm fine,' he said with a faint smile that reassured the Chief Inspector that his Sergeant was OK.

'You were miles away.'

'No, I was just thinking about Samantha; she's been home from university for a few days. When I left, she gave me a big hug, nothing unusual in that, except that this time it was a long one, then she thanked me 'for everything', and gave me a big kiss.'

'You should be so lucky, mine always want money.'

'H'mm, I just hope everything's OK.'

'Jack, if there was anything wrong Jenny would pick up on it straight away.'

'Yes, you're right.' Jack leaned forward until he was almost touching Ripley, 'How long before we arrive, I'm bursting for a pee.'

'About twenty minutes,' Ripley replied, not interested in the reason for the Sergeant's distress.

Snapshot 131

With seating for around fifty people, the Blue Lagoon was a driver's haven. Steam rose from an array of hot dishes at the counter, and lines of drivers queued along a gangway waiting to be served.

George had already spotted the driver she was to meet in a calamitous collision that would hopefully divert attention away from the windows for enough time so Nick could escape with the lorry unheeded.

She watched the driver's progress; he laughed and joked with the other drivers immediately around him. Once he had collected his meal he moved towards his favourite seat by the window, his tray, piled high with food, held out in front of him as he negotiated his way between the tables. George waited and watched his careful progress, then just as he was about to pass her she jumped up, her hand catching the underside of the tray which then spewed a mixture of food and liquid all down the shocked driver's front.

The tray and its contents crashed to the floor, leaving the forlorn driver drenched in gravy and custard, with remnants of potato, vegetables and treacle pudding running slowly down his uniform. George made an instant apology, muttered something about getting a towel to clean his uniform and left.

No one noticed her leaving by the back door; everyone's attention was on the plight of the driver. Small ripples of laughter began to roll around the room as cafeteria staff began to fuss over the driver and clean up the mess.

Snapshot 132

The Iveco Stralis handled well and the noise from its 12.88 litre direct-injection diesel engine was hardy noticeable. With it's 16-speed gearbox in semi-automatic mode, the mammoth 50 ton truck, fully loaded, purred it's way along the road.

Nick was highly satisfied that the hi-jacking of the truck had gone to plan. He was just anxious now for George to ring in and let him know that her exit from the café had gone as arranged. As he continued down the road his thoughts turned briefly to his parents. He was not sure what type of truck ploughed into them, but he knew it belonged to East West Transportation Company, just as this truck did. It was that crash that not only took away his parents, but also changed his whole way of life.

He barely noticed the large chestnut trees standing tall in the twilight on either side of the road as his mood, sombre with thoughts from the past, changed abruptly as he brought himself back to the present. He pulled into a long lay-by, shielded from the road behind the chestnut trees, just as his mobile rang. It was George.

'Hello, did everything go to plan?'

'Yes. Is everything all right with you and the truck?' she asked.

'So far so good, I've pulled into the lay-by. I'm going to prepare the truck, I'll pick you up on Hawes road as planned.'

'Fine. Nick, you should have seen the driver's face as the tray tipped over him, it was a sight to behold,' she laughed, still high from the adrenaline of the moment.

'See you soon,' replied Nick, anxious to start work on preparing the lorry for its Grice Hall debut.

Snapshot 133

'Detective Chief Inspector Martin, your table is ready.' Martin looked round to see the tall thin figure of the manager, Nigel, dressed as always, in his dark blue pinstripe suit. Martin waved his hand, beckoning him to come closer.

'Just call us by our surnames if you don't mind,' he whispered, leaning towards the manager.

'We don't want to frighten the customers.' The manager looked at all three detectives and nodded knowingly.

'Of course, absolutely,' he smiled, turning to make his way back to the dining room.

'Nice chap,' said Martin, taking a drink.

'H'mm, they're not very busy,' observed Jack, leaning back in his chair.

'End of season I expect,' said Martin.

Suddenly, a muffled ring tone could be heard from inside the Chief Inspectors coat pocket. He fumbled around and finally dragged out the blue mobile phone.

'Hello, hello,' he waited expectantly. 'Hello, funny, there's no one there.'

'Excuse me Sir, I think you have a text message,' Ripley leaned forward and turned the phone so the Inspector could see the screen.

'Oh, I can't get used to these damn mobile gizmo's. Let me see,' he grabbed the phone and read the message; 'U won'. He grimaced, then turned to Jack and smiled. 'It says 'U won', sounds like a Chinese takeaway. 'U won', what the hell does that mean?'

'Perhaps you've won the lottery,' Jack said, jokingly.

'I wish,' retorted Martin, still examining the phone message.

'If you let me have a look I can tell you who sent the message, then you can ring them back,' said Ripley, reaching out and taking the phone off his Chief Inspector. Martin watched as Ripley quickly flicked a few keys.

'There you are,' said the young constable, returning the ringing phone to Martin who moved off to make the call.

'It's really quite easy once you get the hang of it,' said Ripley.

'To you maybe, but to our generation they are still gadgets,' Jack said, disdainfully.

'We have to move with the times, Sarge, just like this place has. It was a coaching inn in the seventeenth century in a world far removed from the one we know, yet here it is, still accommodating and serving people just like it has always done.'

Jack stared at Ripley over the pint glass he held, his eyes scanning the young man's face.

'You come out with some stuff at times lad, I make a comment about the mobile, and you give me philosophy.'

'It just interests me how there are so many examples of the old living with the modern,' smiled Ripley.

'Like me and you?' retorted Jack.

'Oh no, Sarge, now you are misinterpreting my meaning.'

'I'm only having a joke, lad,' said Jack, as the Chief Inspector returned.

'Ripley, go and get three pints,' he handed the young constable a twenty pound note.

'The tables ready,' said Jack.

'It will wait, off you go and get the drinks,' he waved Ripley off in the direction of the bar.

'Something wrong?' asked Jack.

'No, not at all. You remember that Sally entered my painting in an exhibition at Hull. Well someone from a gallery in London has bought it for five hundred pounds'

'Five hundred pounds,' gasped Jack.

'Yes, incredible isn't it, and for a load of old bottles,' laughed Martin.

Ripley returned with the drinks, they each took one.

'Well I never, do you think you could give me a few lessons,' cried Jack.

'C'mon, let's eat, fillet steaks all round,' Martin led the way to the dining room.

'I rather fancied the Dover Sole,' said Ripley, unaware of the reason for the celebration.

'Forget Dover, Ripley, tonight your 'sole' belongs to me, you're having fillet,' Jack and Martin disappeared into the dining room followed by a somewhat confused Ripley.

Snapshot 134

It was a dark night; heavy cloud obscured the moon, as if to order. Nick slowed the Iveco Stralis down to around twenty miles per hour, the engine was almost silent at this speed. A cool breeze swept over him through the open window. Outside, the cat's eyes created a line of bright lights, picking out the road ahead. Autumn leaves danced across the tarmac. Suddenly, Nick picked out a figure at the side of the road, a raised arm waved in his direction, it was George. Her hair blew in every direction as she clambered aboard.

'Thank goodness you're on time, I'm freezing, oh my god they don't make it easy to climb into one of these trucks,' she said, rubbing her hands together energetically.

Nick smiled as he gently pulled the truck out onto the dark road.

'You'll soon get warm. Is the car parked OK?' he asked.

'No problems, it's in the disused drive, just as we planned.'

'Good. I was worried in case some courting couples parked there.'

'It must be too cold for them tonight,' she giggled, 'I just want to be home in front of a nice warm fire.'

'Well, we'll soon have one of those, but I don't recommend you stay around to warm yourself. Here's the gate,' Nick swung into the drive, as, on either side the lime trees danced with the breeze. They both watched intently for the lights from Grice Hall to appear through the trees. Everything Nick had said about wanting to hurt Luzhkov was about to happen. Here they were, driving one of his company's lorries into the grounds of his home. George was full of apprehension; would someone see them at the last moment, would they be caught, if so, what could they possibly say. Such thoughts made her uneasy.

'There's the Hall,' said Nick in a matter-of-fact voice. He pulled the truck off the drive onto the grass lawn in front of the steps leading to the oak door that they had so recently entered to view the furniture in the library, although it seemed an age away.

Nick pulled some fuse cabling from the rear of the cabin and fastened it around the steering wheel.

'Lets go. When I light this, we'll have five minutes before the whole lorry bursts into flames. Pity we won't be around to see it.'

'I've had enough excitement for one night. Let's get out of here,' whispered George. A moment later two figures, moving silently, quickly disappeared into the dark depths of the night.

Snapshot 135

With all the guests happily chattering, the dinner had been a success. Mr Luzhkov had nodded his approval to Blandford. Having supervised the whole proceedings, he could now withdraw to relax.

He went into the library, secure in the knowledge that he would not be required for the rest of the evening. He poured himself a large brandy and sank into a comfortable leather chair, then picked up his favourite book, the 'Seven Pillars of Wisdom'.

He was reading it for the third time; the life of 'Lawrence' fascinated him, he was the last great adventurer. Savouring the brandy, he flicked the pages, studying the maps of Akaba and the Sinai Desert.

His thoughts were suddenly disrupted by a loud commotion outside in the hallway. Opening the door, he found guests rushing back and forth, but others were staring out of the windows. He rushed towards the open door where he saw Mr Luzhkov staring wide-eyed at a blazing inferno on the front lawn. He rushed to his side. Luzhkov turned, and in a calm voice, out of earshot of the guests, said, 'Blandford, someone is out to make a fool out of me. I want to know who is responsible, get me some names.' He turned and ushered his guests in the direction of the great Hall.

Blandford walked down the steps towards the fire. He could easily make out the shape of the lorry, with the emblem of the East West Transportation Company on its side through the flames. The heat from the burning cargo was so intense he had to move away. The sound of alarms from emergency vehicles penetrated the night air, adding to the chaotic scene.

Someone had gone to a lot of trouble to make a statement; now he would have to find out who was responsible.

Snapshot 136

Having enjoyed a hearty breakfast, Martin was rather surprised to find himself bundled into a car with Sgt Berry, while Jack and Ripley were following on behind with Constable Dunstan in another squad car.

Being unable to finish reading his regular morning paper was not the best way to start the day, never mind that he liked to enjoy at least three cups of tea before starting out for the office. So, today, he felt a little aggrieved.

Eventually, the car turned into the long avenue leading to Grice Hall. It was a grey day with a stiff breeze. Martin caught his first glimpse of the smouldering wreckage, as firemen were busy clearing away flat lifeless hoses. The smoke drifted over the impressive Hall, and deep ruts, made by the fire appliances, crisscrossed the immaculate lawns.

Martin pulled up his coat collar against the cold morning breeze and looked over the sodden scene. Blackened molten rubber and plastic formed irregular mounds on the remnants of the lorry's carcass. Jack and Ripley joined him to survey the scene.

'Not much left to salvage, why are we here exactly?' asked Ripley, to no one in particular.

'We're here because the lorry was apparently stolen from the Blue Lagoon services, and as luck would have it, that's on our patch, so Sgt Berry thought we would be interested,' growled Martin.

'Well, she would, wouldn't she?' said Jack, sarcastically.

'I briefed her as to why we are here, Jack, so let's just make a few enquiries to keep her happy. Jack, have a word with the fire officer, see if he can throw any light on the cause of the fire, Ripley, find out where the driver is, we need to speak with him.'

Martin walked around to the remains of the burnt out lorry, frequently bending down to inspect pieces of debris. Finding a suitable stick, he poked some smoking remains; eventually he pulled out a blackened square metal plate.

'Anything interesting, sir?' asked Sgt Berry.

'The lorry's number plate, it's about the only thing that's still recognisable. Bloody hell, look at my shoes,' Martin said, holding a foot aloft so the Sgt could see. He walked back to the driveway and wiped his shoes with a polythene forensic bag.

'You've obviously done that before,' she said, watching him expertly clean his shoes.

'Goes with the job Sgt, we get used to cleaning everyone's shit.'

'Let's go and interview the owner of the house to see if they can tell us why anyone would want to dump a burning lorry on their front lawn.' Martin walked off towards the Hall.

Sgt Berry resented his coarse remark, but refrained from saying so. Instead, she followed him up the marble staircase. Martin looked over the Hall, turned and surveyed the grounds.

'This is something special, who lives here?'

'The present owner is a Mr Luzhkov, previously the Hall was occupied by Lord Saville, but he ran into financial difficulties and had to leave.'

'What do you know about Mr Luzhkov?'

'He's an influential financier or banker, he doesn't mix much with the local community.' Coming to the large oak doors, they did not have to knock. Blandford, who had been watching the proceedings, opened the door.

'Good morning, this is Chief Inspector Martin and I'm Sgt Berry, could we speak with Mr Luzhkov please?' asked Sgt Berry.

'I'm afraid Mt Luzhkov is unable to speak with you at this moment,' said Blandford, avoiding eye contact with either visitor.

'Is he ill?' asked Sgt Berry.

'No, just indisposed,' replied Blandford.

'What do you mean *'indisposed'*, we need to speak to him,' said Berry crossly.

'I'm sorry, that's not possible.'

'Who are you exactly?' asked Martin, harshly, pushing his way past the surprised personal assistant. 'Very nice, very spacious,' Martin sniffed the air.

'There's a smell of Eau de Cologne, what do you think Sgt Berry?'

'Definitely Eau de Cologne,' she said, amused at the way Martin was dealing with Blandford.

'I am Reginald Blandford, Mr Luzhkov's personal assistant. You cannot just march into the Hall. Mr Luzhkov will not allow such an invasion.' Blandford protested.

'Mr Blandford, I'm not leaving until I have spoken with Mr Luzhkov. If he does not want to speak with me here, then I will speak to him at the station. Do you understand? Now, please tell him. We will wait outside,' Martin turned on his heels and walked outside, followed by Sgt Berry. A flustered, red-faced Blandford was left to digest Martin's ultimatum.

Once outside, Martin took a deep breath of fresh air, then turned to Sgt Berry with a wide grin, 'It was him who was wearing the Eau de Cologne.'

'I know.'

'I get the impression that they don't want us here dealing with this incident. They're hiding something; most owners would be upset if a great, big, fifty-ton lorry had been driven onto their front lawn and set afire. They would be demanding answers before the flames had died down. But not here, they don't even want to talk to us.' Sgt Berry nodded, but before she could respond, a tall wiry figure, dressed in an immaculate grey suit stepped out to meet them.

'Inspector, you wanted to see me, I am Mr Luzhkov.' Martin turned to greet the Russian owner; immaculately dressed, he betrayed no anger at the Chief Inspector's insistence on the interview. His cold stare was penetrating and having introduced himself he waited for Martin to start.

'Detective Chief Inspector,' Martin corrected him, 'What can you tell me about the fire?'

'Not a great deal, I was enjoying after-dinner drinks with some guests, when our attention was drawn to the burning lorry on the lawn. There was nothing to be done except call the fire service.'

'Can you think of why anyone would steal a fifty-ton lorry and drive it into your grounds, and set it on fire right in front of the Hall. The incident was obviously carried out by someone who bears a grievance against you.' said Martin looking straight at Luzhkov.

'I have a large number of business interests, one of which is the East West Transportation Company. The lorry is from our fleet. Perhaps someone who once worked for the company was responsible. Please speak with Mr Blandford should you require further information; as my personal assistant he is familiar with every aspect of my business interests,' said Luzhkov, with a tight-lipped smile. 'You must excuse me, but I have guests waiting.'

He turned and walked towards the large oak doors with the twisted wrought iron hinges.

'I haven't finished, yet sir,' snapped Martin. His cutting words halted Luzhkov in his tracks; not used to being reined in, he turned to face the Chief Inspector.

'If any of the staff or guests remember seeing anyone in the grounds at the time of the fire, please don't hesitate to leave a message for me or Sgt Berry at the station. Thank you for your assistance, sir.' Martin delivered the comments with consummate ease, knowing that he had irritated the owner.

Luzhkov nodded acknowledgement and left to join his guests, betraying no reaction.

'You managed to get under his skin,' Sgt Berry said with a smile.

'Good. I'd like you to talk with his personal assistant, Mr Blandford, about the transportation company, and we will need a list of the names and addresses of the guests who were here last night. I don't have the stomach for it,' said Martin.

'Sir,' Ripley joined him, panting heavily from walking up the steps. 'I managed to contact the driver, not very helpful I'm afraid. Having parked his vehicle in the normal way, he made his way to café and selected a meal, then before he reached his table, a woman bumped into him and knocked his meal tray all down the front of his uniform.'

'Don't tell me, he can't identify the woman.'

'Afraid not, by the time he had cleaned himself, she had disappeared and so had the lorry.'

'Why am I not surprised?' sighed Martin, disconsolately. 'Come on, Ripley, let's go and find Jack. What the hell are we doing here, dealing with these Hooray Henry's, this was not in our brief.'

'Well, like you said sir, the lorry was hi-jacked from our patch,' said Ripley, cheekily. Martin ignored the boldness of Ripley's remark it did no harm to let him think he had got one over on the old man.

He saw Jack poking around the smouldering wreckage with the fire officer, so he called out to the sergeant, not wanting to get his shoes dirty once again. Jack looked over towards Martin and Ripley when he heard the familiar voice calling his name. He scribbled some notes, thanked the fire officer and joined his colleagues.

'Well, Jack, what have you to tell me?' asked Martin, impatiently. Jack sensed from his tone that the Chief Inspector was ruffled.

Usually, in modern terminology, he was 'cool' or 'laid back'; he could confront most situations with a carefree attitude and make the most complex assumptions look easy. But today Jack detected that he was flustered, someone or something had got under his skin.

'The fire was started deliberately. A number of homemade incendiary devices had been planted in amongst the freight, according to Mr Lane, the fire officer. The accelerant used was a hydrocarbon-based fuel, which was ignited by a fuse from the cab. He'll be able to tell us more after a more detailed analysis.'

Martin stared at the wreckage, digesting the information. Both his hands were sunk deep into his jacket pockets.

'What was the lorry carrying?' he asked.

'Laptop computers, about five hundred, worth at least a quarter of a million,' said Jack.

'A quarter of a million, and he didn't raise an eyebrow,' said Martin, pointing a raised arm towards the Hall.

'Dunstan,' he shouted towards the constable stood by the patrol car.

'Stay here and wait for Sgt Berry, tell her we've returned to the hotel for lunch. Come on, Jack, let's get out of here, it stinks. Oh, and by the way,' he glanced down in Jack's direction, 'your shoes are dirty.'

Snapshot 137

Once Sgt Berry had left with Dunstan, Luzhkov wasted no time in summoning Blandford to his study.

Seated behind an exquisite nineteenth century Napoleon 11 bureau mazarin he tapped a pen rapidly on the boullework desktop, reflecting on his family's gemstone business.

After the break-up of Russia, Viktor Luzhkov had been well placed to benefit from the wealth that ensued. He was now a partner in Group Ivor, the company behind Yukoil, the second largest oil company in Russia. He owned various offshore companies, whose sole purpose was to dispose of several billion dollars of Yukoil's profits. Since moving to the UK, his power and developing influence in the business world had been rapid; he could not afford to let incidents like the fire last night detract him from his business activities. The sound of Blandford entering the room interrupted his thoughts, looking up he signalled to Blandford to sit down in a chair opposite.

'I will be leaving for London first thing in the morning, please make the necessary arrangements. Assign Lorenzo to investigate the hi-jacking of the lorry and the fire, find out what you can.'
He pushed back the chair and walked over to the window. Without turning to face Blandford he continued,

'When I bought Grice Hall I thought it would be a country retreat, without any need for security, cameras, electric gates and the like. I was wrong; someone has penetrated not only the peace and tranquillity of my home, but also my personal life. Ensure that security measures are implemented to bring it up to our usual standard before I return.'

Having delivered his instructions, Luzhkov turned and left the room, leaving Blandford still scribbling notes furiously; he would have a busy night ahead, making arrangements for Luzhkov's departure in the morning.

Snapshot 138

Jack sat by the fire in a large Windsor chair, enjoying a beer. His frame easily fitted the ash-shaped plank seat. The flames from the fire spiralled upwards in a hypnotising dance as Jack's thoughts returned to those last few moments he spent with his daughter, Samantha.

She had said goodbye so many times before, but there was something different about that last big hug, the way she had squeezed him before planting one last kiss on his forehead, just as she had done a thousand times before. Gazing into the flickering flames, he could see the glint in her eyes and hear her special giggle. He was immensely proud of her. If anything was troubling her he was sure that she would confide in him or his wife, so why was he worrying?

The familiar call from Martin brought him back to the present, he sat upright and pushed the chair backwards, aware that the warmth from the fire had made him feel drowsy.

'Jack. I've just had a very interesting talk with the manager. Are you all right'

'Yes I'm fine, just a little tired,' said Jack, finishing his drink.

'It's all this fresh air, we're used to the smell of the streets. Your glass is empty, lets have a refill, then I've something very interesting to tell you.'

He leaned over, grabbed Jack's glass and hurried to the bar. Jack smiled to himself, he could tell from Martin's manner that he had uncovered something of interest.

Looking around the room he noticed a couple in hiking boots and anoraks, who were studying an ordnance survey map. At another table, an elderly couple, each with a half glass of stout, talked quietly, while at the bar sat a burly farm labourer, attempting to engage the barman in conversation. It was a scene similar to one that he would expect to find in this sleepy rural community.

'Here you are, Jack,' Martin passed the sergeant a full pint with its cream collar just rolling over the side of the glass.

'Have you seen Ripley?'

'He's writing up a report of the fire at Grice Hall in the room,' answered Jack, wiping the glass clean of the spilt cream with his index finger and then wiping it clean with his lips. 'You said you had something interesting to tell me.'

'I was asking the manager, Nigel, about what he could remember when Ronson, Fray and Lumpy stayed in the hotel,' said Martin.

'Did he remember them?' asked Jack interested.

'Oh yes, he said they were different from the usual guests they are used to; he recalled they had a meal in the restaurant washed down with a large quantity of a potent beer called La Fin Du Monde.'

'Never heard of it,' said Jack, who was always interested in a new brew.

'Nor me, but this particular beer is 9% proof, and the reason he remembers them is that it was the first time anyone drank them dry of this particular brew. Most people normally just drink two bottles.'

'Most people aren't like Ronson and co,' interrupted Jack.

'That's right, he remembers them being rather loud. I asked to look at the guest book for that night, and guess who was dining and staying on the same night?' Martin waited for Jack to respond.

'Tell me.'

'Our friend the antique dealer, Mr Nick Hartford and his fiance.'

'Interesting, but why would he stay here when he lives locally?'

'The manager said it was not unusual for locals to stay here when they dine, they are very worried about drinking and driving, especially on unlit fell roads.'

'Very sensible.'

'He could have taken the money Jack, he had the opportunity,' said Martin.

'But why would he take money from three people who were complete strangers.'

'That's what we have to find out.'

'Did you ask the manager for his opinion of the antique dealer?' asked Jack.

'They seem to be close friends,' snorted Martin.

'He tells me that Mr Hartford is, as he says, very well off. He travels a lot, but when he is at home he supports many needy local charities.'

'Not the type who would steal money then.'

'Perhaps he had a motive,' said Martin.

'We're going to have to do an awful lot of digging to uncover one,' growled Jack.

'We are Jack, an awful lot, and starting tomorrow, we're going to call on Mr Hartford.'

As Jack shuffled in the Windsor chair, a log on the fire, half-burnt, dropped slightly sending a spray of sparks over the stone hearth.

Ripley, having finished his report joined the two seasoned detectives and offered to replenish their glasses. Before walking to the bar he leant over and announced.

'I've just been studying the hotel register, and guess who was staying here at the same time as Ronson?'

Jack and Martin glanced at each other with a wry smile, handed Ripley their empty glasses, and pronounced, as if rehearsed.

'Mr Nick Hartford.' Both laughed raucously, leaving a deflated Ripley to retreat to the bar.

Snapshot 139

Wilf had been looking after the gardens ever since Nick bought the house. He loved the rolling lawns and insisted on cutting the grass at least twice a week, if the weather allowed. Nick watched as he carefully parked the Atco Royalle lawnmower at the side of the drive.

Wilf produced a long willow stick that he repeatedly swished over the top of the grass to dislodge the morning dew. This allowed the grass to dry out in the morning sun, so the grass would be ready for cutting by lunchtime.

'Morning sir,' Wilf called out, on seeing Nick. 'It's going to be a warm one today.'

'You take it easy Wilf, don't try to do too much.'

Nick had offered to hire another gardener to help the old man but he had insisted he could manage. This time of the year was a busy period; preparing the beds for next year, feeding the lawns and perpetually sweeping the lawns clean of the fallen autumn leaves.

'Don't you worry sir, the machines do all the work, all I do is steer them,' he chuckled, 'looks like you have visitors.'

Nick turned to see a car pull up outside the front of the house. Three men stepped onto the drive and walked towards him. Nick's instinct had already alerted him to the fact that they were police before they introduced themselves. He glanced at the warrant cards waved in front of him by Detective Chief Inspector Martin, Detective Sergeant Jack Blenkinsop and Detective Constable Ripley.

'Very nice gardens, they must take a lot of looking after,' said Martin pocketing his warrant card, while looking around the vast expanse of lawn.

'Wilf over there is the gardener, he takes care of everything,' explained Nick, while wondering what the hell they were doing here. His mind was racing, but outwardly he was calm.

'A lot of work for just one man, he must be a dedicated gardener,' continued Martin.

Nick nodded in agreement, 'Well, I keep offering to get extra help, but he won't hear of it, he likes to do things his own way,' smiled Nick.

'Mr Hartford, we are investigating a number of crimes in and around this area, consequently we are questioning a number of locals,' explained Martin.

'Shall we go inside, its much more comfortable,' suggested Nick, glad now they had made clear the reason for their visit.

Once inside, Nick showed them into the study with its fruitwood bookcases lining the walls.

'Very nice room Mr Hartford,' Martin gazed around the room taking in the sumptuous furnishings.

'Thank you, but just exactly why do you wish to talk to me regarding these crimes you referred to?' asked Nick, biting the bullet before it was fired.

'Well now sir, its quite simple really; you keep cropping up in the course of our enquiries.'

'I do, how exactly?' asked Nick.

'Well sir, it may be just a coincidence, but I'm sure you can clear up the whole question of why you keep popping up once I have explained everything to you,' answered Martin.

'I'm sure I can, but exactly what are the circumstances inspector?' asked Nick, annoyed at the delaying tactics. Martin knew from the young man's reply that he had 'ruffled his feathers'.

'Recently, three villains from our area stayed at the Golden Lion. At that time, you and your fiancée also dined and stayed one night. It was on that particular night that £17000 was stolen from their room.'

'So, I hope you're not suggesting we had anything to do with taking the money,' said Nick indignantly.

'There's more; some time later, while these three men were looking around your antique shop, they overheard a conversation between another customer and your fiancée about how an old Russian gentleman had found a bundle of notes in the street, the same amount it turned out, that had been stolen from these villains in the hotel; a curious tale.'

Martin pulled a Georgian style mahogany armchair into position and sat down, shuffling to make himself comfortable, then added, 'The man who told the tale has never been identified.'

'So let me get this clear, Chief Inspector; because I was dining in the same hotel as these people and these same men overheard a tale while they were visiting my shop, I am a suspect! Really,' laughed Nick, 'that's quite an assumption you're making. Where are these men now?'

'No one said you were a suspect sir, we just want to clear a few loose ends. You see, you do keep popping up. Two of the men are in custody, one is dead'

'So what is the problem?'

'A number of other robberies took place which we know these men did not commit, but the evidence keeps suggesting that there are links to this area,' said Martin, carefully observing Nick.

'Well you've lost me, exactly how can I help you?'

'On the night you were dining at the Golden Lion, did anything unusual happen?'

'Not that I can recall. I do remember that their were some noisy diners, but that's all.'

'You own a BMW X5 sir?'

'Yes.'

'Could we see it please sir?'

'By all means, but my fiancée has taken it while she is shopping in Skipton. She should be back in a few hours,' said Nick, intrigued why they wanted to see the BMW.

'H'mm, do you normally keep it garaged?'

'Yes, would you like to see the garage?'

'If you don't mind sir,' said Martin raising himself from the armchair, 'not really made for comfort.'

'When that was made, people tended to be, how shall we say, smaller,' retorted Nick.

Martin grimaced at the remark, while Jack tried to hide a slight smile at what was perhaps a sideswipe at Martin's portly figure.

Nick led the three detectives to the garage at the side of the house. Martin was surprised at the size of the building, which they entered through a side door. Nick switched on the lights to reveal several bays.

'The BMW is normally in this bay,' explained Nick. Martin and Jack both looked around the empty bay, then over to the next bay which housed an Aston Martin, the next a fully customised BMW van, and the next a Ford Mustang, while in the last bay stood a Gold Wing and a BMW 1200 touring bike.

'Could I have look at the Aston Martin. What year is it?' asked Jack, enthusiastically.

'Yes, of course, it's a Series 3 V8 from 1978,' said Nick, leading the way around.

'My goodness, this is a beautiful machine. My father used to work at David Browns where they developed the engine, he used to ride on the chassis when they tested them.'

'I've had this one three years, but I don't take her out too often.'

'Right, well, thank you Mr Hartford, for your time, we must be on our way.'

Martin had seen enough and couldn't do with his sergeant drooling over the vehicles. He made his way to exit followed by Jack and Ripley. Once outside, Martin turned to Jack and pointed to the driveway.

'Crushed stone, no imprints in that.' They climbed into the car and set off down the drive. As they drove past Wilf, the gardener, riding on the lawnmower, he doffed his cap in the traditional way.

'Bloody old fool,' croaked Martin.

'Did you see that Aston Martin?' cooed Jack, still in raptures at having seen the car with which his father had been associated with.

'What about that Ford Mustang?' replied Ripley.

'Too bloody rich,' snapped Martin.

'Exactly. Collectively, those cars must be worth around three quarters of a million quid, so why would he be involved in some small time robberies?' said Jack.

'All right Jack, you've made your point,' growled Martin.

Snapshot 140

'George, where are you?' Nick asked anxiously.

'At this very moment I am wandering around the open market in the High Street. Is anything wrong?' asked George, sensing the urgency in Nick's voice.

'Listen George, I want you to meet me at the Little Chef on the by-pass outside of town. I've just had a visit from the police and they showed an inordinate interest in the BMW. Park at the rear of the cafe, it'll be out of sight.'

'I'm on my way,' she said, recognising the significance of his message.

'No need to panic George, the police think you are in Skipton not Richmond, but I need to check out the vehicle before you return home. See you shortly.'

Nick donned his motorcycle leathers and helmet; he pushed the BMW 1200 off its stand. The engine roared into life as he slipped out of the bay and onto the driveway. Wilf watched the bike leave the driveway and join the road. The purr of the engine could be heard long after the bike had slipped out of sight.

Snapshot 141

Sitting in the BMW at the rear of the roadside café as Nick had suggested, was not the most satisfying experience after an enjoyable day's shopping.

Having exhausted the limited view, George flicked her way through several magazines. Family cars, arriving and leaving in a steady procession, distracted her attention from anything other than glancing at pictures and the odd advert.

More society wedding photographs seemed to spread over the pages; apart from the facial features, each bride and bridegroom all looked pretty much the same, dresses with light beading or ones embellished with floral embroidery, A-line skirts all with a chapel train. The men were dressed in an array of tuxedos.

The welcome sound of a motorcycle engine distracted her browsing. Nick parked the bike at the side of the car, signalled 'hello', then set about inspecting the outside of the vehicle. It was not long before he joined her.

'I think I've found what they're looking for,' Nick went on to explain in detail about the visit by Martin, and his interest in the BMW.

'Once they asked to see the garage, I just followed their eyes; it had to be the treads on the tyres. I've just inspected the tyres, the offside rear has a marked slash across the tread; that must be the one they wanted to see,' he speculated.

'Why would the police want to see it?' asked a puzzled George.

'It's quite possible that they've seen an impression near to where the men were staying; I did follow them the night they robbed the fur shop.'

'Oh Nick, what are we to do?' she cried anxiously.

'Here's what we'll do,' he explained, almost ignoring her plea. 'There's a BMW garage in Richmond; we'll pretend to be interested in buying a model similar to this, request a test drive, bring it here, exchange the tyres, then return the vehicle and thank them. What do you think?'

'Brilliant, are you sure it will work?'

'Of course it will,' he said, leaning over to give her a hug.

Snapshot 142

The eager salesman, anticipating a quick sale, watched as Nick and George left the forecourt. It was not unusual for couples, having had a successful test drive, to want to talk over the impending purchase.
He took a pride in his ability to read client's body language; he felt confident they would be back tomorrow to complete the deal. Placing the keys on the desk he picked up the paperwork, realising immediately, that in his enthusiastic conversation with his prospective client, he had omitted to obtain the couple's address. Suddenly he didn't feel so jubilant.

Snapshot 143

Returning to the house, George dropped the baggage in the hallway and made straight for the kitchen for a welcome cup of tea. As a street girl, whenever she felt depressed or stressed-out, she always relied on a cup of tea to revive her spirits.

She glimpsed her reflection in the glass cabinet that she opened to reach for a cup and saucer, the warmth of the kitchen had brought a glow to her cheeks.

How her circumstances had changed; from the days when she sat in dingy café's clutching a mug of warm tea, to now, when she enjoyed her tea in a cup and saucer made of the best china.

Seated in the sun lounge, enjoying her tea, George picked up the magazines she had looked at earlier in the afternoon. Flicking through the pages, one society-wedding picture caught her attention; she read the brief summary, and sure enough, there he was again, Luzhkov.

She lay back against the soft leather cushion as the magazine slipped from her grasp to the floor. This was too much of a coincidence. She recounted the detail of the wedding; "Mr Thomas Powys-Smith married Miss Irina Petrova, who was given away by Mr Viktor Luzhkov in the absence of her father who was ill in Moscow".

She picked up the magazine and examined the report; Powys-Smith was Chairman of Compass-Smith Water Company. A search on the computer revealed that the company had recently developed a new type of desalination plant that could potentially alleviate water shortages in many countries.

George was hooked, her imagination was working overtime.
A more thorough search of Mr Thomas Powys-Smith revealed that this was his second marriage; his first wife, Lucy, had died tragically of carbon monoxide poisoning twelve months ago.

Curious, George began another search; this time she typed in the name of Henry Burton, the Home Secretary, whose second wife Yekaterina was also Russian.

Her eyes never left the monitor as she waited for the results of her search to appear on the screen. As she sifted through the relevant entries there was one entry that mentioned the word 'accident' that drew her attention. The open file revealed a newspaper report about how the Home Secretary's first wife, Andrea, was killed in a fire at their country cottage. As she read the details of the accident, she experienced a feeling of elation at the discovery, but at the same time, fear, at the realisation that these two accidents were possibly related.

Snapshot 144

Nick rolled himself halfway from beneath the Ford Mustang on his creeper, his face black with grease; it gave him the appearance of an urban guerrilla often seen in movies. He could see that George was excited, and looked up at her as she told him about the newspaper items.

'Well, that's an interesting coincidence,' he said, when she had finished.

'*Interesting coincidence*,' she said angrily, immensely disappointed at his apparent lack of interest. 'Nick, I need you to listen carefully, there is something not right here. Now get yourself upright and pay attention!' Recognising the sense of frustration and anger in her voice he pushed himself from beneath the car and leaned against the car.

'All right, from what you've said, we have two men who both remarried, whose wives are from Russia and whose previous wives have died in a accident. Right.'

'Yes'

'Well, as I see it, they are both isolated weddings that have taken place independently of each other,' he said, wiping his hands with a dirty rag.

'*Luzhkov* was at each wedding,' George said forcefully.

'OK, we know he's a friend of the Home Secretary, and being Russian he will have friends in the Russian community.'

'But both wives had accidents.'

'So do lots of other people. Everyday someone dies from being run over by a car, or is killed in a fall, and a large number of their partners will probably remarry, but that doesn't mean there's something sinister going on, does it?' he asked.

'I'm really surprised that you can't see that there's something just not right here!' said George, taken aback by Nick's lack of enthusiasm for her findings.

'Look, I don't like the guy Luzhkov, as you well know, but I can't waste my time examining every social event that he attends looking for sinister incidents. I can hit him where it hurts by going after his business interests.'

'Right, OK, fine. You pursue your angle, and I'll pursue mine.' George turned on her heels and marched out of the garage, leaving Nick in no doubt that they had encountered the first real difference of opinion in their relationship.

Snapshot 145

After taking a shower and changing into something casual, Nick made his way downstairs to find George, and to apologise for not showing interest in the results of her research. After a quick search of the house and the gardens, he failed to find her and returned to the house, puzzled, convinced that she must have gone for a walk to cool down.

A note left by the fireplace soon made him realise how wrong he was in thinking that George would resolve her ideas 'with a walk'. In the note she informed Nick that she was going to investigate further her suspicions behind the newspaper articles and would be in touch later. P.S. She would be charging everything to Nick's account.

Snapshot 146

Having taken a light breakfast, George drove to the small village of Aldrich, in the centre of which was a large open pond. Next to it a large willow tree cast a huge shadow over the water. George consulted her notes and started walking away from the pond and crossed a large, well-kept field surrounded by five large cottages, each set in well-stocked manicured gardens.

The middle of the field was fenced off to protect the 'hallowed turf' of an over-used cricket pitch, not a game with which George had any allegiance.

The cottage she had come to see was tucked away behind a row of large chestnut trees. The leaves on the trees were already a golden colour and looked as if they would fall with the next strong wind.

George could see that the estate agent had already arrived and was eagerly waiting to greet her. Not much older than George, dressed in a smart black embroidered blouse with elegant slim cut trousers, she had a wide welcoming smile.

Once the initial formalities had been dispensed with, a tour of the cottage began. As they passed through each room, the estate agent gave a brief description of each room.

Had George seriously entertained the idea of buying a property, this would have been perfect. Unable to betray the real motive for her visit to the cottage, she continued the charade of being an interested would-be purchaser, following the young lady's commentary intently.

Not once during the tour did the estate agent refer to the previous occupants, or the sad demise of Lucy Powys-Smith. George recalled the newspaper account of her death, how she was found by the daily household help in the master bedroom. The recollection of the woman's tragic end spurred George into action, and she asked to inspect the heating supply.

The estate agent led George into the utility rooms, one of which contained the combination boiler for the premises. Whilst listening to a speech on the heating facilities, George noticed a stock of service sheets hanging by the side of the gas boiler. On the top one, she clearly saw the name and address of the servicing engineer. She turned to the smartly dressed young lady and asked how many carbon monoxide detectors were installed in the cottage, 'as I can't see one here.'

The question made the young lady pause in her commentary; she was clearly not prepared for such an enquiry. Thinking on her feet she said that she would go and count them, and rushed off.

Pleased with herself, for catching the lady off-guard and being left alone, George lost no time in examining the service sheets. On hearing the estate agent's returning footsteps, she removed the top sheets from the clipboard at the side of the boiler, and placed them into her bag.

'I've located one in the main hallway,' the girl announced rapidly, catching her breath.

'Just one,' exclaimed George in feigned surprise.

'Yes, just one,' repeated the girl.

'Well that's interesting.'

'Really. Why?'

'Carbon Monoxide is odourless, colourless, but highly poisonous, assuming that the alarm was in good working order, why didn't it warn her?'

'Warn who?' asked the puzzled young estate agent. George looked at the women in disbelief, 'You really don't know, do you?'

'Know what?' asked the women.

'The previous owner died of accidental carbon monoxide poisoning; well, that was the coroner's verdict. But if the CO detector was working, why didn't the alarm wake her?'

'I'm sorry, I don't know anything about the previous owners death, no one told me'. She turned to George, no longer composed, she asked, ' Do you want to continue looking at the house?'

'No, I've seen enough.' George followed the woman up the steps and out through the hall and onto the front drive. 'Thank you for the tour.'

'Were you ever really interested in the house?' asked the young woman angrily, locking the door.

'I was interested to see the house where Lucy Powys-Smith lived and died, I am investigating her death.'

'I see, well, good luck. I really must go as I have another appointment.' She moved quickly down the path and beyond the chestnut trees and was soon out of sight.

George turned to look at the cottage once more. Life must really have been idyllic here, she thought, but what about the neighbours? Time to find out.

Snapshot 147

George walked up the path to the cottage next door to be met by a silver-haired lady, whose appearance was synonymous with country life. With her ruddy cheeks, twinkling eyes and a figure of ample proportions, she greeted her visitor with a warm handshake.

'I saw you looking around the cottage next door, we don't miss much here in Aldrich,' she laughed heartily. George liked her immediately, and explained how she was researching the circumstances surrounding the death of Mrs Powys-Smith for a national magazine.

'Such a lovely lady, please come in, I'll make some tea. What magazine do you write for?

'The Modern Woman,' George said, snatching the title out of thin air.

'Never heard of that one,' the woman laughed, taking two cups from the cupboard, 'I haven't progressed beyond 'Red Letter.''

'Can you tell me anything about the days immediately before her death?'

'Not really, nothing unusual happened as I recall. Lucy always seemed perfectly happy. Our conversations always revolved around our love of gardening, especially her roses, she loved the rose garden. When she was away, I always watered the garden, and the house plants.'

'Yes, but did you notice anything unusual; visitors, something she might have said that struck you as unusual.' The silver haired lady shook her head while as she poured the tea.

'No, nothing unusual happened that springs to mind. Do you take sugar?'

Over the next hour George listened to stories about Lucy Powys-Smith; while it helped to build a profile of interesting minutiae, it did not reveal anything to help her investigation into Mrs Powys-Smith's death.

Snapshot 148

George knew she had found the correct address when she read 'Ezra Ownsworth & Son, Heating Engineer, Corgi Registered, Phone: 01483 608222' on the side of the white van that stood in the driveway of the redbrick detached house.

The man who answered the door wore a green ribbed woollen cardigan and was smoking a brier pipe. A small man with large forearms, he announced bluntly,

'Can I help you? If it's about a repair or a gas fitting, I only take appointments over the phone.' He pointed to the writing on the van with his pipe, the mouthpiece was wet, a small wisp of smoke drifted from the end.

George explained the purpose of her visit and produced the service sheets she had removed from the house.

'Aye, they're mine, you'd better come in.' He led her into a small conservatory with cane furnishings. 'When did she die?' he asked, puffing gently on his pipe.

'Two weeks after you did the last service on her boiler. She died of carbon monoxide poisoning. The coroner said her death was accidental.'

'I see.' Mr Ownsworth placed his pipe on the table at side of his chair and reached over for the service sheets, which he studied carefully. After a moment, and without any explanation, he left the room.

George glanced round the cosy conservatory that looked over a neat expanse of garden, then watched as a robin preened itself in a pedestal birdbath outside the window. 'I keep this for all the jobs I do; it contains everything I think about a job, and the people who I work for. If I don't like someone, it's in the book.' George watched as he waved his book in the air thinking,

'This is too good to be true.' She asked, 'Did you make an entry for the service on Mrs Powys-Smith's boiler?'

'Let's see now,' he flicked the pages, looking briefly at each date entry, 'that's the one, miss.' He handed the notebook to George, who read the page eagerly.

Mr Ownsworth sat back in a chair, picked up the brier, pulled out a Zippo lighter from his cardigan pocket and went through a well-rehearsed routine of lighting his pipe.

'So it was a routine service check, you didn't find anything faulty?' George asked.

'Just routine, that's right. You say it was carbon monoxide poisoning, well I'm pretty sure that boiler was not responsible,' he said, puffing clouds of pipe-smoke upwards.

George watched the smoke drift upwards towards a half-open window above the gas fitter's head.

'There was one other little job I did there.' He leaned over and took the notebook from her. 'There at the bottom of the page in small writing.'

He passed the open notebook back to George. 'Flue screw, what does that mean?' she asked, puzzled.

'The waste gasses and heat escapes through the flue on the external wall. I noticed the flue cover was loose with one screw missing so I replaced the missing screw.'

'I see, and there was nothing else?' asked George despondently.

'No, except that she was a lovely lady, always pleasant.'

He tapped the pipe in his palm, blew down the stem, and replaced it on the table. George was staring at the entry in the notebook. After an embarrassing silence she turned to the gas fitter and asked, 'Mr Ownsworth, would you accompany me to Aldrich? I'll pay you your usual call-out fee.'

'When do you want to go?'

'Now.'

'I'll get my coat.'

Snapshot 149

Mr Ownsworth pulled his white van onto the drive of the cottage and parked it at the side of the house.

'I'll just get the key from next door, I won't be long.' Quickly she darted down the drive and very soon was knocking at the silver haired lady's front door; she didn't have to wait long.

'Hello, it's me again,' she laughed and greeted the old lady, explaining that the estate agent had been delayed and that Mr Ownsworth had agreed to check the gas boiler, but was pressed for time.'

'Oh I know Ezra, he's a lovely man, he does my boiler check every year, a most reliable man.' She gave George the key with the request, 'You must let me read your story as soon as it's published.'

Once inside the cottage, Mr Ownsworth wasted no time in checking the heating system, while George looked around the main bedroom where Lucy Powys-Smith died. She walked around the bare room, creaking floorboards adding to the eerie atmosphere. The walls were covered in a floral repeating patterned paper; a silent witness to what had occurred, betrayed no secrets of what had taken place. From the tightly shut windows she could look out over the gardens. She heard Mr Ownsworth enter the room.

'The boiler is in perfect working order, just as it was when I last serviced it,' he said solemnly.

'Well, the carbon monoxide came into this room, it found it's way in somehow, and poisoned Mrs. Powys-Smith. Of that there is no doubt, the coroner said it was accidental poisoning, and blamed the boiler.'

'Well, Miss, I don't know about that, but I can assure you there's no way that the gas came up those stairs and past the CO alarm system by itself. And if I know that, how come no one else realised it?'

'That's something I've given quite a lot of thought to too. Why did the investigation into her death concentrate solely on accidental poisoning?'

'I don't know Miss. But while you went for the key I examined the outside flue, well you may recall I mentioned replacing a missing screw on the flue cover.'

'Yes I do, but what of it?' George asked.

Chuckling, he pulled out his pipe from his shirt pocket and blew steadily down the stem.

'It's all right, Miss, I won't light it in here. You see, I always start at twelve o' clock with a new screw, its a little ritual of mine, but when I walked round to the side of the house to inspect the flue, I noticed the screw was at twenty after twelve, therefore, someone has removed the flue cover.'

The impact of those final words caused her heart to race; was this the breakthrough she needed?

'Could the gasses from the flue have been fed into this room?' she asked, carefully.

'Look, Miss, I agreed to inspect the boiler, this speculation is a bit out of my league.'

'Mr Ownsworth, I just need to know if the gasses could somehow have been piped into this room from the flue, is it feasible?' she implored him.

He looked at her and walked into the corner of the room waving his pipe towards the window and the air grate.

'It would be possible to feed a pipe through this top window, or I suppose the air grate. I would favour the window; drop the pipe through, stuff a blanket to block off the rest of the opening and there you have it.'

'It's that simple?'

'Yes, the gas is lethal. But thinking about it, someone wanting to do this would really need to be in the house to make sure the bedroom door was shut and sealed, otherwise the gas would have been detected by the alarm.'

'I knew it, now I need to check out the others,' she said, excitedly, to herself. Mr Ownsworth caught the words.

'Look Miss, whatever it is you're involved with, keep it to yourself, I don't want to know. Now, I'm going. If you want a lift, you're welcome,' he turned for the door.

'I'm sorry, you're not involved,' she said. 'You've never been here, right.' She followed him down stairs, locked the front door and leant through the van door.

'Here, take the money, it's what we agreed.'

'Are you really writing an article for a women's magazine?' he asked, curiously.

'No, I'm investigating a series of mysterious deaths, somehow I believe they're all related.' She pulled herself into the front seat. 'Light your pipe, it will help you relax.'

'You don't mind?' He pulled out the brier, flicked the Zippo, placed the stem in between his lips and sucked on the stem gently, and exhaled the blue smoke, which curled slowly upwards, spiralling towards the open window. 'This must be the most exciting thing that has ever happened to me. I don't want the money. You're not going to the police are you?'

'No, not yet. What would I say, too much conjecture at the moment, not enough substance.' she smiled wistfully.

'Here, take the money, we agreed.'

'No thank you,' he reached over and turned the ignition key, and the van's engine spluttered to life.

'Sorry about panicking back there, miss. To be honest with you, I really have enjoyed myself,' he said, chuckling to himself as the van pulled away.

'My name is George, not Miss, and thanks for your help.'

'Don't mention it, my name's Ezra.'

'I know, it's on the side of the van.' They both laughed loudly.

Snapshot 150

As he walked down the corridor of the local station Chief Inspector Martin was feeling cold and wet, though his mood was singularly boisterous, given that he was expecting to return to his own patch in the next couple of days. Walking into the office, which had been allocated to him since arriving, he caught sight of

Ripley closing a book, and was immediately curious as to what his young constable had been reading.

'What's that, Ripley?' asked Martin in a mock serious tone.

Ripley knew better than to play dumb. 'It's nothing sir, just something I'm reading, I've finished the report you wanted.' He passed over a sheaf of papers to Martin, who ignored them.

'The book?' he asked once again, teasingly.

'The Myth of Sisyphus, a philosophical essay by Albert Camus,' said Ripley, meekly. Martin mulled over the words, 'Sissy what?'

Ripley sighed, pulled the book out of the drawer, and placed it in front of the chief inspector.

'It's about man's futile search for meaning, unity and clarity in the face of the unintelligible world devoid of god and eternity. Sisyphus; a figure of Greek mythology, was condemned to perform meaningless tasks; he had to push a rock up to the top of a hill, then when it fell down the hill he had to push it back up again, and again, and again.'

'Really, and is this one of your meaningless tasks?' the Chief Inspector asked, picking up the report and waving it in the air.

'No, oh no,' protested Ripley. 'This,' he picked up the book, 'is just something I picked up in the local bookshop, I studied it years ago, but I never did truly understand it.'

'It's all right lad, I'm only ribbing you. Where's Jack?' A relieved Ripley picked up his book and returned it to the drawer. 'He's just slipped out for some digestive biscuits.'

'Good, I could do with a mug of tea, then you can explain this Greek philosophy to me, should go down well with digestives,' scoffed Martin mischievously.

Snapshot 151

For the last few days Nick had been completing a stock audit at the shop with Spence, but his mind had been elsewhere.

'It really is most inconsiderate of her not to contact me,' he blurted out.

Spence quickly realised that all was not well with Nick. Normally relaxed, he had stumbled around the shop attempting to find and record items that he would have usually located easily.

'I'm sure she'll contact you soon,' she said, sympathetically.

'I hope so. Look, Spence, would you mind finishing off the audit, I really don't have the stomach for it, besides I have to call at the local police station, they want to inspect the tyres on the BMW. If I set off now I should get there before dark.'

'Sure I can, you go. And don't worry, I'm sure George will ring you soon.'

Snapshot 152

'Jack, come in,' Martin greeted the sergeant, 'did you bring the digestives? Ripley has just made the tea. Jack pulled the biscuits from his raincoat pocket and placed them on the desk.

'Bloody awful weather,' he moaned, taking off his wet coat.

'Won't be long now Jack, we'll be home soon,' said Martin, trying to open the packet of biscuits.

'Have you ever heard of The Myth of Syphilis, Jack?' he chuckled.

'The what?' asked Jack, wiping the back of his neck with a handkerchief?

Ripley sighed, took the book from the drawer and pushed it towards the sergeant. It was typical of the chief inspector's humour, to misrepresent the title in this mocking way. Jack studied the book, and then asked, 'Is someone going to explain?'

Ripley took hold of the book and began to slowly interpret what he understood of the philosophical meaning. Martin nibbled his digestives while Jack dunked his half way. Both listened to the detective constable, they didn't have a lot else to do on this miserable day in the middle of the dales.

'...Sisyphus has the conscious power to contemplate and control his fate. Therefore if we know, for example, that everyone faces death as their fate, then consciousness equals the ability to deal with ones fate.' Ripley leant back into his chair, reached for his mug and took a long drink.

Martin looked at Jack, but the sergeant gave no reaction. His silence was the detective's way of giving Ripley some respect; they might not truly understand the philosophical argument, but one of their own did seem to understand, and that was good enough.

A sudden knock at the door broke the silence.

The wet, bedraggled figure of P.C. Dunstan appeared round the door. 'There's a Mr Hartford outside waiting to see you,' he said, looking at the three detectives.

'Well, show him in lad,' replied Jack.

'I've tried that but he says that you want to inspect his BMW.'

'Of course we do, thanks to your report about the tyre imprints. Go and get yourself dry.' Jack pushed the constable back into the corridor.

'Get your coat, Ripley. We'll check out the vehicle's tyres.'

'Hang on, I'm coming too, I love these meaningless tasks, you just don't know where it's going to lead,' he said, sarcastically.

Snapshot 153

One thing that Reginald Blandford hated more than anything was workmen around the hall, he looked upon most of them as a totally alien species.

The necessity for security improvements to the hall meant having these so-called specialists around fitting cameras, upgrading the alarm system and fitting the new central computer system.

Blandford took it upon himself to personally keep his eye on the whole proceedings; he had caught one young electrician chatting up one of the servants, another was caught blowing smoke up the chimney while sat eating his sandwiches in the grand marble fireplace. Episodes like these were not in keeping with the dignity of the hall. These local trades people were just a blip; soon, they would be gone, and everything would be as it should be.

It was late afternoon and the light was fading fast. Outside, it was raining heavily which meant a lot of the security men working outside had gone home early. Blandford was supervising the moving of some furniture when Lorenzo appeared at his side; he tapped the personal assistant on the shoulder and gestured towards the library.

'I need to speak with you.' That was it, nothing else. He moved off towards the library.

Blandford sighed; it was a habit of his when he was interrupted. He gave instructions to the staff moving the furniture, and then joined the Sicilian in the library.

'What is so important that you have to act so mysteriously?' he asked, quietly. Lorenzo threw some objects onto a small side table.

'They are,' he said, smugly. Blandford inspected the objects.

'Are these what I think they are?'

'If you think that they are UHF listening devices, then you're right,'

'Oh God, where did you find them?' asked Blandford, in a state of panic.

'One behind this book,' he threw it onto the table.

'The other was underneath the desk.' Blandford picked up the receivers and examined them.

'How long have they been here?'

'Hard to tell. I did a security sweep of the whole hall just to make sure it was clean shortly after we moved in and everywhere was clean, so they've come since then.'

'Thank you, Lorenzo, will you see what you can find out about these, then we'll get together and see if we can determine who put them here.'

Blandford passed on the listening devices. He picked up the book that Lorenzo had thrown on the table.

'Agatha Christie, 'Sad Cypress', very appropriate, her detecting skills would be most useful at this time.'

He smiled to himself, straightened the dust jacket and replaced the book in its proper place on the shelf. Instantly, in doing so, he remembered seeing the woman who accompanied Hartford from the antique shop replacing the same book, just as was entering the room.

It must have been Hartford who planted these devices.' he paced around the room contemplating the evidence.

'No one else has been in the library, except guests of Mr Luzhkov, and they are beyond suspicion.

Snapshot 154

'Did you really read all that stuff?' asked Jack, walking alongside Ripley along the corridor.

'Yes, Sarge, I did.'

'Well, if you understand all that stuff, you really could do a lot better for yourself than the force,' he suggested.

'No, I disagree, Sarge, I always wanted to join, and I haven't regretted it for one minute,' replied Ripley, pushing open the swing door that led to the front of the building.

'Bloody hell, just look at that,' Jack looked out of the door at the pouring rain.

'It's only water Jack, c'mon,' snorted Martin, as he pushed him through the door and marched up to the waiting BMW X5, followed by Jack and Ripley. Nick watched the trio approaching and waved in recognition.

Martin leant down and inspected each tyre, then asked Nick to roll the vehicle forward a little, and carried on looking at each wheel.

Martin looked up at Jack and patted the tyre, 'Clean as a whistle,' he said, with rain rolling down his face.

'Thank you Mr Hartford, for bringing the vehicle in, especially in this weather.' He waved goodbye to Nick and made for the shelter of the station, with Jack and Ripley following on behind.

Snapshot 155

George looked down the long library reference room while waiting for the assistant librarian to deliver the newspapers she had requested. Polished bookcases, each filled to capacity with reference books, lined the walls. Numerous tables, surrounded by chairs, filled most of the floor space, here she could see people crouching over textbooks, most scribbling notes feverishly.

The assistant soon returned with an armful of newspapers and placed them on the counter. George thanked her, gathered up the papers and found a quiet corner where she could work undisturbed.

As she read, the story unfolded of how the Rt. Hon. Henry Burton's wife, Andrea, perished in a blaze which gutted the family home in Bishop's Castle, Shropshire. The fire started on the ground floor and quickly spread.

A passing neighbour, out walking the dog, after returning home late, saw flames through a downstairs window; he called the fire brigade. Neighbours had tried to gain access to the house but were beaten back by the smoke and flames, which quickly engulfed the whole building.

Each local paper told a similar story, the fire was deemed to be accidental and consequently the case attracted no further attention other than a large out-pouring of sympathy for Henry Burton, the grieving husband whose constituency business had kept him away on the night of the fatal fire.

George left the library, having absorbed all the information she needed from the newspapers. She now felt that she had sufficient background to Mrs Burton's death to carry her investigation one step further; she had already learnt that the dead women's sister lived nearby in Church Stretton.

But first, she was going to seek out the fire officer who had been interviewed for a news report by the reporter representing the local press.

Snapshot 156

George had been driving around the country lanes of Long Mynd for long enough, searching for 'High Tops' cottage without any success. She pulled the car over onto the verge, and switched off the engine.

Now, the only sound that she could hear was the wind blowing over the long stretches of grass over the Mynd, which stretched far into the distance. A lone figure appeared over the brow. At first, it appeared as a blur, but slowly, as it approached her, she was able to make out that it was a man pushing a bicycle.

'Excuse me, but I'm looking for a cottage called 'High Tops', could you help me?' she asked, as the man drew level. He had protruding eyes, a thin nose and thin lips, which were cracked around the edges as he smiled in acknowledgment.

'It's back up the road, turn right onto the airfield,' he said, pointing up the roadway which she had just travelled down.

'The cottage is on the airfield?' she asked.

'Oh yes, right in the middle,' he laughed, showing his yellowing teeth. George thanked him, and turned the car round and headed back up the road, turning into the airfield. A large notice warned all motorists that the maximum speed was 15 mph, and that this was private property.

Looming in the distance she could see several gliders parked on the grass; long wings and slender pencil shaped bodies.

Beyond these, a large building contained several aircraft under repair. She stopped outside the building and walked inside where she saw a couple of men working on one of the gliders.

'Hello, could you help me? I'm looking for 'High Tops?' Both men looked up surprised to see the unexpected visitor.

'High Tops,' they repeated.

'Yes, I'm looking for Mrs Karen Walker.'

Both men laughed, then walked outside with her and pointed in the direction of a high hedge alongside the grass runway.

'That's her house, but she's not at home, she's up there,' the older of the two men said, pointing towards the sky. George craned her neck to look up and saw a glider spiralling through the sky.

'Karen Walker's up there,' she said surprised.

'That's right, she'll be down soon.' The men left, returning inside the building, leaving George watching the circling glider.

Snapshot 157

Blandford was a much happier man now that all the security work had been completed and the household had returned to a normal routine.

As usual, when he had completed his duties, he was in the library relaxing, enjoying a brandy, and reading more of his beloved Lawrence of Arabia. A knock at the door immediately brought him back to the present. Lorenzo entered and stood waiting. Blandford poured a brandy and gave it to the Sicilian, who remained standing.

'I've been talking with Mr Luzhkov, and brought him up to date with our progress in the investigation. Needless to say, he was far from happy to learn about the listening devices, but on reflection, agrees with us that Hartford had the opportunity to plant the devices.'

'Good, and what does he suggest?' asked Lorenzo boldly.

'It's the perfect opportunity to set a trap,' replied Blandford, ignoring the Sicilian's interruption.

'How?'

'I want Angelo to call at Mr Hartford's antique shop and, how shall we say, leave him his calling card.' Blandford smiled while waiting for Lorenzo's reaction.

'I understand,' he said, taking a drink, 'I will instruct Angelo, it is a long time since we left a calling card, how much damage do you want?'

'Nothing permanent. If he is responsible for the listening devices, he'll know who's to blame for the damage, and we are pretty sure that he will retaliate, only this time,' Blandford smiled, and raised his glass, 'we'll be waiting for him.'

Snapshot 158

The Long Mynd was often described as a place of barren beauty, with it's vast expanse of heather and sculpted valleys; the airfield took full advantage of the contours, and the height of the hills, making it perfect for flying gliders.

The wind blew against her face as George watched the glider approaching the landing strip, gently coasting down, drifting first left, then right before straightening as the pilot corrected the flight path, then with a gentle bump, it was slithering along the grass until it came to a halt almost opposite the house where she waited.

The cockpit canopy lifted up and out climbed Karen Walker; a small woman with long red hair, which bounced off her shoulders as she walked towards the cottage.

'Hello, can I help you?' she asked, with a large warm smile.

'I'd like to ask you a few questions about your sister Andrea.' The smile instantly vanished.

'My sister's dead, there's nothing further to discuss.' She walked passed George and through a wooden gate, closing it between herself and George.

'I've travelled a long way to speak with you, Miss Walker, please, I won't take up too much of your time.'

'I'm sorry you've wasted your time, but there really is nothing to discuss,' she said without looking back.

'Look, what if your sister's death wasn't an accident? ' George snapped, trying shock tactics. It worked. Miss Walker turned round and gave George a long, cold stare.

'My sister died in a horrific fire, it was fully investigated, and do you know who my brother-in-law is?' she snapped, angrily.

'Yes, I do.'

'Well Miss what-ever-your-name–is, no stone was left unturned, Henry made sure of that, it was an accident, a dreadful accident, now please go.'

She slammed the front door shut with a loud thud, leaving George standing with only the sound of the wind blowing. Gentle drops of rain started to fall on her face, almost like tears.

Being shunned was something George had experienced many times when she was on the streets, but this hurt. It was like someone was closing a book on her theory of wrongdoing, and she just could not accept that finality. Opening the gate, she marched up the path to the front door and pressed the doorbell. After what seemed an age, the door opened and George faced a stern-looking Miss Walker. From this close proximity George could detect small lines around the corners of her mouth.

'I don't mean to hurt you, Miss Walker, in any way. On the contrary, I really wish to clarify certain details surrounding your sister's death,' she couldn't bring herself to say 'accident'.

Large raindrops began to fall, as if by order. On seeing them, Miss Walker relented and said, 'you'd better come in out of the rain and warm yourself by the stove, the wind up here can get pretty cold.' She helped George remove her coat.

'Please sit down. Would you like a drink? I always have a whisky after a successful flight.'

'Whisky will be fine with some water, thank you Miss Walker,' said George.

'Karen please, I don't use the Miss.' She poured two large whiskies and handed one to George who was sitting by the wood burning stove.

'And what do I call you?'

'George,' she said quietly.

'H'mm, now what's all this nonsense about my sister?'

George began to explain to her host the nature of her investigations into the death of several women. Karen listened intently to every word, getting up occasionally to fill the glasses. When George eventually finished they both sat quietly round the stove, watching the flames from the burning wood, until, after what seemed a long time, Karen broke the silence.

'Well, that's all very interesting, but my sister's death was an accident.'

'Your sister, I understand, was a very competent photographer.'

'Yes, she was; ever since she was a child it was one of her major hobbies. But I don't really see the relevance of this,' she said impatiently.

George wanted to ask her far more questions about her sister to add to the information she already collected, but she felt that unless she gave Karen more convincing evidence, she would lose her attention.

'Forensic investigation into the fire determined that the blaze started as a result of a battery charger overheating and bursting into flames. According to the coroners report, the offending charger was an 'Amtman Digital Delux.' It's a relatively cheap model that you wouldn't normally associate with high-end cameras, and certainly not to be used by a serious photographer. Now I don't know which type of camera your sister owned, but I'm guessing that she would have used reputable equipment.'
George moved away from the warm stove.

'She had two digital cameras, both were Canon, one full DSLR, the other one a top of the range, small camera that she could carry round in her handbag. She was always trying to persuade me to use them during my flights.'

' As I thought, so why would she invest in a cheap battery charger, when, for not an inconsiderable amount, she could acquire a charger which was guaranteed not to overheat.'

'There is a lot of supposition here; perhaps she didn't give it much thought, I don't know,' said Karen fretfully.

'I had a meeting with the investigating fire officer yesterday,' George continued.

'He believed that the charger had been immersed in water deliberately, and that would result in it shorting, overheating and subsequently bursting into flames,' Karen was reliving the pain of her sister's death; tears welled in her eyes as she digested the words.

'Why didn't this come out at the inquest?'

'The fire officer told me that his evidence was thought to be too difficult to confirm with any degree of certainty therefore it was discounted. He also told me that all the batteries had been removed from the smoke alarms.'

'Oh my God.'

Karen took a long drink, and poured herself another whisky.

'Who would do such a thing, we must go to the police immediately,' she said.

'No, not yet, remember the evidence was all there, but it is a matter of interpretation; the batteries may have been removed by your sister, and there is no concrete evidence that the battery charger was immersed in water, therefore, the fire was an accident. If my investigations can show that there is a link between your sister's death and those of these other women, then we can acquaint the police with the evidence. If you could be patient a little longer, please.' George pleaded.

'When I fly, you could say I enter into a relationship with the sky, we are as one, it has turned into a love affair, one that is only satisfied when I am up there. I have learnt to be very patient.'

She gazed into the fire for a long time once more. George waited, she did not know where her host was; perhaps her thoughts were somewhere in her beloved sky. Suddenly, she turned and said,

'You had better stay the night, you can't possibly drive, you've had more than two whiskies. I'll make us something to eat.'

Snapshot 159

Nick finished packing, closed the case, checked his wallet, grabbed his jacket, and made his way downstairs to the study. Walking over to the fireplace he pressed his palm against the bottom left corner of the mirror, the bookcase swung open and Nick walked into the room. He quickly surveyed the computer monitors, then set about tracking all the transactions George had made using his credit card.

Tired of waiting for her to ring, he had decided to try and find her himself. He printed out a list of her withdrawals and was studying it when suddenly, he noticed a light flashing on the monitor recording the activity of the listening devices in the library at Grice Hall. Opening the file, he realised immediately that the two devices were no longer active; he must assume they had been detected. However, the microcircuit board in the phone was still transmitting information.

Nick had to discover if they knew who had planted the devices, so he typed in his surname as a keyword, pressed enter, and waited for the result. Three audio files appeared, which he quickly downloaded onto a memory stick, and placed it into his jacket pocket.

If Blandford and Luzhkov suspected him of planting the bugs, they would retaliate. He grabbed the laptop and left the room, his first priority was to find George.

Snapshot 160

'Jack, what was that program where the main character kept referring to his wife as, 'She who must be obeyed,' asked Martin, looking rather agitated, as he sat down, awaiting a reply.
After some consideration and much face pulling Jack answered, 'Rumpole.'

'That's it, you're right, Jack,' and in a raised voice Martin proclaimed, '**Rumpole**, she who must be obeyed, a good name for you-know-who, upstairs,'

Martin leant forward over the desk. 'Just been to report our progress on the investigation; I recommended that because of the lack of evidence we were unable to justify continuing the investigation. Guess what?'

'She wants the case to remain open,' sighed the sergeant.

'You've got it in one Jack, she who must be obeyed, wants us to continue. I explained that we've no further leads to follow, but she reckons whoever is responsible will ultimately commit further crimes and eventually make a mistake. Bloody fool.'

'Actually I think it was H. Rider Haggard,' chipped in Ripley, who had been sitting quietly.

'What?' snapped Martin?

'H. Rider Haggard, first used the term 'She who must be obeyed,' in her novel 'SHE'.' Jack rested his head on hands and shook his head slightly; actually he was smiling. Martin glared at Ripley incredulously and slowly sank back into his chair.

'Thank you very much Ripley, just what I wanted to know. Now, speaking as one who must be obeyed, will you please make some tea?'

Snapshot 161

After successfully interviewing several people during her enquiries into the deaths of Lucy Powys-Smith and Andrea Burton, George felt, more than ever, that she was correct to follow her instinct.

Now she had travelled to London to follow another hunch; that was to take the top one hundred companies in the FTSE index, find the names of the chief executives from each company, and discover how many of them had recently remarried.

The results more than justified her persistence, out of the top one hundred, twenty-three had married in the last two years, eight of these had had first wives who had fatal accidents, and all eight of the grieving widowers had been introduced and remarried to women from the Soviet Union. Nick would have to take her seriously. She had tried to contact him, but Spence had told her that he had left to try and find her. His mobile was not receiving calls, the battery was probably flat, as usual.

George checked out of the hotel, having decided to continue her investigation. From the list of eight names, she took the first on the list; a Mr. Max Grose, who was Chief executive of the Grose Mercantile Bank in the city. His deceased wife, Angela, had died near their home on the Isle of Weight, and this was the next destination for George.

Nick would have to wait, but she did miss him.

Snapshot 162

After buying their house, Holly Blue, on the cliff top above Compton Chine on the Isle of Wight, Angela and Max Grose had been sublimely happy.

Each day, regardless of the weather, Angela Grose would take her two black Labradors for a walk along the cliff tops. Every weekend, her devoted husband Max would join her from London where he stayed during the week.

When the dogs were found with Angela Grose at the bottom of Compton cliff, it was interpreted as blind devotion, seeing her fall to her death, the dogs followed; 'Faithful to the last' as the headlines in one local newspaper proclaimed.

'This is the spot where she fell,' said Tom Bradley. George had managed to persuade the young newspaper reporter to show her where Angela had fallen over the cliff edge at Compton Chine.

Looking across the open grassland with its lack of cover, she tried to imagine the scene on the morning of the accident. Did she lose her footing trying to rescue one of the dogs that may have slipped over the edge of the chalky cliff? Or was heavy dew responsible for her slipping over the cliff edge?

But George could not rule out a third possibility; that of a stranger, lying in wait for his victim at a predetermined spot, then pushing both her and the dogs over the cliff edge. Surveying the scene, George realised that this was another 'accident' where the police had once again issued a statement saying 'there were no suspicious circumstances'.

'Did anyone report seeing any strangers in the vicinity?' asked George.

'Not that I recall.'

'Approximately what time did the accident happen?'

'Well, according to Mrs Wilson, her neighbour, she was always in the habit of walking the dogs about 7.30 in the morning.

Her body was found at the bottom of the cliff around eleven in the morning, so it was somewhere in between,' the young reporter answered.

'What time was high tide that day?' she looked over the cliff to the sea below.

'I think it would be about 8.15 am,' he replied, puzzled by her question.

'When she was found did she look as if she had been in the water long,' she asked, continuing to quiz young Tom.

'I don't know, I never saw the body.'

'Do you know if anyone found a dog lead,' she asked.

'I don't recall anyone mentioning a dog lead.' Her line of questioning was beginning to annoy the young reporter.

'Doesn't that strike you as odd, would you take out a pair of dogs without a lead?'

'No, I guess not.'

George looked at Bradley, 'I think we should go and talk with Mrs Wilson. There are many gaping holes surrounding this death as far as I am concerned' she said, gravely.

Snapshot 163

Mrs Wilson had a round face with ruddy cheeks, a wide friendly smile, greying hair and a pear shaped figure. She stood no more than five foot two.

George explained the nature of their interest in her late neighbour, and Mrs Wilson proved to be most willing to answer questions, especially from the young reporter whose reports she was familiar with in the local paper.

She said that Mrs Grose always took the dogs for a walk around 7.30 am every day and she always carried a lead. She did not recall seeing any strangers in the vicinity of the house.

The rest of the afternoon was spent recalling how wonderful a neighbour Mrs Grose had been, a friend to many less fortunate than herself. It was not really what George wanted to hear, overall she had been disappointed, she felt frustrated by the lack of anything substantial to suggest anything other than accidental death. George thanked Tom for his help and promised to keep in touch and let him know if she discovered anything new.

Snapshot 164

Early next morning, George was back on the cliff top at Compton Chine. She preferred to be on her own, looking around the scrub and coarse-grassland immediately around the cliff top from where Angela Grose fell to her death. Carefully examining the area, George picked up everything she found; two cigarette ends, three sweet wrappings and a fifty pence piece. She put them all into a plastic bag. Was it any good, she didn't know, but she clutched at anything that may give her a lead.

It was low tide and she wanted to examine the area below, where Mrs Grose and the dogs had been found, so she wrapped her scarf around a large pebble, and threw it down from where she thought the hapless woman had fallen to her death.

She made her way down to the bottom of the cliff where she located the scarf, a search of the area revealed nothing of any worth.

Sitting on a rock, she tried to imagine the picture; the body of Angela Grose and her two dogs. Now, among the rocks there was nothing to suggest anything so tragic had taken place. The sea, with its relentless tidal rhythm, had washed everything clean; the sand and rocks, of the blood from the lifeless bodies.

'Did you find what you were looking for?' The gruff voice, followed by a chuckle, startled George.

'My name's Wilson, you spoke to my wife yesterday. Sorry, I didn't mean to creep up on you, but I saw you walking past the house and my wife pointed you out.'

He sat down on the rock beside her, 'So I thought I would come to meet you.' He held out his hand. George shook it; it was the hand of an elderly person, but his grip was strong.

'You took me by surprise, I was just trying to imagine what it was like.' She smiled, still surprised at being sought out by this stranger.

'It was not something you would have wanted to see,' he reflected, shaking his head.

'You were here?' she asked, surprised.

'I was second on the scene. The alarm was raised by a young surfer, who rang on his mobile for help, then waited on the cliff-top to direct the rescuers,' he explained.

'Did you see anyone else?' she asked, anxiously.

'Not that I recall.'

'How do you think she came to fall?' There were more questions that she wanted to ask, but she was conscious of not seeming to be too curious, or macabre.

'Don't rightly know, the police believe she slipped on wet grass.'

'And the dogs, do you believe they would follow her?'

'Ah, now that is puzzling. Thinking about it afterwards, I was really surprised they did that,' he said, 'it was really weird that those dogs followed her.'

George nodded in agreement. 'You don't believe she fell by accident, do you?' His direct approach startled George, but she responded immediately.

'It does seem strange to me, that someone who walks here daily, and who is familiar with the terrain in all seasons, falls to her death, and not only that, but the dogs follow her to their death.'

'What's your explanation?' he asked.

'I think she may have met someone, and that someone threw both her and the two dogs over the cliff,' she said, never taking her eyes off Mr Wilson.

'Good!' he said, standing. 'I think you may be right, but, I had to be sure, we must be the only two people who believe that she was murdered.'

He rummaged in his pocket and eventually pulled out a black dog lead and thrust it into George's hands.

'I found that up there,' he pointed to the cliff-top; 'it was like she had dropped it. Another strange thing, when someone slips, you expect to see marks scuffed into the cliff face, but there were none.'

'Did you mention this to the police?'

'Yes, they told me to stop playing detective, and leave that to the professionals.'

'Great,' she said, sarcastically.

'Then there was all this hysteria about the 'faithful dogs following their mistress', all over the local papers; that diverted everyone's attention. And then the wife, well, she was heartbroken for a couple of weeks, she couldn't entertain any theory except that of accidental death.'

'It's nice to meet with someone else who believes that it wasn't an accident; even if we don't have any evidence,' she said, commiserating with the old man.

'There was someone hanging around for a few days before the accident. I traced him to a bed-sit in the village, he was Italian, I think.' George listened hardly daring to believe what she had just heard the old man say.

'That's really very interesting indeed, a few days before the accident,' she repeated. 'We must try to find out who he met, where he visited, when did he leave the area,' her mind was racing.

'You can start by checking the bed-sit, its run by Kathleen Flinders, a nice lady,' said the old man standing.

'We'd better start and make our way back up to the cliff-top, the tide is coming in. We could call into the café at the top of the cliff and have some tea,' he suggested.

'Good idea, my treat, now will you please tell me all you know about this man, where did you see him, do you know if he called for a drink, and if so who did he meet?' George's curiosity was aroused and voracious.

They made their way back. Over a couple of mugs of tea and bacon sandwiches, followed by cream scones, they shared information enthusiastically. The old man was pleased that his imagination had not got the better of him; he had started to have doubts about his sanity.

Each piece of information was examined minutely until eventually they could analyze no further. After a couple of hours they had exhausted all possible avenues. Before saying goodbye, they both agreed not to tell anyone what they had discovered until George had gathered more information, then she would contact him.

They parted on good terms, united in their belief that justice would not prevail unless they pursued and found the truth.

Snapshot 165

Nick threw his keys onto the bedside table, walked over to the large picture window and looked out at the people walking around in the busy street below.

He was tired; he'd travelled from Long Mynd all the way to the Isle of Wight in one day, only to find that George had checked out that very afternoon. She had not left a forwarding address, so he had no idea where she was heading.

He had rung Spence at the shop but she had not heard from George. To make matters worse, his mobile was refusing to work. He took out his MacBook laptop and checked the software to see when she had last used her credit card; it was yesterday, here in Ventnor.

He would have to wait for her to use it again before he knew her whereabouts. What progress was she making, he wondered, as he realised that he longed to see her once again.

Snapshot 166

Angelo Leonardo Caradonna, to give him his full birth name, was from the town of Salemi in the province of Tramani, Sicily. Born into a family of seven, he had moved through school without excelling in anything particular. As a child, he spent most of his free time running errands for the local Mafiosi.

Always well dressed, never without money or friends, it was no surprise to anyone when, on leaving school, he was immediately given his own area for the collection of the busterella; bribes and protection payments. Leaving Salemi and joining Mr Luzhkov was on the recommendation of the local Mafiosi boss, and therefore seen as a great honour. His allegiance and the strict observance of 'Omerta", the code of silence, was absolute and never questioned.

Across the road from the antique shop in Hawes, Angelo waited in a shop doorway. There was a steady drizzle, the type that is almost synonymous with the dales.

A cold wind blew down the High Street, which made for a very miserable afternoon. Few people walked along the street. Angelo didn't feel the cold, even though he had been raised in a warmer climate.

He watched a local paperboy make his way along the street, stopping to push an evening paper through various letterboxes, some positioned near the floor, others halfway up the door. His cap was back-to-front. As he pushed by Angelo he murmured a 's'cuse me mister,' as he pushed the paper through the letterbox and then disappeared down the street on the rest of his round.

Suddenly, another figure caught his attention, that of Spence walking down the street towards the shop. She greeted a passer-by and waved to another shopkeeper on her way, then, having reached the antique shop she opened the door, switched on the lights and went inside.

Angelo checked up and down the High Street before crossing the road to stand outside the entrance. He could see her at the rear of the shop, taking off her coat and straitening her hair before moving into the back room.

He gently lifted the catch and slipped inside, then, quietly pulled the door blind down, turned the key in the lock, and moved silently towards the back of the shop.

Spence, still in the back, hung up her coat and changed into more comfortable shoes. She filled the kettle for a welcome cup of tea, then collected some papers and returned to the shop. Seeing a customer in the shop startled her, as she had not heard him enter.

'Oh, I'm so sorry,' she said, embarrassed at being caught off-guard. 'How can I help you?'

The customer said nothing, but simply stared at her. His eyes were cold.

'Can I help you with anything?' she asked, perturbed at his lack of response. Out of the corner of her eye, she noticed that the door blind had been lowered.

She asked once more, as calmly as she could manage, 'Is there anything that I can show you?' She moved towards the door.

As she passed the stranger he turned and lunged forward. Grabbing her hair, he pulled her back sharply into a mahogany chest of drawers, sending a Meissen Harlequinn figure smashing onto the floor. Spence dragged herself up from the floor but the stranger still had hold of her hair; she tried to escape from his grasp.

'What are you doing?' she yelled. The searing pain was intense. Blood trickled down her face, into her eyes and mouth, still she managed to protest.

'Who are you, what do you want?' she cried. Ignoring her plea, he swung her against the wall with a sickening thud. Before she could sink to the ground he yanked her again, this time he swung her into the upturned chest of drawers. The ball and claw feet dug deep into her ribs as she fell to the floor.

He bent over her, 'I want to see Mr Nick Hartford,' he said, calmly pulling her round so she could smell his breath.

'Nick Hartford, where is he?' he repeated. Bleeding and racked with pain she somehow managed to blurt out,

'He's not here, he's gone to meet his girlfriend,' she cried. The pain was unbearable. Once more taking a handful of her hair, he pulled her limp body upright, then, as if losing his composure, he yelled, ' Where is he, bitch?'

When she failed to reply he flung her over the desk, grabbed her breast, which he twisted and squeezed until she croaked in agony, 'I don't know.'

Her arms were stretched out across the desk. She felt something metallic touch her fingers; it was her paper knife. She grasped the handle, then, mustering what strength she had left, she swung her arm round and plunged the knife into side of her attacker.

Angelo felt a sharp pain as the knife entered his side; almost synonymous with the thrust into his side, as a reflex action, he swiftly jerked her neck sideways, releasing his grip as he felt her body fall limp.

Angelo pulled out the paper knife, placed his free hand over the wound and swayed unsteadily through the shop towards the back door. He anxiously looked out into the drizzle, and then, still clutching his side, he lurched forward into the drizzle and disappeared.

Snapshot 167

His round finished, the paperboy made his way back to the shop, the empty newspaper bag slung over his shoulder. He stopped by the window of 'Slater's Hobby Shop,' leant against the wall and gazed longingly at the new Formula One model cars.

In another couple of months he might be able to afford the red Ferrari or the new silver Honda. He saw Mr Slater, the elderly owner, peering at him from behind the counter in the shop. The old man waved his arm at him to move on, as usual.

How could a mean old man like Slater run a model shop that was mainly for children, when he didn't get on with them? Returning to his journey, he threw down the ball and began kicking it in front of him.

Suddenly, a stranger approached; he seemed to sway from side to side and didn't seem to see the ball, which inadvertently hit his shoe, and then was propelled into the road.

'Oy mister, careful, that's mine!' cried the boy, running after the ball. The man, oblivious of the boy's protest, swayed his unsteady way down the street.

Back on the pavement, the boy shoved the ball into his pocket, and slowly continued his journey back to the newspaper shop. Suddenly, he noticed a small spot of blood on the pavement, then another, and another.

He quickened his pace, following the spots, thinking they must have come from the stranger who had just passed. The spots were distributed unevenly; one near the wall, another near the edge of the pavement, then he noticed a spot of blood in the antique shop's doorway.

The paperboy saw the door was ajar, which was unusual, so he pushed it open slowly and immediately noticed more spots of blood on the floor. He looked around the shop and called out,

'Hello, hello anyone here?' Moving inside slowly, he suddenly froze as he noticed the prone figure of a woman stretched out over the table, her eyes open, staring in his direction.

Terrified, he bolted out of the door and up the street as fast as his legs would take him until he reached the newsagent's. Bursting through the door, he excitedly told the shopkeeper what he had seen.

Snapshot 168

George had tried ringing Nick at home but had been unable to contact him; she had also tried to ring Spence, hoping she would know where Nick was, but with no success. Perhaps they were out buying some antiques.

Having devised an investigative method that had proved successful she saw no reason to change her approach. She had now moved to Wiltshire to look into the life of Susan Raines, who had, until her death, lived a busy life.

She had been head of 'Raines Equine Research Laboratory,' a highly successful horse breeding business, which was developing methods for equine cloning. She had been considered the leader in her field, and many of the world's leading equine experts travelled to visit her laboratories at Hindon, Wiltshire. Her husband, Charles, was head of the Raines Group, a flourishing investment company.

As usual, George had sought out the local library and made copies of all the relevant news articles into the woman's death. It was late when she booked into the Lamb Inn, a thirteenth-century building which still boasted original heavy oak beams and a large inglenook fireplace, where she now sat reading through the copies of the newspaper articles while drinking a brandy.

'Excuse me Miss, the landlord, Frank, said you would like a word with me. My name's Johnny.'

George looked up to see a small, wiry man in his early sixties, wearing a tweed jacket that was worn and faded with use. He had a short crew-cut haircut, which, like the stubble on his face, was silver-grey. His bronze face was deeply lined, but she thought his stubby nose and light blue eyes softened his features.

'Yes, Frank said you used to work with the horses at 'Raines' before it closed down.'

'That I did; to be more exact I worked with Miss Susan's horses,' he said, taking off his flat cap.

'Please sit down, can I get you a drink?' She pulled over a chair next to hers, near the fire.

'Not just now thanks, perhaps later when I've finished this,' he held up his pint pot to show that it was half full.

'When you say Susan's horses, didn't all the horses belong to her; she did own the business,' she asked, trying to break the ice.

'Indeed she did, and a very successful business it was too. Miss Susan went out riding everyday; she had three horses that she rode regularly. She loved those horses. It was my job to look after them and make sure they were ready when she wanted to ride them,' he explained.

'I'm writing a feature on 'Raines Equine Research Laboratories,' and the innovative techniques they pioneered in genetic cloning. I thought you might be able to help me with some information on Susan Raines, you know, what sort of a person she was, that sort of thing.' She finished her drink and waited for Johnny's reaction.

'I certainly can. She was a wonderful woman. When she died I didn't think I would ever get over it. I knew her from when she was a young girl; I used to work for her father you see. He bred horses, that's really how she got started, you could say it was in her blood.' He chuckled, then continued.

'She could be difficult at times. Knew her own mind, but she was determined to show the 'horse world' that she could clone a horse that would be the exact replica of it's parents, and with the same abilities. You know that she cloned 'Red Sunset', who won the Derby three times. Now that really upset a lot of race-owners and other 'toffs' in the 'hoof world' as she called them.'

He continued to talk about his former employee and friend for quite some time, painting George a good picture.

'It was tragic that she had to die while riding her favourite horse, 'Pepper Corn'. He was a beauty. Mr Raines had him shot after the accident, then, as soon as he could, he sold all the rest.'

'It must have been difficult for him,' she said, sympathetically.

'Difficult for him, not at all, he was never close to the animals or the business. That's probably why he couldn't wait to dispose of the business after her funeral,' he said bitterly.

'Oh, I didn't realise, but he must have been devastated after the accident.'

'I doubt it; they hadn't been close for a long time. They both had,' he paused awkwardly, 'someone else.'

'They did?' His revelation surprised her.

'Oh yes, it was no secret, She had been seeing Mr Fleiter, one of the genetic boffins, for some time.'

'Really? About the accident, the papers said she fell while jumping a wall.' The old man shook his head slowly.

'Strange, I still can't understand what happened. The horse could easily make that height; goodness knows what happened. They said he might have slipped; it had been raining, but the horse was unscathed. Whatever it was, it killed her outright. They said she hit her head on the wall.'

When the old man spoke George could see he had large gaps between his teeth. He sat back in his chair and finished his drink, then leant forward and said,

'You say you're writing about the business, so you'll not be interested in her accident. Sorry about rattling on, but I really miss her, and the horses.'

'On the contrary, I'm most interested. Could you possibly spare the time to show me where the accident happened, tomorrow?' she asked, looking into his misty eyes. His face lit up and the sparkle returned to his eyes as he gathered up the empty glasses.

'Time is one thing I have plenty of, I'd be only too glad to show you.'

Snapshot 169

Jenny returned the letter to its envelope, glanced at her computer screen, and quickly read the answer to her correspondent's plea for help.

Sometimes being the agony aunt for the Weekly News emotionally exhausted her. The people whose problems she addressed were sometimes highly emotional, and most genuinely depended upon her advice. Satisfied with her latest work, she pressed the send button; that would be in her column next week.

But there was one problem that she still had to deal with, closer to home. Her daughter had been seeing someone that she met during her last holiday.

When her daughter divulged the name of her boyfriend, stating that they hoped to be seeing each other frequently during the Christmas holidays, she asked Jenny if she would inform her dad about the relationship, especially since the name of her new friend was Harry, otherwise known to her husband as Detective Constable Ripley.

Snapshot 170

Jack had been home for two days and had already filled the lounge with an assortment of railway pamphlets, magazines and postcards, which could not be moved because he was 'sorting' them. Moving between rooms, wearing an old green cardigan with his half-rimmed glasses resting on top of head, he cross-referenced his railway memorabilia.

Jenny brought a tray of tea and biscuits into the room and sat down beside him. 'I've brought some tea. Have a rest, Jack, you've been at it all day.' She passed him a mug of tea.

'I enjoy sorting the cards, it's like the Forth Bridge; I'll never complete the work,' he grinned, taking a drink.

'I have something to tell you about Samantha.' Hearing this, Jack put the postcards onto the chair. He immediately recalled, how, when he was sat in the Windsor chair in front of the fire at the Golden Lion, he had pondered over the last meeting with his daughter; worried that something was bothering her.

'Is something wrong, what is it?' he asked, anxiously. Jenny half-smiled,

'She's all right, nothing to worry about.' She reached out and placed her hand on his knee to reassure him.

'It's just that she's seeing someone.'

'I knew there was something! Is this someone at university?' he reeled the words off quickly.

'No, it's here at home,' she explained quietly.

'Well, she isn't seeing much of him then, is she,' he said, relieved.

'They text and e-mail a lot, she sounds quite keen about him, she seems very happy.'

'Who is it? Do we know him?' In those two questions lay the concerns that Samantha had expressed when she first spoke to her mum about who she was seeing.

'Yes, we know him quite well.'

'We do?' said Jack, looking at Jenny, waiting for her to continue.

'Yes,' she said, teasing her husband.

'Well, are you going to tell me, or is it a secret?'

'No, it's not a secret. Samantha wanted you to know before she came home for the Christmas holidays,' she continued, spinning out the conversation.

'Jenny, I'm getting nervous.' He sensed his wife was playing with him.

'I know,' she giggled.

'Tell me!' he asked.

'It's Harry Ripley,' she blurted out, relieved at last to have told him.

'Ripley, my Ripley,' he stood up and walked around the room.

'Yes, apparently they met in the library, enjoyed talking, went out for a coffee, then later arranged a date. They got on really well and it wasn't until the second date when Harry told her what he did for a job that they realised a potential problem.

'Ripley; but he's much older than Sam.'

'He's five years older. She seems to like him a lot.'

'Well, I never,' he exclaimed.

'So, are you happy?'

'Are you?' he asked.

'Yes, he seems well behaved, and, like I say, Samantha really likes him.'

'Well, that's it then, I can understand they will have a lot in common.'

'You can?'

'Yes, he's very well educated; she could do a lot worse than young Ripley. God knows what the chief's going to say when he hears about it.'

'As long as you're happy about it, that's all that matters,' she said, taking hold of his hand.

'Does it really matter what we think?'

'Yes, it does to Samantha, and to Harry'

'Harry, I'll never get used to that, to me he's Ripley.'

'While you're on duty Jack, but in this house, he'll be Harry,' she said, firmly. The phone ringing interrupted the family discussion. Jenny answered, and then handed the phone to Jack with a knowing look that told him it was connected with work.

'Jack, sorry to disturb you at home, but I'm afraid we're off to Settle tonight.' The voice belonged to Chief Inspector Martin, and he didn't sound best pleased.

'Settle, tonight, why?' asked Jack, stunned.

'There's been a murder; someone's bumped off the lady who looks after the antique shop in Hawes, the one owned by Nick Hartford. I'll pick you up in one hour.'

'Him again! Right, see you then.' Jack replaced the phone, and turned to Jenny who was waiting for him to finish.

'Guess what.' She recognised the tone.

'I'll pack your bag.'

Snapshot 171

At last Nick had found the Lamb Inn where George was staying, only to find, disappointingly, that she had left for the day with one of the local residents. She was not expected back until later that afternoon.

Knowing that he would meet her later, he'd booked in to the hotel.

After unpacking, he enjoyed a warm bath. He had no idea what had brought her to this lovely village, but was sure he would find out when they met.

This time he would listen to her, and if he could, assist her. But, before she returned, it was time to try and grab some sleep.

Snapshot 172

Johnny led the way over the fields, through the woods and over the many gates; finally, just before George thought she would collapse from exhaustion, he signalled they had reached their destination.

'She loved riding in this area. I think she knew every blade of grass, so I suppose it was fitting that she died here.' His knuckles were bare-white as he leaned on and gripped the top bar of the five-bar gate, as he gazed out over the fields.

'She died near here?' asked George, having regained her breath.

'Right here; this is the wall where she fell.' He pointed to the wall next to the gate.

'What happened exactly?'

'Who knows? She must have somehow struck her head on the wall; even with her helmet on, it killed her.'

'When we spoke yesterday, you mentioned that 'Pepper Corn' could easily jump this height?'

'That's right, he could clear it with two feet to spare.'

'Two feet,' she exclaimed. 'Something must have happened to frighten her horse, to distract it perhaps?'

'You may be right, I've considered every possibility over and over, but I can't explain what happened,' he said, quietly.

'How long was she here before she was discovered?'

'When she didn't return, I grabbed Willie the stable lad and we went out to look for her and found 'Pepper Corn' grazing in a field over there, then I found her.'

He opened the gate and walked over to a spot covered in faded blue cornflowers. Bending down, he signalled to George to join him.

'This is the exact spot. I stayed with her while Willie went to meet the police and doctor.' He waved his hand over the grass.

'The doctor said she had a broken neck; death must have been instantaneous, she wouldn't have suffered. The police agreed with the doctor's assessment, and that was that; suddenly life changed for everybody.'

George left Johnny reflecting on the fateful fall that killed his employer and changed his life. She walked slowly along the wall, looking for anything that might give her a clue as to what spooked the horse into failing to clear the wall.

About sixty feet away from the wall, an old oak tree, bent and weathered, stood alone, it's branches reaching up into the sky like a giant umbrella.

She walked over and searched below the trunk, where its artery roots reached out before burying themselves into the earth. Her mind was working overtime; if anyone had wanted to spook the horse, this tree would have provided adequate cover. Looking over the wall, they would have seen Susan Raines emerging from the woods and riding over the field towards the wall, and then just as she was about to jump, they did something, but what?

She walked round in a wide circle looking, searching, for anything that would give her a clue.

'Find what you're looking for?' She looked up to see the old man grinning.

'Just looking to see if there are any clues to tell us why the horse was frightened,' she answered, shrugging her shoulders.

'I've already looked. After the doctor and police had reached their decision that it was just another riding accident, I scoured the area looking for clues to prove them wrong. Would you be interested in these?' He opened his left hand to reveal two cartridge shells.

'Where did you find them?' she asked, eagerly.

'Just there, where you were looking.' He pointed to the base of the oak tree.

'If these were fired, would it have been sufficient to scare the horse and cause the accident?'

'I've been around shotguns all my life. These,' he held them up, 'are 12 gauge steel magnum shot cases for use in a gun with a 76mm chamber; it's a high velocity shot for use with special gun barrels. Believe me, they would make a noise sufficient to startle any horse.'

'Well, you certainly know your guns. Did you show these to anyone, like the police?'

'Yes, I did, for what good it did. They suggested that a poacher would have used them. The case was wrapped up; everyone was happy with the accidental death verdict. Within ten days, she had been cremated, the horse put down, and the work force given one months notice. Susan Raines was history.'

'That's terrible.' She took the cartridge shells and examined them. 'What do you think may have happened?' she asked him.

'Like you suggested, if someone lay in wait here by the tree, he or she could have discharged the shotgun just as 'Pepper Corn' was about to jump. The blast would have been sufficient to make him pull away in mid flight and throw her. It would have been over in seconds. Then they could have made good their escape down the fields.'

He pointed down the field.

'Beyond the ridge there's an old road, it's mainly used by the farmer, but if they had some form of transport they could have disappeared easily that way; it leads to a minor B road after a couple of miles.'

'I think you're right, Johnny; someone was here waiting for Susan Raines and fired the shotgun.' She passed back the shot cases. 'But why, why would anyone want to do that?'

'That's a question I've been asking myself ever since that fateful day,' he said, reflectively.

They walked slowly back to the gate just as it started to rain.

Snapshot 173

'All very professional, Jack, do you think they're trying to impress us?' Martin said loudly as he got out of the car.

'Not at all, Detective Chief Inspector. We may be a country force but we are familiar with procedure,' called out Sgt Berry, surprising the three detectives.

'Oh god, it's that woman again,' whispered Martin to Jack. 'Hello Sergeant, didn't see you there. Now, what's so important that we've been dragged here once more?'

He ducked under the police tape surrounding the crime scene.

Sgt Berry grimaced, she resented his matter-of-fact manner, he should realise that 'the dead woman was highly respected in this tight-knit community.'

'This way, sir,' she opened the door and allowed both Martin and Jack through. They looked over the shop from inside the door, before moving carefully towards the back of the shop and the body of Spence, still sprawled over the table.

'Have your boys taken photographs?' Martin asked, casually.

'Yes,' she answered, following the two out-of-town detectives. Jack examined the body and pointed out the heavy bruising and cuts to her face and forehead.

'Paper knife on the floor, blade covered in blood,' called out Jack.

'No visible knife wound to the body that I can see. This is where her head has been banged against the wall; see the tiny fragments of blood and hair on the wall,' Martin pointed to a spot on the wall.

'More blood here on this chest of drawers, and on the floor,' continued Jack. They were both absorbed in the analysis of the murder scene. They moved round carefully, scribbling notes, calling out to each other. Jack moved over towards the door, following the trail of blood. Leaning out of the door he motioned over to Ripley who was setting up the camera on a tripod.

'Take some photographs of the murder scene,' he said as he patted Ripley on the back, 'note especially these points of interest.' He handed Ripley some scribbled notes, and then joined Sgt Berry.

'I know your lads have taken some photographs, but we always like to take our own snaps to study. Ripley's very good, does some wonderful close-ups; he has a fine eye for detail. Approximately what time was the victim found?' he asked the sergeant.

'Mrs Spencer was found by a paper boy at about 5.15pm,' she replied. The cold detachment they showed towards the victim made her shudder.

'Did he enter the shop?'

'Yes, you can't see the body from the doorway; he'd followed the trail of blood up the street.

'Right, we need to know what, if anything, he touched in there. Will you send someone to collect whatever he was wearing on his feet?' He smiled at her and returned to the shop.

She moved outside and found herself thinking of her twins, Nathan and Jessica, who were with their grandma; they would have had a late tea and would probably be playing with granddad. Her husband, Chris, would pick them up after his evening surgery and take them home.

'Sgt Berry.' A voice calling brought her back to the murder scene. 'Sgt, can you make arrangements for the body to be taken away?' Martin walked over to her, fastening the buttons on his overcoat.

'Have you any thoughts about the murder?' His directness surprised her.

'I don't really know sir. From what I've seen, she may have disturbed a robber; once discovered, he turned nasty.' She waited for Martin to offer some reaction to her suggestions.

'H'mm, perhaps. She has a broken neck; snapped like a chicken. We need to know if there's anything missing from the shop. Find Mr Hartford please, I need to speak with him,' he moved towards his car.

'Where did she live?'

'She shares a cottage with her husband at the end of the village, going up towards the fells.' Sgt Berry replied.

'Not anymore she doesn't. Anyone told her husband yet?' asked Martin.

'No sir.'

'Well, it would be better coming from you, being local to the area. Oh, and we'll need a formal ID, so please ask him if he'll do that tomorrow, say, about 10.30am. I'll see you at the morgue in the morning; there's nothing more we can do here tonight. Jack, let's be on our way, my throat's parched.'

'Ripley will be staying here for a while, he's very good at what he does, but best left alone to work.'

He climbed into the car. June Berry was fuming at his cold-hearted manner.

Suddenly, she heard his voice call out once more, as he leant out of the car window, and bellowed.

'This may be a long shot, but would you find out if any of the shops down this street have security cameras. If so, we want to see all the recordings made today. You can contact me at the Golden Lion. Oh, and can you give Ripley a lift back when he's finished?'

'Bloody cheek,' she muttered to herself as she watched him drive off.

Snapshot 174

'I need a doctor, I've been hurt bad, I'm bleeding pretty bad,' Angelo rapped off four word descriptions of his condition. Blandford immediately recognised the distress in Angelo's voice.

'What's happened?' asked Blandford, nervously.

'I've been stabbed.'

'Where are you?

'I'm in my car, I'm feeling faint… just pulled in… bleeding pretty fast… needed some fresh air…'

'Can't you come in?' Blandford enquired tactlessly.

'I need medical attention… I don't think I can make it.'

'Did you leave your calling card?'

'Yes… but it's damaged…'

'How badly?'

'The woman was difficult…

she found a knife…

plunged it into my side…

I took her out, it was a reflex action…she's dead...'

Blandford listened carefully to the Sicilian's explanation; already he knew what had to be done.

This was not the first time that he had cleaned up, but he hated it each time, and this would be no different.

'Ok, tell me where you are? Don't worry, I'm coming to bring you in.'

Blandford barked orders to a couple of young assistants; within five minutes they had all climbed into a Land Rover and were heading down the driveway.

Snapshot 175

The knock at the door woke Nick, then a quick glance at the alarm clock told him he had overslept. He opened the door to find George waiting impatiently.

'You've been sleeping, I can tell your eyes are still half shut,' she pushed her way past him and sat by the window.

'Why didn't you wait for me to return?'

'I wasn't sure how you would be with me; when you left, you were rather angry. When I didn't hear from you, I wasn't sure how you would be!' He walked over to sit with her. He was really pleased to be with her once more.

'I've tried to ring you but your mobile was either switched off or your battery had run out.' She reached forward and planted a wet kiss on his forehead.

'There, I forgive you for being such a stubborn so-and-so. Now get yourself decent and we'll go down and eat. I'm absolutely famished, and I have absolutely tons to tell you.'

Snapshot 176

Blandford parked the Land Rover twenty yards behind Angelo's car at the top of Sheepshead pass. He motioned to his two assistants to wait in the vehicle, grabbed a bag, and walked along the road to Angelo's car.

The Sicilian was covered in blood from the waist down. Blandford quickly assessed the situation; he lifted clothing to reveal the puncture wound. Angelo talked incessantly, most of it he ignored.

'I shall have to apply a large dressing before we move you, I afraid it's going to hurt,' he opened the bag and pulled out a silver flask.

'Here, take a drink of this brandy, it will help numb the pain.' Blandford stood back and waited as Angelo took off the top and took a large swig. The Sicilian let out a short sharp, groan; he tried to move his hand to reach for his throat, but never made it.

His lifeless body slumped onto the steering wheel.

Blandford signalled to the others, who then joined him and quickly doused the interior of the car with petrol.

Then they rolled it steadily to the edge of the roadway, struck a match and threw it into the car, which immediately burst into flames.

One final push, and the flaming car dropped into the valley below. Before the vehicle exploded at the bottom of the pass, Blandford and his two assistants were driving away.

Snapshot 177

Through most of the dinner, the wild trout starter, the fillet steak main course and the jam roly-poly with custard, George talked about her investigations into the deaths of the four women.
She continued unabated during the coffee, and now, when he was hoping to relax with a large brandy, unceasingly, she recounted every detail.

If the truth be known, he was full of admiration for all the work she had done and the ground she had covered. It seemed, from what he had heard, that she had uncovered a series of deaths, which, if they could be positively linked to Luzhkov, would finally bring him down.

He mulled over the information. If they could only show that these seemingly innocent deaths, were in fact murders…

'Nick, are you listening to me?' her raised voice interrupted his thoughts.

'Yes, of course, It's just such a lot to take in at one sitting,' he smiled.

'I know. What do you think?' she asked, looking at him wide-eyed.

'You were right. I think you're onto something. I want to help you.'

'Good, that's what I wanted to hear. This is the list of eight women who died in accidents.' She handed Nick the list of names.

'And you obtained this by just taking the top list of one hundred names in the FTSE index?' he asked, full of admiration.

'Yes.'

'So which name on the list are we investigating next?' George was thrilled with Nick's use of the word 'we'.'

'Jane Corsellus, she died in a climbing accident in the Lake District,' she answered.

'Where in the Lake District?' he asked.

'Buttermere.'

'Not too far from home,' he added, 'and which particular mountain was she climbing when the accident happened?'

'One called the Haystack.'

'Ah yes, it can be very difficult. Did she live in the Lake District?'

'No, their first home was in Mallord St, Chelsea. They had a second home in Buttermere, which is where she spent a lot of her time. She was also an accomplished watercolorist, apparently her work sold quite well. I did some research on her while I was in London.'

'You have been busy. And I suppose that after her death her husband remarried?'

'That's right, her husband Digby, is head of the Corsellus Fund Management Group. According to the papers, it's an extremely prosperous business on both sides of the Atlantic. And yes, eleven weeks after the funeral he remarried; the bride's name was Olga Preskaka, from Kiev.'

'Any connection with Luzhkov?'

'Not that I know of, yet.'

'Well, George, like I said earlier, I want to help, the more I hear of your investigations, the more I'm convinced you're onto something. Have you wondered why the police haven't been involved?' he asked searchingly.

'Well, they have as far as the individual accidents are concerned...'

'Exactly,' interrupted Nick, 'individual accidents dealt with by individual forces. You've brought them together and identified common links. Namely, each husband has taken a new wife of Soviet origin, but there the commonality ends. There's no contact between the couples, they are strangers; we must assume the common link to each of them is Luzhkov.'

'We know he attended a couple of the weddings,' said George.

'Yes, but I think he's known to each bride. But what is he up to?' quizzed Nick.

'I've been thinking about just that,' said George excitedly, 'and the answer I've come up with is **information**!'

'Information,' Nick whispered, thoughtfully.

'Information about each company passed to Luzhkov by the wives,' she suggested.

'Brilliant! He has an endless source of information about each business; collectively, that information could give him the edge in insider dealings on the stock market.'

'But how do we prove it?'

'By continuing what you've already started, George. We keep on sifting, investigating each name on that list for that one piece of evidence that may connect Luzhkov to the murders.'

'Great, then we'll make our way to the Lake District tomorrow,' she smiled, raising her glass to toast the idea.

'Cheers,' the glasses clinked together. 'Sounds good to me, but right now, let's have another large brandy each, we have to celebrate finding each other.'

He collected the glasses and made his way to the bar.

Snapshot 178

The flames lashed around the garments in the oil drum, burning ferociously. The white-hot fibres crumbled in the furnace-like fire, like Angelo, his personal belongings were being cremated in the flames until there was nothing left. Lorenzo stood watching as Blandford dropped the last papers into the flames.

'That's it, there is nothing to connect us with him, he was never here.' Blandford spoke coldly, without emotion.

'He was a good man,' Lorenzo murmured. On hearing this, Blandford turned angrily and snapped,

'He was careless; he did not obey my instructions. That's why he's dead to the world and dead to us; there's no room for sentiment in this organisation. Now I want you to hang around the fur shop; keep your eyes and ears open. Listen to the local gossip; find out what you can about the investigation. What have they discovered, listen to rumours, anything, and let me know if you see Hartford,' snapped Blandford.

'Yes Mr Blandford.' Lorenzo knew that Mr Luzhkov's personal assistant was not a man to be crossed.

Snapshot 179

The local farmer's market was held on the third Saturday in the month and was popular with locals and visitors alike. With about a dozen stalls selling local produce from meat, cheese and vegetables to home made jam and pickles, from eight in the morning until around mid-day, it was always busy. Jack and Martin had been wandering around, inspecting the produce and listening to the local gossip surrounding the murder in the local antique shop in Hawes. Martin bought three jars of relish, and then moved on to the next stall, where customers were invited to sample a variety of local cheeses.

'Have you tasted that Wensleydale Cheddar? There's no taste like it,' whispered Jack over Martin's shoulder.

'They all taste good to me. Do you know, moving between these stalls, tasting various foods, you could have a good meal out, and it's all free,' laughed Martin.

'Try that Cheddar,' coaxed Jack. Martin reached over and grabbed a lump, took a look at it then dropped it in his mouth and started chewing slowly, savouring the flavour.

'By God Jack, it's a bit strong, that.'

'A bloke over there told me that it's made in Hawes, from milk collected from within a thirty-five mile radius. All the cows, he said, 'graze in sweet limestone meadows rich in herbs.'

How about that, it's almost like poetry,' laughed Jack, grabbing a large slab of Cheddar and handing it to the young girl behind the stall.

'The only sweet things I've seen in the meadows round here are large lumps of cow clap, and that certainly smells rich,' laughed Martin, shaking Jack's shoulder with his large outstretched hand. The pair walked off between the stalls and up the street towards the Golden Lion.

'Detective Chief Inspector Martin, what time do you call this?' The voice had an unmistakeable tone; Martin looked up to see Sgt Julie Berry standing beside an unmarked squad car.

'I've been waiting forty minutes, you do remember asking me to collect you at 9.30am.' she said sharply.

'Yes, I remember very well, thank you Sergeant. We've been shopping, mixing with the locals. When I've put these in my room I'll join you,' Martin held a plastic bag high for her to see.

'That man is so exasperating,' she said, loud enough for Jack to hear.

'We were down in plenty of time to meet you, but then noticed the market,' said Jack, trying to placate the Sergeant.

'We wandered over, had a look and, with so many people around we took the opportunity to mingle, and see if there was any local gossip about the murder. We also bought a few items, sort of blended in.' Jack showed his bag to the Sergeant, and then also left her to go inside.

'Oh, I've never heard so much bullshit,' she muttered under her breath.

Snapshot 180

It was already past lunchtime when Nick and George arrived outside the Bridge Hotel in Buttermere.

'Well it's too late to do any serious walking today, George, so once we've settled into the hotel why don't we split up. If you want, I'll see what I can find about Jane Corsellus in the local press while you visit the family home; what do you think?'

Nick pulled out the bags from the boot and started carrying them into the inn.

'Sounds good to me,' said George, following Nick into the bar that also doubled as a reception area.

Snapshot 181

Sgt Berry emerged from the last shop on the main street carrying a bag full of CCTV camera tapes from the shops near where the murder took place. Walking back towards the antique shop, she greeted a number of locals, in addition to policing the community, she and her family lived here and knew most people.

The murder of Mrs Spencer had shocked the whole community of Wensleydale. Spence belonged to a family spanning four generations; they had lived and worked the land, keeping large flocks of tough Swaledale sheep high on the fells while looking after herds of cows on the lush pastures of the low land.

Now the community closed ranks; they knew how to look after their own. If anyone had seen or knew anything about the murder they would inform Sgt Berry, that's how it was here in Hawes, and that was something that Detective Chief Inspector Martin and his sergeant could never appreciate coming as they did from a widely dispersed built-up area like Huddersfield. She could see Martin talking to Jack outside the shop; they both turned and waited as she walked slowly towards them.

'Are those the videos?' asked Jack politely.

'That's all of them,' she handed over the bag to the sergeant.

'Forensics have finished their work here. Is there any news of Hartford?' asked Martin abruptly.

'I'm afraid not, no one seems to know where he is.'

'Well keep at it, we need to establish if any antiques are missing from the premises and Hartford is the only person who can give us that information.'

Martin seemed distinctly grumpier than usual, Berry thought.

'How did the ID of the victim go?' he asked.

'Mr Spencer was very brave,' she replied.

'I'd like you to ask him if his wife had mentioned anything unusual, you know, strangers hanging round, anyone taking an interest in a particular antique, anyone asking questions, you know the sort of thing,' Martin reeled off the instructions to Sgt Berry.

'I'd rather not if you don't mind,' she replied.

'But I do mind sergeant; you know the man, he knows you. Now we want to make this as painless as possible for him at this particular time. Contact me this evening at the Golden Lion.'

Sgt Berry stared at the Chief Inspector who had admonished her, but he turned away and walked back inside the shop.

Jack, sensing that she was about to follow him inside and possibly protest against her treatment, stepped between her and the door.

'If you don't mind sergeant,' he placed his hand gently on her arm.

'Best thing would be, if, when you've spoken to Mr Spencer, ask for me at the hotel, and I'll pass the information on.'

Jack spoke in a low, soft, tone, contrary to that used by the Detective Chief Inspector. Jean Berry relaxed.

'Do you always protect him?' she asked, with a hint of a smile.

'Not often, but we are away from everything that is familiar to him. We don't think it was robbery; there was still money in the till, we just have to make sure it wasn't robbery to order, and the only way we can do that is to establish if anything is missing.'

'Alright sergeant, I'll ask Mr Spencer, but this is not my enquiry.'

'I know…' Jack was interrupted by Sgt Berry's phone ringing. She listened briefly, acknowledged the call politely, then, the call finished, she returned the phone to her pocket.

'That was the station in Settle, a car has been found by some walkers, burnt out at the bottom of Sheepshead Pass. There's a body inside, probably the driver. I have to go and investigate. Don't worry, I'll see Mr Spencer and be in touch.' She emphasised the last three words.

'I thought you said this was a quiet patch,' said Jack, jovially.

'It was before you came.'

Snapshot 182

'I love this part of the country; imagine what it must have been like before the invention of the motorcar,' mused Nick, pouring more wine.

'Lots of horses,' teased George, holding out her glass for a refill.

'Seriously, it must have been wonderful. I could almost imagine we were about to bump into Wordsworth and Coleridge strolling through the meadow, in deep conversation, when we met by Lake Buttermere this afternoon,' Nick laughed.

'Well, don't get too carried away with romanticising about the past, because tomorrow, we have a long day ahead of us trying to determine how Jane Corsellus met her death,' George countered.

'I know, you don't need to worry, I shall lead all the way to the very top of Haystacks.'

'Will you indeed?'

'From the reports in the local press, printed at the time of her death, Jane Corsellus must have been at the summit of Haystacks when she got caught in low cloud. The reports said that instead of staying where she was, she tried to make her way down, took a wrong turn and fell about 150 feet to her death. Seems straightforward really.'

'They always do. Someone is extremely proficient at making murder look accidental,' George said forcefully. 'That's why we have to sift through every clue that is available to us.'

'What about the house?' asked Nick.

'Beautiful, it's a sixteenth century whitewashed cottage sitting in its own garden with a fast running beck at the back. A perfect setting for someone who spent a large amount of her time painting the local scenery.'

'What did you find out about her apart from her love of painting?' asked Nick.

'I spoke to the local Vicar who knew her well; he told me that she was an avid fell walker who loved nothing more than to set off shortly after sun-up, reach the peaks and spend hours sketching before coming down before the light faded. According to the vicar, she actually took part in several rescues from the surrounding peaks,'

George sipped her wine and waited for Nick to respond.

'So it seems as if she knew the surrounding area intimately and walked extensively. Mrs Corsellus assisted in mountain rescue; doesn't suggest that she was someone who would take unnecessary risks. This all has a familiar ring to it! Tomorrow, let's try and follow the route she took, see what we can discover,' suggested Nick.

'I've invited the vicar to accompany us, he often walked with Jane and knows the routes she would have followed.'

George finished the last of her wine at one go.

'Early start, so I'm off to bed.'

Nick was left pondering about their new companion for the next day's climb. It was a good idea to have someone accompany them who was familiar with Mrs Corsellus, perhaps he would be able to provide them with clues. If this was another murder, then someone knew her movements, habits and vulnerability. Nick took a stroll round the gardens.

The night was warm, the early evening stars twinkled against the dark shadows of the fells, and as he walked slowly, his mind turning over endless possibilities.

Snapshot 183

Jack settled into the now familiar Windsor chair at the side of the stone fireplace in the Golden Lion. Martin was still getting changed and Ripley was attending the post-mortem on Mrs Spencer. No sooner had he settled than he heard the familiar voice of Sgt Berry. To his surprise, she had discarded her familiar uniform and was wearing a brown and blue floral print dress. She sat down next to him.

'This is a surprise. I expected you to ring,' he said, standing. 'Can I get you a drink?'

'My husband is getting me one, thank you, Sergeant,' she said, giving him a large smile. 'We're on our way to the annual cricket club dinner dance.'

'Sounds good fun. Please call me Jack, we're off duty,' he said, settling into the Windsor once more.'

'I spoke with Mr Spencer; he hasn't heard from Mr Hartford. He can't recall his wife mentioning anything unusual about customers in the shop. She often used to chat with him about large or unusual purchases, but had not done so for a while. He just assumed the business had been quiet.'

'Fine,' said Jack.

'There was something you might be interested in; you remember I received a call about the vehicle which had been found at the bottom of the Sheepshead Pass?'

At this point her husband brought over a drink, acknowledged Jack with a raised hand and returned to the bar.

'The car and the driver had been burnt out, but we're pretty sure it was alight before falling down the fell, and we also believe that the driver was dead before it was set alight.'

She took a sip of her gin and tonic, letting Jack digest the information, then added.

'Forensics found a stab wound in the corpse. We'll know more after the post-mortem.'

'Now that is interesting. Forensics is sure it was a stab wound?' Jack asked.

'Absolutely; despite the burning, when they pulled back the victim's clothes, you could clearly see the puncture wound,' she watched as Jack churned over this information.

'What time is the post-mortem?' asked Jack.

'Eleven in the morning; pretty early for a Sunday. Shall I tell Dr Blears you will attend?'

'You bet. Make sure you don't drink too much tonight, Sergeant, I think it would be a good idea if you picked us up in the morning. I want to see if the puncture wound could have been caused by the paper knife we found on the floor of the antique shop.' Jack was excited by the information that Sgt Berry had given him.

'It looks like Mrs Spencer stabbed her attacker; probably from sheer terror, then he finished her. Were there any clues as to the driver's identity?' he asked, almost willing Berry to answer in the affirmative.

'Afraid not,' she answered, finishing her drink. 'I'll have to go now, see you tomorrow.' Turning towards Jack she said, 'I'll pick you up about 10.30, please make sure you're all ready this time. Especially you know who!'

'Have a good evening Sergeant, and don't you worry about tomorrow,' Jack raised his glass towards the departing June Berry and her husband.

'Jack, was that Sgt Berry I saw just leaving?' asked Martin.

'Yes, it was, and I have some very interesting information for you. Sit down, I'll go and get the drinks.'

Snapshot 184

A stiff, constant, cold breeze made the excursion much more difficult than Nick or George had imagined. Long, steady slopes, together with the narrowest of paths made the journey tiring.

The vicar accompanying them stopped periodically to point out places of interest, but otherwise he set a cruel pace that they found difficult to maintain.

'I never realised I was this unfit,' moaned George.

'By the time we had passed the old slate factory and quarry I was knackered,' joined in Nick. 'And that seems ages ago, we seem to have been climbing for ever.'

'Don't worry, the vicar says we're stopping at Innominate Tarn for a hot drink,' called George breathlessly.

'I would much prefer a stiff drink, thank you,' groaned Nick, struggling to keep his foothold on loose stones as he followed the vicar.

After weaving along and amidst the rocky landscape they eventually reached the desolate tarn, where the vicar, who was carrying the largest backpack, produced two flasks of hot tea, which he handed to his two exhausted companions.

'That must be the best tea I've ever tasted,' said Nick, sprawled over a rock.

'I agree wholeheartedly. Could I have some more, please Vicar?' George held out her cup, awaiting a refill.

'When we've rested a little, we can take the path up to the summit of Haystack, or if you wish to see where Jane was found after her fall, then we could follow that small sheep trail around the side.' Having given them a choice, he waited until the two of them discussed the options. Although tired, Nick wanted to reach the summit to see the area from where Jane Corsellus fell. George agreed, but thought a visit along the sheep trail would be useful. The vicar suggested showing Nick to the summit, then descending to join George so he could show her the exact spot where Jane was found after her fall.

Nick couldn't help but admire the wiry old man's endurance.

'God, where do you get all your stamina from?' blurted Nick without thinking.

'Exactly, he is my inspiration in all things,' chuckled the vicar, much to Nick's embarrassment. George giggled so much at Nick's gaffe she made an excuse and escaped down to the tarn.

'Look, vicar, I didn't mean to blaspheme or anything like that,' explained Nick.

'Don't give it another thought. Now, shall we get going; those clouds in the distance look very heavy, we don't want to get caught up here.' The ascent was arduous with twisting paths and deep gullies on either side, dropping down a few hundred feet.

The views, when Nick could bring himself to look, were outstanding, but mostly he was too busy making sure he didn't lose his foothold.

Each step up the incline was, for him, an effort of intense concentration. The vicar, on the other hand walked with a spring in his step and a smile on his lips, much to Nick's annoyance. He never stopped pointing out the various beauty spots;

'Over there we have High Stile Ridge, while to the left we have Buttermere and Crummock Water,' cried the vicar. 'Just a little more and we'll be there, Nick.'

George found following the small sheep tracks around the side of the steep slopes precarious, and her progress was slow. At various intervals she came across large clusters of boulders that offered her a welcome breather.

It was during just one such rest she began to recollect how she and Leslie would often take off and spend hours walking hand in hand, talking, talking, talking. They would share every secret, every thought, and every wish. Two friends so devoted they could not imagine a time when they would not be together. Their plans included joint weddings, houses next to each other, babies growing up together; they even agreed that if one divorced the other would follow! Dreams that disappeared forever with Leslie's death after she threw herself off the multi-storey building.

'Why?' the question had been asked a thousand times.

The memories of her beloved friend she would cherish forever, but right now they belonged in the past, and George had no intention of going there again; her life had changed considerably since those days.

She continued her journey round the slope looking for any clue that might indicate how Jane Cornelius's accident had occurred in this empty rocky landscape.

Nick clambered up the last stone-strewn path and suddenly found himself at the summit. The vicar was collecting a couple of large stones; he passed one to Nick.

'We must put one at the top of the cairn; it's tradition when you reach the top,' he said, excitedly. Nick knew better than to argue, he just followed obediently and placed his stone onto the top.

'Now, let me show you where I think Jane fell from,' the vicar moved quickly along the top until he came to a spot that was extremely narrow.

'It must have been somewhere here, presumably, because we found her body at the bottom below.' Nick kneeled down to peer down the steep rocky incline in the direction the vicar indicated.

'I'll leave you to wander round; I'll go and join George. Meet us later,' the vicar called out already scrambling over the rock-strewn path.

Nick pulled himself upright; there was nothing to see down the slope except rocks. He studied the stony pathway; it was easily wide enough for two people.

'Let's suppose,' he thought to himself, 'that she was carrying 'bits and bats' when she fell, they would have gone with her. But nothing apart from the back-pack she was carrying was found near her body.' 'Let's imagine,' he thought, 'that someone was here, and they fought, and he pushed her, she could have dropped something.

Nothing was reportedly found, so her attacker must have taken whatever it was she dropped, or, he had disposed of the 'bit and bats', but where?' Nick looked around but there was nothing. *'What if,'* he thought, suddenly, *'her attacker had thrown everything down the opposite slope, the rescuers would not search there, why would they, she was just another statistic; accidents were a regular occurrence in this part of the country.'*

He retraced his steps back down Haystack until he reached the point where George took the sheep trail. Carefully, he inched his way along the opposite slope, loose rocks made finding a firm foothold difficult, but over the years hundred of sheep had moved along the side and left a firm and definitive narrow track.

Shuffling forward, arms outstretched he moved along, steadily grabbing tufts of blue moor grass and rigid buckler fern where he could, all the time searching the area for any sign of discarded belongings.

The vicar spied George resting between two rocks, gazing out over the expanse of the lake below.

'Buttermere, it's beautiful from here isn't it. The name literally means 'the lake by the dairy pastures.' Jane never tired of painting it,' he called out.

'I wonder if she did any sketching on the day she died,' said George, glad to see the vicar.

'I doubt it, no sketch pad or pencils were found on her to suggest she did,' said the vicar.

'If we continue just a little further I'll show you where we found her.' He scrambled past George and edged his way along the narrow path. After a short while he pointed out the spot where they had found the body. George looked around; an ice axe stuck in-between the rock was all that could be seen.

'Not much left to celebrate a life,' said the vicar taking a white ribbon from his pocket and tying it around the ice axe handle. 'I always leave a ribbon as a tribute to her life whenever I come up here; she was a dear friend.'

'Well,' he said, 'if you've seen enough we should be making our way down, those dark clouds look menacing.'

With that, he once more pushed past her and started back along the ridge. George had not noticed the clouds until he pointed them out, then for the first time she realised how close they seemed and was surprised at how fast they moved over the summit.

Nick had progressed around the slope, and, much to his satisfaction had come upon a wide expanse of fallen rock that gave him some respite from the narrow sheep ledge. He estimated that this would have been below the path he had trod at the summit above. He began searching the area, looking for any clue, but the surface revealed nothing. Recklessly, he climbed up over the rocks, looking and feeling in between rocks. Eventually, he could go no further up the surface safely.

Looking up, he could barely see the outline of the top of Haystack. He noticed the dark misty clouds edging their way over the first lip of the rocky outcrop at the summit, so carefully he tested each foothold and gradually manoeuvred his way back down to the narrow ledge from where he could retrace his steps back to the main route. Suddenly, out of the corner of his eye he saw something glistening between two folds of rock. He reached down and grasped a round metallic object, he pulled it out and rubbed it on his sleeve to clean the surface to reveal the initials J.C. It was a compact. Elated, he shoved it into his pocket.

More aware of the advancing cloud, he, quickly as safety would allow, made his way back to the main pathway.

Snapshot 185

Having scrambled his way down, with the low swirling cloud moving just behind him for most of the way, Nick was worn out. Having reached the slate factory he slumped down on the grass to catch his breath. The path was wide enough now to follow despite the mist. Where were George and the vicar?

He fully expected meeting them on the descent. He pulled out the compact and examined it more closely. Apart from the initials J.C. it was just like any other compact he had ever seen. He opened it; one side was a mirror, the other, contained a small pad and compact powder. He held it to his nose and took a sniff; it was very pleasing. A voice disturbed him.

'Hello there, we wondered where you were.' There was no mistaking the voice of the vicar; he still had a spring to his step as approached. Nick closed the compact and slipped it back inside his pocket.

'We fully expected to meet you on the way down, George was quite worried about you, so here I am,' he said, sitting next to Nick.

'Is she alright?' asked Nick.

'Exhausted, cold and hungry, she's returned to the hotel' said the vicar.

'Did you find anything interesting?'

'No, not a thing,' lied Nick.

'We'd best get back then,' said the vicar, picking up Nick's backpack, 'I'll take this for you.'

Snapshot 186

'Sgt Berry do you ever put the heating on, it's absolutely freezing in here?' asked Martin, sitting behind his desk with his overcoat fully buttoned and the collar pulled up.

'Certainly not, it's far too early. We don't usually put it on until we've had the first frost,' she said, winking at Jack.

'Come on, Jack, let's finish off here and get back to the hotel, at least they'll have a warm fire,' grumbled Martin, ignoring Berry's sarcasm.

'I've nearly finished this report. Cheer up, Ripley's gone to make some tea,' Jack turned to Sgt Berry.

'Sgt, do you think you could find us some biscuits, digestives preferably.'

'I'll see what I can do,' she said.

'That woman gets on my nerves. We don't put the heating on until the first frosts,' mumbled Martin.

'I think you'll find the feelings mutual. She'll be glad when we've finished here and returned home. She was only ribbing you about the heating,' said Jack.

'I know, Jack, I know, but she still irritates me. She makes it perfectly clear that this is her station, and we're in the way. Where is Ripley with that tea?'

'That's finished my report,' Jack leaned back in his chair, ignoring Martin's whingeing, he continued. 'It's not been such a bad day; the post mortem on Mrs Spencer was straightforward, we know she died from a broken neck. The spots of blood left in the shop were group A+. We know the dead man found in the car had the same blood group, and his puncture wound matches exactly the length of the paper knife found in the shop. The man in the car killed Mrs Spencer.'

'But who was the man in the car?' asked Martin.

'Good question. Well, we know he didn't die from the stab wound, but from cyanide poisoning; there was no smoke in his lungs from the fire in the vehicle. He was dead before it was pushed over the fell. So we are looking for the man who administered the cyanide; find him and we'll know the identity of the dead man and the reason why he killed Mrs Spencer,' reasoned Jack.

'Another bloody dead end. Where the hell is Ripley with that tea?' growled Martin.

'We still have forensics working on trying to identify the owner of the vehicle, and the results of dental checks with local dentists are due tomorrow. I'll find out where Ripley is.'

Having tried to reassure Martin regards the investigation, Jack went off to find out what had happened to their refreshments.

Snapshot 187

When Nick reached the hotel he had just about used all his energy reserves. The climb up Haystacks had been more arduous than he had anticipated. Almost tumbling into the bar he ordered a double brandy, found a quiet corner and slumped into a deep armchair.

Having refreshed herself with a soak in a hot bath, George threw on some casual clothes and went down stairs to wait for Nick in the bar. When he did finally return, she guessed, this would be his first stopping off point. Armed with a large refreshing gin and tonic, she walked round the large lounge bar looking for a suitable seat, and recognized Nick slumped in an armchair by the corner window, fast asleep.

'Nick, are you ready for another walk?' she teased, then repeated her question until he started to stir.

'You really are joking, every bone in my body feels like it's been displaced,' he said, grabbing the glass of brandy and finishing it off.

'Come on sleepy head, what you need is a long hot soak, then you'll feel great,' she signalled the waiter for service.

'What did you discover?' asked Nick.

'Space, and lots of it. The only evidence that the body of Jane Corsellus was ever there is a makeshift memorial with an ice-axe.' She ordered more drinks from the waiter, who upon hearing the word 'body', made a quick exit. 'Did you come up with anything?' she asked.

Nick fumbled inside his crumpled jacket pocket and pulled out the powder compact. He placed it on the table in front of George, who looked it over.

'J.C., her initials,' said Nick. 'I found it down the slope on the opposite side to where she fell. My guess is that she dropped the compact during a struggle, then, when she was tossed over the side, her attacker disposed of the compact by throwing it away. I found it lodged in between some rocks.'

'That's great, another clue.' She opened the compact and sniffed. 'Nice smell,' she said, closing the compact.

'Yes, I thought so,' agreed Nick.

'But it doesn't get us any closer to finding the killer. If only we could find something that would lead us to who is responsible for the deaths of all these women,' George said as she put the compact in her bag.

'Well, if Luzhkov is behind these killings, we'll need to start digging into his business affairs if we are going to find any evidence,' said Nick, taking a drink. That's where the answer will be; it's my guess that everything has been to done to give him an advantage.'

'An advantage, what sort of advantage?' asked George.

'Financial muscle, power, status, call it what you will. He'll always want to be one step ahead of the big game, without ever being seen to get his hands dirty.' Nick finished off his brandy.

'Now I'm off to have that hot bath, then I'm going to ring Spence; she worries when she doesn't hear from me for a while. I'll meet you here for dinner in one hour.'

George was left pondering over what Nick had said. Certainly, in each of the murders so far, a great deal of planning had been undertaken to ensure that each woman's death looked like an accident. If Nick was right, then each woman must have been selected simply because she had the misfortune to be married to a husband who Luzhkov had chosen because of his financial or business acumen, and one that would be most beneficial to the Russian's business empire.

Snapshot 188

Having satisfied himself with the quality of the pictures from the night vision lenses on the outdoor security cameras, Blandford signed off the final checklist. Mr Luzhkov, still in his London residence, was not due back for at least another two weeks, by which time all the new security features would be fully working. Blandford noted on screen four that Lorenzo had just entered the building, so he left the security office to meet him.

'Lorenzo, what have you to tell me?' He guided the Sicilian into the library.

'Not a great deal.' Lorenzo said, as he sat uninvited in leather Queen Ann chair, which, although irritating to Blandford, he let pass without comment.

'Surely the police investigation is causing some comment in the village,' suggested Blandford.

'A little; these people, they do not say much. Everyone is distressed by the death of the lady in the antique shop. But all they do is gather together, and gossip in the street or in the local pub,' drawled Lorenzo.

He took out a packet of cigarettes and pulled one out as if to smoke. This was too much for Blandford, who rushed over to the Sicilian, and snatched the packet out of his hand.

'What is this, have you no respect. Who do you think you are, here, in Mr Luzhkov's library, sitting down uninvited, then daring to light a cigarette?' With one sweep of his backhand he caught Lorenzo across the cheek, drawing blood where his gold signet ring cut deep into the startled Sicilian's flesh.

'Now you tell me if you have seen or heard anything that would suggest a connection to us!'

'Nothing, nothing at all,' cried Lorenzo anxiously.

He had misread Blandford's friendly manner in ushering him into the library as a gesture of comradeship in the light of everything that had taken place. It was a mistake; he staggered backwards, holding his hand to the bleeding wound.

'They found Angelo's body in the car, but do not know his identity. The word on the streets is that the woman in the antique shop was killed when she disturbed someone trying to rob her.' Blandford listened and stared angrily at the Sicilian, whose blood had began to seep through his fingers.

He dismissed the injured Lorenzo with a curt gesture of his hand.

'I will speak to you later,' said Blandford, dismissively.

Lorenzo made a hasty exit, glad to be out of the personal assistant's company. He had misinterpreted Blandford's friendly gesture; he would not make that mistake again.

He shuddered, as his thoughts turned to his comrade Angelo, and how he had met his death at the hands of Blandford.

Snapshot 189

After changing for dinner George ordered two cold beers and settled down to read the menu, while waiting for Nick.

The day's strenuous exercise, walking up Haystacks, had sharpened her appetite. Very soon, Nick joined her; he sat upright, no greeting or gesture. She sensed his unease and realised immediately something was wrong. She didn't have to wait long.

'Spence is dead!' he blurted out. The words hit her consciousness, but were immediately rejected; the meaning of what she heard was unacceptable. She knew he would not utter such a sentence unless it was true, but how could this have happened to Spence and why?

'Dead?' she uttered, feebly.

'Yes.'

'But how?'

'She was killed in a robbery at the shop.'

'Oh, my God. Nick I'm so sorry.'

'We have to go home,' he said.

'Go?'

'Yes, straight away.'

'Of course.'

'The police have been trying to trace us, they want to interview me,' he said, as if in a trance.

'When did it happen?'

'Thursday or Friday I think, I'm not sure. I couldn't concentrate on what they were saying.'

'I can't believe it,' she gasped, tears rolling down her cheeks. The menu she had been reading so enthusiastically fell to the floor. Nick moved over to sit beside her.

'I know, it seems unreal,' he said holding her. Unable to contain the tears any longer, George, once in his arms, cried unrelentingly.

Snapshot 190

'Ah, Ripley, I'm over here,' shouted Jack, to the young detective who made his way over towards his sergeant.

'Where have you been, we've all been wondering where you were?'

'The antique shop, I went over to take one more look. While I was there the phone rang, it was Hartford.'

'Really, did you tell him?' asked Jack.

'Yes.'

'How did he take it?'

'Much as you'd expect, he was pretty cut up. I advised him to return immediately as we need to speak to him about the crime. Do you want another drink?'

'I thought you'd never ask, bitter please.' Ripley took the glass.

'Oh, and bye the way, Jenny told me about you and Samantha. You have my approval Harry, just let's keep it separate from work,' said Jack, taking Ripley by surprise.

'Right Sergeant, thank you, err... I'll get the beer,' he turned and left Jack smiling with satisfaction.

Snapshot 191

The police tape, cordoning off the antique shop, blew gently in the breeze. Having driven straight to meet Detective Chief Inspector Martin at the station where they were both interviewed, Nick and George were now given protective clothing before they could enter the 'crime scene,' as it was now referred to.

'The sergeant is going to take you into the shop, you will follow him; remember this is still a crime scene. What I want you to do is look around the premises and tell him if anything is missing,' explained Martin.

'I understand,' said Nick, unsure about how he would feel looking over where Spence had been killed. The sergeant fumbled with the keys in the door, then groped for the light switch on the inside several times before successfully locating it.

'Try to follow in my footsteps if you can sir, feel free to look around, but please, don't touch anything without asking me first,' the sergeant said bluntly before moving inside.

Nick followed; he could see that items were strewn where they had fallen during the attack. After a few steps he noticed the blood stains on the floor, carefully marked out with yellow tape. The sergeant explained that these belonged to the assailant. Nick caught sight of a broken Meissen harlequin figure; the sight of it reminded him how Spence used to give it prominent position, he could clearly see the impressed 'OD45' on the rockwork base.

'You noticed something?' asked Jack, curiously.

'A broken figure.'

'Was it valuable?' The question was asked in a routine, matter-of-fact way. The sergeant stood close to Nick looking at the broken pieces.

'She loved this figure more than anything else in the shop, I swear, sometimes she would go out of her way to put off prospective buyers,' said Nick.

'Worth a lot then, was it?' Jack repeated his question.

'About two and half thousand,' said Nick.

'Blimey, mind you, you'll have it insured I expect,' said Jack, unaware of the hurt his casual remark had caused.

'Money is the last thing on my mind at this moment sergeant,' snapped Nick incredulously. Jack winced at the callowness of his own remark.

'I'm sorry, I didn't mean any offence,' said Jack, placing his hand on Nick's shoulder. Nick nodded, acknowledging the sergeant's apology.

'We really need to know if anything is missing, to try to establish the motive for this attack,' explained Jack. 'We couldn't find a safe; did Mrs Spencer take home the takings each day, or did you put them into a safe deposit box?' asked Jack.

'The safe is there,' Nick pointed to a plain-framed mirror on the wall.

'Clever stuff, let's have a look inside to see if anything is missing,' suggested Jack, moving over to the mirror and trying to move it. 'It's fixed!'

'There's only one way anyone could get into this safe, and that is, if either Spence or I opened it. The mirror is part of the security unit, there's also a camera in there that operates on sensors; it starts filming whenever anyone enters the premises.'

'Well, I never, open it please,' Jack requested firmly.

He suddenly realised that when they questioned Mrs Spencer and Mr Hartford earlier, about the man who had spoken with Ronson, Fray and Lumpy in this shop, no-one had mentioned the hidden camera, but that would wait.

Nick placed his hand on the bottom right corner of the mirror, a small red square appeared and Nick leaned forward and looked into the square. Within moments, the mirror moved and slid out of sight to reveal a door and various slots to the left.

Nick opened the door and looked inside and pulled out a leather satchel.

'Everything is as it should be,' He thrust the satchel towards the sergeant, who examined the contents.

'And the film from the camera?' asked Jack. Nick closed the door, pressed a button, and a silver-cased hard disk was ejected, he passed it to the sergeant and explained,

'It's 120 gigabyte, we found it films, on average, a week's business.'

'Thank you, but you never mentioned this before, ' said Jack, unable to resist the challenge.

'Before?'

'When we visited your house, we specifically told you about the old Russian gentleman who had found a bundle of notes in the street, and how he related this story to your fiancée and other customers. You didn't mention the camera then.'

'Like I've just explained, sergeant, after one week of filming, the hard drive is wiped clean, and we start again. There would have been no point.'

Jack examined the silver box; the fact that they had not known about this vital piece of evidence earlier, and how it may have changed the whole course of the investigation, was a huge misjudgement on someone's part.

'Please continue looking around the shop, but remember, don't touch anything. I'm just going to see the Chief Inspector.'
Having heard what Jack had learnt in the shop, Martin was livid and without hesitation proclaimed loudly,

'Bring them both in to the station. I've always had a feeling about this bugger. Ripley, you go with Miss Sanderson. Jack, we'll take Mr Hartford. Oh and Ripley' he called out loudly.

'After you've made a copy of this, I want it sent to the local whiz-guys, let's see if they can retrieve anything.'

Snapshot 192

Sgt Berry could not remember a time when the visiting detective team had behaved with such professionalism. Ever since returning to the station, having detained Mr Hartford and his girlfriend for questioning, they had busied themselves with interrogations, corridor conferences, phone calls and further interrogations. Eventually, after an hour, they brought her up to date with their progress. It was the first time since the investigations began she had seen them smile. PC Dunstan even commented that both the Chief inspector and the sergeant had declined tea and biscuits, digestives even!

Now she watched as all three stood in the corridor and watched as Mr Hartford and his girlfriend left the station.

'Ripley, as soon as you learn what is on that disk, let me know,' Martin gathered his coat and joined Sgt Berry.

'Somebody fouled up big time in not telling us about that internal security camera Sgt.'

'His fiancée was in the shop at the time the alleged conversation took place,' said Sgt Berry.

'I know, but she says she didn't know about the safe or the camera behind the mirror, and I believe her, dammit,' said Martin.

'But Mrs Spencer and Hartford knew, but said nothing. Why?' Martin shook his head and slipped on his coat, then added,

'You look tired Sgt; look after yourself. C'mon Jack, Ripley, I fancy some egg and chips, and perhaps even some sausage and steak to go with it, I'm starving.'

Sgt Berry watched them all leave, then walked over to the mirror and examined her looks. ' Its hardly surprising I look a little jaded, looking after that lot,' she thought.

Snapshot 193

Nick and George slumped into the soft leather chairs. Very few words had passed between them on their way back to the house in Hawes. It had been a long stressful day.

'I'll make something for us to eat, we've had nothing since our breakfast this morning in Buttermere, and that seems an age away,' said George, tired from the strain of being questioned.

'I still can't believe that Spence has gone, I keep thinking about what she must have gone through, it's dreadful.'

'I must contact Mr Spencer, they were a devoted couple.'

'Yes, but not tonight, it's too late. Ring him tomorrow,' replied George, moving off to the kitchen. 'I'll have something ready in half an hour.'

Nick heard what she said but couldn't muster a reply. His mind was awash with the events of the last twenty-four hours. Facts, suspicions, and descriptions swirled around, mixed with images of the bloodstains and the broken Meissen figure.

There was no escape from the enormous hatred he felt towards the perpetrator of this act. Spence was an innocent victim, of that he was convinced. He must learn more about the man who was found dead in the car, the detective sergeant had already told him they knew he was responsible for killing Spence, but why?

Nick dialled the number to speak with Mr Spencer, but the line was engaged. He would try again tomorrow.

Snapshot 194

Nick walked slowly up the crunchy gravel drive. The house looked quiet. He recognised the family car parked outside the garage. Downstairs, the curtains had been closed as a mark of respect, an old established tradition, still adhered to in these parts.

Nick rang the doorbell. When no one answered he walked around to the rear of the house. Through the glass windows of the conservatory he could see Mr Spencer sitting in a large wicker chair. He tapped lightly on the window, but received no response so he walked alongside the curved window until he could see why.

Mr Spencer was dead; one bullet wound in the middle of his forehead, a trickle of blood, long since dried, ran down the corner of his right eye socket down the side of his nose and over his thin lips.

Nick stood staring at the body for what seemed an age; had life without his beloved wife become too much to bear; surely not, what about the girls, where were they?

He walked around the house once, there was nothing out of place, all the doors and windows were closed. Time to ring the police.

Snapshot 195

As they parked alongside Nick's car outside the Spencer residence, Jack was already drooling, much to Martin's annoyance.

'Look at that magnificent machine, what a sight,' said Jack, unable to resist showing his admiration for the Series 3 V8 Aston Martin.

Nick watched as they all clambered out of their vehicles. Martin ambled over to Nick, his hands sunk deep into the pockets of his heavy open coat.

'Where's the body?'

'In the conservatory, I'll show you,' Nick moved to make his way once more up the drive. Martin reached out and gripped Nick's arm to restrain him.

'If you don't mind, it's a crime scene now. Jack, Ripley, take a look let's see what we've got. Now, Mr Hartford, please tell me why you called here, and what you found.' He removed his hand from Nick's arm.

'I visited to pass on my condolences at Mr Spencer's loss, we were friends,' explained Nick. 'He was an early riser, so I rang him but there was no answer, so I called to speak to him. No one answered the door, so I walked round to the conservatory, thinking perhaps he was in the garden. I saw him sitting in the chair, at first I thought he was asleep, then I saw the bullet hole; looks like he shot himself.'

'You didn't go inside the house?'

'No, but I would have done had I thought the girls were at home,' said Nick.

'How did you know they were not there?'

'Their cars were not parked in the drive, they both drive identical Citroen 2CV's, I assumed they're staying with relatives or friends,' explained Nick.

'H'mm, OK, just wait here with Sgt Berry. I'll need to talk to you later.' Martin turned, and made his way up the gravel driveway.

Snapshot 196

George came in from the garden having had a long conversation with Wilf about the damage that can be done by moles on the lawn.

'Did you know they tunnel more than one foot a minute?' Wilf had told her. 'They do untold damage to the lawn by creating ridges. The only way to get rid of them is by trapping, but the 'man in the house' won't let me set the traps.'

His words were still ringing in her ears. She loved the way the old gardener referred to Nick as 'the man in the house', and she was full of admiration for Nick for refusing to let him set traps to catch the moles.

Hearing the phone ring she picked up the receiver.

'George, it's me,' she smiled at the way he always stated the obvious. 'I'm at Spence's house, more bad news I'm afraid, Mr Spencer is dead, looks like he shot himself.'

'Oh, my God, no,' she gasped.

'It's unbelievable, I know. I've called the police. Detective Chief Inspector Martin is here, he wants me to hang around, so I'll see you later when they've finished with me.' George replaced the receiver.

'What on earth is going on?' she thought. A little unnerved by the latest news, she made her way round the house making sure all the doors and windows were tightly locked.

Snapshot 197

'Here's a mug of tea and some biscuits. Look after that mug; according to P.C. Dunstan it's a collector's item. He won it by guessing the correct year on 'The Daily Politics' programme.'
Sgt Berry put the tray on the Formica topped table.

'The Chief Inspector will be with you shortly.'

'Thanks,' said Nick, watching the Sgt move back into the corridor. The station looked as if it had been built in the early 1920's, and had had several major refurbishments since. He inspected the mug; it didn't look special, but the tea tasted good although the digestives were rather dry. Before he finished the tea, the Chief Inspector, his Sgt and D.C. Ripley joined him.

'Those look suspiciously like my digestives,' growled Jack.

'Sgt Berry kindly brought them to me, I haven't had anything since early this morning,' explained Nick. 'Actually, they're a little dry.'

'Dry?' Jack leaned over and grabbed one.

'Do you mind Jack! There are more important things to discuss than your digestives,' interrupted Martin.

'They're your digestives as well,' protested the Sgt.

'Jack,' snapped Martin. 'Right now,' he continued, addressing Nick, 'we're pretty sure that Mr Spencer did not commit suicide. There was no gun found at the crime scene. There was no sign of a break-in, which suggests that the victim possibly knew his killer.'

'Why on earth would anyone want to kill Mr Spencer, or, for that matter, Mrs Spencer? It doesn't make sense,' protested Nick.

'Exactly so, why?' smiled Martin. 'We do know who killed Mrs Spencer, we found him at the bottom of Sheepshead Pass. Guess what we found on your hard disk from the security camera in the shop,' teased Martin.

'What?' asked Nick anxiously.

'Ripley, do your stuff,' Martin said gruffly, taunting Nick.

'What you are about to see are edited highlights from the security camera in the shop,' Ripley switched on the machine.

In the first clip, Spence was seen entering the shop, followed shortly afterwards by a smartly dressed man; he released the door blind.

'We can see, in clip one, the killer entering the shop.' Ripley blanked the screen. 'Mrs Spencer must have heard him; she comes from the back and asks him if there is anything he would like to look at. He ignores her, she becomes suspicious, sees the closed blind, and walks towards the door. He grabs her, they struggle, she asks him what he wants, another struggle. In clip two, you will see the attacker asking three questions. That's all you will see, I have purposely omitted the struggle, it's very distressing,' explained Ripley.

'Get on with it, Ripley,' said Martin, dispassionately.

Nick watched the edited clips, the man angrily asking Spence questions, there were three such scenes in clip two, but no sound. When Nick installed the security camera he was only concerned with capturing film of customer movements, not the sound.

'Well, I hardly think he would shoot him, then give us a ring, do you?' said Martin.

'The Sicilian influence in the first killing, and the way we found Mr Spencer this morning, I think, suggests an execution,' interrupted Ripley, still clearing away the recording equipment.

Martin and Jack pondered the young man's comment.

'So you are suggesting the killer of Caradonna also killed Mr Spencer?' said Jack.

'Possibly, he's clearing up loose ends,' added Ripley.

'He could be right,' reflected Jack.

'But we still come back to the same question. Why was Caradonna looking for Hartford?' said Martin, smacking the desk with the flat of his hand in a gesture which made both Jack and Ripley look at each other in surprise.

'I don't know. Hartford insists that he has never met, or heard of him,' protested Jack.

'Perhaps he's telling the truth. Perhaps Caradonna, and the man who killed him were both employed by someone else who really did have a grudge against Hartford, so much so, that he wanted to hurt him, or those connected to him,' speculated Ripley.

'Not another Mr X,' cried Jack.

'Why not?' asked Ripley.

'Let's just concentrate our efforts on trying to find out more about the man who we know poisoned Caradonna. The more I think about it, the more Ripley could be right; he could be the one who killed Mr Spencer. But we'll talk more with Hartford. Ripley, go through his books again, note all the names connected with his business trips. Let's see if there are any links. Jack, let's me and you go for something to eat.'

Snapshot 199

George watched the data on the screens. Nick worked vigorously, typing out endless instructions on the computer keyboard, then analysing the information that scrolled onto the screen, before repeating the whole process.

It was almost three hours since he had returned from being questioned by the police; once he had explained to her what had taken place over a quick snack, he excused himself and retreated here to the secure room.

'Look at this, George,' he pointed to the laptop widescreen. 'I typed in Angelo, the name the police gave me, and 'bingo', it appears three times in conversations.'

'How,' she asked?

'It's recorded on the hard disk from the UHF listening device I planted in the library at Grice Hall,' explained Nick, his face contorted, he gazed at George. 'The memory stick – of coarse, that's the answer!' He rushed from the room and before a puzzled George could leave, he returned, waving the memory stick in front of her.

'I downloaded some audio files onto the memory stick just before I left to find you on the Isle of Wight. Only you had already moved on, what with everything that happened, I forgot all about the files on the memory stick, until now!'

Nick pushed the memory stick into a USB port on the computer and quickly typed in instructions; suddenly voices crackled into life over the speakers, small excerpts of conversation, meaningless in themselves, except for one thing; Nick's name.

'That's why they targeted the shop, they were looking for me.'

'So Luzhkov could be behind the killings!' George gasped.

'Without a doubt. Once they showed me the clips of the man attacking Spence, and mouthing my name, things started to fall into place.'

'Why would he suddenly launch an attack on Spence?'

'My guess is that they stepped up their security levels shortly after we dumped the lorry on their lawn. They must have done a security sweep and found the two listening devices I planted; but luckily, they didn't discover the microchip I placed underneath the microcircuit board in the telephone,' Nick explained.

'Look at this,' Nick pointed to another monitor.

'Data received from the two listening devices stopped here; that's around the time when Spence and I were doing the shop audit, that must be when they discovered the devices. After that, the computer only received data from the chip in the phone.'

Nick switched off the laptop.

'I'm assuming they thought I was responsible for planting the devices, especially since my name comes up in conversation.

They wanted revenge, so they sent their man, Caradonna, to find me, and as Chief Inspector Martin so aptly put it, Spence got it because I wasn't there.'

'Oh my God, what are we going to do?' said George, anxiously.

'I've been thinking mulling over that. I want Luzhkov more than ever, but the police are over me like flies at the moment, so we'll have to be careful. Once things get back to normal, we can continue with your investigation.'

'Will they come after us?' she asked, nervously.

'Possibly, but with the police presence I doubt it. My guess is that they'll be waiting to see what I do.'

Nick placed his arm around George's shoulder and whispered. 'Don't you worry. I'm going to continue analysing all the data on the hard disk as it comes in, it may yet give us some interesting information. We are not going to do anything to intimidate them. On the contrary, we'll attend the funerals, reorganise the shop, and lead what appears to be a normal life.'

'A normal life, with you, wow.' George threw her head back, laughing at Nick's suggestion of a normal life. 'Now *that* is going to be a first.'

'Really? Well, let's start right now, we'll drive over to the Crown at Horton in Ribblesdale; they do a wonderful meat and potato pie, and I'm starving. Are you coming with me?' he asked, teasing her.

'You bet, so this is normal. Let's go, I'm not letting you out of my sight.'

Snapshot 200

The converted redbrick stables housed mostly staff. Blandford was not a frequent visitor, nevertheless he knew his way around, as he knew every member of staff, especially those who lived on the premises. He knocked on the door loudly and wiped his brow with a large, yellow, silk handkerchief. Lorenzo opened the door, curious to see who was knocking so loudly.

'I need to speak to you urgently,' Blandford pushed past the Sicilian. The room was clean, but untidy. He sat on the window seat overlooking the courtyard.

'I've just heard that the police have found the body of Mr Spencer. Rumour has it he had been killed with one bullet to the forehead.' Blandford lifted the handkerchief once more to his brow, mopping lightly. He could see that Lorenzo was nervous, his head hung low.

'It is the Sicilian way,' snarled Lorenzo, in a low voice.

'What is?'

'Anyone who has a connection to us, you said.'

'What is it exactly you are trying to tell me Lorenzo.'

'When you did this,' the Sicilian pointed to the cut on his cheek,

'You said, anyone who has a connection to us, did I know of anyone?' His bumbling manner irritated Blandford, who looked around the room once more and could see from empty wine bottles that Lorenzo had been drinking heavily.

'Did you kill him?' he asked, outright.

'Yes, I killed him, the Sicilian way. Get rid of family before they come looking for you. It is the way,' he said.

'This is England, not Sicily, you fool,' roared Blandford; pushing Lorenzo away with such a force he fell backwards into an armchair. Blandford towered over him.

'Now you listen to me, you little worm. Stay on the estate, don't go anywhere, or see anyone without my say so.' He whipped the full force of his hand across the Sicilian's cheek, tearing open the previous wound with his ring.

'Do you understand?' Lorenzo cowered low in the chair, fearful of further blows.

'Yes, yes,' he whimpered. Blandford made for the door, and, just before leaving growled.

'Just remember what happened to Angelo.' He strode off, leaving Lorenzo reflecting on those final words.

Snapshot 201

The meat and potato pie arrived steaming hot and proved to be as good as Nick had said it would be with a golden crust and succulent meat, smothered in a gravy that was simply delicious. George slumped back into the old, wooden, high-backed chair and surveyed the empty plates. She watched as the slim, blonde, green-eyed waitress let the dessert menu, and then cleared away the used plates.

'I'll leave you to consider the sweet menu, I'll be back shortly,' she said, while balancing plates, the large meat and potato pie dish and cutlery on one arm.

'No sweet for me, I can't eat another thing. I'm pogged,' said Nick.

'Me too,' replied George. Suddenly she sat bolt upright 'Oh shit,' she whispered over the table to Nick. 'There're coming over here, they've seen us'

'Who?' asked Nick, curiously.

'Inspector bloody Clueso and his sergeant' she whispered sarcastically.

'Fancy meeting you two here, we do keep bumping in to each other, don't we,' smiled Martin. 'They tell me the food here is marvellous, especially the meat and potato pie. Home-made, so Sgt Berry tells me.'

The hairs in the nape of Nick's neck stood on end, he was so surprised to see the superintendent and his sergeant standing at the side of the table.

'That's right, I can recommend the food here, especially the pie.' Nick blurted out.

'Is this meeting a coincidence, or are you following us, Superintendent?' Unruffled at the young man's direct approach, Martin assured Nick that their present meeting was purely coincidental.

'However,' he leaned over closer towards Nick, 'I can tell you that we know you didn't kill Angelo Leonardo Caradonna and Mr Spencer,' it was delivered as if rehearsed.

'But, whoever did,' he hesitated slightly, a smile still on his lips, 'wants you dead.' For a second Nick stared at the superintendent, digesting what he had said, then fired back in a calm voice.

'Well we can't have everything, can we?'

'You're a cool customer Mr Hartford, but there are still many unanswered questions,' He had not expected this reaction from the young man.

'We'll meet again,' said Martin, deliberately being casual.

'Oh yes, I nearly forgot to mention it, but I thought you'd like to know. We've released the bodies of the Spencers, so no doubt we'll meet up at the funeral. Now, Jack. We really must go and find a table, I must say I'm looking forward to some wholesome meat and potato pie.'

'I hope it chokes him,' said George, bitterly, 'his callous attitude about releasing the bodies was done deliberately to goad you.'

'I know, keep calm, don't give him the pleasure of seeing you angry or upset,' said Nick.

'Everything he does is deliberate; he's trying to coax a reaction out of us that may help him in any future questioning. Smile, he's looking this way.'

'The way he referred to Spence and Mr Spencer, as the '*Spencers,*' and his use of the word 'bodies' like it was some kind of dog meat,' she said, forcing a thin smile.

'And if that wasn't enough, he then went on to tell you that the killer 'wants you dead'. What a pillock.' Still smiling, she took a sip of wine.

'Well, he wasn't telling us anything we didn't already know. What about the sweet?'

'No, thank you,' she said, gulping the last of the wine. 'Let's get out of here.'

Snapshot 202

'Now that's put the cat among the pigeons, lets see how they react to that information being dropped in their lap while they digest their meal,' said Martin, chuckling with mischievous intent.

'They look calm enough,' replied Jack, having thrown a glace over towards Nick and George.

'And how would you feel if I had told you someone was out to kill you. Calm, I don't think so. Don't be fooled Jack. Inside, he will be scared. We're going to be seeing quite a lot of Mr Hartford, of that I'm sure.'

'Maybe so, but right now they're going.' Martin turned to see George and Nick leaving. Now let's sample this meat and potato pie we've heard so much about, my stomach thinks my throat's been cut,' said Jack, picking up the menu.

Snapshot 203.

The elevated position of St Margaret's gave the church an excellent vantage point over the winding streets of Hawes, and on this blustery winter day it's exposure ensured that everyone was wet, cold and miserable.

Nick mused that this was how it was at funerals; it had been a similar day when he buried his parents. Why was it, he thought, that the only funerals he had ever attended were always for two people?

Ridiculous feelings on this sombre occasion, George had wept for most of the service, as had most of the women, especially the two Spencer girls. The wind blew the vicar's surplice in all directions, and the rain splattered down onto the two coffins, making a drumming noise as they were lowered into the ground side by side.

At last, walking away was a welcome relief to many. As a solitary chime from the church bell rang out, a group of crows flew off, wings beating against the wind and rain, lifting them higher and higher into the grey sky. Each of their resonant squawks rang out as if it was a triumphant call against the elements.

Nick watched as people dispersed, some in cars, others trudging off in a line down the small ginnel by the side of the graveyard to the main street.

The gravedigger, who had kept a respectful distance from the funeral party, now hung around awkwardly. The smell of death was in the air; there is no beauty in death, only sadness thought Nick.

'Time to go,' said George, quietly.

She grasped Nick's arm as they followed the others down the drive, leaving the bleak figure of the gravedigger to complete his task.

Snapshot 204

Viktor Luzhkov was pleased with the new security system and congratulated Blandford on the unobtrusiveness of the installations.

Blandford savoured these rare moments when his superior took him into his confidence and almost treated him as an equal.

Having acquainted him with some of the detail of his business in London he had gone onto tell him that the business was going into one it's most prosperous periods, but that there was no room for '*loose ends*'.

Luzhkov as usual was not interested in handling any trivial detail, that was Blandford's department, but he did make one small suggestion; leaving Lorenzo's body on Hartford's land.

'This little man Hartford will not cause us any further embarrassment, he will be hurting too much,' he had delivered these last words with the thinnest of smiles, betraying satisfaction.

Blandford cupped the brandy glass in his hand to give it warmth, while subconsciously swirling the liquid around while reflecting on his most satisfactory meeting.

Snapshot 205

For the last few days George had rarely ventured out of the house; the weather was deteriorating, and her mood, since the funeral, had been sombre.

Nick, on the other hand, had flung himself into tidying up the shop ready for opening again. Apart from meal times and a few short amicable words in the evening, little had passed between them. George had spent some of her time reading and watching TV, but most importantly she had started researching into the lives of the three remaining women who had died in seemingly tragic accidents.

Lydia Mackintosh killed in a tragic car accident; Gemma Edge lost at sea and finally Priscilla Hedgecoe, who died of an anaphylactic shock due to a nut allergy. From what she had gleaned from her investigation, there was doubt in her mind surrounding the deaths of all three women. She had not mentioned any of this to Nick, as she did not feel he was in any mood to pore over her research just yet.

He was still grieving over the loss of Spence, but he was coping with it in his own way; this side of Nick was new to her and she had decided to leave him alone to deal with it as he saw fit.

Snapshot 206

Being used to waiting on both the sergeant and the Chief Detective Inspector, Ripley knew it was no use returning to the office after completing his journey to Skipton, without taking in some steaming hot tea, plus the digestives. Opening the solid, wooden, green-painted door he confronted the two, busily reading the daily papers.

'Tea, anyone?' He slid the tray onto the sergeants' desk, dislodging several piles of papers, though neither of them noticed as they each grabbed a mug.

'Just what I needed,' snorted the sergeant.

'Too true, Jack,' agreed Martin, 'Anything new, Ripley?'

'Not really, the hard drive from the shop contained only what we have seen, normally we can recover items that have been deleted. But not in this case.'

'Why?' asked Martin, taking two biscuits much to Jack's consternation.

'Because this type of disk,' he held up the disk, 'does not retain any deleted data.'

'Now, why doesn't that surprise me, what's he got to hide?'

'We'll ask him about this Jack, don't forget,' said Martin.

'A fat lot of good that will do, he's always one step ahead, is young Mr Hartford.' Jack drawled over the name, emphasizing the consonants.

'What about Hartford's business books, was there anything there?' asked Martin, hopefully.

'No, just records of sales and purchases, outgoings and incoming goods, details of previous owners, itineraries of expenses abroad, hotel bills, travelling expenses and shipping cost, etc, etc, nothing out of the ordinary. No names to match up with any names we are aware of, a total blank.'

Ripley took a sip of tea, while observing both men's reactions, but only silence ensued which made him feel uncomfortable.

'So,' he continued, 'the question remains. Who wants to kill Nick Hartford and why?'

'Bring him in again Jack, first thing Monday morning.'

'What's wrong with tomorrow?'

'It's Saturday, Leeds are playing M.U., let him stew.'

'He's been sorting out the shop in Hawes, looks like it's nearly ready for opening,' chipped in Ripley.

'H'mm, has he now?' pondered Martin, thoughtfully. 'Tell you what Ripley,' he said briskly, 'Tomorrow, you can return the disk and the books, let's see if you can get anything out of him.'

'But I was rather hoping to watch the match.'

'Ripley, I didn't know you liked football, never mind, there'll be other matches, think of it as a wonderful opportunity to test out all your theories. Besides, Jack and I will keep you right up to date with all the action, won't we Jack?'

'No problem, Ripley,' Jack agreed, chewing on a biscuit, while crumbs tumbled over his grey cardigan.

Snapshot 207

Nick's eyes rested with pleasure on the many antiquities around the newly rearranged shop; it still gave him a great deal of satisfaction to see the many pieces he had purchased from around the world. His eyes rested on the empty space previously occupied by the Meissen harlequin figure, this would always remind him of Spence; a space never to be filled.

It had taken a lot of work to get the shop ready for opening, but there was to be no ceremony, just business as usual in a week's time.

'Tap, tap, tap,' he turned towards the hollow sound that came from the glass door, 'tap, tap, tap,' he moved the blind to one side to be confronted by a smiling Detective Constable Ripley.

'I've brought your books back, together with your the hard drive,' he shouted through the glass, holding up a brown paper parcel.

'There can't be many years between us,' thought Nick, 'but what different directions we have travelled in.' He slid the bolts, turned the keys, and opened the door.

'I'm glad I've found you in, we've finished with these,' gasped the detective. He handed the parcel to Nick and strode into the middle of the showroom.

'You've made quite a few changes.'

'Yes, we had to.' Nick unwrapped the brown paper parcel to reveal the shop books and the hard disk.

'I'm glad you've brought the disk, especially with us opening in a weeks time.' He walked over to the wall mirror and once it slipped open he gently slotted the hard drive into place and closed the mirror door.

'How long exactly has the shop been open?' asked Ripley.

'More questions.'

'It goes with the job, explained Ripley, trying a softer approach.

'About three and a half years.'

'Did you come straight from London or Hampshire?' asked the young detective.

'You've been doing your homework, if you know the answers, why ask?'

'Just answer the question please'

'London.'

'Not Hampshire?'

'No, London.' 'How much did he really know,' thought Nick.

'It must take a lot of money to move up here, buy property and open a business.'

'Enough.'

'I mean, how much can you make in an auction house in London enough to buy all this, and your house and all those cars?'

'Why don't you come to the point, OK, so you know where I worked, where I gained my knowledge of antiques and made lots of contacts in the business.'

'Just part of the picture, Mr Hartford,' smiled Ripley. 'But you still haven't explained about the money,' persisted Ripley.

'When my parents died they left me well provided for, not that it's any of your business,' snapped Nick.

'Ah I see, sorry, I didn't know about your parents.' Ripley felt slightly uncomfortable, but decided to continue. 'The question remains, why was the man who killed Mrs Spencer, looking for you, *what* did he want?'

Nick glanced at the empty space where the Meissen harlequin figure stood and then at Ripley. It was obvious to him that the police were going to continue with this line of questioning, so he just had to refrain from giving them any information about Luzhkov.

'As you know, constable I was elsewhere when the murder of my business partner took place. I did not know this man, have never met him, I am as much in the dark as you and your colleagues appear to be.'

'Detective constable,' added Ripley.

'What? Oh yes, of course. Do you have any more questions? It is getting rather late.' The dismissal of his title irritated Ripley, but he had not finished yet. He fired another question,

'But this man knew you, he asked for you and killed Mrs Spencer as a consequence of not being able to find you.'

'Why he killed Spence is a total mystery to me, why someone who I have never met should ask for me is a mystery,' replied Nick, adding,

'Perhaps if you could find the person who killed the killer, it would answer many of these questions, including, why Mr Spencer was killed, or should I say, 'executed,' so soon afterwards.'

Ripley, who thought he had the advantage, suddenly felt the position had been reversed.

'Quite, well, rest assured we'll be pursuing our investigation.' With that stock reply Ripley suddenly felt it was game, set, and match to Hartford.

'We will be speaking with you again Mr Hartford.'

'I never doubted it,' quipped Nick, realising he had got to the young detective.

Snapshot 208

Blandford knocked firmly on the door and waited patiently.

'Lorenzo, look I'm sorry for being so harsh with you the other day,' he said to the pensive figure who was standing in the doorway,' he continued.

'As you may know, Mr Luzhkov has returned, I have a job for you to do, get ready. I'll wait here.'

Lorenzo knew better than to ask any questions, if he was being given a second chance he was going to grasp it with both hands.

He quickly washed his face, dried it roughly on a towel, combed his hair grabbed his coat, and rushed out to meet Mr Blandford.

'Ready. Look, I'm sorry about that last job, it was a misunderstanding. You can count on me, I won't let you down again, Mr Blandford,' said Lorenzo, following hurriedly behind Blandford; quite pleased with the way he had delivered the well-rehearsed speech.

'What's the job?' he asked. Blandford turned sharply.

'Look, keep quiet; it was not my idea to give you this job. Get into the land rover and I'll tell you about the job on the way, OK?'

'Yea, sure,' Lorenzo slid onto the seat, shut the door and waited for Blandford to join him. If it wasn't his idea, then it must have been Mr Luzhkov.

Blandford must have told him about the last job and he must have been pleased, yes, that was it,' he smiled at the thought.

Blandford knew that any softly, softly approach would not have worked with the Sicilian. By suggesting it was not his idea to give him a second chance ensured his complicity. Blandford always prided himself with the knowledge that he knew how to handle men. He climbed into the cab, turned the key in the ignition and set off down the drive.

'Mr Luzhkov has suggested its time we hit Hartford's place, give him something else to think about,' said Blandford.

'Great, what exactly do you want me to do,' asked the Sicilian, enthusiastically.

'I'm going to drop you outside Hartford's place and you're going to give him a little present which I have in the back.' Lorenzo peered round and saw a black bag on the rear seat.

'Great, I won't let you down Mr Blandford, you and the boss can count on me.'

'I know,' said Blandford, reassuringly. 'I'm sorry about striking you the other day,' he added. 'It's been tough supervising all these security changes, having all these different people tramping inside the grounds and in the Hall, day in and day out. I'm sure you will understand.'

'Sure, I understand, Mr Blandford, don't you worry. Lorenzo understands,' he said, forgivingly. After a few miles Blandford pulled over at the side of a darkly lit road.

'We're here, now remember, if you see anyone, pull back. Just deliver the package to the front door, and leave, understand?'

'Sure, sure, don't worry, there will be no mistakes this time,' whispered Lorenzo.

'Ok, here's the package,' Blandford turned round and reached over to the bag on the rear seat, his every action followed by the Sicilian.

'Open your window. Is the road clear in both directions,' asked Blandford.

The Sicilian did as he was told then, turned his head to reassure him about the road. Blandford fired at almost point-blank range; the schsplat-sound from the silencer was followed by a gasp as, in a split-second, the bullet forged its way through his skull and disappeared through the open window into the night.

Blandford quickly undressed the lifeless body, pushing all the clothes and possessions into the bag on the rear seat. He had enjoyed the role-playing with the Sicilian, fooling him into believing that he had been given another chance.

There are no second chances in this game, that's how you end up being caught; he chuckled to himself. He had thought through every detail in advance, true they were going to surprise Hartford, just like Mr Luzhkov wanted, but the surprise package was Lorenzo himself.

He started the land rover and drove slowly up the road until he came to the drive leading to Hartford's place. He pulled over, looked around, silence. Quickly, he opened the door and using the Fireman's lift hoisted the lifeless body onto his shoulders. He then walked down the drive a hundred yards from the main road then laid the body down face-up, with its arms outstretched.

Once inside the vehicle he started the engine and drove quite fast down the drive and over the body, making sure his nearside tyres drove over the Sicilian's head. He continued down the drive until through the trees he could see the lights of the house. Turning round, he drove back down the drive

'You often talked about the Sicilian way,' he shouted, 'well, this is the Russian way,' as he drove once more over the lifeless body, then out of the drive and into the night.

'Would you like buttered white or brown bread, with your boiled eggs, or some more toast?' Nick, biting into a slice of toast, looked up and mumbled an incoherent reply.

'What?' bellowed George, frustrated at his inability to answer.

Nick swallowed some tea then answered. 'Toast please.'

'At last.'

'Are you feeling alright?' asked Nick.

'Yes.'

'Oh good,' Nick returned to his paper, crunched on his toast and continued once again to talk while chewing.

'Nick, it's impossible for me to make out a word you are saying while you are eating.

'Sorry, habit I suppose,' he drank some more tea. 'This must be what it's like when you're an old married couple,'

'Well, I am neither married nor old, so I wouldn't know.'

'Are you sure you're alright, there's nothing wrong?'

'What could possibly be wrong, you've hardly said two words to me for the last few days, you're out most of the day, and I'm left here alone, what could possibly be wrong?'

'Ah, I see, you're lonely without me.'

'Don't kid yourself, as a matter of fact I've been quite busy.'

'Ah good, I'd hate to think that you were just stuck here all alone, pining for me,' he smiled.

George brought a small tray with a plate of toast and some boiled eggs. She took one egg and planted a kiss on top of the shell, and then put it into the eggcup in front of Nick.

'That's not very hygienic,' chuckled Nick.

'It's the end you chop off,' she said, sitting opposite him at the table.

'H'mm, even so. Look why don't we...' before he could finish there was a loud knock at the door and Wilf burst in.

'Sorry to bother you sir, but you'd better come and look at this,' he said, breathlessly.

'Calm down, Wilf, whatever's the matter?' asked Nick, moving towards the gardener.

'You'd better come with me, Sir,' he beckoned Nick to follow. Nick did as the old man suggested.

Pulling on an old coat, he followed him around the back of the house and onto the drive leading to the main road. Wilf was in front, but kept turning round, urging Nick to follow.

'Quickly, sir, quickly,' he continued to encourage Nick to follow up the slight gradient of the driveway.

'Just ov'er here, sir,' he was now almost scampering over the last few yards,

Once over the brow looking down the long stretch of driveway to the road, he stopped. When Nick reached his side he looked down the drive and could just make out a naked body halfway down the drive. An old bike with green mudguards and a front wicker basket was laid down at the side of the body. Nick knew that the bike belonged to Wilf.

As he approached the corpse laid almost on its side, he could see massive bruising and what looked like tyre marks on the body.

He walked around until he could see the face. He called out,

'Wilf, go back to the house, ring Sgt Berry at Settle and tell her what we have here.'

'Do you know him sir?'

'No, now please go to the house and do as I say.'

'Right sir, straight away sir, a real rum do this is and no mistake, never seen anything like it in all my life,' he mumbled as he turned towards the house. 'What is the world coming to when you can't go to work without all this business?'

Nick did not recognise the person but he felt immediately that the incident was connected to Luzhkov. Taking care not touch anything, he moved in to take a closer look at the face, which had been run over by a vehicle, resulting in substantial facial injuries. The forehead was clearly visible and Nick could see he had been shot. Speckled skin around the point of entry told him that he had been shot at close range.

The body, having been stripped, was dumped in the drive, then a vehicle had been driven over him a couple of times. Some tyre marks could be clearly seen on the body and Nick was pretty sure he recognised the tread, Pirelli scorpion zero.

He looked up and saw George coming towards him.

'Stay there George. This is not pretty,' he called out to her. He could see Wilf was hanging around the bottom of the drive.

'Oh, my God, who is it?' asked George.

'I've absolutely no idea.'

'Here, I've brought you a warmer coat. What is happening, Nick, why does this keep happening to us?' she said, glancing at the body.

'Luzhkov, it must be, everything points to him,' said Nick, with an air of resignation.

'What are we going to do?' she pleaded.

'Well, presumably, this is a warning, back off, leave me alone or else. If he wanted to harm us, he would have done it by now, he's telling us he knows.'

'Great, so he knows what?'

'He knows I planted those two bugs in the library, that's enough. I don't think he's aware of your investigations.'

'What do we do, Nick.'

'Luzhkov knows that we'll have to call in the police, they are going to be all over us'

'They already are!'

'I know, he's done this to increase the pressure on us, but we cannot, must not tell the police anything about what we know, its too early, we have to find conclusive evidence before we move in that direction.'

'Did Wilf ring Sgt Berry?'

'Yes, she's on her way.'

'OK, there's nothing to be done here now. Go back to the house; it would be a good idea to give Wilf a brandy or some tea. I'll go and wait by the gate for the police.'

'Yes, sir,' she gave a mock salute.

Snapshot 210

The trip over the fells was always inspiring for Sgt Berry, having lived here since she was a child she knew them very well.

She had known old Wilf since she was a teenager, when her father found he was no longer able to care for their extensive garden Wilf had been hired to care for it.
She recollected how he sounded very distressed on the phone.

'Come quickly Juniper, its terrible, come quickly, there's a body.' Juniper was his name for her when she was a teenager and he used to fascinate her with tales of the dales people.

It was a cold crisp morning, the sheep grazed amongst the fells and along the roadside, oblivious of her presence.

As she dropped down into the valley, the land was more cultivated, divided up into fields by rough limestone walls, further down trees, which had lost their leaves, could be seen in clumps or along the roadside, all adding to the tapestry of the lower dale.

She spotted Hartford waiting outside the drive gates, which were closed. She pulled up her car by the verge, grabbed her hat, and walked towards him.

'Morning,' she shouted.

'Morning, Sgt,' he replied.

'Now whatever is this all about, Wilf mentioned something about a body.'

'That just about describes it, a naked body in the middle of my drive, and before you ask I have no idea who it is, or how it got there.'

'Well, I never,' she had reached Nick and the gates to the drive, 'we'd better have a look then, show me the way.' Nick pushed open the gates and led the way up the drive. Pretty soon, the body came into view, sprawled across the drive; arms and legs bent in ways that are only possible when severe fracturing has occurred.

'Right you stay here, I'll take a look.'

Nick did as he was told and watched as she bent over the body and walked around carefully looking from all angles, after a few moments she returned to where Nick was standing.

'He's been shot; the bullet went straight through, probably lodged over there in those trees. I'd better call for assistance. This is now a crime scene Mr Hartford, can you access your house another way.'

'Yes, I'll go down the old path through the wood. For what it's worth, I don't think he was shot there.' He pointed at the body.

'Really, and what makes you say that Mr Hartford.'

'Obviously, I had a look when Wilf first alerted me about finding the body, you can see the speckled skin around the point of entry, which suggests that when he was shot the gun was between six inches to two foot away, that's pretty close, and when the bullet exited through the rear of the skull it would have taken with it bone fragments and a splattering of blood. There is none in the immediate vicinity of the body, which suggests to me he was shot elsewhere.'

Finished, Nick stood waiting for a reply.

Sgt Berry looked at him for a long time, as if she was digesting everything he had said. After what seemed a long, embarrassing silence, she returned to the body for a further examination, after which she returned to him.

'What a remarkable man you are, Mr Hartford, how come you know so much?'

'I don't know, it's just something I picked up over the years working with antique weapons, and basic observation.'

'Basic observation,' she repeated,' remarkable. Have you anything further to add?'

'Well you'll note the marks of a tyre tread on the skin, its quite distinctive, and goes in both directions, which suggests that he was run over twice. It's my guess, and it is only a guess, that those tread marks were, made by Pirelli Scorpion Zero tyres, I had them on a land rover I once owned, they're quite distinctive.' Sgt Berry listened to his analysis and found it hard to hide her admiration of his knowledge.

'Well, you may be right, our forensics will sort all that out, but I'll pass on your observations. Now, I would like you to return to the house, but we'll need to talk to you all later.'

'Right, oh, one more thing while I'm at it. While I was waiting for you to arrive, I had a look around, and to the right of the driveway along the road you'll find where a vehicle has pulled over onto the verge. If I'm not mistaken it had the same tyre tread as those found on the body. I'm pretty sure that's where this chap was shot, but I expect your forensic team will sort all that out.'

With that Nick walked back along the road to where he could join the path, leaving a rather submissive Sgt Berry to follow his progress.

Snapshot 211

'Sunday mornings, Jack, are the one time when a man can really enjoy himself; a hearty breakfast, read the papers undisturbed and afterwards visit the pub for a nice chat with your mates, then back home to enjoy your Sunday dinner.'

Martin laid back into the wooden chair by the open-hearth fire and dwelled on his proclamations. Jack, who had been half listening while attempting to read a Sunday tabloid, looked up in disbelief.

'I don't know where you've been living for the last few years; it's nothing like that at my house. First and foremost, there's work, which doesn't always recognise Sundays. Secondly, I'm expected to make breakfasts on a Sunday morning if I'm home and thirdly, with the kids around the house it's anything but quiet. Fourthly, since Sunday opening the wife usually takes me shopping, and Fifth and last, my local pub closed its doors three months ago.'

'Bloody hell, Jack, you're a right killjoy; I was telling it how I'd like it to be. And today, we can enjoy just one of those days. Come on, the bars open, it's my round.'

Snapshot 212

Ripley replaced the phone, and sighed at the thought of having to leave the warmth and comfort of his room, where he had been catching up on his reading. He pulled on his jacket and made his way down the curving staircase, past the tall grandfather clock perched precariously on the landing half way down the stairs, he caught sight of Jack and Martin at the bar, before he reached the last step.

'Fancy a pint, Ripley?' asked Jack, on seeing the young detective approaching.

'No, Sarge, bad news I'm afraid.'

'Oh no, keep it to yourself, please, Ripley,' pleaded Martin, turning his back on the young detective.

'Sorry, Sgt Berry's just phoned me, there's another body, she wants us to join her.'

'Oh that woman, where does she conjure them up from, she's a right Jonah,' moaned Martin taking a long drink, then standing up and pushing his chair backwards.

'Come on Jack, where are we going Ripley?'

'Hawes, the body was found in Mr Hartford's drive.'

'Bloody hell, that man again. Jack, are you going upstairs.' Jack nodded. 'Good, fetch my coat will you. Ripley, give me all the information.'

Snapshot 213

Stepping from the car into the cold air Martin pulled up his jacket collar. He walked up the drive to where could see Sgt Berry waiting for them to join her.

After a cursory examination of the body and a full report from the sergeant, he joined Jack and Ripley.

'A right bloody mess, he fell out with someone big time. Have you got any ideas Jack?' he asked.

'No, and I can't see how the post-mortem's going to enlighten us much either. Shot from close range, and from the look at the marks on his body he was run over twice. This was an execution, and the body was dumped here to cause as much embarrassment to Mr Hartford as possible. The question is, why?'

'Sergeant,' Martin called over to Sgt Berry, 'lets see if we can retrieve the bullet, at least that may tell us something'

'Already started sir, nothing as yet.'

'Ripley, take some photographs, the usual, you know what to do. Jack, we'll go up to the house and question Hartford and the gardener.' The pair started the long walk up the drive. Sgt Berry acknowledged Ripley as he started taking photographs with the camera that he always carried with him.

She could just not come to terms with why Martin relied so much on the young detective to replicate work that had already been undertaken by the crime squad.

'Does he ever look at the official photos, she asked Ripley as he was busy taking shots.

'Oh yes, very much, but he likes certain angles and close ups, 'as seen with his own eye', he always tells me.'

'What's your impression of the scene?' she asked, curious to learn of the young detective's views.

'Well, it's a little early, but its definitely an execution, and in my opinion, it's linked to the other deaths, but how and why, that is what we'll have to find out. There's something going on here that's evading us.' Sgt Berry listened and nodded in agreement, but left the young detective to let him get on with his work.

So many deaths in such a short space of time, and in a rural community not used to such events. *What is going on,* she asked herself, *and when would it end.*

Snapshot 214

Having spoken to the gardener about how he had discovered the body, he had sent him home in a squad car as the discovery had shocked the old man and there was no need to detain him any longer. Together with Jack, he now faced Hartford and his fiancée across the large, oak, kitchen table.

'Well, Mr Hartford, here we are again, your presence is starting to really irritate me; every time we have another crime or an incident, your name comes up. Today you have a dead body in your drive, I don't suppose you can give me an explanation for this latest episode?'

'No,' said Nick, with a half smile.

'And you, Miss, do you know anything?'

'No,' replied George quietly.

'I thought not. Well now, let me tell you what I think. Someone in this community of yours does not like you Mr Hartford, and I think you know who it is, but for some reason, you're refusing to tell me. Normally in a community like this when people fall out they can reconcile their differences, or even agree to differ while still remaining on good terms. But you have really pissed someone off so badly, that they want to dump a body in your drive, and kill off your business partner and her husband,' said Martin. Finishing off with a crescendo he continued, 'now that is being pissed off big time, don't you agree?'

'It's time you gave us some honest answers, Mr Hartford,' said Jack. 'We have a body count of four, and everything points to you knowing something that you are refusing to divulge. People don't kill for no reason, it's time you started being straight with us.'

'Gentleman, I realise how this looks, but believe me if we could help you, we would. But the plain truth is we are as mystified as you are,' explained Nick coolly.

There was a long silence, with each party looking at the other; Nick and George trying to sound convincing while not betraying any knowledge of Luzhkov, Martin and Jack hiding their frustration at not being able to shake the truth from their suspects.

'Well, let me tell you, I will find out what's behind all these murders, and I will find out if you are involved

I just hope that the next time we meet Mr Hartford you will be ready to tell me what you know, because the next body may be even closer to home, and you ought to seriously consider that Mr Hartford, before it's too late.' Martin delivered his final words without taking his eyes off Nick.

'Believe me, Chief Inspector, I've nothing to fear, because I,' Nick looked at George, 'we, are in no way involved in any of this sordid mess. We will cooperate with you in any way we can, but I can't conjure something out of the air just to satisfy your mistaken belief that somehow we are involved.'

'Very well, Mr Hartford, have it your way for now, but we will be interviewing you again. In the meantime, your drive is out of bounds, it's still a crime scene. Good day to you.'

Jack and Martin let themselves out; walking up the drive towards the crime scene, each was convinced that Hartford knew more than he was telling them.

Snapshot 215

'I feel like a punch bag that's just been given a right pummelling,' said George, clearing away the mugs.

'It was to be expected,' replied Nick. 'We've featured so much just recently in his investigation, we're bound to be the No 1 suspects.'

'What do we do now?'

'Just a few days ago I said we should keep a low profile, but I'm afraid that's all changed now. Luzhkov has brought the fight to our door and it looks like he means business. We have to collect hard evidence of his involvement and his shady business interests.'

'You're sure it was Luzhkov?'

'No doubt about it.' Nick moved over towards George and resting his arm on her shoulder continued. I've been thinking it over, I'm pretty sure I've seen the dead man before.'

'You are?'

'Yes, I'm sure that I saw him at the fur shop and at Grice Hall when we collected the furniture.'

'His face was a bit mangled, how can you be so sure?' she asked.

'His facial features, well, the ones still left, and his distinctive olive skin.'

'If you had mentioned that to the Inspector it could have diverted attention away from us.'

'Let's get some evidence.' Nick sat down at the kitchen table. 'Can you continue your investigations into the remaining women on your list while I supervise the opening of the shop next week, after which I can continue sifting through the computer data?'

'Gladly,' she walked over to where he was sitting and placed her arms round his neck, whispering, 'when I go off this time, please keep in touch.'

'I certainly will, just let me know where you are going to be.'

'Just a phone call away, wherever.'

Snapshot 216

'Did we glean anything from the pathology reports?' asked Martin, sifting through photographs of the body found in Hartford's drive.

'Blood was A+, the bullet was fired about eighteen inches from the victim's forehead, clean entry, came out the back of the skull, leaving a larger hole with bevelling around the edges. Traces of blood and small bone splinters found on trees nearby came from the victim,' replied Jack.

'Any news on the bullet?'

'They found it burrowed deep in a tree, pretty poor specimen, we're awaiting the ballistic report,' explained Jack.

'And the tyre marks on the body?' Martin continued, looking at the photographs.

'The tread belonged to a Pirelli Scorpion Zero tyre, no doubt about it, although we can't accurately pin point the tyre size; our experts guess at 265/65.'

'So, what does that tell us Jack?'

'Well, if I was making a guess, given this area, I would say it was a 4x4, probably a Land Rover. The imprint at the side of the verge was too deep for a saloon car.'

'Anything else?' asked Martin penetratingly.

'The victim had been drinking some wine, and had had some type of pasta about an hour before his death.

The crush injuries to his head, chest and limbs were inflicted after he was already dead,' added Jack, nonchalantly.

'No pain then,' smiled Martin, looking up at Jack.

'No pain,' answered Jack, used to the Chief Inspector's ways.

'What a way to spend Monday morning, Jack, I don't feel like we've had a weekend.'

'Goes with the job.'

'I know, Jack, ignore me, I'm just fed up of getting nowhere.'

'Well, I think we have a good chance at identifying this victim. Given his skin colour he could well be Mediterranean, if so, he would be easily recognisable in this area. He could have been a casual farm worker, but I doubt it, his hands are too smooth, they haven't done much hard grafting. There were also two cuts to his face, one had been made earlier, then another on top of the old scar tissue, as if he had been hit across the face quite violently. The pathologist guessed that he could have been cut with a ring when he was slapped.' Jack, having updated Martin, slumped into his chair.

'Very good, well let's make a photo fit picture and circulate it in the area.'

'Already done, Ripley got straight onto it early this morning.'

'Splendid, let's hope someone recognises the victim quickly. Shall we have some lunch, then we'll get in touch with Ripley to see what progress he is making,' said Martin, collecting his coat before Jack had time to reply.

Snapshot 217

Having got rid of Lorenzo, Blandford had given orders for all traces of him to be removed.

He looked around the empty rooms, which used to be occupied by the Sicilian; his staff had done a thorough job. He closed the door, walked over towards the smouldering brazier and poked the last embers with a stick and turned to the young man supervising.

'When this has finished, collect all the ashes up and dump them into the river. Afterwards, collect some rubbish from around the house; leaves, branches and grass cuttings and burn the lot slowly,' ordered Blandford to the young man who acknowledged his instructions by nodding acquiescently.

Blandford knew the staff were pretty nervous; two of their number had been dispensed with as a necessity to maintain good order. Nevertheless, they were uneasy, even though some of them would benefit by moving up in the pecking order, that's how it was.

Snapshot 218

The sticky toffee pudding and the spotted dick were brought to the table steaming hot, along with a jug of thick custard. Both men viewed the dishes with delight and promptly poured the thick custard over their chosen dishes as Ripley joined them.

'Have you had lunch, Ripley?' asked Martin.

'No sir, not a scrap,' answered the young detective, watching the two tuck in.

'Well get something ordered lad, we don't want you to waste away,' laughed Martin, devouring a large portion of the sticky toffee.

'Any news?' asked Jack.

'Well, yes, Sarge, a girl in Hawes at the General store recognised the photograph of the victim.'

'The shop which sells railway magazines,' interrupted Jack.

'I don't know about that, Sarge.'

'What was the girl's name?'

'Maxine,' replied Ripley, slightly bewildered.

'That's her, bright girl, she recognised the photograph of Frey,' said Jack.

'Do let him finish, Jack. When did she see him?' pleaded Martin.

'At the opening of the Fur shop a few months ago, she admired his tan, that's why she remembered him,' explained Ripley.

'Bright girl that Maxine, and they do sell railway magazines in the shop, very good selection,' said Jack.

'Get on with your spotted dick, Jack, you and your bloody magazines,' protested Martin. 'Isn't that shop something to do with Mr Luzhkov up at Grice Hall, Ripley?'

'Yes sir.'

'I thought so. Hurry up Jack, we're going to pay Mr Luzhkov a visit. You drive, Ripley.'

'But what about my lunch sir?'

'Grab a sandwich lad, grab a sandwich. Work comes first, isn't that right, Jack?'

'Absolutely.'

'This sticky toffee is excellent, Jack, how's your spotted dick?'

Snapshot 219

Once he had been informed that a police car was making its way up the long drive towards the hall, Blandford nipped quickly into the security office to watch its progress on the security monitors. The car stopped at the newly installed barrier and the driver pressed the buzzer.

'Hello, I have Detective Chief Inspector Martin who wishes to speak with Mr Luzhkov.' Ripley's voice delivered the message to Blandford, who nodded to the security assistant who then pressed a button to raise the barrier.

Blandford moved into the hall to await his unexpected guests, having already alerted Mr Luzhkov, who had made it quite clear to his personal assistant that he had no desire to meet with the uninvited guests unless it was absolutely necessary.

The butler opened the door and the three detectives entered the hall. 'How can I help you?' asked Blandford in his usual overbearing manner.

Martin surveyed the lavish scene with disdain. He pulled out a photograph and thrust it at Blandford.

'I believe this man worked for you.'

The Chief Inspectors forthright manner came as a shock to Blandford who tried to maintain his detached air of authority. He looked at the photo of Lorenzo.

'I don't think so Chief Inspector, I would certainly have remembered him, I....' Martin abruptly interrupted him, still holding the photograph in Blandford's face.

'This man was seen at your fur shop in Hawes,' growled Martin. Both Ripley and the sergeant glared at the personal assistant, waiting for a reaction.

'This man, I can assure you, has never been in our employ. I know all the staff personally, and I have never seen this man. What has he done?'

'He's dead, murdered in cold blood,' said Martin.

'I see, goodness me. I'm sorry but I cannot add to what I have already told you,' lied Blandford cordially with a hint of a thin smile.

'We would like to look around and show this to your staff, is that OK?' asked Martin.

'If you must, but I must protest at this unnecessary intrusion; Mr Luzhkov has some very important guests arriving soon, so this is most inconvenient.' He delivered this last sentence as smoothly as he could without wishing to antagonize Martin further than he had already.

'Ripley, take the back, Jack, interview all the staff on duty.' Martin rapped out the orders.

'Mr Blandford, I would like to speak with Mr Luzhkov now, if you don't mind,' Martin said firmly. Blandford did not protest further, realising it would be futile, so he decided to let them get on with it. He was confident that the strict code of silence amongst the staff would not be broken.

'If you wait here I will ask Mr Luzhkov if he can spare the time to see you,' said Blandford.

'He'd better, or else,' muttered Martin, under his breath.

Snapshot 220

'Did you find anything Ripley?' asked Jack, walking back to the car.

'There was a Land Rover, but the tyres were Dunlop. I spoke to several staff, no one recognised the photo fit,' replied Ripley.

'Same here, a complete blank. One thing though, each and every one of them gave me stock answers, it was if they were rehearsed,' speculated Jack.

'I got the distinct feeling I was shown what they wanted to show me. Three members of staff are away, either off-duty or on estate business. I left instructions for them to report to the station before the weekend. I came across a burning brazier, but it was only garden rubbish.'

'Good lad. Look out, here's the boss,' laughed Jack, waiting for Martin to join them in the car.

'That bloke Luzhkov really gets up my nose. Who the bloody hell does he think he is?' moaned Martin, settling into his seat.

'No success?' asked Jack.

'What makes you think I would know anything about a man who met his death in this way,' mimicked Martin. 'Find out all you can about this man, Ripley; what business is he in, how does he make his money, how come he has so many influential friends. I mean everything,' rapped Martin.

'Will do.'

'Let's get out of here, I need a drink.' As they approached the barrier it opened to let them through, then they sped off down the drive, comparing notes with each other.

Snapshot 221

Nick's progress was slower than he would have liked; he kept stopping and listening for any unusual sounds above the noise of the swaying branches and the rustling of the leaves in the cold, night wind. He looked through the night vision monocular in a sweeping arc, and when he found the area was clear, he continued his trek, stopped, and repeated the process with the night vision scope.

Nick had decided to visit Grice Hall from the rear by approaching from over the fields and through the forest. He guessed they would not have as many security cameras at the rear of the hall as they did at the front.

Suddenly, he heard the unmistakable shree scream of an owl hunting its prey somewhere close by. He checked the area with the night scope; once again he did not see any guards patrolling the perimeter of grounds. As he emerged from the forest he lay flat in the grasses and crawled on his stomach the rest of the way.

Taking no chances, it took him over an hour to reach a low wall overlooking the rear hall garden and outbuildings. He was surprised how dimly lit it was. Cautiously, he moved around the outbuildings, examining each one carefully. He could hear people laughing and the sound of applause from some function inside the hall. His real purpose in coming to the hall clandestinely was to visit the offices in some converted stables that he had noticed during his previous visit.

The windows were old and he easily forced one open and slid inside. Using a pencil torch, he examined the various rooms until he came across one where a number of cardboard boxes were stored. Quickly, he looked in the boxes searching for anything that would help him to delve into Luzhkov's business dealings. Finally he opened a box and found several notebooks and diaries. He pushed some into his bag, replaced the boxes and left through the same window that he had used to gain entry.

Outside once more, he retraced his route back over the fields, soon he was making rapid progress and soon found the car he had left earlier.

Snapshot 222

June Berry finished opening her personal mail and turned her attention to the pile marked 'Settle Police Station'. Before she had untied the string securing the bundle the phone began to ring, the start of another day.

'Hello, Sgt Berry, Settle.'

'June, it's Larry from Low Blean Farm.' She immediately recognised the sharp rasp of the old farmer, Larry Marsett, who farmed by Semer Water, a beautiful valley in Ryedale.

'What's the problem, Mr Marsett?' she asked.

'Someone's gone and set fire to what looks like an old Land Rover down by Semer Water Bridge. I had a lot of hay stored down there, that's all gone too. It'll 'ave to be moved, June, it looks a mess,' he protested.

'Make sure no one touches anything, Larry, we'll be over soon. Did anyone see the fire, do you know when it started?' She asked the questions without expecting any positive reply.

'I've been away since Saturday, over at our John's farm in Wharfdale, just got back this morning. Florrie looked after my place, feeding the chickens and what have you. Dog's been with me, an' all the sheep are on the fells,' he explained.

'OK Larry, I'll put the phone down now; I'll be with you shortly.'

Snapshot 223

'Phone call for you,' said the waitress, a short plump girl with a pleasing face, who pointed in the direction of the table in the corner of the room, where they ate all their meals.

'Go and see who that is, Ripley, there's a good lad, and tell whoever it is we've only just finished breakfast,' grumbled Martin.

He hated to be disturbed at his morning nuptials, especially before at least two cups of tea had been consumed over the ritual of reading the morning paper.

'It was Sgt Berry; a local farmer has found a burnt out Land Rover, she's on her way to pick us up,' said Ripley, sitting down to complete his breakfast.

'That women is a bloody nuisance,' snarled Martin.

'Well, if she's on her way, we'd better get ready. Come on Ripley,' urged Jack.

'Jack, what's the rush? The car's burnt out, it's not going to go anywhere,' pleaded Martin.

'I know, but if she's on her way, we'd best meet her.'

Reluctantly Martin folded his paper and followed Ripley and Jack.

'I sometimes wonder if it isn't time for me to take my pension and disappear into the sunset,' he mumbled to himself.

Snapshot 224

All three were quite surprised at the change in the countryside; all round Settle and Hawes there was plenty of fertile land which then gave way to the high fells, but here, suddenly, the green pastures rolled down to meet a stunning expanse of blue water.

'This is really beautiful,' proclaimed Jack.

'Very impressive,' replied Ripley in response. They all clambered out of the squad car and stood gazing over the vast area of water, as several wading birds clung to the shore while a gentle breeze sent ripples scurrying across the surface.

'It's one of our secrets, we tend to keep it to ourselves, otherwise the area would be inundated with tourists. Ah, there's Farmer Marsett,' said a smiling Sgt Berry.

The three turned to see, hurrying towards them, a tall, well built man with a ruddy complexion, dressed in a collarless shirt with a green, hand-knitted jumper and an old overcoat, not fastened, but tied around the middle with string. Wearing a pair of well-used Wellingtons he took long strides that quickly brought him to where the four officers waited.

'It's o'wer 'ere,' he pointed away from the lake.

'What did he say?' asked Martin, unable to understand the accent of the old farmer.

'It's over here,' explained Sgt Berry as they followed the farmer's quick strides down a bank and through an open gateway, the open wooden five barred gate leaned precariously against a stonewall.

"Thar' she is, not much left of 'er." They surveyed the burnt-out wreck of what had been, unmistakably, a Land Rover.

'Take a look, Jack, there's no point in all of us getting our shoes dirty,' reasoned Martin, pushing Jack gently forward.

'Well thank you very much,' said Jack, walking carefully down towards the vehicle.

'Over here, sir,' called Ripley to Martin. 'I'm quite sure these tracks belonged to the Land Rover, definitely Pirelli Scorpion Zeros.'

'Good lad, Ripley. Take some photographs of the burnt out wreck and the tyre tracks. How many people live around here sergeant,' asked Martin.

'Well, there's Larry here, he lives at Low Blean Farm, then there's a family at High Blean house, up there on Blean West Pasture. Back there about half a mile there's the small community of Countersett, and further on there's Countersett Hall. Then way down the road around the lake and beyond there are a few houses at Stalling Busk,' explained Berry to Martin, who followed her outstretched arm describing each location with interest.

'Beautiful place to live,' said Martin. 'How many people in total then?'

'About thirty-six, wouldn't you agree, Larry?' Sgt Berry asked the old farmer.

'Aye, that's about right. Now, what are you goin' to do about moving this 'ere vehicle?' asked the old farmer?

'We'll let you know when it can be moved,' said Martin, looking the farmer up and down.

'Nothing there, everything has been destroyed in the fire, including the tyres,' called out Jack, clambering back up to join the others. 'A total burn-out, efficiently carried out.'

'Ripley,' Martin called out to the young detective, 'Constable Dunstan is going to join you, then make sure you question everyone around here to see if anyone saw anything. Come on, Jack, lets go.'

Snapshot 225

George had been scouring the Internet looking for various press stories as her investigations into the deaths of the women associated with Luzhkov continued.

Tired, she closed her laptop sending it to sleep, and then she went into the secure room where she found Nick turning the pages of one of the books he had taken from Grice Hall.

'Found anything yet?'
'Just an assortment of entries and odd initials.' Nick explained, 'I'm scanning the pages into the computer so we can search through and sort all the information; hopefully it will reveal something of interest. But it's time consuming and very boring, we both need some refreshment.'

'Good idea,' agreed George.

'How are you doing with your investigation?' asked Nick, filling the kettle.

'Well, I thought I would start by looking for press reports on the husbands whose five wives died, to see what, if anything, is happening in their lives. Who knows, some reports might mention their business. I'm just looking for any scraps of information which might lead back to Luzhkov,' she explained, while leaning back in the chair and running her hands through her hair.

'Great, if we could just find some positive evidence between any or all of those businesses that prove he's exploiting them to his own advantage,' said Nick while making the tea, 'we would have him.'

'I'll keep on looking.' The sound of the doorbell interrupted their conversation. 'I'll go,' said George, jumping up. She returned with Detective Chief Inspector Martin and his Sergeant, who both immediately noticed the two mugs of tea on the kitchen table.

Surprised, but not unphased by their presence, Nick asked if they would like some tea, which they gladly accepted.

'Sorry for disturbing you, but we were in the area, so I thought it easier to call round and tell you that forensics will be finished tomorrow, so you'll have full use of the driveway once again,' explained Martin, taking a mug of tea from Nick.

'Thank you for taking the time. Have you discovered who the unfortunate individual is yet?' asked Nick.

'No, not yet, but we located the Land Rover which was parked on the roadway on the night of the murder,' explained Jack.

'That's good news,' jumped in George.

'Not really, Miss, it was completely burnt out, but it might still yield some clues,' continued Jack. 'One positive piece of evidence is that we've found a young women who remembers seeing the dead man at the opening of the fur shop in Hawes.'

'We were there,' added George.

'Really, and yet you don't remember seeing him,' asked Martin. No, but the shop belongs to Mr Luzhkov of Grice Hall,' said George, thoughtfully.

'That's right Miss, but they have no knowledge of him either,' added Martin, interested in where this was going.

'It's quite possible the victim worked in one of the hotels around the area, they are the only ones to employ foreign labour,' chipped in Nick, 'most of the farms only employ family members or locals.

'We're looking into that possibility. You've not recollected anything that could help us?' asked Martin.

Shaking his head, Nick said, 'I'm afraid not, it's a complete mystery.'

'A total mystery,' agreed George.

'Not a mystery, Miss, murder. We have four murders; two of the victims are local, as you well know. And two are strangers, who no one seems to know. But all the murders seem to be connected to each other in some way; it's my job to find the evidence that connects them.'

'But Chief Inspector, you already know who killed Spence,' Nick hesitated, 'I mean Mrs Spencer.'

'True, but then the killer became a victim, who murdered him?'

'I don't know, but it wouldn't surprise me if that same person wasn't the one who was responsible for this latest murder,' speculated Nick.

Martin finished his tea and walked around the kitchen, studying the various ladles and spatulas. 'Do you use all these?'

'Yes, they each have a specific function,' said Nick, curiously.

'Quite, now you stick to your antiques and we'll solve the...' he ran his fingers along the line of ladles so they bumped into each other, 'what you referred to as the mysteries. But don't forget, Mr Hartford, you're still central to our enquiries. Thank you for the tea, we'll be seeing each other again soon.'

Snapshot 226

'Well what did you make of that little episode?' George asked, returning from showing the visitors out.

'Interesting; they seemed quite friendly, but they're constantly digging, just waiting for one of us to slip up.'

'H'mm, that's their job. What are you going to do now?' she asked, recognising a sudden change in Nick, who, realising she was studying him, smiled and came to sit beside her.

'I feel like confronting Luzhkov and his sidekick Blandford with the fact that we know it was them who dumped the body in our driveway.'

'You must be joking; this guy is crazy! We already have four dead. We need to continue with our investigation regarding his shady business deals, until we find something, till then, we are low key, strictly low key,' beseeched George.

'Alright, but I can just see them laughing; it's as if they've dumped their rubbish on our land and there's nothing we can do about it.'

'Meeting them head on is not the answer. God knows what they'll do next time. Let's continue gathering evidence, until we know, for certain, that Luzhkov is benefiting financially or politically from his conspiratorial connections, then we'll act.'

Nick listened to her outburst and nodded approvingly.

'What would I do without you, George? Of course we'll continue gathering data,' he placed his arm around her shoulders and drew her close.

Snapshot 227

George woke up early, showered and had already enjoyed a light breakfast before the sun came up on a cold Wednesday morning. By the time she climbed into the BMW, Wilf, who had returned to work, was busy sweeping leaves off the lawns.

'Morning, Miss, are you going far?' he called out.

'Just over to the farmer's market in Settle,' she replied, cheerily.

'Well, best watch the roads for ice over the tops, Miss.'

'I will, thank you, Wilf.' With that, she drove off steadily down the drive before turning into the road towards Settle.

The sky was a lovely watery blue with just a few wisps of cloud, and a stiff northerly breeze was blowing. A typical cold winter morning, she thought, as she started to climb higher and looked out upon the undulating fells rolling out ahead. Outside, she could see a few hardy grazing sheep dotted around the green expanse, otherwise, she was quite alone.

At the very top of the climbing road she pulled into a lay-by, specially created for summer tourists who enjoyed taking photographs or who just wanted to gaze out over the landscape while enjoying a sandwich and a flask of hot tea.

She pushed the door open and the side of the 4 x 4 rocked, as it caught the full force of the wind. Her hair flew in every direction as she walked the small distance to a limestone wall that helped keep the sheep away from the road.

The Enigma Variations by Elgar was playing on the radio, these fells, which were mild and tranquil on this winter morning ideally suited the music. But these same fells had known harsher times, with many people having to scratch out a meagre living from the poor soil, or else having to endure backbreaking hours in the many small stone quarries. These fells have seen their fair share of spilt blood and tears; lashed by the fierce winds and diluted by the driving rain they have been tamed by machine and man but even now could deliver a harsh lesson to those who ignored the climate.

The chill breeze on her cheeks soon became uncomfortable and she returned to the warm cabin of the BMW, continued her journey, rejuvenated by the surroundings and enthusiastic for the day ahead.

Snapshot 228

Molly Marshall was bright, exuberant and blonde, with a large, warm smile. As the leader of the 10th Queensbury Green Guides Troop she had her work cut out supervising her guides.

They were a lively bunch of ten to thirteen year olds who enjoyed being together doing 'girlie things', but were currently camping down by the river on the outskirts of Settle. On this Wednesday morning, Molly had brought a group of eight girls to collect some provisions from the local market, plenty of sausages, beef burgers and beans. Some of the girls wanted to buy some sweets and their favourite magazines, so Molly was making sure they only bought age-appropriate material. In the small shop they eagerly looked at what the store had on offer, scanning and sharing the material with each other.

Most of the regular customers ignored the laughter and chatter from the small group while calling in for their regular purchases. As usual most stopped, and past a few pleasantries between themselves. It was like this most days, so when George entered she was greeted with the usual array of smiling faces and small gossipy exchanges.

'Your usual papers and magazines, there's a full report in the Dales Magazine on the proposed new hydro scheme; now that will turn a few heads,' said the newsagent, handing George a small bundle.

'I expect it will,' agreed George, pretending to be interested.

'How is Mr Hartford, is he getting over the shock of all these deaths, and when is he opening the shop again? It was such a shock, poor Mrs Spencer and her husband,' the newsagent continued to talk to the group, all these murders, robberies, and endless questions, when is all going to end.

'It's been a very difficult time for everybody,' interrupted George, not really knowing how to respond to the gossip, but then added as an afterthought, 'the shop opened on Monday.'

She excused herself and left to a round of sympathetic nods from the locals.

Molly Marshall decided the girls had had long enough to choose their purchases and started encouraging her young guides to move to the counter to pay.

'Come along now girls, Lucy, Bethany, Charlotte. Sarah, make your way to the counter,' she ushered them forward, all except Sarah, she stood perfectly still, oblivious to the heeding from her patrol leader.

'Sarah, please, it's time to go,' urged the guide leader. But the girl didn't move.

Molly became concerned and, walking towards the young girl, repeated her request, much to the amusement of the other guides finalising their purchases. By the time she reached Sarah's side her gentle concern grew to shock as she observed that the young girl was frozen by fear; she stood, transfixed, staring straight ahead, oblivious to the guide leaders coaxing.

Snapshot 229

Sgt Berry watched as her husband treated the young Girl Guide for shock. He had already questioned the guide leader about any history that could have led to such a reaction, but she knew of no reason why the girl should behave in this way.

'I'm going to admit the girl for observation, I think it would be a good idea if you accompany her Miss Marshal,' said her husband, and then added to his wife, maintaining a professional approach,

'I think you should notify the girl's parents, Sergeant'.

'But what about my girls?' pleaded the leader.

'Don't you worry, I'll make sure they all get back to the camp safely,' Sgt Berry assured her.

Snapshot 230

Sarah Hawks was a perfectly normal 12-year-old girl; she enjoyed her school, her friends and a happy home life. She had eagerly looked forward to this trip with her guide troop.

In the newsagents she had been reading extracts from the Mizz magazine with her friend Lucy.

Suddenly she had become aware of a familiar voice above the chattering and laughter of her friends. At first, she failed to place it then slowly, with the realisation of where she had last heard the voice a feeling of apprehension swept over her. Was something awful about to happen? Fear spread, quickly numbing her small frame, inducing a paralysis.

Snapshot 231

Having overheard Sgt Berry recounting the story of the young guide in the newsagent's to PC Dunstan, Martin showed little interest until he heard her name, Sarah Hawks.

He had spent the last half hour outside the young girl's room, awaiting the arrival of her parents. Jack flicked through some well thumbed magazines while Martin paced the corridor, looking up each time the door swung open as yet another nurse, doctor or orderly entered or left.

'Nobody seems to do anything here, Jack, they seem to spend most of their day walking up and down,' he grumbled.

'Isn't that what we do?' said Jack, replacing the magazine. 'I'm off to find a tea machine.'

Martin watched the sergeant disappear through the swing door, and then he glanced back at the limp figure of the girl through the window.

'What could possibly have traumatized her so much to evoke such a severe state of shock?' he wondered. *'Such innocence; sometimes we forget how vulnerable our children are.'*

The swing door opened and Jack walked in backwards, carrying two cups.

'Best they have,' he thrust a plastic cup towards Martin, who inspected the contents then took a drink.

'Bloody hell, Jack, its witch water.'

'At least its warm,' said Jack, sitting down.

The door swung open and Mr and Mrs Hawks rushed through, looking extremely anxious. They acknowledged the two detectives briefly, before, as if out of nowhere, a nurse appeared and ushered them into the room where their daughter lay.

Jack watched as Mrs Hawks hugged her daughter, tears streaming down her face.

The sound of her mother's voice, together with her comforting hugs, triggered something in the girl's psyche; suddenly she cried out, 'Mummy, mummy, it was her,' then collapsed into her mother's embrace.

'Did you hear that, Jack?' whispered Martin.

'I did.'

'I want an officer posted here immediately. Tomorrow we'll question the girl with Sgt Berry,' retorted Martin.

'Oh, and will you suggest she leaves her uniform at home.'

Snapshot 232

George pored over the press cuttings from The Invernesshire Courier about the car accident in which Lydia Mackintosh died. Driving from Oban after a celebration dinner, she was involved in what was described as a road rage incident, in which her car was pushed off the road, the car went through a fence, overturned and rolled down a cliff into the sea.

'Here we go again, this sounds familiar,' thought George already excited at the prospect of visiting Oban. She sifted through more papers and learned that the dead woman had been married to Hamish Mackintosh, who was chairman, and the largest shareholder of Scottish Pharmaceuticals.

'Now what has he been doing since his late wife's death,' she pondered, typing his name into her laptop. It seemed the company's shares had increased in value considerably since successful new drug trials in the USA and Europe. A new drug due to be released onto the market shortly was to be used to treat patients suffering from cancer.

After his wife's death, Mr Mackintosh had moved out of the family home, Bermaldine Castle just outside Oban, and moved to London, where he was remarried within six months to a Latvian beauty, Anzhela Nazarov.

Later, having packed her bags into the BMW George checked with Nick to see if he had found any references to Scottish Pharmaceuticals on the database of Luzhkov's business interests.

'Nothing as yet, but there's still a lot to upload. I'll contact you the minute I find anything.'

'Don't forget,' she chided him.

'I'll join you as soon as I've finished my work here.'

'You continue your work here, the quicker we find more information about Luzhkov's business insider dealing, the better the understanding we'll have of any corruption,' she came up close to Nick and grasped his hand tightly.

'I'll work flat out,' he pulled her close into a long embrace.

Snapshot 233

Martin had successfully persuaded the ward staff nurse to allow the auxiliary nurse to make him some tea rather than use the vending machine. He sipped it slowly, savouring the liquid while he waited for Jack and Sgt Berry to emerge from talking to Sarah Hawks in the side room. The young girl had made a remarkable recovery, and was enjoying her brief celebrity status.

Fellow guides had made visits, most bearing gifts of sweets and flowers, which along with the presence of her parents had assisted in her quick recovery. She was now sitting up in bed chattering away to the two sergeants. Martin decided to leave it to them, while he observed through the window as he enjoyed his tea.

'Tea alright for you?' asked the auxiliary nurse with a big smile, as she pushed a trolley down the corridor leading into the main ward.

'Very good, thank you,' said Martin, lifting his cup to the departing figure.

'If you could somehow devise a method to encapsulate the energy generated by the constant traffic of numerous bodies in every corridor in the hospital, it would provide enough power to supply the whole hospital,' mused Martin, chuckling.

Sgt Berry, dressed in civilian clothes, emerged from the side-room with Jack following behind. They both waved to Sarah, who then resumed talking to her parents.

'Well?' asked Martin, anxious to learn what they had found out.

'Where did you get the tea?' asked Jack, eying the steaming mug enviously.

'Trust you, Jack. This way,' said Martin, moving off down the corridor and into the kitchen, 'There's the tea, now tell me, what did the girl say?'

'She remembers talking to her friend Lucy about their horoscope in the Mizz magazine. There was a lot of chattering, then, from the front of the shop, she picked out a familiar voice. At first she did not recognise the voice, but it was familiar. Suddenly, it dawned on her that the voice belonged to the woman who kidnapped her and her mum.'

'Did she see her?'

'No,' Jack poured another tea, 'once she realised who it was, she was frightened.

She describes feeling cold and being unable to move. She doesn't remember anything else about what happened afterwards until she heard her mother voice calling her name here in the hospital.' Finished, Jack leant against a large double cooker and started to loosen his tie.

'Jack, drink up, we need to get to the shop and see if they can remember who was in at the time,' urged Martin.

'It's in hand, I rang Ripley and told him to get round there, pronto.'

'Well done, Jack. In that case, I suggest we all take advantage of the staff canteen. The staff nurse said we could eat there, and they have stew and dumplings on the menu today,' said Martin, rubbing his hands together.

'Hospital food,' responded Jack, nonchalantly, with a twinkle in his eye.

'I don't remember you turning down a free meal before,' teased Martin.

'And I don't intend to start now,' laughed Jack. Sgt Berry followed the two detectives, who were still ribbing each other, down the corridor and out of the ward.

Snapshot 234

Ripley couldn't believe his luck when the shop assistant had suggested they go to review the CCTV tapes, to establish who was in the shop on Wednesday when young Sarah Hawks heard the voice that had terrified her.

He was full of admiration at the way the assistant wound the tapes and handled the controls, not only to show him who was present, but to be able to put a name most of the faces.

Explaining that the tape would be returned in due course, he left to report back to Detective Chief Inspector Martin.

Snapshot 235

Sgt Berry went through the photographs that Ripley had produced from the newsagents CCTV tape. She checked faces against the names that Ripley had supplied, conscious that Martin was watching her.

'Well, can you confirm the list?' asked Jack, anxious to move forward in the investigation. This was a break they had not expected, and it had come from a very unlikely source, but if they could put a face to the woman's voice the girl heard, they would be well on their way to perhaps finding someone for the robbery at Computer International and the kidnapping of the Hawks.

'Yes, the names are correct and I've added two more. I agree with Ripley that nine people entered or left the newsagent's during the time spread of, say, four minutes.'

Jack picked up the photographs and scrutinised the faces once more, his eyes screwed tight in concentration, his eye lines deepened. Martin was waiting for his sergeant to confirm what he had been thinking since Ripley produced the photographs.

Jack looked up. 'Its Hartford's girlfriend.' He looked once more at the photographs.

'She must be our prime suspect; we need to play a recording of her voice to the girl.' Jack sat down still clutching the prints. Both Martin and Ripley watched him, each knew that he had not finished talking.

'If the girl correctly identifies her voice, we have them.'

'By God, Jack, I was waiting for you to say that,' said Martin, jubilantly. 'Ripley, we have her voice on tape, can we use it?'

'Legally?'

'Of course, legally, it has to be watertight,' stressed Martin.

'Come on, Jack, we'll show Mrs Hawks these photographs. Let's see if she can identify anyone. Ripley, prepare a tape for the girl to hear.'

Snapshot 236

'Jack, surprise me! Why have you just bought two pints, when I expressly said we were going to interview Mr and Mrs Hawks. Not that it's not welcome, are you having one of your moments?' asked a puzzled Martin. '

Jack raised his glass and took a drink, then waved it in the direction of the fireplace. Martin followed his sergeant's outstretched arm, and, just beyond his pint glass, were Sheila and Stephen Hawks sitting at the corner table enjoying a bar-meal.

'You knew they were here?'

'Of course, I'm a detective,' chuckled Jack, 'They're staying in room 12, checked in last night.

'What would I do without you?' Martin raised his glass in acknowledgement. Jack leant towards his chief inspector,

'What did you mean, 'having one of your moments,' are you trying to suggest something?'

'You know, Jack, sometimes you can be a little forgetful, a senior moment,' laughed Martin.

'Cheeky bugger, what about you, you can't think of anything more interesting to paint than some empty green bottles.'

'And sold them for five hundred quid,' laughed Martin.

'I can't believe it, why don't you get your brush out and paint this,' Jack held up his empty glass.

'You show Mr and Mrs Hawks these photographs, and I'll fill that for you,' said Martin, passing over the photographs.

'Sounds like a perfect division of labour,' said Jack, acquiescing to Martin's suggestion by faking a stiff bow.

Snapshot 237

Jack weaved his way round the tables and haversacks strewn on the floor on his way back to Martin.

'Well, any luck?'

'No,' Jack lifted the glass and inspected the clarity of his beer, 'just reiterated what she told us before; the woman who entered her house had dark hair with a long fringe that covered a lot of her face.'

'Then tomorrow, we'll have to play the tape to the girl, and hope she recognises the voice.'

'That's what I explained to them. I said we would be there early. Oh, young Sarah is being, discharged tomorrow,' explained Jack, 'Now we have time for a few more.'

'Good idea, by the way, where's Ripley?'

'He's preparing the tape and filling in the reports,'

'Poor sod,' they both laughed and downed another drink.

Snapshot 238

Blandford entered the library and was surprised to see Mr Luzhkov sitting in the red leather chair, perusing his well-thumbed 'Seven Pillars of Wisdom'.

'I've never read it, is it interesting?' asked Luzhkov.

'Yes, very, I have a long standing fascination for the exploits of T.E. Lawrence,' said Blandford eagerly.

'H'mm, a somewhat odd fellow, wasn't he a homosexual?'

'There was a strong homoerotic element in Lawrence's life that is still debated amongst scholars of his life,' explained Blandford.

'An adventurer; someone prepared to stand up for his own principles, but he had a weakness; his vanity.' Blandford shifted uneasily from one foot to the other. Luzhkov tossed the book onto the side table.

'Please sit down Blandford,' he motioned to his personal assistant. 'Is everything satisfactory?' Though not visible, the tension in Blandford's shoulders disappeared upon hearing the question.

'There has been no further contact with the police. I understand they have questioned Hartford a few times.'

'Good. That thoroughly unpleasant little man, let's hope that is the last we hear from him.'

Luzhkov stood to his full height and walked over to the bookcase running his fingers along the spines of the books.

'Let's hope our actions has successfully deflected police attention away from us. I would like you to arrange for Thomas Powys-Smith and his wife Irina to be picked up from the airfield this weekend.' Luzhkov's fingers stopped on a well-worn brown leather spine embossed with gold lettering.

'"Hard Times' by Charles Dickens,' he said brandishing the book, 'an attempt to attack the Utilitarians of the nineteenth century. Do you know they actually believed in the 'greatest amount of happiness for the greatest number of people. What nonsense. Would you get me a whisky and soda, please, Blandford?' Luzhkov replaced the book while his personal assistant poured out the drink.

'I have decided it's time our friend Powys-Smith assisted us in our plan to develop the water supply in Cyprus. Irina tells me that 'Compass' requires more money to undertake further development and research. But they are already facing demands from the banks to pay off some existing loans. We now hold twenty eight per cent of shares in the company and I think we can promise to supply the extra money they need, at a price, of course.' He lifted the heavy cut, crystal glass and took a small sip.

'Have our people in Limassol set up the first round of talks with Government representatives.'

'Yes, the first meeting is scheduled to begin at 11pm our time on Sunday,' replied Blandford.

'Good We'll tell Powys-Smith about the talks on Friday evening.'

Snapshot 239

Ripley watched Sarah's reaction closely as she looked at the photographs; the girl shook her head slowly.

'Sorry, I don't recognise anyone from them,' she said, flashing her large, clear, green eyes at Ripley.

'I'm going to play you a recording of four voices, before each, I'll say one, two, three, four. After you've heard all the voices I want you to tell me which number you recognise. Do you understand?' The girl gave Ripley a large wide smile and nodded in acknowledgement. Ripley pressed the button on his Olympic voice recorder, *'I hate working with kids, you never know what they will do next,'* he thought.

'One,' the voices began.

'Two,' no reaction.

'Three,' immediately her eyes narrowed and her hands pushed hard into the bed sheets.

'Four'.

'Number three, it was her, definitely, it was her,' she said, hurriedly.

'It's OK, don't you worry, no one is going to bother you again,' he reassured the young girl, while at the same time indicating to her parents, who had been watching from outside, that he had finished.

Snapshot 240

'So, the young girl identified Miss Sanderson's voice as that belonging to the woman who kidnapped her. But she failed to identify her from the picture in the shop.

Well, I think we have enough to pull her in.' Jack, take Ripley and bring her in,' Martin folded the newspaper, and then turned to Ripley.

'What did you discover about Luzhkov?'

'He runs a large haulage business and has numerous business interests in the city; buying and selling into companies, asset stripping, and some hedge funds. He is extremely wealthy with some highly influential friends.'

Ripley put on his jacket and pushed his Olympic voice recorder into the inside pocket.

'Legitimate?' asked Martin.

'Seems to be. He has interests outside the UK, deals in the US, Europe and Eastern financial markets. That's all I managed to find.'

'What does it all mean?' asked Jack, pulling on his dark blue jacket.

'It means he thinks he's untouchable; they live in a different world from the likes of us. Jack, take Ripley and bring Miss Sanderson in for questioning.'

Snapshot 241

Nick was busy on the computer when he saw two familiar figures walk up to the back door on the security monitor. He sighed, closed the bookcase door to his private room and went to meet his visitors.

'Good afternoon Inspector, constable,' he let them into the breakfast room.

'It's Detective Sergeant, and this is Detective Constable Ripley,' said Jack, correcting Hartford.

'Of course, how can I help you?' said Nick, knowing full well their correct titles.

'We would like to speak with Miss Sanderson,' said Ripley.

'Well, I'm sorry but she is not here,' explained Nick.

'When do you expect her back, sir?' asked Jack.

'I don't, she's gone off to visit some girlfriend of hers down south, family trouble I think,' Nick lied, suspicious of their officious attitude.

'Is there anything I can help you with?'

'Can you give me an address where we might contact her?' asked Jack sharply.

'No, I don't have one, its somewhere in Billericay.'

'Billericay! But she's your girlfriend, surely she'll be ringing you.'

'Well, I hope so, but you'll never believe this; she broke her mobile the day we found that corpse on our driveway and she hasn't replaced it yet. She said she would get one of the latest models in Billericay. When she rings, I'll tell her to get in touch with you straight away,' Nick lied, yet again. There was nothing Jack and Ripley could do but leave, but not before they warned Nick to get in touch as soon as she made contact.

'What do you think Sarge?' asked Ripley, as they trudged back to the car.

'That it's a bloody long way to come for nothing,' moaned Jack.

'I meant do you believe he doesn't know of her whereabouts?' said Ripley.

'Do I hell, but what can we do?' said Jack, climbing into the car.

'Wait,' sighed Ripley despairingly. 'We have a young girl who has recognised a voice but not the photograph. Her mum is unsure about either; without Miss Sanderson we have nothing.

Snapshot 242

As soon as the police left, Nick rang George to tell her they wanted to speak with her, and that they had not explained why, but it was official.

He advised her to unscrew the rear number plate, once free it would open to reveal a rear storage compartment in which she would find alternate safe number plates. Also, she should buy a new pay-as-you-go phone.

'I've been talking to you all this time and I don't even know where you are,' they both laughed heartily.

'I'm going to investigate the death of Lydia Macintosh in Oban.' She explained the detail of her enquiry then they talked for a long time, each realising they missed the other.

Snapshot 243

Martin reacted to the news about Miss Sanderson's absence with a typical tirade of frustration.

'Why is it every time we think we're making progress the rug gets pulled out from beneath our feet,' he moaned before ordering Ripley to put out a description of the woman.

'We must find her. Get to it Ripley, when you've done you'll find us at the Golden Lion.'

Snapshot 244

George took an apartment on Corran Esplanade overlooking the bay of Oban rather than book in to a hotel. Small but well equipped it had a panoramic view of the mountains on one side of the bay and the far distant isle of Kerrera on the other. After Nick's phone call she had changed the number plates as he had suggested. Afterwards she had taken the A85 to Dunbeg to view the scene of the accident in which Lydia Mackintosh had died.

The fence through which she had driven when pushed off the road had been repaired, but, to her horror, the wreckage of the car still remained at the bottom of the cliff. It was a desolate place where the road twisted and turned along the cliff edge. She could find no one in the locality with whom she could discuss the accident; it seemed the only witness to the accident was the person who pushed her off the road, and no one had come forward.

Here in the apartment she studied a road map; was it possible that Lydia's car and that of her pursuer could have been captured on CCTV camera in Dunbeg just a couple of miles away. Perhaps the local constabulary had already checked, she must find out.

Snapshot 245

Thomas Powys-Smith had never felt completely comfortable in the company of Luzhkov; tonight was no exception.

He took a strong puff on a Cohiba cigar, its rich aroma suited him and he blew out a long stream of smoke across the green baize of the snooker table.

'Excellent cigar, as always, Luzhkov,' said Thomas Powys-Smith, rolling the cigar gently between his fingers.

'I get them from Davidoff's, London,' said Luzhkov. 'Blandford, put a box aside for Thomas.'

'There's no need, really,' said Thomas.

'Nonsense, not at all, as a matter of fact I have some news for you,' said Luzhkov striking the white ball strongly towards a lone red in the corner of the table. He watched the ball's progress along the green baize, and then pressed a remote control. Thomas watched as a giant TV screen unfurled from the ceiling. Luzhkov pressed more buttons and Sky News appeared on the screen.

'If my information is correct there should be some breaking news from Cyprus that will be of interest to both of us,' said Luzhkov.

Thomas watched as the adverts disappeared and the news screen appeared. Sure enough, just as predicted, the scrolling Breaking News banner contained a report that major talks were planned to discuss the building of three desalination plants at a cost of over five hundred million euros.

Thomas was puzzled; he took another long drag on his cigar, not sure why this should be of interest to him.

'Those three desalination plants, when completed, would supply the majority of water to the populous of the island. There are no natural rivers in Cyprus.' said Luzhkov.

'You seem to be remarkably well informed, how did you know about the talks?' asked Thomas, sensing both he and his company were being manipulated. He wished he was far away.

Blandford handed a mobile to Luzhkov, who walked into the corner of the room to take the call. Thomas stubbed the cigar into an ashtray forcefully, as he realised the whole visit had been stage-managed, and wondered what new surprises lay ahead.

He watched while Blandford, the lap dog, took the mobile from Luzhkov, who having finished the call seemed ebullient.

'How would you and Irina fancy a visit to Cyprus? I have a wonderful villa in the Troodos mountains near Platres, where you will be comfortable,' he announced.

'That's impossible, out of the question, why should I go?'

'Because I want you to take charge of the negotiations on behalf of 'Compass-Smith',' said Luzhkov, placing one arm around his shoulder.

'Ridiculous,' protested Thomas, 'we cannot be involved in such a huge contract at this time,' he protested, shrugging off Luzhkov's arm.

Luzhkov turned and stared at him with his blue steely eyes and announced calmly,

'I own 28% of the shares in 'Compass Smith Water Co', and, I know the banks are going to call in some rather large loans. You will attend the talks; with my contacts and backing you will immediately enter into negotiations with the Cypriot government for the contract to build the three desalination plants. What is more, 'Compass-Smith' will provide half the cost; the EU will provide the rest. In return, Cyprus will pay back the whole cost over fifteen years to 'Compass-Smith'. In the meantime, I will promise to pay off the bank loans.'

Thomas listened, seething; he could feel the Russian's warm breath on his face. He met his gaze but knew the battle was lost; he could taste the bitterness of his defeat.

Without the backing of Luzhkov, in the face of the bank's threat to call in the loans, he would be ruined.

'Blandford will drive you and Irina to the airport,'

Luzhkov continued, then handed him several folders all neatly tied with ribbon.

'Read these, they will brief you on the Government ministers you will be meeting on Sunday. I will be in touch.'

He turned and left the sad figure of Thomas clutching the files.

Snapshot 246

The sixteenth century Creran Castle lay two miles from Oban. Having parked the car George tramped up the drive on a bitterly cold morning.

The castle had been the ancestral home of the Mackintosh clan since 1605 and Lydia Mackintosh had lived here with her husband Hamish until her death. The raw, grey, granite building towered over George as she reached the large, oak door at the top of the giant steps. She raised the iron doorknocker three times to announce her presence; the resulting thuds rang out deep inside. She pushed her cold fingers into her coat pockets and waited for a response. Gradually the door opened to reveal a wizened old lady in dark clothes, her silver hair was tied back in a neat bun.

'Can I help ye?' George noticed three large chains fixed across the doorframe that restricted the door from being opened any wider.

'My name is Sanderson, I write for a London Society Magazine and we are doing a feature on the late Lydia Mackintosh. I was hoping you could give me some information on the circumstances surrounding her death,' said George, through the tiny gap.

There was a long pause while the old lady studied the shivering stranger, George lifted up her hands and breathed warm air onto her chilled fingers.

'You'd better come in out of the cold,' the words sang out in a rhythmical lilt.

The door closed and George could hear the chains being removed. When the great door opened once again it revealed the tiny frame of the lady with the creased face. Once she was inside, the door shut with a loud clatter.

'Since the lady went, we only use the kitchen.' George followed the old lady through the large baronial hall into the corridor and down some tiny stairs.

'It's warm in here,'

She pushed open another large oak door to reveal a kitchen that was warmed by a three oven Aga.

'You'll be warm in here.' The old lady walked towards the Aga and opened the oven door. She pulled out a tray of hot scones, put two on a plate and pushed them towards George signaling her to sit down.

'These will warm you.'

'Thank you.' George cut her scone and buttered the two halves.

'Did Mrs. Mackintosh spend most of her time here?'

'She did, born and raised in the castle she was, married here and laid to rest, all in the castle. Aye it was her home, as well as being her ancestral home.'

'And Mr. Mackintosh, did he live here as well?'

'He did at first, but his work kept him away a lot. The mistress would go and visit him down in London, but she couldn't stomach it down there for long.'

It was the first time that George had seen a wry smile cross the old woman's face.

'He's married again,' she continued, 'didn't wait too long before he was bedding another,' she scowled, 'a foreign woman so I'm told, never seen her myself. He doesn't come here anymore. He was never a full Mackintosh, never will be.'

George did not quite understand the relevance of this and asked.

'So he no longer owns the castle?'

'Never did, never will, it's all passed to Master Robbie, the mistress's brother.'

'On the day of her death, was everything alright,' asked George.

'Aye, she'd been down Dunbeg Marina to make arrangements for her boat to be fitted out for a journey she was planning. Then she called at the Kirk to see the Reverend, to arrange a remembrance service for her mother. Little did she know, the next time she saw the Reverend it would be at her own funeral.'

George quickly gathered the old women was a lonely old soul who liked nothing better than passing away the time chattering, especially about her mistress. After more than an hour of pleasant conversation George left and made her way back down to her car.

Snapshot 247

George walked along Camus Road in Dunbeg and observed that it did not have any CCTV cameras that could have captured vehicles passing on the nearby main road that Lydia Mackintosh would have used on her final fateful journey.

Disappointed, she walked down Kirk Road that had shops on the left and a beautiful bay on the right where the yacht 'Misty Isle' owned by Lydia Mackintosh lay at anchor.

'Hello there, could you take me over to a boat?' George called out to a man clad in yellow oilskins sitting repairing nets in the bottom of a small fishing craft. Unshaven, with deeply tanned features and small blue eyes, he looked out over the bay where she was pointing.

'There's a lot of craft out there, any one in particular?' his voice was deep but soft.

'The Misty Isle,' said George.

'Miss Lydia's boat, an' what would ye be wanting with that?' he asked.

'The old lady up at Creran Castle gave me permission to have a look at the boat. I'm writing a feature on Mrs. Mackintosh.'

'Are ye now, an what sort of thing would ye be writing about her?'

Without hesitating George answered. 'There are a number of women who have met there deaths in the last two years, all were married to successful businessman who all remarried very quickly to young women from former Russian states.'

'Lucky them, never been married myself. Climb down slowly,' he said, holding out his hand to help her negotiate the steep steps down to the swaying craft.

'She's a 32 footer built in Bristol in the seventies. She has five sails and five berths, lovely craft, very easy to handle. Last year Miss Lydia sailed her across the Atlantic and back, I was one of the crew,' he told George casually, while steering his small boat alongside the yacht.

Climbing aboard 'Misty Isle' George could almost feel the sense of adventure from sailing the seas.
She was narrower than George had imagined, her 32-foot length stretched out into the distant lapping water that produced a rocking motion, accompanied by the rappings of the swage ends of the rigging against the metal mast.

'I can certainly understand why she would want to spend a lot of time on board.'

'Aye, she was here that last morning planning her next voyage,' said the boatman.

'Was that the last time you saw her?'

'Alive, yes,'

'What do you mean?' asked George.

'I saw her at the crash site.'

'Oh my God, what did you see exactly, could you make out what had happened?'

'When I reached the vehicle she was already dead, the car was a mangled wreck, she didn't stand much of a chance once it left the road,' he said, unlocking the cabin door.

He signaled George to go below where she found the tables still strewn with maps and charts. On one area of the seating a heavy beige Arran jumper lay crumpled where it had been thrown. The galley area was neat; tins of stewing beef, curry, soups and rice pudding lined the shelves behind protective rails.

'What do you think happened?' asked George.

'The general consensus seems to be that she was driven off the road. There were traces of green paint on the mangled pieces of metal that was the side of her car,' he said quietly.

'Why didn't the police remove the wreckage?'

'You've seen the area, too steep, and almost inaccessible. The sea washed the area clean as soon as the tide came in, smashed the wreck against the rocks a hundred times before the next low tide,' he explained, then added, 'I did find her mobile before the tide came in.' George could hardly believe her luck.

'Have you still got it?'

'Yes, would it be of any use?'

'It may be. Why didn't you hand it to the police?' she asked.

'Didn't think it would help them, so I brought it back here,' he opened a drawer in the radar and satellite navigation area and handed George an iPhone.

'It will, need charging, I'll bring it back as soon as I've finished looking at it.'

'Lights fading, we'd better get back ashore,' he said.

'Did she say anything about seeing any strangers around?' she asked.

'No, but when I returned her mobile I was sure someone had been aboard.'

'What made you think that?' asked George.

'Just a feeling, and there was a faint smell.'

'It may have been her perfume.'

'No, I know her perfume. This was different, strong.'

'Like Ea de Cologne?'

'Perhaps'

Snapshot 248

Having finished scanning the notebooks and diaries into the computer, Nick analyzed the data. The repetition of several pairs of initials and numbers puzzled him; there was no sequence that made any sense. But the more he looked at them the more he felt that there was a hidden significance.

Taking the list of eight firms, each belonging to men whose wives had mysteriously died, and which George was currently investigating, he attempted to find a link-up between them with the data he held on the computer. It reminded him of a giant Samurai Sudoku puzzle.

Snapshot 249

Jack almost felt at home now in the tiny police station at Settle, as he gazed out of the window onto the main street. It was bitterly cold and the wind tossed the remaining leaves around in a circle.

The traffic was light and consisted mainly of local tradespeople, some of whom he now recognized.

'What are you staring at, Jack?' asked Martin

'Oh, nothing in particular, just watching Malcolm the dairy farmer making his usual deliveries and Gordon from the cheese factory carrying out his stock.'

'Bloody hell, Jack, don't tell me you're becoming one of them!'

'No fear of that, but they're a nice crowd,' said Jack.

'Any news of Miss Sanderson yet?' asked Martin, expectantly.

'Afraid not, Ripley put a bulletin out about her vehicle, but there have been no sightings.'

'Well, she's got to be somewhere, people don't just up and disappear. That bugger Hartford knows where she is but he's not letting on. Keep leaning on him Jack.'

Snapshot 250

George returned the iPhone to the fisherman still in his yellow oilskins. She had found a couple of photographs and several unfamiliar names in the address book, but other than that nothing useful to her investigation. The last number she had rang was a local number and she was on her way there to see if she could speak to the last person Lydia had spoken to on her phone.

'The Wide-mouthed Frog' was on Dunstaffnage Bay and its warmth was very welcome on this cold morning.

A red haired woman, whose smile was as warm as the surroundings, met George.

'Will ye be eating with us this lunchtime, or is it a drink you'll be wanting to warm you up? It's terribly cold this morning, with snow forecast before the days out,' she said, never once losing her smile. George explained the reason for her visit and asked if she could speak to the person who had spoken to Lydia Mackintosh on that fateful day.

'Of course, what a tragedy, the poor woman. That would be Miss Morag she spoke to; they were best friends and Miss Morag often accompanied her sailing.' Still smiling, she left, leaving George to explore the bar.

When she returned a tall, sporty looking woman with short blond hair accompanied her. Having made the usual introductions, George explained the reason for her visit. Miss Morag, the owner of 'The Wide-mouthed Frog', was visibly upset at the very mention of her late friend Lydia. Yes, she had indeed rang, and it turned out it was while she was being perused by another car.

'She was very distressed; this other car kept trying to overtake and seemed to be trying to force her off the road. She was very frightened, she said the man had been following her all morning. She had seen him at the Kirk and at the marina, but thought it was a coincidence,' she spoke very quickly with a soft voice.

'Did she describe the man or his car?' asked George.

'Yes, she said it was a green Land Rover and that the man was well dressed but with fiery eyes, he had a handkerchief in his top pocket. What silly detail to give me while she was fighting to stay on the road. The last thing she said was, 'What does he want, why is he doing this?' and then the line went dead, that was the last time I heard her voice. She was so distressed,' the blond haired woman recalled sadly.

'Did you tell the police about the call?' asked George.

'Yes, I did, they actually thought the accident might have occurred because she was using the phone. Outrageous, and of course they never found the other car.'

As George left the warmth of the hotel and emerged into the cold of the morning, the first light flakes of snow were falling gently. Time to head south George thought, before the snow makes travelling difficult.

Snapshot 251

Nick looked tired; his eyes were streaky red, his hair tousled and the dark shadows on his face betrayed the fact he had not shaven for thirty-six hours. In fact, apart from a few catnaps, he had not slept at all. Three mugs and several plates, some with half-eaten sandwiches and an empty carton of Chinese sweet and sour all bore witness to the fact that he had been working straight through.

Surrounded by paper, pens, pencils, books and flickering screens he scrutinized another list of data one more time, flicked a button on a control panel and listened once more to now familiar voices discussing share price movements in onerous detail over and over again.

Sometimes a new voice would break the monotony, then more information, and more detail. The hard disk had captured hours of conversation and presented it in one long stream of statistics and text.

He now had the evidence that he had been looking for, confirmation that Luzhkov was personally benefiting from insider dealing in a way that was almost unimaginable. The sheer amount of money he was moving around was staggering, most of it right under the eyes of the FSA, the regulatory body that was supposed to monitor shady stock movements.

On the surface he was a respectable businessman, but in truth, he was a gigantic fraudster, who, if George was right, was also responsible for multiple murders.

Now he had to bring all the evidence together so that it made sense. He had encountered some names that he would investigate in further detail. He felt sure that perhaps the key to unlocking the secrets of Luzhkov insider dealing could lay hidden amongst this new evidence.

Snapshot 252

The fire spit and splattered as more logs were thrown onto the burning embers, where large red and orange flames rose up out of the red furnace-like grate throwing off welcome heat.

Luzhkov's gaze was penetrating; he raised his head slightly without seeming to notice the maid fulfilling her duties. His blue eyes were firmly fixed on Blandford sitting opposite, who had just finished giving his update on the talks in Cyprus.

'Did Powys-Smith seem hopeful of an imminent successful conclusion to the talks?' Luzhkov asked.

'He estimates another two to three weeks followed by further meetings to discuss the logistics of building the dams. They would like to use as much local expertise as possible, 'Compass' of course want to use their own men. It's all open to negotiation,' said Blandford.

'Good, we now need to look at our strategy for expanding our shares in 'Compass'. Get in touch with William in London; tell him to buy 360,000 shares at around the present price of £8.45 per share. Once we leak news about the successful conclusion of the talks into the public domain, the share price of 'Compass' will climb very quickly. When it does, tell him to then sell all our shares in the company immediately, Afterwards, Willy is to disperse the money to our accounts in Venezuela, Estonia and North Cyprus so it cannot be traced in the usual way.' Luzhkov smiled when he had finished giving Blandford instructions.

'And Thomas Powys-Smith?' asked Blandford.

Viktor Luzhkov ran his thin fingers through his blond hair and walked over to the fire, where he grasped a brass ornate poker and stirred the fire, sending sparks flying up the chimney.

'We don't need him at the talks anymore. As we previously planned, send a small charter jet to collect Irina and Thomas, then 'poof,'' he dug the poker into fire, sending a scurry of sparks and flames up the chimney once again, 'they disappear from the radar.'

Blandford watched as Luzhkov replaced the poker, turned and left the room quietly, leaving his loyal personal assistant gazing into the flames.

Snapshot 253

The sun was sinking lower in the watery blue sky, a stiff breeze blew the branches gently to and fro, and the sound of the crunching gravel beneath Jack's feet rang out eerily through the trees.

Jack had decided to leave the car at the bottom of the drive and walk up the long twisting driveway to see Nick Hartford once more. The carefully attended lawn beds came into view, then the house, as he walked around to the rear looking into each window as he passed.

The building where Hartford kept his cars was shut tight, no vehicles were to be seen anywhere. Jack climbed the steps and knocked on the door.

He could hear someone behind the door moving around, when it opened to reveal Hartford, Jack was surprised at his appearance. Unshaven, his blond hair unkempt and eyes that were normally bright were now reddened.

'Sergeant, please,' Hartford hesitated, obviously caught unawares, 'please come in. I'm sorry, I was not expecting anyone.' Jack was taken aback at the state of him, and wondered immediately if he had been on the bottle.

'Are you alright?' he asked.

'Oh, yes, sorry about all this. He moved several groups of papers into a neat pile. How can I help you?'

'We were wondering if you had heard from your girlfriend yet,' Jack asked.

'No, no I haven't.'

'H'mm, and you've still no idea where she is?'

'Billericay, like I told you before.'

'It's very important we get in touch with Miss Sanderson,' emphasized Jack.

'Is she in some kind of trouble?' asked Nick.

'She might be, we would like to eliminate her from our enquiries. Are you sure you are alright?'

'Oh yes, I've been working long hours, burning the candle at both ends, you could say,' Nick laughed limply.

'You look like you've burned quite a few candles Mr Hartford. Is there anything you want to tell me?'

'Tell you, like what?'

'I don't know, anything,' asked Jack, probingly.

'No, nothing, nothing at all, unless you like figures.'

'Figures?'

'Stocks and shares, all that sort of stuff, I've been working on the movement of shares, really boring stuff.'

'I see. Well, I don't have much to do with stocks and shares in my line of work.'

'No I suppose not, nor me really, I'm just doing some work for a friend. I offered, stupid really, it's driving me crazy,' Nick was trying to bring the whole ridiculous conversation to a conclusion without giving anything away. If he hadn't been so tired he would never have got into this conversation, he told himself.

'Well, you get some sleep, and if you hear from Miss Sanderson, let me know.' Jack left Hartford promising to get in touch as soon as he heard anything.

Stocks and shares, what was so important that he had to work so many hours without sleep, doing it for a friend, movement of shares, what does it all mean?' Jack mulled over the details of the meeting as he trudged back down the drive to the car.

Snapshot 254

George threw her bags onto the bed and collapsed at the side of them, she had set off from Oban just after lunch and arrived in Whitby just after seven in the evening.
But there was no time for sleep just yet, first she must ring Nick and bring him up to date. The phone rang out for what seemed an age; she had missed Nick and looked forward hearing his voice.

'Hi Nick, it's me, I'm exhausted having just driven for over six hours,' she said.

'Oh, I'm so glad you called, George, where are you?' he asked.

'Whitby,' she cried.

'You're so close, less than a hundred miles.'

'I know, actually I nearly called in.'

'Glad you didn't, the police still want to talk to you, they've been around again asking after you.'

'Why?'

'I don't know, but I'll try to find out. In the meantime, stay away.'

'Can you join me here?' asked George.

'Perhaps, what are doing in Whitby anyway?'

'Do you remember Global Investments based in London, a big player in the stock market, the owner was a Mr. Harry Edge whose first wife died at sea?' she reeled off the data.

'Yes, I think so.'

'Well, his wife owned and moored a converted trawler called "Harry O" here in the marina. When she was not living in London, she lived aboard the trawler which coincidentally was named after her husband,' she told Nick.

'What happened to her?'

'She took a party of guests out for cocktails one evening sailing around the coast and when it returned she was missing. The police investigated her disappearance but later the coroner gave a verdict of death by misadventure,' she said.

'Sounds familiar.'

'I know, very familiar territory. I'll see if there is anything that I can dig up tomorrow, but right now I'm going to have something to eat.'

'Keep out of trouble, and please don't leave there until you either hear from me or I join you,' said Nick.

'Yes, sir,' they chatted for a while longer, each talking about their respective investigations and the possibility of any links.

Snapshot 255

William Montessori Berg previously had worked for 'Credit Agricole' and the Bank of America where as a currency investor he bet on fluctuations in the value of foreign currencies and also traded in stock.

He was less than six foot tall with a slight stoop, probably from hours hunched over computer screens; he was blessed with a generous round figure, a double chin and perspired most than most men. His spectacles lenses were thick and left a deep mark on the end of nose where they were generally perched. Berg was always immaculately attired, all his suits made in Hong Kong and each had a canary yellow lining.

Since forming his own company, 'Berg International Investment Fund', he had been an active trader in the London markets, and acting on inside information given to him by his so-called *sleeping partner* Viktor Luzhkov they had both prospered. He didn't know precisely where Viktor got all his information and to be honest, he didn't much care.

Much of his time and expertise was spent in devising new ways of concealing many of his financial transactions and depositing monies in accounts beyond the reach of the taxman and the regulatory financial authorities.

Life was good to him and his family and he was a well-known patron of the Arts and a variety of charitable causes as well as pursuing his lifetime hobby of sailing.

He had recently purchased a 62 foot reconverted trawler from a colleague, Harry Edge of 'Global Investments', whose wife had been tragically lost overboard on the vessel.

William had spent most of the day in his prestigious office on the twenty-ninth floor of St Mary Axe, it was cold outside with a persistent drizzle of rain that made the City of London look bleak.

It was late evening when he received a phone call from Reginald Blandford wanting to discuss the acquisition of shares in 'Compass-Smith Water Co'.

Having been fully briefed he later rang several well known trusted dealers to leak information about the talks in Cyprus that should result in 'Compass' being given the lucrative contracts to build three desalination plants.

Snapshot 256

Early the next morning, just after the market opened, William watched the stock price of 'Compass' climb steadily.

The news of the lucrative contracts had filtered through to various dealers, the share price flickered and continued to move upwards as buyers purchased more and more shares and confidence grew in an upward spiral.

William had spread his share purchases carefully earlier in the day; he now held over 360,000 shares. He waited patiently, not daring to take his eyes of the screens; trickles of sweat ran down a plump fold of flesh under his chin, his glasses perched precariously on the end of his nose, as still the price moved upwards. After what seemed an age, it steadied out at over seventeen pounds, the phones were on standby, he quickly made several phone calls giving the order to sell all the stock at the inflated price of seventeen pounds ten pence. Within minutes, the deal was closed. He had made millions.

Now, more relaxed, he watched as the price began to fall, someone was selling, who, why, panic, offload, he knew how other dealers, uncertain, would quickly sell, sell, sell.

His next task was to prepare the way for the monies to be dispersed throughout a network of prearranged deceptive links whose paths led over three continents.

Soon the money was secreted away with no links leading back to the 'Berg International Investment Fund'.

Finally, he picked up the phone and informed Blandford of the successful conclusion to the transactions.

Snapshot 257

A very satisfying conclusion, very satisfying indeed, Mr Luzhkov would be well pleased that his carefully constructed plan for buying and selling 'Compass Water Co' shares had gone like clockwork.

Reginald Blandford checked the time; Thomas Powys Smith should have been in the air for two hours, time to implement the finale. He carefully pressed the numbers on his mobile phone and waited for the familiar, ringing to signal a connection.

'Could I speak with Mr Powys-Smith, please,' he asked the cabin staff. He tapped his fingers impatiently while waiting, 'Thomas, hello, its Blandford, is everything alright with your journey?'

'Yes thank you Reginald. Have you seen the share price crash, what's happening, first they increase now they've plummeted. What on earth is going on?'

'Now, look, Thomas, don't you worry about the fluctuation in prices, when they hear about the new contracts, the price will take off once more,' Blandford said reassuringly.

'Did you get the attaché case I sent you?'

'Yes, its here, what's in it, not more papers for me to digest? Anyway I don't know the combination,' he said, in an off-hand manner.

'No papers I assure you, but a pleasant reward for a job well done. The combination is 562134, have you got that, 562134,' Blandford repeated.

'Oh, right, thank you, 562134....'
A crackle then silence.
Blandford put the mobile away, he poured himself a brandy, *'now you don't need to worry about plummeting shares, in fact you won't be worrying about anything ever again.'*
He raised his glass as a silent tribute to the vanquished.

Snapshot 258

The long sleep had invigorated George, and after enjoying a leisurely breakfast she eagerly set off for the harbour to find the trawler "Harry O".

Walking alongside the harbour, she passed lines of carefully coiled ropes that were all the colours of the rainbow, lying amidst piles of lobster pots and rows of netting.

Here old men, who all wore large woollen jumpers and had deeply furrowed brown skin with grey hair, sat in circles and repaired the nets while chatting amongst themselves.

Tourists mingled with locals on the busy pavements; some just hung over the railings looking out over the water, while gulls dived crazily over the bows of boats looking for any abandoned fish. Overlooking the harbour on the opposite side were the steep cliffs of West Bay and perched on top lay the old ruins of the Abbey with it's magnificence defying the years.

George soaked up the atmosphere but did not let it detract her from the business in hand, to find the trawler.

She did not have to wait long. Moored in the deeper water of the harbour, a converted trawler lay at anchor, her flag fluttering in the stiff breeze. The first thing George noticed was that a man was seated over the side, painting a new name.

She called out, but failed, amidst all the resident noises, to catch his attention. Not for the first time recently, she quickly persuaded a local boatman to take her out to the Atlantic trawler. Once alongside the sixty-two foot vessel she climbed up the rear ladder onto its magnificent teak decks with polished handrails and shiny brass fittings.

Almost immediately, a young man dressed all in black appeared from the wheelhouse.

'You have no right to be on deck, young lady, you must leave immediately,' he called out sternly.

George screwed up her face in her puzzled fashion trying to weigh up the best way to confront this situation. *'Young lady indeed,'* she thought, she guessed he was not much older than she was. Standing with arms folded he was waiting for her reply.

'Are you the captain?' she asked, having decided to flatter him, and approach this gently. *He looks officious,* she thought.

'The man who brought me over has gone.'

The young man looked over the side to confirm that the boat had returned, then turned to face her once more with a stern, disapproving look.

'I will make arrangements for you to be taken ashore.'

'Hang on a minute,' she interrupted, 'Can I explain why I am here, it's very important, you could say it's a matter of life or death. *Oh God, why did I say that?'* she thought.

'What I have to ask you will only take a few moments of your time, Captain,' flattery again, she thought.

'I am not the Captain; I simply look after the boat while the owner is ashore. You cannot board the boat without an invitation, any boat,' he said harshly.

'I did actually try to get the attention of the man painting over the side, but he did not hear me,'

'He is a painter, he has no authority on this boat,'

'OK, we've established that, and you have? So can we start again. My name is George Sanderson, I write for a well known woman's magazine, and to cut a long story short I am doing a story on the owner of this boat.'

'Mr William Montessori Berg.'

'Who?'

'Mr William Montessori Berg, the owner of this boat,' proclaimed the young man.

'But I thought this boat was owned by the late Mrs Gemma Edge,' exclaimed George, she had been caught off guard.

'She was indeed the previous owner, but the boat is now owned by...'

'Mr William Montessori Berg, yes, yes you've told me that already,' she interrupted, much to the young man's annoyance.

'Look, I'm sorry for coming aboard unannounced and all that, but what the hell, I'm here now, so can I just ask you a few questions, then I'll go?'

'What is it you want to know?'

'Do you know anyone locally who was aboard the night when Mrs Edge went missing?' she asked.

'Yes, I was.'

'You were?' wonderful she thought a break at last. She was beginning to find this young man irritable.

'So, you are like a fixture, you come with the boat. Sorry, I don't want to sound disrespectful or anything like that, but you worked for Mr Edge, and now you work for Mr Berg.'

'That's right, I come with the boat, as you so aptly put it, there are three crew, an engineer, a navigator and the steward,' he explained.

'And you're the steward,' she nodded.

'That's right, I look after the guests, the owner is the Captain.'

'So, on the night in question, you were looking after the guests, can you tell me what happened?'

'We were sailing back from Scarborough, it was late evening, they had enjoyed dinner and were on deck having drinks, listening to music and generally enjoying the voyage. When we came around the coastline towards Whitby someone pointed out that Mrs Edge had not made an appearance for some time. We searched the boat, but she was not on board. We put out a mayday call for a lifeboat, we doubled back and searched the area, but she was never found.'

'They never found her body?' asked George.

'No, the currents are strong, she could have been swept out to sea, she could be anywhere, it was all very sad.'

'Can you remember the names of the guests who were on board that night?' she asked.

'Of course, that's a guest list I'm hardly likely to forget,' he said, haughtily.

'I would very much like to speak with these people to gather material for my article. Could you give me their names?' she asked, pencil poised, ready to scribble down the information.

He pursed his lips and almost shut one eye while he recalled the names of the guests, anonymous names to George, until he came to the last one.

'And finally, Mr Blandford from Grice Hall.'

George almost swallowed her tongue and she put too much pressure on the pencil so that the lead point snapped off and rolled onto the teak decking. The young man immediately retrieved the discarded tip and threw it overboard.

'Will that be all, I really have to go?' Without waiting for a reply, he leant over the side and arranged for the painter to take George ashore.

'Goodbye,' and with that he disappeared into the wheelhouse.

Snapshot 259

Nick surveyed the neat piles of documents on the floor. In front of each was a sheet containing records of price movements and acquisitions of shares. Altogether there were eight piles; each representing a specific company, each led by a man who had lost his first wife and had then remarried to a Russian national.

He surveyed them with some degree of satisfaction; at last he felt he had made sense of the data he had collected. After hours of monotonous deliberation poring over codes, figures and listening to hours of conversations, he suddenly, over a cold bacon sandwich, had had his Eureka moment.

The code lay bare, it was ball-achingly simple.

For every name take the last letters, so Thomas Powys-Smith became SSH, Benjamin Hedgecoe became NE, and so on.

Once he had the names of the men he found the names of the companies they ran; 'Compass-Smith Water Co' was SHRO and 'Hedgecoe Investments' was ES respectively. So the initials SSH=SHRO and NE =ES began to have meaning, and with this information he had began to unravel large portions of the data.

Nick brought one file to the large rosewood dining table where he had been reading the morning paper. On page five he had ringed the story about a private jet exploding over the Austrian Alps, because Thomas Powys-Smith and his wife Irina had been on board.

Hours prior to the death of SSH there had been a lot of buying and selling of his company shares. Someone had made millions, but, following the announcement of the jet explosion, shares plunged. Banks called in all of their loans, the talks in Cyprus over possible contracts for desalination plants collapsed, and a mysterious backer withdrew his support.

He tied a ribbon around the file; for now it was a closed case, but ready for examination by the authorities when the time came.

Snapshot 260

Liam Stafford, the steward, was alone aboard the trawler, the painter and engineer having gone ashore. He had made the boat secure, and was enjoying some time on his own.
The visit by the inquisitive journalist was worrying him, 'I should never have given her the guest list,' he had this nagging doubt. Perhaps he should ring Mr Edge and tell him about the enquiries regarding his wife's disappearance.

'Mr Edge would understand,' Stafford convinced himself a call to the previous owner was the proper course of action to take.

Snapshot 261

'Yes, well, I'm ringing everyone who was on board.

That blithering idiot, Stafford gave this reporter the full guest list. So, anyway, Reginald, I'm just letting you know,' spluttered Harry Edge.

'Have you informed William?' asked Blandford.

'Yes, I rang him first, and I advised him to get rid of that nincompoop Stafford,' he bellowed down the phone.

'Never did like the fellow, gave me the creeps, always dressed in black, you could hardly see him on deck when it was dark. I used to remind him 'Why do you think Navy personal always wear white,' blithering idiot, but Gemma liked him.'

'Well, thank you for calling,' and then as an afterthought.

'Oh, do you have a name for this journalist, or the name of the journal he writes for?'

'It was a woman, her name is George Sanderson. For God's sake, the last thing I want is for Gemma's name to be dragged through the bloody tabloid press. You do understand, it was all too painful then, I don't want to go through all that again, you do understand.'

'Of course, Harry, of course, I will have a word with William and sort something out. Goodbye Harry, you needn't worry anymore, and thank you for ringing.'

Blandford replaced the receiver, 'Sanderson, I know that name,' he puzzled for a moment, but could not recall from where.

Snapshot 262

'William, has Edge rang you regarding the enquiries from the journalist?' asked Blandford.

'Yes, I must say he was in a bit of a state,' replied Berg.

'We can't have someone snooping around asking questions William, after all, my name is on that list.'

'Ah, I see, well, what do you suggest?'

'Tell that steward of yours to find this Sanderson woman and ask her to return to the trawler on the pretence he has further information which might be of interest to her. Let's say about nine tomorrow night,' said Blandford.

'I say, is all this necessary?'

'Absolutely, William, we must find out what this journalist is really after; who knows, she may work for the financial regulators,' Blandford knew that would do the trick. The thought of someone snooping into Berg's financial dealings would produce the desired reaction.

'Come now, Reginald you don't really think,' he hesitated as the possibility sunk in.

'You're right, we must be sure. I'll ring Stafford immediately and tell him to arrange for her to call.'

'Good, I will arrive on the trawler tomorrow afternoon,' said Blandford.

Snapshot 263

George climbed the 199 steps from the old town to the top of the east cliff, between the beautiful ruins of Whitby Abbey and St Hilda's church. She looked out over the vast expanse of sea and then over the bay to the quilt-like array of red clay cottage rooftops.

Originally founded by St Hilda, the abbey had become a Benedictine Priory in the eleventh century, until in 1539 King Henry VIII ransacked the place. It had remained empty since then, ravaged by the wind, the rain and local inhabitants.

She walked slowly amongst the old gravestones dotted around the church. The strong sea breeze almost took her breath away as her hair blew freely. She touched the cold, rough-hewn stone gravestone of 'Albert Beaumont, forty two years, lost at sea, trying to save crew from the shipwrecked boat 'Cooks Drift'.'

'Hi, I thought I might find you here,' a voice rang out and startled her. She turned to see the steward from the trawler.

'I called at the hotel, they told me you were looking around the old town,' he continued. George was taken by surprise and took a moment to compose herself.

'The hotel; how could you know where I was staying?' she asked.

'When you left the trawler, I saw you walking along the harbour towards the railway station, so I guessed you must be staying in one of the hotels in that area.'

'So you've found me, what do you want,?' she asked bluntly, annoyed at having been disturbed.

'After you left I found some photographs that were taken on the night Mrs Edge disappeared, there's also a diary. I found them stashed in a drawer, thought they may be useful for your story,' he explained, leaning casually against the fisherman's gravestone.

'Did you bring them with you?' she asked sharply.

'No, I wasn't sure that I would find you. I have some errands and shopping to complete today, and early tomorrow we are stocking up with water and diesel, so if you come around nine in the evening, I will show them to you,' he said.

As George listened, her instinct told her not to trust the steward. Suddenly, he was falling over himself to assist her, whereas earlier he had been rude and obstructive.

'Thank you, it sounds as if they will be very useful. OK, I'll call at nine,' said George. With that the steward left.

She watched as he made his way down the 199 steps holding onto the iron railing. She waited until he was well down the steps before she followed on slowly, and by the time she reached the bottom he had disappeared into the narrow alleyways of the old town.

She had decided to ring Nick and bring him up to date, but first she was going to check out of the hotel and find somewhere else to stay.

Snapshot 264

Passing through Pickering and making his way up onto the North York Moors was a delightful journey. Nick had heard it said that this is a place where dreams are made; in every direction you are confronted by vast open swathes of rich undulating moorland.

In spring and summer, the moors are inhabited by a rich variety of bustling wild life hidden in the lush green heathers. In autumn the moors are a tapestry of rich purple for miles in every direction. Right now as winter creeps over the moors it becomes a bleak uncultivated place where the driving rain, sleet and snow falls with a wild rage across the landscape.

Only the hardy Scottish Blackface and Swaledale sheep can survive here in this rugged land, nibbling grasses and heather shoots, annoyingly, Nick thought *'they always seem to be grazing near the road's edge'*.

He pulled over where the road widened. The wind blew fiercely. He could see the bays of Whitby in the distance as he pulled out the new number for the pay-as you-go-mobile that George was now using; he dialled and waited.

The cold wind was beginning to seep into his bones, but he had to be outside, as there was a signal problem in this area. He pushed the phone under his woollen hat that he had pulled well down over his ears.

'George, is that you?'

'Yes, where are you?'

'Up on top of the moors looking down on Whitby. Tell me where you're staying and I'll join you.'

'Great, I'm at the 'Jolly Sailor'. I have some information for you; you'll never believe what I've discovered. Shall I order breakfast for you?'

'Yes, please, and a large pot of extra hot tea please, its freezing up here. Be with you in a jiff.'

Within minutes he was roaring down the road, the lure of the hot breakfast was irresistible, and so was the thought of seeing George.

Snapshot 265

First thing in the morning was not the best time to confront Mr Luzhkov with anything, let alone unwelcome news.

Having discussed the successful conclusion to the share dealing in 'Compass', Blandford then acquainted him with the phone call from William Montessori Berg regarding Ms Sanderson, and immediately his attitude changed.

'Of course you know her, it's Hartford's fiancée,' he said bluntly. 'I remember reading details of the Spencer's funeral ceremony in the local press.'

Blandford felt embarrassed at not remembering, especially as he had met her, but he said nothing.

'Hartford does not learn,' Luzhkov continued, 'I thought the body in their driveway would be sufficient warning, but obviously not. He is a menace and I will not tolerate his interference into our affairs any longer. Bring this matter to a conclusion.'

Luzhkov's voice trembled with anger, although he did not raise the pitch of his voice, Blandford recognised the tone.

'I'm leaving to go to the trawler straight away,' he said.

'Who are you taking with you?'

'No one, I will deal with her myself.'

'Bring her in undamaged, Blandford; we must ascertain what she is doing and how much she knows about our affairs,' said Luzhkov.

'Very well, and if I should find Hartford?'

'Take Ilia with you; he will prove useful if you meet with resistance. Should Hartford be there, bring him back with the woman. I will return tomorrow to Grice Hall, and we will conclude this business for good.'

He delivered the whole sentences without emotion, the trembling of his voice had subsided, it was as if he was discussing a share price or arranging one of his shooting parties.

This was Luzhkov at his worst, as Blandford well knew.

Snapshot 266

The Jolly Sailor pub on St Anne's Staithe is situated close to the harbour. It has been patronised by Whitby fishermen, boatmen and locals in general for over two hundred years. It's small dark bars, with shining brass pumps, welcome the roving drinker who can enjoy real ale and home cooked food in a bar that had changed little over the years.

Having ordered breakfast for two George climbed up the dimly lit narrow twisting staircase to her small rooms that overlooked the harbour. The dark stained floorboards creaked and groaned with each step she made. A large double bed occupied most of the first room. Through a dividing door was a small sitting room with one settee, a single rocking chair and a low glass topped coffee table and against the wall stood a chest of drawers.

'It's above the bar, so it does tend to be noisy, especially in the evenings,' the landlady had explained when she was showing George the accommodation.

But for George it was ideal; the view over the harbour was the reason she had chosen these rooms, from here she could spy on the trawler.

Her suspicions about the steward's offer had not diminished, on the contrary, she was convinced the steward was lying and was trying to entice her aboard, but why?

She had chosen to take all her meals in the sitting room so she could watch the trawler undisturbed.

Through the small diamond shaped windows over the grey seawater she could observe the trawler, that dwarfed the smaller boats that were anchored nearby, her black and red hull bounced up and down repeatedly on the tidal water.

'Anyone home?' Before she could answer, the door opened and in walked Nick. George rushed forward and flung her arms around his neck. His flesh was cold from the stiff morning breeze, but she squeezed him hard.

'Hey OK, OK, I know you've missed me but lets not overplay our hand,' he feigned a choking noise.

'I've been so worried, I'm so glad you're here,' the tension of uncertainty suddenly lifted in his presence and her calmness gave way to a wave of tears, tears of relief.

'Hey what's this, what's happened to my solid, dependable, soul mate?' Nick sat next to her on the settee, and gently dabbed her tears with a handkerchief.

'I'm frightened, Nick. I feel that I'm being drawn into a trap, Blandford was on the trawler the night Mrs Edge went missing. Thank God you're here,' she pulled him closer once more.

A sudden, sharp knock at the door startled them both. The door opened and in walked the landlady with a large tray.

'Two breakfasts as ordered, my dears,' she observed George's tears.

'Pleased to see him, ah, I used to feel like that once,' she laughed, 'I'll bring up the tea in a jiffy.'

Snapshot 267

Nick pulled his woolly hat down, then pulled up the collar of his Berghaus jacket against the biting wind blowing off the sea. He walked slowly across the narrow cobbled street to the harbour's edge; he leant against the black iron railings that ran along the sea front.

From here he gazed down into the grey murky seawater, debris floated on top of the waves lapping the large stones of the harbour wall. Stone steps leading down to the stirring sea were covered in green slippery slime that would make climbing them hazardous. Nick figured this was where tenders and small boats would tie up when people travelled ashore.

He turned and surveyed the surrounding area; several shops had already opened, trying to tempt customers inside.

Winter was not the busiest time for tourists. Nick spied a small alleyway opposite; it took him exactly eight strides to cross the road. He walked up the narrow alley, he counted fifteen strides along its length, on each side there were deep doorways, most in a state of decay, there were no windows.

The alley led into Haggersgate, a narrow cobbled street with rickety narrow red-bricked buildings on either side. Nick retraced his steps once more to the main street overlooking the harbour; from the entrance of the alleyway he could see the top of the opening leading down the steps to the sea.

He stood there for a long time gazing over the harbour. Boats, including the trawler were bobbing up and down on the tidal waters, the ropes securing the boats moving in concert.

There were the beginnings of a plan of action taking shape inside his head, he juggled around with the if's and the but's, ran through different scenario's, but much depended on the behaviour of the steward.

The cold wind seemed to be blowing stronger with just a hint of rain, time to leave and do some shopping. George was in the warmth of the Jolly Sailor watching the trawler; no one could come or go without their knowing about it.

Snapshot 268

Blandford pulled into the marina car park and found the vacant spot by the water's edge reserved for him. Climbing out of the car he looked around the harbour, pulling up his coat collar against the cold wind.

Whitby, with its smells and tourists was not to his taste, all this oldie worldly charm stuff was nonsense, he preferred modern; Grice Hall was the exception. This visit was business occasioned by the appearance of Miss Sanderson and Hartford prying once again into Mr Luzhkov's affairs that were none of their business, he had been prepared to give them the benefit of doubt, but the recent visit to the trawler was the last straw.

Ilia Laskin, who, as instructed, accompanied Blandford came originally from Irkutsk in Siberia.

He was Mr Luzhkov's trusted personal bodyguard; he performed a variety of services, as required, and always completed them with the minimum of fuss. As a member of the Russian Army he was trained as a sniper, and had seen service in Afghanistan and with the KGB. Still sitting in the car, he was equally unimpressed by what he had seen of the surroundings.

Blandford watched as the steward, dressed in black, manoeuvred the rubber dinghy over to the small landing pier, tying it up carefully before approaching his guests.

'Welcome Mr Blandford, I trust you had a good journey; everything is ready for you onboard. Can I take your luggage?'

The steward eyed Mr Blandford warily, he had been warned to give him every courtesy by Mr Berg.

'There is no luggage, we do not plan to stay any longer than is necessary.' Blandford made a signal to Laskin who joined him.

They boarded the dinghy and sat with their backs to the steward who started the outboard motor and set off for the trawler.

The wind had whipped up the sea until it was quite choppy. The steward could tell his passengers felt uncomfortable on the short journey by the way each gripped hard onto the side ropes.
Once aboard, Stafford showed them around and then announced much to Blandford's annoyance.

'I have left you some food. I have to go ashore, I shall be back by about seven.'

'Where are you going?' asked Blandford.

'There are some provisions I have to collect. Actually it's my half-day off. I shall be back on board before the girl comes,' said Stafford, casually. Blandford stepped forward and grabbed the steward by his shirt collar and flung him against the cabin wall. He moved his face close to the steward's.

'I've come a long way to see this woman, and I will not tolerate anything going wrong. Make sure you are back on board before seven,' he growled, 'if you let me down I will send my man after you,' he dragged Stafford's face down the side of the window, so that his face, pressed up against the glass, was distorted. He could see the Russian Ilia outside on deck staring at him. 'He can be very nasty.'

Blandford lifted him and threw him against a table on which sandwiches and cakes had been neatly arranged. The steward fell clumsily onto the deck surrounded by the fillings, bread and cakes from the upturned table.

Blandford went down below, leaving him sprawled out, dazed and shocked by the ferocity of the unprovoked attack. Stafford stood up to his full height, but his legs were shaking; he wiped his mouth with the back of his hand, and straightened his clothes.
His face was porcelain white, he looked almost ghoulish in his black clothes.

'That was totally uncalled for, Mr Berg will hear of this,' he said meekly, but Blandford had gone, no one could hear his protest at the indignity he had suffered.

He moved across the deck and down the steps and into to the dinghy once more. Laskin watched as he made his way across the water to the steps by the harbour side and secured the dinghy once more.

Snapshot 269

In the cosy, warm sitting room George had seen Blandford arrive with a companion. Immediately she knew her hunch about the phoney invitation to view the diary and photographs aboard the trawler was a setup.

His very presence was almost an admission that he was responsible for the disappearance of Gemma Edge from the trawler on that fateful night over a year ago. Shortly after they had gone aboard the trawler, she had observed what looked like an angry scuffle between Blandford and the steward. Since then, Blandford and his companion had stayed below deck.

She had watched the steward come ashore. He moored his dinghy almost opposite the Inn window that she was looking through, and if that wasn't enough he had entered the Jolly Sailor. She could hardly contain herself, but dare not betray her presence here in the rooms above the bar.

Fortunately, Nick had returned from his exploratory jaunt and she quickly brought him up to speed; he had eagerly gone down to the bar to meet the man in black.

The waiting was agonising for her, what were they talking about, how had Nick introduced himself, it was almost too much to bear. Why didn't he ring and let her know what was happening. Suddenly, her attention was diverted when the aft and port lights on board the trawler came on. It must be automatic, she thought, as there was no sign of any activity aboard

Snapshot 270

The bar area in the Jolly Sailor was L shaped. Nick leant against the corner of the bar facing the door and between him and the end of the bar were four more customers.

The bar man kept trying to engage his customers in conversation, but no one was particularly interested, so he returned to polishing his wine glasses from the shelf above the bar.

The old man nearest to Nick wore a thick, olive, woollen jumper that was threadbare around the elbows; his head hung low over his half full glass, he was unshaven. His watery eyes were fixed on the dark liquid that he sipped at irregular intervals.

Beyond him three other customers adopted a similar stance, as if the vitality of life was played out. Was this the final episode, or the final showdown of life frittered away?

Nick found it too morbid and depressing to contemplate and moved away, so he could observe the Trawler steward who sat by himself at a table in the far corner of the room.

Dressed in his black pea coat and dark blue roll neck jumper, Nick fitted in well with the surroundings. He had an uninterrupted view of his quarry through a mirror on the opposite wall; the steward sat alone. From Nick's observations, he appeared to be nursing a grievance, probably from the skirmish that George had seen.

The light outside was fading fast, it was time to move in and introduce himself. He waited until the steward's drink was almost empty, then he ordered two lagers and moved over to join him in the corner bay.

'You look as if you are ready for another,' he announced, thrusting the drink towards the surprised steward.

'I saw the big guy pushing you around this afternoon, no need for that, some of these owners treat us like dirt.

'Your good health, I'm Gordon from the 'Endeavour4', just got in on the morning tide,' Nick lied.

Stafford looked at Nick suspiciously, he was thoroughly fed up, the last thing he needed now was for some Happy Joe to come and make light conversation.

'Never heard of 'Endeavour4',' he croaked.

'No matter, as I say, we just came in on the morning tide all the way from sunny Newcastle. Saw your shenanigans when we were passing you, looked nasty, very nasty.' Nick took a large drink then waited for the steward to reply.

Stafford watched then took a drink himself, perhaps this guy was OK.

'I like Newcastle, love it when we go up there, great atmosphere,' he said, to get things going.

'Me too, great atmosphere, an' the beer's great too, and the girls, wow,' said Nick. 'Where else do you sail to?'

'We spend a lot of time in the Mediterranean, especially Turkey.'

'Oh' that must be terrific, all that sun. We don't go anywhere except round the British coast, working boat you see.' They talked a while over another couple of drinks. Nick knew he had gained the steward's confidence, but time was passing, it was nearly seven o clock.

'Why don't we have one more at the pub next door,' Nick suggested.

'No, I have to be back on board soon,' said the steward.

'Me too, but we could have one more next door then say goodbye until the next time.' Stafford considered the friendly proposition, downed his drink and nodded his approval.

'OK, just one.' Outside, in the dark, Nick led the way up the cobbled street. Outside the entrance to the alleyway he had inspected earlier in the day he paused, waiting for his companion to join him.

The street was deserted.

'Come on my friend, hey, I don't even know your name,' he called out.

'Liam,' he announced as he drew level with Nick, 'Liam Stafford.' Nick grabbed his coat collar and roughly bundled him into the alleyway, dragging him into the first doorway where he threw him against the door.

'Don't say a word.'

'Take my money, I've only a few pounds,' the steward cried out in sheer panic, ignoring Nick's warning.

'If you want to live, listen to me,' Nick said, banging him once more onto the doorframe.

'Oh God,' snivelled the steward, holding his head.

'Quiet,' Nick jammed his elbow into the steward's throat.

'Now listen to me carefully, things are not what they seem I don't want your money. I want information about Mr Blandford. Do you understand?' Stafford nodded, the very mention of Blandford's name ended all resistance.

His protestations ceased, and Nick's elbow in the throat didn't help as he gasped for breath. For the second time in a day he found himself a victim of an assault. Nick relaxed his grip on the man.

'Now listen, I know about the disappearance overboard of Mrs Edge, I know about your invitation to Miss Sanderson this evening and how your guests are planning to welcome her on board. What time do they expect you to return?'

'Seven, seven,' he repeated, ' I want to be sick,' Nick stood back and let him puke against the wall, to anyone looking on, it was just another drunk throwing-up, except there was no one about. When he had finished, Nick passed him a handkerchief and he wiped his mouth, hardly able to support himself he leaned against the corner of the doorway for support.

'Your time aboard the trawler is over, you can never return. You have to get as far away from here as you can, no clothes, no luggage, nothing. If you return you will die.'

'Oh God,' the steward sobbed, he was barely audible.

'Here,' Nick fumbled for his wallet and thrust a wad of notes into the steward's pocket. This will see you through. 'You do understand, you must leave right now.'

'Yes, you won't see me again, I promise.' And that was the last Nick saw of him, a broken figure staggering along in the shadows of the main street, heading towards the railway station.

Snapshot 271

'I can see Blandford talking on his phone, the other man is sat reading a newspaper.' George was using binoculars to spy on the trawler and was giving Nick a running commentary.

'They're waiting for your arrival,' said Nick, packing his backpack.

'Do you really need that,' asked George, on seeing Nick pack his Glock 17 semi-automatic.

'Insurance,' smiled Nick, 'just insurance.'

'Do be careful, remember, if we're right Blandford is a cold-blooded killer,' she said.

'Don't worry; if everything goes to plan I'll be OK. Just make sure that you are in the car park at exactly nine. Check your watch.' Nick looked at the watch she held up.

'Right, I'm off.' He fastened up his pea coat and put on his black wool balaclava hat.

George left the window and helped him on with the backpack, then she reached over and held his face in her hands and gave him a long sultry kiss.

'H'mm, I could become addicted to those.' Without a backward glance he walked over to the door, the floorboards creaking with each step, and disappeared into the night.

Snapshot 272

Nick checked the time, ten past eight. The street was empty. Nick crossed over the cobbles, a light drizzle making them shine under the streetlights. He looked around once more, still no one in view. He made his way steadily down the stone steps until he could see the dinghy that had been left by the steward. It was tied up by a huge chain that was secured to the harbour wall. The dark water lapped the sides of the dinghy as he climbed in; he felt the cold breeze off the sea for the first time. He pulled down his woollen balaclava so it covered his face, untied the boat and started rowing; the outboard motor was too noisy to use.

Soon he was several yards from the harbour wall, but he was careful to row in between the other boats that were anchored so they gave him cover.

He pulled on the oars gently, each stroke deliberate. Luckily, the moon was hidden behind some fast moving clouds.

The stiff breeze whipped off the sea and rattled the rigging of several large boats. He rowed steadily until he was at the stern of the Trawler where he quietly secured the dinghy and stowed the oars.

He climbed the swim ladder until he could see onto the deck; he could hear conversation from inside the saloon. Nick pulled out the Glock pistol from his backpack and climbed the few extra steps onto the deck. He moved forward until he could just see inside one of the fixed windows of the sliding door that led into the saloon. Two figures were seated on the starboard settee with the adjustable table in situ, *'couldn't be better'* thought Nick, *they can't move too fast because of the table*. Holding the semi-automatic pistol in front of him Nick slid the door open.

'Good evening gentleman, please keep your hands on the table where I can see them.' Blandford and Laskin could not have been more shocked if Nick had caught them with their trousers down. They were sitting ducks, and they knew they had been completely outmanoeuvred.

'Hartford!' gasped Blandford.

'You, big boy, over here and lie down on the floor with your head facing the galley. Quick, move it,' Nick waved the pistol menacingly at Laskin who reluctantly moved around the settee and then onto the floor as ordered. Nick pulled out some nylon plastic ties from the backpack.

'You, Blandford, tie one of these around his feet,' Nick moved back to allow Blandford carry out his instructions. *This was too easy*, Nick thought. He watched as Blandford made the tie secure around Laskin's ankles.

'Right, put your hands behind your back,' Nick called out,
'Here, tie them, make sure they're tight,' he instructed Blandford, who had started to sweat profusely.

'Right now it's your turn, hands behind your back.' He pushed Blandford against the sliding door and slipped a plastic tie over his wrists and pulled tight.

'It's too tight, oh, my God,' Blandford croaked in a self-pitying way.

'Now you can sit,' Nick pushed Blandford roughly and he fell onto the settee.

'You'll pay for this, Hartford, just you wait and see,' he whined. Nick checked the ties on Laskin, firm enough, but just to make sure he put two more on his wrists and ankles.

'You were expecting to see Miss Sanderson at nine, I believe. I wonder what sort of a reception she would have received.'

He checked Blandford's pockets first, then the bodyguard Laskin, on whom he found a knife and a small handgun. Nick opened the sliding door and threw them both into the sea.

'You pig,' roared Laskin, as he tried to get free. Nick deliberately stepped onto his back, reached down and grabbed his hair, lifting his head.

'Are you talking to me?' Without waiting for an answer, Nick swung the pistol and smashed it into the Russian's temple, then let his head crash back onto the floor with a thud.

'There now, I don't think we'll hear from him for a while.'

Nick checked his watch, almost nine. 'Time to go,' He dragged Blandford out into the cold night air.

'Be careful going down the steps, I would hate to loose you overboard,' he joked, but Blandford was not amused.

'Where are you taking me?' he asked defiantly, carefully stepping into the dingy, then sitting down. Nick joined him, started the outboard motor and steered the craft towards the opposite shore. The dinghy bounced off the waves, and unable to hold on, Blandford toppled backwards much to Nick's amusement. Soon they had reached the landing bay, Nick tied up the dinghy, and then dragged Blandford ashore. He quickly spotted George waiting in the car nearby. They walked over and he opened the boot of the car.

'You were waiting for Miss Sanderson, well, here she is,' Nick waved to George, 'but this is your accommodation for the rest of the journey,' Nick pointed inside the boot. The bedraggled Blandford tried to resist.

'You can't,' he protested, as Nick pushed him into the dark, large, empty space.

'Oh, you'll be fine, a little bumpy perhaps, but at least you'll be warm,' with that Nick slammed down the boot lid and ignored the muffled protests.

'Hi, George, been waiting long?' he joked, climbing into the car.

'Am I glad to see you,' she reached over and grasped Nick's hand, 'everything OK?'

'A lot easier than I thought it would be.'

'What about the other guy?'

'Oh, he's sleeping,' laughed Nick.

Snapshot 273

'Has he said anything yet?' asked George, watching Blandford eating the last remnants of a sandwich.

'Not yet, but when he's finished breakfast I'm sure he'll tell us all we want to know,' said Nick, pouring some tea into a mug and passing it to Blandford.

George moved over to Nick and tugged his sleeve, signalling to him she wanted to speak out of earshot of their guest.

'I'm very nervous about him being here. Look at him he just does not seem to be agitated one bit. It's almost as if he's expecting to be rescued any minute, then what happens to us?'

'Try to keep calm; don't let him see you're nervous. The house is secure, we're going to be alright, just remember, if he'd had his way it would be you that would be his prisoner, or worse, you could have been feeding the fishes.' Nick's words sent a cold shiver down her spine.

'I want to ask him about the women,' she said.

'Soon.'

Blandford was just finishing the tea Nick had given him. He felt very unpleasant, his clothes were crumpled and dirty, and he felt unclean and longed for a hot shower. He watched them talking in the doorway, and wondered how had it come to this.

God knows what would happen when Mr Luzhkov realised he was missing; he could not tolerate failure. How could he have let himself be caught so easily? He drank the last of the tea and noticed that Hartford was coming towards him once more.

Without a word being said he was manhandled into the study and pushed into a large, solid, oak chair. More plastic ties secured him to the chair, except that this time his left arm was bared before being firmly tied down.

'Mr Blandford, I am going to ask you some questions about Mr Luzhkov's business ventures, especially his insider dealing activities, with regard to certain key businesses. Miss Sanderson, who you were so anxious to meet, wants to ask you about the mysterious deaths of some prominent women whose husbands run these businesses.'

'Absolute nonsense, I have no idea what on earth you are talking about,'

'Really, how interesting. Let me suggest to you that each of these influential businesses were specifically selected by you, that the wives of each of the owners was murdered by you and then women under your influence were introduced to these owners with the sole intention of marriage so they could then pass back vital business information.'

'You're crazy, you have a very vivid imagination Mr Hartford, but you cannot prove a thing. When Mr Luzhkov realises what has happened he will crush you both, you are already dead.'

'Crush us both,' Nick repeated, 'just like he did my partner Mrs Spencer and her husband.'

'You really are crazy, why would Mr Luzhkov be so concerned with an inconsequential shop keeper.'

Nick nodded slowly, digesting those words, 'of little importance', that summed up their attitude to the deaths of people who got in their way. He opened a drawer and pulled out two syringes that he held in front of Blandford.

'This syringe contains a drug which, when I inject it into your vein, will make you nauseous within one minute, then you will begin to feel drowsy, in three to four minutes your blood pressure will rise dramatically, then you will fall asleep. In eight minutes you will be dead.'

Nick held the second syringe in front of Blandford.

'This syringe contains the antidote, if I administer this within four minutes you live. Now you have choice to live and talk, or to stay silent and die.'

Without waiting for a reply, Nick took the first syringe and, finding a vein, emptied the contents of the syringe into Blandford's writhing arm.

Blandford's face was ashen; he clearly had not expected this unfolding drama in which he was the principle player. He stared at his forearm where a speck of blood marked the entry point of the drug now circulating in his system. He was already aware of his heart beating faster, trickles of perspiration fell into his eyes making them smart, or was it the drug? His mouth was dry, and yes he was beginning to feel drowsy, he must act before he lost consciousness,

'Two minutes,' Nick leaned against the desk, as he held out the other syringe.

To refuse the antidote meant the end of his life, he felt tired. It was ridiculous, but an image of T.E.Lawrence sprang into his thoughts. There was Lawrence held captive by the Turkish troops, how did he react? He shook his head to rid himself of the intrusion, his lips were so dry -- pulse racing –- so tired -- don't fall asleep.

'Three minutes.'

'*Hartford's counting out the last minutes of my life,*' thought Blandford, '*I must act now before it's too late.*' He attempted to open his eyes wide, but it was increasingly difficult.

'Yes, yes I agree,' whimpered a terrified Blandford.

'Did Luzhkov orchestrate the deaths of Gemma Edge, Andrea Burton, Angela Grose, Susan Raines ---'

'Yes,' interrupted Blandford, 'yes, yes give me the injection I will tell … you… all..' his voice trailed off as he fell into a deep sleep, his head falling to one side.

'Did you get that, George?' asked Nick, throwing the other syringe back into the drawer.

'Yes, that was brilliant, it's on the recorder. The four minutes are almost up, give him the second injection quickly,' she said, anxiously.

'Oh, he doesn't need it,' said Nick laughing, 'I just gave him a mild sedative; when he wakes he'll think I gave him the antidote and sing like a bird.'

Snapshot 274

Luzhkov paced angrily up and down the library, he should have returned hours ago from his trip to the trawler. Neither Blandford nor Laskin were answering their phones and all his attempts to contact the trawler had failed; something must be wrong.

Finally, he had rung the harbourmaster at Whitby and relayed his concerns that he had been unable to make contact with the trawler. They had promised to investigate and ring him immediately but that was over thirty minutes ago. Why didn't they ring?

Snapshot 275

The last few days had passed slowly and Martin was prowling around in a mean mood. Jack had seen him like this many times before, when a case had run cold.

Daily reports had failed to find any trace of the Sanderson woman; it was as if she never existed. Ripley, always resourceful, had kept himself fully occupied attempting to delve into the background of Mr. Luzhkov; it also kept him away from Martin.

In the meantime, Jack, had paid numerous visits to the railway yard where they kept a few old railway engines that were being renovated, of course he did not let the boss know.

Snapshot 276

The phone call from the harbourmaster confirmed Luzhkov's worst fears; sure enough, burglars had caught the steward unawares, and left him bound and gagged on deck. Apart from bruising around his limbs and on his temple where he had been coshed, he was in good health.

'Could I please speak with him?' asked Luzhkov.

'Of course, we will make a full report to the police and ambulance services who are on their way, here is the steward now,' said the harbourmaster.

'Hello,' Laskin was a man of few words.

'Can you speak?'

'Yes, they have gone up on deck to meet the ambulance,'

'Tell me, quickly, what happened, where is Blandford?' rapped Luzhkov.

'We were surprised by Hartford, he had a pistol, a Glock 17 I think. One minute we were talking, the next he is in the cabin waving the gun around, shouting out orders. He smashed me on the head; I didn't wake up until this morning. Blandford's gone, Hartford must have taken him. They think I'm the steward,' he explained.

'Listen, get out of there now, return here immediately, do you understand?'

'Yes sir, immediately,' replied the obedient Laskin.

Luzhkov banged down the phone. 'Hartford again, that snivelling insignificant man, he has been a thorn in my side ever since he first made my acquaintance,' he raged. His thought processes raced at times like these, while he tried to work out what could have possibly happened. One thing for sure, he was determined to remove Hartford for good, and his girlfriend with him. But where was Blandford now; the logical conclusion must be that he is at Hartford's home.

Snapshot 277

'How is he?' asked George, eyeing the slumped form of Blandford.

'Still sleeping, I thought he would have been awake by now,' said Nick, lifting one of Blandford's eyelids.

'Oh, how can you do that?' cringed George.

'I've been thinking, perhaps it's time we rang the police and told them what we know, before this situation becomes a fully fledged war,' said Nick.

'Yes, let's ring them straight away, this is way too heavy now,' agreed George.

'You do realise they want to bring you in for questioning,'

'When they hear what we have to tell them, surely they will forget me,'

'Maybe, maybe not, we might be able to strike a deal. We could come clean about everything and who knows, perhaps we could negotiate a deal.

Whatever happens, it's time we came clean.'

'Let's do it.' George picked up the phone, 'the sooner we get him off our hands, the better I'll feel.'

She handed the phone to Nick.

Snapshot 278

Almost four-thirty, it was already almost dark, too late to organise another visit to the railway yard, still, there was always tomorrow. The phone was ringing; none of the others seemed in a particular rush to answer it, so Jack walked slowly over to the desk and picked up the receiver.

'Hello, Settle Police Station, how can we help you?' asked Jack.

'This is Nick Hartford, could I speak with Chief Inspector Martin or his Sergeant, sorry, I've forgotten his name.'

'This is the sergeant speaking, Sgt Bellows is my name, thank you for calling, Mr Hartford. Have you heard from your girlfriend, Miss Sanderson yet?'

'Yes, as a matter of fact she is here with me now,' replied Nick.

'And where is 'here'?' asked Jack.

'At home in Hawes.'

'Well, we need to question Miss Sanderson before we can eliminate her from our enquiries. Will you come round to see us here at the station in Settle today?'

Nick was a little impatient with the small talk.

'No, we really can't do that, let me try to explain. We have information that will be of great interest to you concerning Mr Luzhkov, but we are unable to leave the house just at this moment. It could prove to be dangerous. Will you please call round to speak with us here, its very important.'

'Danger, what sort of danger, Mr Hartford?' asked Jack.

'It's difficult to go into detail over the phone, it's rather complicated.'

Jack pondered for a moment, it all sounded very dramatic.

'It really would be better for Miss Sanderson if we questioned her at the station,' pressed Jack.

'Look, I'm sorry, that's out of the question, you must come round straight away. Its vitally important.'

''Must' Mr Hartford?' Jack was losing his patience.

'We know who killed Mr and Mrs Spencer,' Nick blurted the words out. Jack did not respond immediately, he twisted the phone cord round and round in his fingers while turning the last sentence over and over, 'We know who killed Mr and Mrs Spencer,' what have they been up to, he wondered.

'Alright Mr Hartford, we'll come over, but this better be worth the journey,' said Jack, stressing the last part of the sentence.

'Oh, it will be Sgt, it will be.'

Jack replaced the phone.

'Anyone important, Jack?' asked Martin.

'That was Mr. Hartford. Miss Sanderson has turned up. I explained about us wanting to question her here at the station, but he said they were unable to make the journey. They wants us to call round to their home.'

'Does he now, and why would we do that?' scoffed Martin.

'Because he said they know who killed the Spencers,' said Jack.

'Do they now?' said Martin, already grabbing his coat, then shouting out 'Ripley! Drop what you're doing lad, you're driving us to Hawes right now.'

Snapshot 279

Luzhkov was still in the library, busy working when Laskin was shown in by one of the maids. Luzhkov saw the bandages on his forehead and wrists, and noticed that he walked with a noticeable limp.

'Sit down, Laskin.' Luzhkov poured him a brandy, and then listened to his account of the evening's events on the trawler. When Laskin had finished recounting the detail Luzhkov fell silent. Laskin sipped the brandy slowly. He avoided looking at his employer, he felt guilty over the way they had been caught off-guard so easily. He didn't have long to wait for a response.

'You will reconnoitre Hartford's grounds; you are the sniper once more,' he said tapping him on the shoulder.

'Observe the house for any sign of Blandford. We must find him. Do you have your equipment here?'

'Yes, sir' replied Laskin, forthrightly.

'Good, you will need it; tonight we will clear up this mess. As soon as you have surveyed the area, report back by phone. We will take it from there,' Luzhkov returned to his chair and sat down, then waved his hand in the direction of the door. Laskin had been given his orders; it was time to leave.

Snapshot 280

'Nick, he's starting to move,' George watched as Blandford shook his head from side to side and screwed up his eyes several times. Nick moved over towards his captive, and began to wipe his face with a wet cloth.

'You are a lucky man, Blandford, I was beginning to think perhaps we had given you the antidote too late.'

'Can I have a drink of water please?' he asked.

'Of course,' Nick pushed a large ice cube into his mouth, which Blandford welcomed.

'Enough of the pleasantries. You agreed to talk to us; first I would like to ask you about these codes,'

Nick held up a notebook and waved it in front of Blandford.

'On page 3 we find this code; 'AE on LS +78542 @ 2.51–5.32' Am I right that this translates to; Oksana Edge passed on information about Global Investments (LS) and 78542 shares were purchased for £2.51 and were later sold for £5.32.'

Blandford listened as Nick quoted from the notebook and although still groggy from the sedative he could not hide his surprise.

'Where did you get that notebook?' he asked.

'I removed it from a box I found in one of the offices in the converted stables at Grice Hall. Now, can you please tell me was I correct that you acted on inside information about Global Investments and purchased shares anticipating a significant rise in their price?'

Blandford nodded his head.

'Therefore every line of code represents a purchase of stock.' Blandford once again nodded in acknowledgement, then asked limply.

'Could I have some more ice?'

Nick continued to question Blandford about the business transactions and the involvement of Luzhkov, he confirmed most of the data that Nick had found in the notebooks and captured on the phone from the bug in the library of Grice Hall.

Snapshot 281

Laskin moved slowly until he was able to see the house clearly, through the night sight binoculars he identified the alarm wires, telephone cables and security cameras. He was able to observe and identify Blandford sat in front of a large desk; Hartford and Sanderson were in the same room.

'Luzhkov.'

'Laskin here, I have found him,'

'Blandford?'

'Yes.'

'Describe it to me.'

'He's sat in front of the window, he may be tied to the chair, it's difficult to see. Hartford and the girl are in the room; it appears they are talking to him, possibly asking questions. When Blandford talks, they listen.'

'Take him out, take them all out,' snapped Luzhkov.

The order was precise, Laskin understood. He closed the clamshell phone. Then, unzipping the leather gun case he slid out the Dragunov SVDS sniper rifle. Quickly, he fitted the N2 night-sight and swung the rifle up so it rested on a tree-branch. It took only a few seconds to make some quick adjustments to ensure perfect single shot accuracy. Looking through the night-sight he carefully moved the rifle round until Blandford's head appeared in the calibrated green screen.

Snapshot 282

Nick scribbled more notes then closed the notebook, George turned off the hand recorder, withdrew the memory stick and shoved it into her pocket, then looked at Nick. It had been an eventful day. Now they were waiting for the police; surely when they heard all this evidence they wouldn't be still interested in her.

'I'll make you something to eat, you must be hungry,' George looked up about to agree, but he wasn't talking to her, he was asking Blandford.

She was just about to remonstrate with him when she heard the sound of breaking glass, followed by blood mixed with shards of bone and brain shooting across the room, splattering everything in it's path.

Nick immediately threw himself on top of her and they both fell to the floor as automatic fire sprayed across the room shattering the windows, lights, mirror and the wall. The ear-splitting sound of the gunfire and fragmenting wood and glass took her breath away. Nick's weight on top of her didn't help either; she shoved him off. There was a sudden lull in the fire.

'Crawl over to the bookcase quickly, keep down,' Nick shouted to her. She didn't have to be told twice and followed him obediently.

'The mirror is broken, how do we get into the security room?' she felt a sudden overpowering feeling of fear when she caught sight of the limp body of Blandford.

'Always have a back-up plan.' He winked at her, then reached up to the forth shelf and removed a leather book, pulled a hidden lever and the false bookcase door swung open. Instantly the firing started again, spraying across the room. Nick pulled her into the secure room and banged the door shut.

'Are we safe?' she asked, relieved to be out of the line of fire.

'Absolutely, there are steel doors lined with Kevlar, behind the bookcase.'

'Did you see Blandford?'

'Certainly did, hit by a trained sniper probably, must be using night sights, straight through the back of the head,' he said, in a calm voice that took George by surprise.

'Oh, well, that's comforting, and now he's after us.'

'Correct, you can stay here or join me outside,' he said.

'You have got to be joking, there's no way I'm staying here alone, I'm coming with you,' she cried.

'Right, then, put these on,' he handed her a black jump suit and a woolly balaclava. He then lifted the door in the floor to reveal the tunnel slide.

'Remember this?' Without waiting for her to reply, he unfastened a steel lock, opened a steel cupboard and removed two weapons. He shoved the Glock 17 pistol that he had used the previous night into his backpack. Next, a night vision monocular, finally he grabbed a M249 light machine gun.

'I'm ready, you first,' he pointed into the tunnel.

'You thinking of starting a war?'

'It's already started.'

'It was much easier on the street,' she gasped, in amazement, looking first at Nick then down into the depths of the hole.

'But not half as much fun.' With that he pushed her.

She slid down and suddenly automatic lights came on to reveal the stainless steel tube through which she was falling, it reminded her of a giant slide. After what seemed an age, she dropped onto a mat, quickly followed by Nick crashing into her.

'There now, I told you it was fun,' he said.

'Where are we?' she asked looking round.

'Well, I suppose you could say this is an extension of the safety room. But I'm afraid we don't have time to explore, follow me and be quiet.' With that he opened a door, looked around, and then they were out into the chilly night.

'Pull down your balaclava,' he whispered. George could hear the sound of water and looked down to see the river running close by. They climbed up through the woods and eventually came out onto the road.

'Nick what are we doing?' she whispered.

'Looking for whoever shot Blandford.'

'Are you crazy?'

'Look, it's my guess Luzhkov has sent someone to finish us off. There's no escape, we have to confront whoever it is,' he reasoned. 'Follow me.' Nick spanned the landscape with the monocular night scope, and then moved off followed by George.

Snapshot 283

Once he had killed Blandford he switched the rifle to automatic fire. After spraying several rounds into the room, Laskin cautiously moved forward. He climbed through the broken window to find the room was deserted. The body of Blandford remained tied to the chair. He quickly searched, but the house was empty, perhaps Hartford and the girl escaped through the back of the house.
He decided not to hang around.

Snapshot 284

A speeding car, headlights blazing, screamed round the corner, hogging the middle of the road and almost crashed into the oncoming car, which was forced halfway up the grass banking.

'Who the bloody hell was that Ripley, he almost killed us, did you get a good look at him?' roared Martin.

'No, he had his headlights on full beam,' said Ripley, shaken.

'Do you want me to turn round and follow him?'

'Follow him,' Martin roared once more, 'he'll be halfway up the bloody fells by now, total madman. It'll be one of those silly bloody local yokels, must have had some loopy juice. Carry on.'

Ripley started the engine, reversed the car, and then drove back onto the road.

'Well done, Ripley, you kept your cool there, good driving,' said Jack, reassuring the young man.

'A damn sight better than that bloody maniac, yes, well done Ripley,' agreed Martin.

'This is Hartford's house,' Ripley pulled into the drive and up to the house.

'What the hell's been going on here?' Martin blurted, seeing the shattered windows.

'He did mention the possibility of danger when he spoke to me,' said Jack. They climbed out of the car and walked up to the house. The side door was open, so they walked into the hall across broken glass and shattered ornaments.

'Hello, Mr Hartford, Miss Sanderson,' called out Jack.

They walked into what was left of the library, Martin followed by Jack then Ripley bringing up the rear. The three of them stared first at Blandford, then at the destruction in the room.

'Bloody hell, Jack, sheer carnage. Ripley, check him out, will you?' he pointed towards the body in the chair. 'Jack, better check the rest of the house to see if you can find Hartford and his girlfriend.'

'Dead, very dead, looks like he was shot through the back of the head, then there are lots more wounds from what looks like random automatic fire,' reported Ripley.

'Yes all right, no need for the grizzly detail, thank you, Ripley,' said Martin.

'Let's keep to the basic facts. If I'm not mistaken he's Luzhkov's personal assistant from Grice Hall. What the hell is going on?' shouted Martin, at no one in particular.

'No one upstairs or in the kitchen,' said Jack, returning from searching the house.

'Is he dead?' asked Jack, looking at the body.

'Very, there's more lead in him than there is left in Cornwall,' quipped Martin. Suddenly, the three turned as they heard the sound of scrunching glass and debris underfoot. Each looked in the direction of door at the sound of the approaching footsteps.

'Sgt Bellows, Chief Inspector Martin,' a voice called out, and all three sighed with relief when they recognised the voice of Nick Hartford.

Snapshot 285

When he saw the headlight's high intensity beam sprawling across the driveway he made his way to the front entrance to meet Laskin.

'What have you to report?' he asked immediately, holding Laskin by the arm.

'Blandford is out of the game,' he said quietly.

'And Hartford and his woman, what about them?' he asked, shaking his arm.

'I missed them, somehow they escaped from the room, I don't understand how they could, I fired automatic fire into the room many times; they really should be dead.' Luzhkov let go of Laskin's arm, his head dropped momentarily.

'I searched the house, it was empty, I can't understand how they could have escaped the repeated firepower I poured in to the rooms,' said Laskin, in an attempt to appease his boss.

'Are your weapons still in the car?' asked Luzhkov.

'Yes.'

'We'll return to Hartford's house immediately. We are going to find them both, they will not escape this time,'

Snapshot 286

'Jack, what do you make of all this? We've gone from investigating a robbery, kidnap and the deaths of two prominent local people, to insider dealing on a massive scale. Then we have anything up to God knows how many killings of women whose husbands run high-flying businesses,' Martin said, taking Jack to one side in the library.

'Well, he has the evidence to support his allegations,' offered Jack.

'We'll have to arrest them and take them in to custody. I want you to call in forensics and the crime scene people; it's going to be like a bloody circus in a couple of hours. And you know what that means Jack, an awful lot of bloody report writing, and God knows how many meetings when 'she who has to be obeyed' get's involved.'

'All part of the job,' said Jack, giving Martin a friendly pat on the back.

'Bollocks, Jack, you and me belong on the streets, not investigating all this crap. I feel like I've got a bit part in a film script. One day we're investigating the accidental death of the owner of an Italian restaurant and robbery back home, then all this.'

'Must be our biggest case yet,' said Jack, reassuringly, 'this will make them sit up and take notice back at the station.'

'Will it, do you really believe that Jack? Well, I've got news for you, this crime scene has to be cleared up before we can start taking standing ovations.

First we've got the body of some poor sod whose body is leaking blood like a sieve, because he's been shot through the back of head and God knows where else,' Martin pointed at Blandford's limp body, and then pulling Jack closer whispered.

'And if what Hartford and Sanderson have told us is correct, then we are going to have to arrest Luzhkov and his henchmen before the night is out.'

'OK, I'll contact forensics and the crime scene people immediately, then I'll ask Ripley to arrest those two and take them to the station,' said Jack.

'Fine Jack, the sooner we....' Martin was interrupted by the sound of gunfire, Ripley fell to the floor, holding his arm as blood poured from a wound. Bullets spat into the walls and the furniture, light fittings swung wildly and the air was filled with flying debris.

'Get down,' shouted Nick, pulling George to the ground for the second time in one day.

'Keep low,' he quickly squirmed his way over towards the bookcase and reaching up pulled the lever down to gain access to the secure room, the door swung open.

'Come on, George, keep down. Quickly you two, get inside,' Nick helped them inside then returned crawling to help pull Ripley towards the safety of the secure room.

'Who the hell are you?' shouted Martin, above the sound of rapid gunfire.

'Just your friendly antique dealer,' said Nick, closing the door, then flicking switches to turn on the security monitors.

'Friendly antique dealer my arse,' retorted Martin, 'who the bloody hell is firing at us?' Nick ignored the Chief Inspector and rapped out instructions to George.

'George see to that wound, put on a tourniquet.' Turning to Martin and Jack he pointed to the monitors,

'Look there on the camera, that's the man who I left on the trawler last night, see him, he's hiding behind that silver birch tree.'

Martin moved nearer the screen for a closer look.

'What the hell is this room and why do you have all this sophisticated equipment in here?' asked Martin.

'This is my secure room; they are becoming quite common. There's someone else, look behind those rhododendron bushes, see,' said Nick, pointing once more

Both Jack and Martin glanced at the second monitor.

'It's Luzhkov,' cried Nick, 'He's finally broken his cover, come to finish us off, no doubt. But he didn't know that you were visiting.'

'And what are we supposed to do locked up in this place?' said Martin, 'they've got weapons.' Nick opened the steel cupboard once again and pulled out three Glock 17 pistols and two M249 light machine guns, together with ammunition,

'Do you know how to use these?' he said, smiling and passed one each to Jack and Martin.

'Now, wait a minute, you can't go charging round the countryside fighting your own personal war, son,' said Martin, throwing his M249 onto the table.

'What do you propose to do, march out there and start firing into the night.'?

'No, Chief Inspector, but just remember this, they've come here to kill us, they started this, they don't want a truce, and I don't intend to give them one,' Nick opened the door to reveal the slide.

'Now you can join me if you wish, but I'm going to finish this once and for all, with or without you.' Jack and Martin stared with incredulity as Nick grabbed his backpack and disappeared down the tube.

'Who the hell are you?' shouted Martin after him.

'I told you, your friendly antique dealer,' came the reply from the tube.

'There, that should be OK, just keep releasing every two minutes, the dressing will hold. You're quite safe here, it's totally secure,' said George, reassuring Ripley.

Martin and Jack were watching the monitors; she donned her balaclava and gloves.

'Luzhkov indirectly killed his parents, that's how all this started. One way or another, it will end tonight.'

'Where are you going and where does this contraption take you?' asked Martin.

George sat on the edge of the tube.

'Comes out by the river at the bottom of the garden. Sorry I have to leave you like this, you'll be safe here,' with that George slid into the hole and out of sight.

Jack and Martin watched her disappear out of sight, then for a moment just stared at the screen and the weapons on the table.

'Friendly antique dealer my arse,' repeated Martin. 'Who the hell's in charge here, Jack. Were supporting players in their private game. We can't just let them leave, come on, Jack, we'll have to follow,' pleaded Martin.

'Are you sure? What about these weapons, they're firing real bullets out there.'

'Yes, I know, Goddamit. How does this damn thing work?' he asked, picking up the machine gun.

'Here, pass me the automatic.' Ripley took the weapon, flicked it onto single fire and knocked off the safety switch. 'Its armed and ready, flick this lever to switch to automatic fire.'

'Thanks, you stay here Ripley, and keep watching those screens, oh, and by the way, don't forget that tourniquet.'

'OK sarge, be careful.'

Snapshot 287

As Nick moved up the riverbank, the wind was light, the moon glowed brightly, and the branches waved in tandem. After a while, he moved away from the river and around the vast expanse of lawn, keeping in front of the shrubs that adorned the edge of the green expanse. Suddenly, he heard the gentle crack of a dry twig from behind him, and looking through the monocle he recognised the crouching figure of George. He waited for her, then whispered,

'You're making too much noise, what are you doing here?'

'My place is with you.' It annoyed him a little having to look after her, but realised it was too late to argue.

'Alright, but follow in my footprints.'

Nick moved off, carefully checking the landscape with the night scope at regular intervals, with George following on behind him.

Suddenly, there was more gunfire; someone was moving around the house, spraying each window with fire, waiting a moment, then firing once more.

He signalled George to lie down. If his hunch was correct, then whoever was firing was coming toward them. Luzhkov, probably, would be staying back, waiting for them to try and break free.

Soon he spotted movement just in front of the main entrance to the house, another burst of fire, and Nick had the outline of the figure in his sights. He pulled slowly on the trigger moving the weapon from left to right, keeping low, aiming about knee height.

'Aaarrrgh,' a cry of anguish spilt into the night as the gunman collapsed to the ground firing wildly into the night as he fell; bullets ricocheted off the walls of the house.

Soon they heard groans of anguish and pain. Nick picked out a prone body writhing on the lawn through the monocular scope.

He guessed the bullets would have torn through the muscles and tendons as well as smashing the bone. He would not be going far, but he still had a weapon. He signalled to George to follow, then they crawled through the shrubs slowly until eventually they were out of sight of the main building and into the trees on the edge of his land.

'We can move around here pretty freely,' he whispered to her, 'We'll aim for the road beyond the woods, then circle around and wait opposite the drive entrance.'

They made rapid progress and soon came to the road. Nick checked in each direction, all clear. They walked slowly along the grass verge towards the corner where they should have a clear view of the entrance to the driveway some three hundred metres ahead.

Rounding the bend they stopped suddenly; up ahead they could just make out, in the shadows, a parked vehicle. As they cautiously approached, they could make out it was a Land Rover.

Nick, crouched low, moved forward to the cab until he could see it was empty. He leaned into the cab then stood upright and dangled some keys in front of George.

'Someone's been careless,' he said, in a low voice. George suddenly tagged his sleeve and pointed down the road.

'I'm sure I saw someone moving about.' Nick used the scope but the road and the verges ahead seemed clear.

'If there is someone there, then it is probably Luzhkov waiting, probably watching the drive. Let's see if we can flush him out with the headlights. Climb in.'

'What, do you really think that's a good idea,' cried George.

'It's the best I've got. Listen, if that is Luzhkov down there he'll think it's Laskin driving. We must take a chance, climb aboard.'

'Why is it you always sound so convincing, I really must be crazy for following you.'

'You can always stay here alone,' laughed Nick.

'Forget that.'

'That's what I thought', he whispered. 'Now look, I'll drive slowly towards the driveway entrance, if Luzhkov is hiding there, he will think Laskin has finished the job up at the house and is picking him up.'

'Yes, you've said that already. OK, but what happens when he realises it isn't Laskin.'

'We give him what he wanted to give us,' he lifted the automatic on his knee.

'Here we go.'

'I've got a bad feeling about this,' George said nervously.

He turned the keys in the ignition, the engine started immediately. Nick pulled forward slowly and switched on the headlights to full beam. The road suddenly unfolded before them, grasses on either side moving gently in the breeze, the cold grey stone of the walls stretching out into the distance.

'See anything?' he asked.

'No.' The vehicle moved forward steadily, slowly.

One hundred metres, everything well illuminated, the road disappeared under them.

One hundred and fifty metres; each of them peered out into the distance, Nick to the left, George to the right.

Two hundred metres, still the roadsides were clear, now Nick could just make out the entrance ahead. Trees and bushes passed slowly by on each side, still nothing.

Two hundred and fifty metres, almost there, the headlights captured the road sliding past.

Suddenly a figure jumped out.

'Oh my God Nick, its Luzhkov,' cried George, grabbing Nick by the arm.

'Let go,' Nick yelled. 'He can't see us the headlights are blinding him.'

Nick pressed down on the accelerator instinctively; he needed to get a little closer. The land rover jerked forward.

Luzhkov waved and peered towards them. Suddenly, through the glare of the headlights he was able to make out the outline of two figures; it could not be Laskin!

He raised his automatic and fired towards the cab. Nick watched with horror as Luzhkov raised his weapon.

'Get down,' he shouted at George at the same time pushing his foot down hard on the accelerator.

The vehicle lurched forward in response, tyres screeching. A single bullet punctured the windscreen, only narrowly missing Nick and George. Luzhkov stood his ground; he must switch his automatic from single fire to rapid fire. He was fumbling with the switch, the Land Rover was closing in on him, he flicked the switch. The glare of the lights dazzled him, he lifted the automatic, at the last moment he saw Hartford in the cab. Nick looked up simultaneously to meet Luzhkov's glaring enraged stare, just as the Land Rover smashed into him.

Momentarily he was knocked forward with a sickening jolt, he tumbled onto the road, instantly the Land Rover ran over him rocking the cab from side to side as he passed under the tyres.
Nick slammed on the brakes to bring the vehicle to a sliding halt, then turned the Land Rover around in the drive so the headlights could pick out the lifeless body slumped in the road.

They both slumped back into the seats momentarily, just gazing out at the still figure. Nick slowly climbed out of the cab and walked cautiously over to where Luzhkov lay. He kicked away the automatic, then turned over the lifeless body with his foot.

George joined him, but looked away, her head rested on his shoulder as she clung tightly to his arm.

'It's over,' said Nick and put his arm round her as they walked slowly away towards the house.

Snapshot 288

Sgt June Berry looked around the station; Dunstan was busy at the desk dealing with a local farmer concerning some ponies that had wondered through an open gate onto the highway just outside the town; a local matter concerning local people.
She greeted the farmer, then headed out into the main street. A light snow was falling as she headed for the Golden Lion to wave goodbye to the trio of detectives who were finally leaving.
She felt that things would soon return to normal, just like it should be in Settle nearing Christmas.

Snapshot 289

Back in the office, Jack sifted through a pile of documents and files that had accumulated while they had been away.
Since their return they had enjoyed a brief period of celebrity status for their part in solving one of the largest cases of the decade.
They had featured in the national and local press for solving what had been dubbed 'the invisible murders' of eight women, on account that no one had known about them in the first place.
For his part, Jack was glad it was all over. It felt good to be back on his home patch, except for the paperwork. Ripley was enjoying a period of sick leave, due to the gunshot wound to his arm. He was becoming a fixture in Jack's home with Samantha caring for him.
As for Martin, well, some people never change do they?

Snapshot 290

The sun was high in the blue sky, the sea was crashing onto the long sandy beach and Nick, having enjoyed a late breakfast, was reading the morning paper.
'There's a very interesting story on page four,' he called out to George, who joined him on the balcony.

She leaned over and grasped the paper,

'Let me see, 'The FSA are investigating several cases of insider dealing which it believes are taking place in the city. It has announced that it is to introduce tighter regulation.''

'You see,' said Nick, 'there are more people like Luzhkov out there who always believe they will get away with playing the market. It will take more than tighter regulations to stop them.'

'Really, we are on our honeymoon, remember,' she said, letting the paper fall over the balcony.